KU-451-863

Practically Perfect

Katie Fforde lives in Gloucestershire with her husband and some of her three children. Her hobbies are ironing and housework but, unfortunately, she has almost no time for them as she feels it her duty to keep a close eye on the afternoon chat shows. *Practically Perfect* is her twelfth novel.

KATIE FFORDE

Practically Perfect

CENTURY · LONDON

First published in the United Kingdom in 2006 by Century

3 5 7 9 10 8 6 4 2

Copyright © Katie Fforde 2006

The right of Katie Fforde to be identified as the author of this work has been
asserted by her in accordance with the Copyright, Designs and Patents Act, 1988

This book is sold subject to the condition that it shall not, by way of trade or
otherwise, be lent, resold, hired out, or otherwise circulated without the
publisher's prior consent in any form of binding or cover other than that in
which it is published and without a similar condition including this condition
being imposed on the subsequent purchaser

Century
The Random House Group Limited
20 Vauxhall Bridge Road, London, SW1V 2SA

Random House Australia (Pty) Limited
20 Alfred Street, Milsons Point, Sydney, New South Wales 2061, Australia

Random House New Zealand Limited
18 Poland Road, Glenfield,
Auckland 10, New Zealand

Random House (Pty) Limited
Isle of Houghton, Corner of Boundary Road & Carse O'Gowrie,
Houghton 2198, South Africa

The Random House Group Limited Reg. No. 954009

www.randomhouse.co.uk

A CIP catalogue record for this book is available from the British Library

Papers used by Random House are natural, recyclable
products made from wood grown in sustainable forests.
The manufacturing processes conform to the environmental
regulations of the country of origin

ISBN 978 1 8441 3675 9 (from Jan 2007)
ISBN 1 8441 3675 2

Typeset in Palatino by Palimpsest Book Production Limited,
Polmont, Stirlingshire
Printed and bound in the United Kingdom by
Mackays of Chatham plc, Chatham, Kent

To Louise Ratcliffe, Interior Designer,
who was the original inspiration for this book.
Lots of love and many thanks.

Acknowledgements

This book was inspired by the major re-working of my own house. As I never waste anything that happens in my own life, everyone mentioned below were extremely valuable research assistants.

Victoria Kingston and Hilary Johnson who first alerted me to the plight of ex-racing greyhounds.

Someone who works with rescue greyhounds but who wisely prefers to remain anonymous and was really helpful.

Melanie Foster, who was kind enough to share a lot of her knowledge about the listed buildings business.

Tim Poole and the Stroud Building Company and all their skilled craftsmen whose high standards, attention to detail and (mostly) cheery dispositions were exemplary.

To Bill Thorne and Olly from Abacus Removals who made a grisly process a lot more bearable.

Jonathan Early and later, Arthur Early, as colour consultants.

Briony Fforde who has to take her share of responsibility.

As usual, to my darling and long suffering husband, Desmond Fforde.

Also to my wonderful editors at Random House – Kate Elton and Georgina Hawtrey-Woore. The brilliant art department and the audacious and wonderful sales force who are in a class of their own. And not forgetting the stunning (in all senses) Charlotte Bush with whom I have such fun each year.

To Richenda Todd, as ever, meticulous but sympathetic.

To Sarah Molloy at A. M. Heath who has always been such a support to me over the past ten years or so. To Sara Fisher, who has a tough act to follow but who has my complete confidence.

You've all been brilliant, thank you so much.

Chapter One

❧

The candle at her side flickered, and Anna shifted her position on the pair of steps where she was perched. She was beginning to regret having the telephone connected so promptly. There was very little mobile reception and without a conventional phone she'd have been almost unreachable. As it was, her ear was getting hot and her hand was getting cold, but her sister was still interrogating her. Anna didn't bother to cut her short – it would only involve another telephone call later – she tucked her free hand into her sleeve and listened politely. The bib-and-braces dungarees she was wearing were fairly warm when she was moving around, but now she was getting chilly.

'So why was it you moved there again?' asked Laura for what felt like the hundredth time. 'You know, property's much cheaper up here in Yorkshire. We could have done the project together. Much more fun.'

Anna embarked on her explanation again – rather patiently, she thought. 'I didn't want to be so far from London, and Amberford is a much more desirable area. Commutable from London, just. We've been through this.'

Laura sighed. 'I just don't like you doing it all on your own, so far from us. And I really wish you hadn't rushed into buying it, without me having a chance to see it first.'

In fact Anna did feel a bit guilty about this. 'I'm sorry, but I had to decide very quickly. There were lots of other people after it. It was such a bargain.'

'You were a cash buyer,' Laura pointed out rather snappily.

1

Anna sighed. 'I know, and that's partly thanks to you. But so was the other guy. It would have gone to him if I hadn't been in a position to write a cheque for a deposit on the spot.' She paused. 'I'm eternally grateful, Lo. Without that loan I couldn't have done it.'

'You know I was happy to lend you the money, and you're paying me more interest than I'd have got from anywhere else, I just don't trust you to buy—'

'I know you don't,' said Anna, quite gently considering her frustration. 'But it's time you did. I know you're my older sister, but I am an adult, you know.'

'Twenty-seven is not—'

'Yes it is.'

'I don't mean that, of course you're an adult, but this is all your capital and a bit of mine. It's your inheritance.'

'I know the money didn't come from the tooth fairy.'

Anna wished she'd supplied herself with pencil and paper and a space to sketch – she could have got on with some drawings while all this was going on. Not that it would have been possible in this light. She just hated wasting time.

'What I'm saying is,' Laura continued, 'you won't get that money from Granny again. And you could lose everything, you know.'

Anna shifted uncomfortably on the step. 'I watch all the same television programmes you do. I'm just as aware that the property market goes down as well as up, all that stuff. I haven't lived the last five years with my head in a sack.'

Laura sighed again. 'I expect I'm just jealous. It was such fun doing up the flat in Spitalfields together.'

'It *was* fun,' Anna agreed, 'but I'm a big girl now. I'm a qualified interior designer. It's time for me to go it alone.'

There was a silence. Laura was obviously still not convinced. 'So how much money have you got left to live on?' she asked, setting off on a new tack. 'You won't be able to do everything yourself, however handy you are with your Black and Decker and your Workmate – and I admit you are quite handy. And you still need to pay the mortgage.'

'I took out a slightly larger mortgage so I can use some of it to pay it—'

'That doesn't sound sensible—'

'But I thought I might get a part-time job anyway,' Anna said soothingly before Laura could get any further, 'just to get to know people.'

'Ah! So you're already worried about being lonely and you haven't even spent a night in the house! Sell it quickly, and do the same thing up here, where I can keep an eye on you. You might still make a bit of a profit. You could get in touch with the other man who was interested—'

'No, Laura! I love this house! I'm not going to sell it.'

Laura pounced like a cat on a daydreaming mouse. 'Ah! I knew it! You've fallen in love with an investment project. Fatal mistake.'

Anna cursed herself for letting slip this sign of weakness. 'I didn't say "in love",' she said, knowing she sounded pathetic. '"In love" is quite different from loving it.' She bit her lip while she waited to see if her sister bought this rather specious argument.

'OK.' Laura seemed resigned at last. 'Just promise me you'll sell it when it's done. Falling in love is always a mistake.'

'I know.'

'With men or with property,' she continued menacingly.

'Come on, Laura! You and Will are ecstatically happy. You and the boys could rent yourself to cornflakes ads as the perfect family!'

Laura laughed, trapped by her own argument. 'I know, but—'

'You've all got good teeth and shiny hair. You eat the right food—'

'This conversation is not about Will and the boys,' said Laura firmly.

'I know,' Anna admitted, 'but I was hoping I could steer it in that direction. How is Edward's spelling coming on?'

'Anna!'

'OK, but I really want to know if Jacob has got off that vile reading book.'

'Oh yes.' Her sister was momentarily diverted from sorting out Anna. 'At last. But getting back to you, and falling in love—'

Anna accepted the inevitable. 'You don't trust me to fall in love as sensibly as you did?' Will was the perfect husband: not only loving, good-looking and a good provider, he also did DIY.

Laura was silent for a moment, possibly realising that falling in love with the right person was about luck as much as anything else. Anna enjoyed the respite.

'You make me sound terribly bossy.'

At the other end of the phone, Anna nodded agreement.

'But I'm just looking out for you,' persisted Laura. 'Mum's a bit taken up with Peter these days and doesn't pay attention to what you're getting up to.'

'Mum's entitled to be obsessed with her new husband. I am an adult.' Although Anna was beginning to wonder if this was true, her sister seemed so unable to accept it.

'And of course you're just as capable of falling in love with the right man as I am. As long as I've checked him over first.' But at least there was a smile in her voice now.

'Fine. I promise I won't marry anyone without consulting you. Oh, I can hear the boys. You're needed, Laura.' Never had her nephews' shrieks sounded so endearing.

'Oh yes, better go. Speak soon!'

'Right.' Anna uncrossed her fingers, and then replaced the receiver on the handset and tucked it back into the little niche in the wall. It was only a white lie, she told herself as she stepped down to the floor. And you have to fall in love with a project a little bit, to really throw your heart into it. As for falling in love with the right man, that ship had sailed, too. She'd fallen in love with the wrong one years ago, and even knowing he was the wrong one didn't affect her feelings. One of the reasons she had come to look at the house in the first place was because she remembered Max saying that his mother lived near here. It had seemed like a good omen.

Anna blew out the candle and then reversed carefully down the ladder that was currently her staircase. Sometimes she let herself fantasise about meeting his mother, or running into Max while he was visiting her. She always chuckled at this dream in spite of herself. If he did run into her, she'd more than likely be wearing dungarees and builder's boots, and while she had always been a jeans and sweater girl, her clothes were even more utilitarian now than they had been when she was a student.

Still, she'd carried the torch for a very long time and it still burned as brightly as when Max had been the guest lecturer at college.

He'd been the hot young architect, coming in to talk to them, and she'd just been one of the students, taking notes. She was willing to bet she wasn't the only one who'd fallen in love with him, either. He'd been so dynamic and vital. Not really handsome, but with such a massive personality that his looks didn't matter. But she'd never talked about him to anyone else and, thank God, this included her sister. She hadn't wanted to find out that he'd slept his way through half the class but passed over her. Then, at their Graduation Ball, he had picked her out and danced with her. It was right at the end, and Anna had had to leave because there was a whole group of them sharing a minicab home. There'd just been time for Max to write his number on a bit of cigarette packet. 'Call me,' he'd said, his voice a husky whisper.

Anna had fully intended to call him, even though the thought was more scary than finals had been, but some hideous bug had laid her low for days. The first day she felt well enough to go out she had been on her way to the chemist when she saw him – with a woman. She had rushed home and torn up the bit of cigarette packet and then burnt the pieces. It was only a couple of days later, when the last remnants of the bug had left her and she felt less wobbly, that she realised she'd been incredibly stupid. The woman could have been just a friend: his sister, a colleague, anyone. She'd regretted her folly ever since.

Anna went to the place where the electric kettle and the toaster were plugged into the only part of the house where they could be. There was also a small wash-hand basin there, so it counted as a kitchen. To satisfy the demands of the building-society-turned-bank, she had left the slightly rusty cooker and cracked sink in place until after she'd been given a mortgage. Luckily for her, the address, and the relatively small amount she needed to borrow, meant the valuer didn't actually need to go into the property. She had secured her money on a 'walk by' – which normally would have been a drive by, had it been possible to drive past the cottages – and it was hers.

Of course the mortgage didn't seem small to her, it seemed enormous, but from the building society's point of view, it was fairly insignificant.

While she made herself a cup of tea, using the last of the milk, she forced herself to stop thinking about the man she hadn't seen for three years and calculated how long it would be before Laura could stay away no longer and would descend, handyman husband in tow, to 'sort her out'.

Anna loved her sister dearly, and when they'd lived together they'd got on fine. But since Laura was no longer able to supervise her dates, steer her wardrobe in the right direction, and generally mother her, the word 'bossy' was becoming more and more appropriate. If she'd known where Anna intended to spend her first night in her very own home – investment project, she corrected herself hurriedly – she'd have had a blue fit. She would not consider a sleeping bag and a camping mat a suitable resting place, even if Anna did have a couple of blankets she could pull over herself. But without Laura adding her capital to hers, her mortgage would have been much larger.

And surely Laura wouldn't blame Anna for falling in love with the cottage, at least a little bit. It was heavenly! Or it would be when it had floors, a staircase, a proper kitchen and a bathroom. The previous owners had ripped all these things out and then either run out of money or interest. The estate agent was rather cagey about it.

Anna had tossed and turned her way through a week of sleepless nights while she waited for the surveyor's report. She was certain he'd discover some major problem: the reason why the previous owners had abandoned something with 'such terrific letting potential' as the estate agent put it. When no such reasons were revealed, Anna felt it was probably because there was so little left in which to discover death-watch beetle, dry rot or perished timbers. The ground floor had been stripped of almost everything, including most of the floorboards. There was no staircase, so the only way to the first floor was via a ladder. Here there was at least a floor to walk about on, but there was no bathroom. And the very top floor, the attic, which in Anna's mind's eye was already the most wonderful bedroom-bathroom-dressing-room suite, was very much as it had been hundreds of years ago. Anna planned to sleep up there when everything

7

was straighter downstairs, but at the moment she felt she needed to be nearer things. Up in the attic, the rest of the house could burst into flames and she would be unaware of it until it was too late. She'd bought and installed a smoke alarm, even without her sister's prompting.

Its lack of amenities had made the house very cheap, considering its position, both in the country as a whole and in Amberford in particular.

It was part of a row of cottages at right angles to the road. A path led between the houses and the gardens which overlooked the village. When the houses were built, the gardens would all have produced vegetables and not been used for leisure purposes. Even now, there was no space wasted in high hedges or fences. It gave the area an open-plan, allotment-like feel, that Anna loved. Laura would say that having the garden open plan would detract from the value. But there was a smaller, enclosed garden at the back, and if your children needed lots of playing space (and Laura's two boys definitely did) there was an attractive bit of common land not far away. A church, a school and a pub, and an easy journey to a mainline station, made it a very desirable spot. There was even a shop and a post office and, not too far away, a Chinese takeaway.

Of course it only had two bedrooms, and Laura would say that cut Anna's target market down considerably. Anna had already prepared her speech saying it made it an ideal second home, although she didn't like the idea of second homes making once-thriving villages barren and empty during the week.

She had yet to meet her neighbours, and because it was beginning to get dark and people would be putting their lights on, a walk along the row would tell her which cottages were occupied permanently, and which were not. She needed a few things from the shop anyway; now would be a good time to investigate discreetly.

It seemed strange walking so close to people's windows and although she couldn't quite resist looking inside, she made her glances oblique and fleeting. She was grateful that she was the end cottage (she would tell her sister that 'end of terrace' was better than 'mid') so no one could look in at the building site she currently called home.

Her immediate neighbour was definitely a permanent resident. Anna could hear children and there were lights on everywhere. A sideways glance through the kitchen window as she passed showed a reassuring amount of mess. Anna's sister was terribly organised and it was what they argued about more than anything else. Anna didn't want to find herself living next door to another neatnik.

The next house was either a holiday home or belonged to someone not yet home from work: a commuter, possibly. The curtains were open but no light showed. Anna could see hints of a very stylish, modern kitchen, full of expensive appliances.

The house next to that was clearly occupied by an elderly lady. Her windowsill was covered with china ornaments, visible in front of the curtain that was already drawn. A cat sat on the porch, evidently dismissing Anna as a blow-in, and refusing her offers of friendship.

The first cottage in the row, and the last one Anna passed before she reached the main road, was definitely a holiday cottage. The Christmas decorations were still up, even though it was mid-March. Going by the quality of the decorations, which were of the tasteful corn-dolly and red-ribbon type, she judged the house was not owned by disorganised people who just didn't get round to taking them down. More likely they were spending the winter somewhere warm.

Out of the five cottages, three – possibly four – including her own, seemed occupied which, considering how small they were, was not a bad ratio.

The shop bell jangled in a friendly way. It was a small

supermarket, with a couple of short rows of goods and a counter for bacon and cheese. The man who stood at the counter, doing the crossword, looked up when she entered and smiled. 'Evening.'

'Evening.'

'Can I help you?'

'I think I can probably manage,' said Anna, feeling a little shy. She was used to the anonymity of London shops, where only the proprietors of shops you used very frequently ever spoke to you.

'Well, let me know if there's anything you can't find. Just moved in, have you?' he added later, when Anna had put a few things into her basket.

'That's it. I just need some basic provisions.'

'So you've moved into Brick Row?'

'Yes. How did you know?' This omniscience took some getting used to.

The shopkeeper smiled. 'It didn't take much detective work. We knew the house had been bought by a young woman; you're obviously dressed for work; and who else would come in here just before closing, at this time of year, who I don't know?'

Anna smiled. 'I suppose it does make sense.'

'Don't worry, we're not all nosy round here, and those of us that are are well meaning on the whole.'

Anna placed her basket of goods on to the counter so he could ring them up. 'I'm sure you are.'

She walked home feeling very satisfied. The shop didn't sell fresh meat or fish but otherwise it seemed to have everything else Anna might need and the town of Stroud was only a short bike ride away. Amberford was perfect, well worthy of being fallen in love with, and if being there without a car caused a few problems, well, she'd deal with them as they came up.

As Anna walked back along the lane she saw a young woman standing by the front door next to hers, looking out anxiously. Anna was pleased to see her as she'd been intrigued by the row of three small pairs of wellington boots, arranged in size order, on the windowsill of the porch. She overcame her shyness and smiled. The young woman smiled back, still preoccupied.

'Hello,' she said. 'You've moved into number five? You're very brave! It hasn't even got floors, has it? I was going to invite you round for a bath, but just now we can't even have one ourselves. I'm waiting for a plumber. He promised he'd be here before two, but I don't suppose he'll come now.'

'Oh dear, what's the problem?' Anna asked.

Presumably hearing her voice, three small boys abandoned their toys of mass destruction and clustered round their mother, eager to see whom she was talking to.

'Blocked drain,' the woman said with a grimace. 'I've pulled out the plug and nothing happens. It's full of cold soapy water. If these three don't have a bath at night, they take ages to settle. And it's beginning to smell.'

'Well, I might be able to help,' said Anna.

The woman's face lit up. 'Really? How?'

'I have a few building skills, which is just as well given the state of my house, but, more to the point, I have a tool that unblocks drains. I'll just pop home and get it,' Anna offered, 'if you'd like me to.'

'I'd love you to! I'll put the kettle on. Or open some wine?'

Anna grinned back at her. 'I'll be back in a minute.'

It took Anna a little longer than that to find the tool that she and her sister had had cause to use so often in the Spitalfields flat. When she knocked on the door of her neighbour's house and was let in, she found an agreeable amount of chaos.

'I'm Chloe,' said the woman.

'Anna.'

'And these are Bruno, Tom and Harry. Two, four and six, only in reverse order.'

'Hello,' said Anna, suddenly shy in front of three pairs of inquisitive eyes. 'I've got my gadget, if you'd like to show me upstairs.'

They all went up the steep and very winding staircase to the second floor, where the bathroom and the boys' bedroom was. The boys grabbed hold of her and towed her towards it.

'We haven't had a bath for two days!' said the eldest, who was probably Bruno, but might have been Harry.

'My husband's away,' said his mother. 'He would be, just when there's an emergency.'

Anna didn't think a blocked bath plug quite qualified as an emergency, but accepted that Chloe obviously did. She rolled up her sleeve as far as it would go, which was not far enough.

'I don't suppose you'd all like to go downstairs while I do this?' she suggested. 'I want to take my jumpers off.'

'We want to watch,' announced one of the boys.

'Yes, we do,' said another.

Anna sighed. 'OK.' She undid her bib and peeled off the two jumpers that covered a long-sleeved T-shirt. Fortunately that sleeve rolled up obligingly high. She plunged her arm into the cold, scummy water. 'Right, pass me my plunger, would you?'

'This is so cool,' murmured Bruno.

'You're right there,' said Anna, shivering. 'Very cool indeed.'

Chapter Two

❧

When the bath was both empty and clean, Chloe filled it again and then went downstairs to make supper while Anna sat on the floor of the bathroom and read stories to the little boys. She was accustomed to small boys, having nephews, and enjoyed their choice of reading matter hugely. Eventually, when the littlest one showed signs of becoming drowsy, she whipped them out, one by one, and enveloped them in towelling. Then, as instructed, she sent them downstairs to sit by the fire.

By the time she had cleaned out the bath, collected the bath toys, done her best to dry the floor, and gone downstairs again, the boys were sitting at the table in their pyjamas eating spaghetti and meatballs.

'We get a bit casual when my husband's away,' Chloe explained. 'It's better to feed them then bath them, but what with one thing and another, it just didn't happen. It was very kind of you to read to them in the bath. I'd never thought of that.'

'I have a couple of nephews and when I had them on my own one weekend, I discovered reading to them in the bath was a really good idea. And then we played dentists.'

'What?' Chloe handed Anna a glass of wine.

'They take turns to lie on my sister's bed, with the reading light on, and I say, "Open wide, E to E sound," while I brush their teeth.'

Chloe regarded her sons, one of whom was sucking up a strand of spaghetti, the end of which had just flicked his nose. 'That sounds a brilliant idea!'

Anna laughed. 'I don't think my sister was that impressed when she found toothpaste on her duvet cover, but she was so thrilled to find us all alive and well, she overlooked it.'

'I think I'm really going to like having you as a neighbour, Anna.'

While Chloe tried out this new tactic in the tooth-cleaning battle upstairs, Anna stacked the dishwasher, wiped all traces of spaghetti and meatballs off the table, and then set it again, for their meal. She wouldn't have told her sister unless given a truth drug, but she was as thrilled as Chloe to have such a jolly, friendly family living next door. It would make being on her own, on a building site, much more bearable.

Chloe came down and collapsed on the sofa. 'Putting them to bed is so exhausting. Mike does it, when he's home. He's my husband,' she added.

'And he's away?' Anna asked.

'Yup. He's a consultant engineer and works abroad quite a bit. He's due back quite soon, but you can never be sure how long a job will take. I used to go with him, before the boys came along.'

'Do you miss it?'

Chloe considered this. 'Not as much as all that. I miss Mike, of course, but being an ex-pat wasn't all joy. Although I'd worked as a temp in offices all my life, it wasn't easy to get work when they knew you'd be off soon. That's how I met Mike,' she added. She looked at Anna, retrospectively mischievous. 'I was working at his office. We met in the morning, went out for lunch, and never went back! I felt awfully guilty, I usually took my temp work very seriously.'

Anna laughed. Although Chloe did a lot of talking she was fun, and could be a useful source of information. 'So have you lived here long?'

'Bruno – he's the eldest – was a baby when we

14

moved here. It seemed ideal for us then. Now, two more babies later, it seems a bit cramped.' She smiled sleepily. 'You wouldn't tip a bit more wine into my glass, would you?'

Anna obligingly tipped.

'It's not that I'm an alcoholic or anything – or at least, I don't think so – but it's so nice to have company in the evening, and I never drink when I'm alone.' Chloe sipped and then, as if going over old ground, said, 'We'd move if we could afford to, probably, but it took all our money just to get our foot on the property ladder.'

'You don't seem exactly cast down by your poverty, if I may say so,' said Anna.

Chloe laughed. 'Well, no! Being broke can become an absorbing hobby and it makes you terribly resourceful.' She undug herself from the sofa and crossed the room. 'See this table?'

Anna nodded. It was holding a small table lamp.

'Nappy box, with a cloth over it. But don't look too closely – there isn't a hem on the cloth.'

'Wow! That's such a good idea,' said Anna.

Now she was on her feet, Chloe drained her glass. 'I'm going to put the kettle on. Mike's parents think I'm a terrible slut. They don't think making furniture out of cardboard boxes is clever.'

'I do, but I usually use something more substantial myself . . .'

'You probably don't have access to nappy boxes like I do.'

'Well, no.'

Chloe frowned. 'I did use cloth nappies as well, but when you've got three . . . So, coffee, tea, or hot choc?'

'Coffee please.'

'And grown-up biscuits?'

'I didn't know biscuits grew, I thought they just came the size they were always going to be.'

15

Chloe laughed. 'You are funny. I mean biscuits I don't let the boys have except for a treat. Too expensive.'

'So why did you move to this area? Do you come from round here?' Anna asked.

'It's more or less equidistant between the parents,' replied Chloe as she filled the kettle, 'which is a bit of a mistake, but I'd spent holidays here as a child and have always loved it. And I must say, although property prices are obscene, it's a great place to live.'

'That's good to hear.' Anna got up from the rather low armchair that was beginning to make her back ache and sat down again on something more upright.

'Oh yes, it's got everything,' said Chloe from the kitchen. 'Lovely countryside, views . . . a really good primary school, playgroups, things like that in the village. You probably know about the shop and the post office, but there's a great market on Saturdays, although there's another one in town, too. We have a pub that does really good food, a Chinese nearby—'

'I know about that. There were menus from it stuck up on the wall in my house.'

Chloe smiled and rummaged in the cupboard for the grown-up biscuits. 'And we've made some good friends here, all within pushchair distance, which is great when you go to dinner with each other: you just totter home on the stroke of midnight for the babysitter.' Chloe stopped and sighed. 'Sorry! I've completely run off at the mouth again. I do that. Mike's always telling me off, but when he's away I do miss adult company in the evenings sometimes. Feel free to tell me to shut up.'

Anna chuckled. 'I wouldn't dream of it! I wasn't terribly looking forward to sitting on my own next door, and you've taken me in, fed me, got me drunk—'

Chloe looked shocked. 'Surely not!'

'Well, a bit tipsy then, but it's been a lovely evening. Thank you.' She smiled happily. Having Chloe as a neighbour was going to be a real boon. She was kind and funny and knew everything. It made her decision to buy the house even more right.

'There's your coffee,' said Chloe, placing a mug of steaming black coffee in front of Anna. 'Milk? Sugar? And have a biscuit.'

Anna helped herself as Chloe sat down on the rather uncomfortable armchair and put the plate of biscuits down on the floor beside her; there didn't seem to be room anywhere else. She turned to Anna. 'Aren't you going to be frightened, sleeping on your own in that house?'

'I don't think so,' said Anna. 'But I never have lived on my own, so I might be.'

'I was always hopeless before I had the boys.'

'Who protect you if the bogeymen come?'

Chloe laughed and shook her head. 'No, but they're company, all the same. You should get a dog.'

'A dog?' That didn't seem terribly practical in a tiny building site of a cottage.

'Mm. I'd have one like a shot if the house wasn't so small and I didn't have three children.'

Anna looked around the room. 'Yes, I did notice quite a lot of pictures of greyhounds.'

Chloe nodded enthusiastically. 'I think I must be the only person who works at rescuing greyhounds who hasn't actually got several herself. One woman I know has got four.'

'Oh my goodness.' Anna couldn't help wondering if this was sensible.

'Yes', Chloe continued excitedly. 'They're very easy. They sleep most of the day, and only need quite a small amount of exercise.'

'I see.' Anna didn't believe it for a minute.

'In fact, I know of a greyhound that's desperate for a home, right now.'

'Do you?' Anna's dismay could no longer be disguised – it was horribly clear where Chloe was going with this.

'Mm. The most lovely brindle bitch. Her owner's going away, and if she can't – or we can't – find a home for her, she might have to be put down.'

'Couldn't you have her to stay?' Anna was positively alarmed now. 'Just while this woman is on holiday?'

'Chloe raised her eyebrows. 'Have you ever seen a greyhound in real life? They're enormous. This house is bursting at the seams anyway. We couldn't possibly have a dog – at least, not a greyhound.'

'Well, I'm afraid I couldn't possibly have one either. I haven't got floors in all the rooms, there's only electricity in one room downstairs and I've only got a cold tap,' Anna explained.

'Then you'll need a dog for company until things are a bit more civilised,' Chloe said triumphantly.

'I really don't think—'

'Honestly,' Chloe wheedled. 'You could just have her on trial. We're between homing officers at the moment, but I'm sure if you and she got on, the new one would let you keep her.'

'My sister would have forty fits!' Actually, this made Anna a little bit tempted.

'It's nothing to do with her, is it?' Chloe looked confused for a moment.

'No, but that wouldn't stop her telling me what she thought about it. She's really put out that I bought a house so far away from her.'

'But it's a wonderful investment, surely?'

'Oh yes, but she doesn't want me to do it without her. We did up a place in Spitalfields together. We did really well, selling right at the top of the market, and I'm doing up next door with the proceeds. Or at least, the proceeds should pay for half of it, if it doesn't go too badly over budget.'

'Wow, all on your own. You are all on your own, aren't you? You haven't got a boyfriend?'

'Nope.'

'You're so brave.'

Anna liked hearing herself described as brave even if it wasn't how she always felt. Her sister's 'foolhardy' seemed like a better description sometimes. She reached for another chocolate biscuit, and suddenly caught sight of her watch. 'Gosh, its late! I'd better go home. It's been a lovely evening though.'

'Hasn't it? I haven't had so much fun in ages. And thank you so much for unblocking the bath. You must come and use it whenever you want to.'

When the last goodbyes had been said, Anna let herself into her own little house. After the warmth and life of Chloe's, it seemed very desolate. The torch she used in order to get to the kettle sent huge shadows everywhere, and until Anna had plugged in an old Anglepoise lamp, she did feel that staying there on her own would be scary.

However, with more light, a hot-water bottle and all the blankets arranged over the sleeping bag, things looked a lot better. She had a portable radio to go to sleep with, so the only trouble was that she couldn't put the lamp near the sleeping bag and the room seemed unbearably spooky with the lamp out.

In the end she found a tea light, put it on an old saucer and lit that. As she realised that she was like a child, afraid of the dark and needing a night light, she thought that perhaps a dog was not such a bad idea after all.

Chloe knocked on Anna's door at half past nine on Monday morning, holding two mugs of coffee. 'I'm so sorry to call on you so early, but I was dying to see the house. Bruno's at school and I've just dropped the other boys off at playgroup. I wanted to come without them or I'd have been round yesterday.'

Anna chuckled at Chloe's eagerness. 'Quite right. It wouldn't be safe for the boys just yet.' And she was quite pleased that she'd had one more day of getting things vaguely organised before her first visitor. She took the offered coffee and sipped it. 'That's delicious. Come in.'

Chloe took the two steps that were possible before the floorboards ran out. 'It could be lovely,' she said eventually, not commenting on the fact that it was not in a state any normal person would consider habitable. 'How on earth did you get a mortgage?'

Anna laughed. 'A "walk by". Fortunately the area is expensive enough not to need too close an inspection for the house to be valuable. And it will be gorgeous eventually. There are some joists that need replacing, then I'll get the floorboards back down. They're mostly lovely wide elm boards that'll look gorgeous.'

'There's a reclamation place quite near,' Chloe offered. 'I could give you the address.' She paused. 'Why no staircase?'

Anna shrugged. 'The people I bought the house from took it out to move it and then ran out of money. Or at least I think they did. Didn't you know them?'

Chloe shook her head, clutching her coffee as if it was her last contact with civilisation. 'They used to come down at weekends and rip things out. They didn't seem to get round to putting anything back in.' She teetered along a joist towards the back of the house. 'This will be the kitchen, presumably.'

Anna nodded. 'With double doors leading out to the garden. They've already knocked the wall down for me.'

'And they got listed buildings consent? I'm surprised. They're very fussy about this particular row of cottages. We applied to move an internal door and they wouldn't let us.'

'Oh.' Anna's enjoyment at showing her new friend her

20

house dimmed. 'I don't think they were the sort of people who'd bother about things like that, were they?'

Chloe shrugged. 'Two men, trying to make a quick profit – probably not.'

Anna chewed her lip and swore softly. 'I really want to do things by the book or it can make things so difficult when you come to sell.'

'You can apply for retrospective consent,' Chloe suggested. 'Perhaps you should go to the offices and ask advice.'

'Mm. I might wait until I've got some floors before I start panicking about that sort of detail.' Anna decided to worry about it later. 'Are you OK with ladders? Would you like to come upstairs?'

'Would you call this a property ladder, then?' Chloe asked with a grin as she got to the top, aware that her information about listed buildings consent had not been welcome.

Anna regarded her for a few seconds and then smiled. 'I suppose so. The floors are fine up here. Come and look at the view.'

'It is wonderful, isn't it? Is that what made you come to Amberford?'

'Partly. It's such a lovely area, and I wanted to buy something that was within reasonably easy reach of London.'

Chloe nodded. 'People do commute from here, although it must cost a fortune. So is this an investment? Or do you want to live here?'

Anna sighed deeply. 'I can't afford to live here, not really. I'll have to sell to pay back the mortgage and my sister. I borrowed some of the money from her.'

'Shame,' said Chloe quietly. 'I was looking forward to having you as a neighbour.'

'Well,' Anna smiled, 'you're having me for a neighbour for quite a long time. Besides, you may not stay here for ever, either.'

'No. If Mike was promoted, he wouldn't have to travel so much, but he couldn't commute from here.'

'Shall we go on up to the attic? I think I'll sleep up there once I've got the wiring done.'

Chloe started up the stairs. 'Do you know good people to do things like that? I can give you some names, if you like.'

'I hope to do as much as I can myself,' Anna replied. 'I'll have to have it checked, of course.'

'I'm very impressed. I can hardly change a lightbulb,' Chloe admitted rather ruefully. 'No, actually, I can change one, perfectly well, but Mike always says I've used the wrong wattage or something, so I leave it to him, mostly, to save the argument. I think it means I've been de-skilled. When he's away I get a bit more self-sufficient.'

Anna nodded in understanding. 'My mother was a widow when my sister and I were growing up. She certainly couldn't change a lightbulb. She was always getting neighbours' husbands to come and fix things for her. It made me determined to learn to do things for myself. My sister and I did loads in the Spitalfields flat.'

'But your sister's got children! How did she manage?'

'This was a few years ago. She didn't have them then.'

Chloe nodded. 'So what have you been doing in the meantime? Sorry! That sounded dreadfully rude. I'm awfully nosy. Lonely, I expect.'

Anna laughed. 'It's a perfectly valid question. I'll tell you my CV. I trained as an interior designer, couldn't get a job—'

'Is that like they have on *Changing Rooms*?'

Anna frowned. 'Not really, I'm not an interior decorator. I'm an interior *designer*. Another four years, plus some more time working in an architect's practice, and I could have been an architect.'

'So why didn't you, then?'

'Money,' said Anna bluntly. 'My mother couldn't

22

support me and I got fed up working in bars and things while I studied. I wanted to earn real money.'

'And did you?'

Anna laughed. 'For a bit, before I got made redundant. Interior designers are the first to go, before architects, when there's any sort of slump in the building market.'

'So then what did you do?'

'I had various jobs and then my sister and I were left some money. Quite a lot of money. We decided to buy a flat together, and we did really well. We were really lucky with the timing, of course – buying at the bottom of the market and selling at the top. That makes such a difference. It's why my sister is so worried about me losing all my money with this place. It was such a golden time for property then, and now it's not.'

Chloe nodded again. 'So your sister got married and had babies. And did you go back to doing interior design?'

'Sort of, but I was working for other people, on their projects, in between having other jobs. I was saving and looking for the right property all the time, but eventually I realised if I wanted a project, I'd have to move out of London. Too expensive otherwise.'

'You didn't feel all weak and feeble when you saw how much work needed doing?'

Anna shrugged. 'I did, a bit, but it was such a bargain. I couldn't *not* buy it, in spite of what my sister said.'

'Which was?'

'That it would have been better to have bought near her, so she could help me. She lives up in Yorkshire now, so I could have afforded something bigger than this.'

'But you chose Amberford?'

Anna couldn't decide if Chloe was digging for more information or if it was just her own guilty conscience that made her think that. Either way, it was a bit early in their friendship to confess about the good omen she felt

23

that finding a property in Amberford was. It was such a ridiculous secret. Like her feelings for Max, which, however deep and lasting, were definitely ridiculous.

'It's such a heavenly spot,' she answered evasively.

'It is.' Chloe seemed content with that, and she moved on. 'So what else are you going to do here? How many bedrooms?'

'It's difficult to make space for more than two, however you look at it. But would you like to see the plans?'

Anna had set up her drawing board and other equipment in a corner of the attic. Next to her drawing board was a pasting table that served as a desk. There was a pile of plans laid neatly next to her pens, geometrical aids, tracing paper: all the sundry bits and pieces of her trade. Now, she pulled off the dust sheet and revealed the plan that was on the drawing board.

Chloe came close and looked admiringly. 'Goodness, you have worked out every detail.'

'Not every detail, but the broad plan. You have to know where all your soil pipes are now, and where you want them to be. Better not to move them if you can avoid it.'

'What I don't understand,' said Chloe after staring at the plans for a while, 'is how you seem to have room for an en suite on the attic floor. Our houses must be almost identical. Have you just drawn a tiny loo?'

Anna laughed, refusing to be offended. 'No! I measured it all out on graph paper. A mistake in the plans could cause hell in a bucket later, when you come to the actual installation.'

'Where have you got the space from?'

'I've just stolen it from here and there. It's easier if you look at the space without anything in it, only on paper, of course. But it's only a shower room and loo and a space for a walk-in wardrobe. It's tiny really, though I hope it will be lovely.'

'What I wouldn't do for a shower room and loo! I hate

24

having to go down those steep stairs in the night. I would have resorted to a potty when I was pregnant if squatting had been an option.'

'I thought people had their babies squatting these days.'

'Only when supported by lusty helpers.' Chloe shuddered at the memory. 'It's been so nice seeing it all,' she said, 'but I'd better get to the shops before it's time to pick up the boys. Do you want anything?'

'I think I'm all right at the moment. I'll have to go to town myself a bit later.'

'Oh,' Chloe paused on her way down the ladder. 'I was going to ask you: where have you parked your car? I didn't see one up at the top.'

'I haven't got a car,' said Anna a little defensively. 'I've got a bicycle.'

'Oh my God,' said Chloe, reaching the bottom of the ladder. 'You really are mad!'

Anna understood a little of Chloe's horror a couple of hours later as she pushed her bike up the long hill from town, but she'd been managing by bike for so long, she felt she could get round the worst of the disadvantages. After all, she had explained to her sister, while fending off another barrage of objections to her project, you can pay for an awful lot of taxis with the money you'd spend on a car.

Now, all her purchases fitted neatly into her panniers. At other times, when she was buying materials, she could get them delivered. She was jolly hot by the time she finally got home, though.

As she got off her bicycle at the top of the lane, a van whizzed by and hooted. She realised it was the man from the shop and smiled. It was nice to be recognised.

A few days later, Anna had finally replaced the joists, which turned out to be a much bigger job than she'd anticipated, but had still not got her floorboards back in place. Sheets of plasterboard would have to suffice until she had time to do it. She recognised Chloe's knock on the door. She was by now a regular visitor and Anna was always glad to see her.

'Come in,' she yelled. 'I'm upstairs. Down in a minute!'

It seemed to take Chloe longer than usual to get in, but it had become her habit to bring coffee from home, and perhaps she'd brought biscuits, too. Anna knocked a pin delicately into the bit of skirting she was fixing to the wall, looking forward to a break and a caffeine hit.

Then there were more strange noises, voices and, eventually, a strange scrabbling sound. Anna wrinkled her brow. What was going on down there? Reluctant to leave her task unfinished, she carried on.

When she did finally negotiate the ladder, and emerged backwards into the downstairs space, as yet undefined by room names, she got a shock. Cowering in the corner, terrified, was the most beautiful dog Anna had ever seen – or at least so it seemed to her, possibly because the fear in its eyes made them huge, dark pools, standing out against the cream and brown stripes and velvet ears. It had very long legs that were waving helplessly as the dog lay on its back.

'Oh, you poor thing!' Anna moved towards it and then stopped. 'You're petrified! What are you doing here?' She turned towards Chloe and a woman dressed in layers of purple muslin and partially spun wool.

'I brought Caroline to meet you,' said Chloe, tentatively.

'Hello, Caroline,' said Anna to the woman, hoping she didn't sound as confused and unwelcoming as she felt. Why had this woman brought her extremely nervous dog with her?

'I'm not Caroline, I'm Star. Caroline's the dog. She's an ex-racing greyhound.'

Thinking that she must have got her wires crossed

somehow – the woman seemed to have a dog's name, and the dog a woman's – Anna said, 'But why have you brought her? She's scared witless.'

'We were, er, hoping you'd like her,' said Star hesitantly. And then added, 'I'm going travelling.' She looked down at her hands nervously and Anna noticed that the fingernails were bitten to the quick.

'She's lovely, I'm sure. But you can't go travelling if you've got a dog.' Anna felt rather uncomfortably as if she was missing something.

'You can't put your life on hold for a dog,' said Star, sounding as if the words may not originally have come from her. 'And she's never really settled with me. If you could have her . . . until she can be rehomed of course . . . I'd be really grateful.' She picked up the tiny bells that were attached to a piece of braid hanging from her dress and started winding them round and round her finger.

Finally, Anna realised exactly what Star meant. 'But I can't have a dog! I told you that, Chloe. Look at the place! Besides, I've never had a dog in my life before!' Giving Star a good chance to see the fact that her house wasn't fit for a human to live in, let alone a nervous dog, Anna turned to Chloe, who was now looking agonised.

'I only mentioned you in passing to Star,' Chloe said guiltily. 'She told me she was going abroad and asked – well, begged, really – if you'd have Caroline. I said it was unlikely but there doesn't seem to be any alternative.'

Not satisfied with this explanation, Anna said, 'But, Chloe, the house isn't fit for a dog! Let alone one with legs as long as that!' She couldn't quite believe that Chloe had put her in such an awkward position.

Caroline was no longer lying on her back, but was now trying to make herself as small as possible. Although she hadn't been shouting, Anna lowered her voice, feeling a bit desperate. 'You must see that I can't have her, although she is beautiful.'

She knew this last remark was a grave mistake before she'd uttered it. She sighed, and went over to the frightened dog. She crouched down, keeping well out of snapping range, in case Caroline's fear got the better of her. 'Hello, Caroline. How are you?' she said in a low voice.

She realised she was talking to the dog in exactly the same way that she talked to children, and as she talked to them in more or less the same way that she talked to adults, she felt this probably wasn't right. But not knowing any other way, she continued.

'You don't need to be frightened, you know. No one here's going to hurt you.' Anna cast a resentful glance at Star who might not have hurt Caroline, but was prepared to abandon her, and another at Chloe, for good measure.

'She is very nervous,' said Star apologetically. 'She's terrified of my partner. He does shout rather, but he says dogs have to know their place.' The braid and bells were showing signs of serious wear as Star continued to wind and unwind them. 'He did kick her once.'

Anna stifled a gasp of horror, put out her hand and very gently stroked Caroline under the chin with her finger. Caroline looked frightened, but didn't say anything. 'Darling, it's lovely to meet you, but I'm afraid I can't have you to live with me. I haven't got stairs, or a bathroom, or anything.'

'She won't care about the bathroom,' said Chloe, gaining in confidence. 'And if she did, she could always come over to our house to have baths, like you do.'

Aware she was being teased into making a bad decision, Anna ignored this. 'She *would* mind about the stairs. A dog like this would want to be near you all the time.'

'She is very clingy,' said Star. 'It's one of the things about her that annoyed my partner.'

'I would have thought that the rehoming people would check out that both partners liked the dog before they let you have it,' said Anna sniffily.

'Usually they're very strict,' explained Chloe, still somewhat abashed, 'but the person in charge of rehoming had left the area and no one else wanted to take it on.'

'Can I look round your house?' asked Star, changing the subject. 'I love what you've done to it so far!'

Taken aback, but suppressing her irritation, Anna said, 'Help yourself. Be careful going on the ladder though, there are no stairs.'

'I can see that.' Star gathered her skirts and made her way up the ladder.

When they could hear her clumping around in her walking boots, Anna whispered to Chloe, 'She's mad! Why did she want a dog in the first place?'

Chloe shrugged. 'Lots of people want dogs.'

'Yes, but they don't have them if their houses aren't suitable or whatever! Look at you, you love greyhounds, but you haven't got one!'

'No,' Chloe conceded.

'I think she's totally irresponsible. As for her partner – he should go to prison.'

'I couldn't agree more. And you must see, she's totally unfit to have a dog.'

'So am I!'

Before Anna could say more, they heard Star making her way to the top of the ladder. 'Can I look round the garden?' she said as she climbed down. 'I want to see the view from the end of it.'

Star didn't wait for permission before going out of the front door.

'Oh, for God's sake!' Anna said to Chloe. 'The woman's completely off her tree! Honestly, Chloe—'

Chloe put up her hand. 'I know, I know, really I do, but I only mentioned your name and she fell on me. I think she was frightened the neighbours might call the RSPCA or something.'

'I think they should!'

Chloe was biting her lip. 'You're perfectly entitled to be furious, with me and with Star, and I'm really, really sorry, but Star . . . she's more barking than Caroline is.'

Anna, who had started to forgive Chloe the moment she apologised, knelt near the unwitting cause of all the upset. 'That's not hard! She's too terrified to say a word!'

Chloe joined them on the floor. 'I wonder if she chases cats. Lots of them do.'

'Surely all dogs chase cats,' said Anna. 'Which is why you really couldn't have one here with so many cats and no fences. Nor could I. Even if I had a staircase.'

The dog looked from one to the other, and it seemed to Anna that she was calmer than she had been. Now when Anna put out her hand, Caroline gently sniffed it.

'The thing is,' Chloe said sadly, 'if you don't have her, she'll have to go to a kennel miles and miles away. It's really very important that now she's experienced life in a home, even a really bad one, she keeps it up. I promise you it won't be for long.'

Anna sighed and said nothing. They stayed silent, letting the dog get used to their nearness.

It was only after a while that they realised Star had been in the garden a long time. But when they got up to see where she'd got to, the garden was empty.

'Perhaps she went round the back to the privy,' said Chloe, referring to Anna's only form of sanitation.

Anna shook her head. 'No. If she'd wanted the loo she'd have ask you if she could use yours. I think she's gone.'

'She can't have!' said Chloe, genuinely concerned now. 'I'll go and see if her car's down the lane.'

Chloe sprinted up the path, but came back almost immediately, panting, but otherwise silent.

'She's gone, hasn't she? And she's left Caroline here!' Anna exclaimed.

Chloe nodded, biting her lip. 'It's like leaving your baby

on the doorstep of the hospital! I'm terribly sorry! I had no idea she'd do something so irresponsible. She's away with the fairies, no other word for it, but this is the limit!' Chloe was mortified. 'I really didn't know she was going to do that. Please believe me!'

Anna, who had allowed a thread of suspicion about Chloe's part in this to run through her mind, let it go. Chloe might be impulsive, but she was caring.

'So what shall we do? There must be a number you can ring. An emergency rescue service or something. It's not that I don't want her, I just think it's far more than I can take on just now. I know nothing about dogs!' Anna was beginning to feel panicky. If it turned out Star really had gone, Anna was determined not to be backed into taking on a dog, albeit a very endearing one.

'There is a number,' said Chloe calmly. 'I'll go and ring. But in the meantime, we'd better find Caroline something to sleep on. Greyhounds get cold easily.'

'Poor thing! I'll get my sleeping bag.'

'No need,' Chloe called back as she went out of the front door. 'Star's left her bedding. And a note: *Please look after Caroline. I'm sorry.*'

The two women regarded each other in silence. 'That's it, then,' said Anna after a few moments. 'She's dumped Caroline on me.' Disconcertingly, she found she wasn't quite as displeased as she knew she ought to be. 'The woman's totally, recklessly, irresponsible. I only hope she hasn't got children.'

'Oh, she has, several. They mostly live with their fathers.'

'A good thing too,' Anna replied sharply. 'But what would you expect from a woman who's got a dog's name, and who gave a dog a person's name?'

'I like proper, people's names for animals,' said Chloe.

'Actually, so do I,' said Anna. 'But what sort of a mother would call their child Star? No wonder she's batty.'

'Oh, it wasn't Star's mother who called her that. It was Star herself.'

'Figures,' murmured Anna. 'Come on, let's get Caroline settled on her bed. I'll get the fan heater. You go and ring the emergency number,' she said firmly. 'This can't be a permanent arrangement.'

Caroline was shivering and Anna had put this down to nerves, but then she realised it was with cold as well. Even when she had the old duvet that was her bed under her, she still shook, so Anna filled her hot-water bottle, glad that Chloe wasn't there to see her. When she had tucked it under Caroline, and pulled the duvet over the dog, she said, 'You need a coat, darling. You've got no flesh and very little hair, really. Perhaps I'll find a jumper for you to wear in the meantime.'

As she rummaged in the black plastic sack that was her clothes storage and found a very nice warm sweater that had shrunk a little, she realised a familiar emotion was forming in her heart. 'You must stop falling in love, Anna,' she said aloud, reversing down the ladder. 'It just gets you into trouble.'

But the trouble with falling in love was that it was involuntary, and no matter how well you knew it was a bad idea, if it was going to happen, it happened, and you couldn't prevent it, however much you wanted to.

When the phone rang at nine-thirty that night, Anna picked it up half in hope, half in dread.

'No good, I'm afraid. There isn't a foster carer in the area who isn't full to the gunnels.' Chloe paused. 'If you could hang on to her until morning, there's someone in Wales who might be able to have her . . .'

Anna sighed and succumbed to the eloquent pause at the end of Chloe's sentence. 'Obviously, I'll keep her for tonight and we'll see how it goes.' She knew she should be insisting Chloe took Caroline away first thing, but looking at her curled up on the sleeping bag, she just didn't have the heart. 'But if there are any problems . . .'

'The Trust will have her off you in a jiffy.' Chloe sounded exultant, and possibly sensing this she added, 'It really is very kind of you. I'm going to have a dinner party in your honour the moment Mike's back. You'll get to meet some local people and it'll be a reward for being such a star about Caroline.'

Anna grinned. 'I'm not sure about being a star . . .' She couldn't help thinking of the woman who had abandoned Caroline.

'Oh, you know what I mean! I'm going to ask you about all your favourite foods. But not now, it's bedtime. See you soon. You're a honey.'

Anna brought her sleeping bag down from the attic and arranged it near Caroline's duvet. She sipped her cup of hot chocolate by the light of the candle flame and shared a biscuit with Caroline. Caroline, who was looking very fetching in a Fair Isle jumper that had originally come from a charity shop, licked her hand. The falling in love process was complete and irrevocable. And having a warm back against hers did have its compensations. Even Anna's sister might agree with that.

Chapter Three

The following day was mostly taken up with the getting-to-know-each-other process. Chloe, still racked with guilt about Caroline being dumped on Anna, had rushed out to the pet shop, leaving Anna in charge of not only a large, nervous greyhound, but, because it was Saturday, three small boys as well. Fortunately the boys and dog got on very well, mostly because Chloe had explained that Caroline was very nervous and they were only allowed to whisper in her presence, and not touch her unless she invited them to. The boys played with their toys and, indeed, only whispered. Whispering involved a lot of giggling, but Caroline didn't seem to mind that.

Chloe came back with a carload of equipment. 'I've done really well! If you lot could come and help me unload it all, that would be fab!'

Making sure the door was safely shut, they left Caroline in Bruno's tender care, while Anna and the other two boys walked up the lane to where Chloe's car was parked.

'I couldn't get a dog bed,' she announced to Anna, 'but I got an Army camp bed from that little shop in Hamilton Street. Do you know the one I mean?'

Anna didn't, and received the bundle in silence.

'There was an offer on dog food. Here you are, Tom, can you manage that?' The little boy took hold of a sack that was marginally taller than he was, and staggered along the lane with it.

'I got the food and water bowls from the pound shop. Oh, and these.' She handed Anna two red plastic buckets.

'Why does Caroline need buckets?' Anna was confused. 'I know she's large, but she's not a horse.'

'I know. But it's very bad for them to eat at floor level,' Chloe explained. 'You can buy proper dog-feeding stands, but a bucket works just as well. You put the bowl, which is just a washing-up bowl, you know, in it, and it's the perfect height.'

'I know I haven't got much of a kitchen yet, but I do know a washing-up bowl when I see it. You must let me pay you for all this,' Anna offered.

'Nonsense! It wasn't all that much, really, and I feel responsible.'

'What will Mike say about it?'

'He won't notice, and when he realises the alternative was having a greyhound living with us, he'll feel it was a good deal!'

The two women were now walking down the path, Chloe clutching a bundle of toys for Caroline. 'But he does like dogs?' Anna had yet to meet Mike, as he was still in whichever strange country he was currently working in, and she was intrigued to find out what he was like.

'Oh yes! He loves them! Never marry a man who doesn't like animals.' Chloe was very definite about this, and Anna's mind flicked to Max. Did he like animals? She had no idea. 'Mike just says we haven't the space,' Chloe continued, oblivious to the fact that Anna's attention had wandered, 'and he's right.'

'Now I see how much gear comes with having a greyhound, I'm not sure I've got the space, either!'

'Nonsense,' said Chloe. 'Now let's see how Caroline likes her things.'

It turned out Caroline liked her things very much, especially her lead with its beautiful wide leather collar, so it only seemed fair to abandon work for the morning and take her up to the common for a walk. She trotted along so elegantly and politely that Anna felt quite proud – as did Chloe and the boys, who came with them – and all was very well until Caroline saw a cat. Then only Chloe's added strength on the lead prevented Caroline disappearing over the horizon.

'You can't blame her,' said Chloe, panting and wiping her hand over her forehead. 'She's been trained to chase small furry things.'

'I know,' said Anna, equally out of breath. 'I just wonder if she can be trained not to?'

'Can I hold her?' asked Bruno, the eldest of the three.

'Only if Chloe holds her at the same time,' said Anna. 'Just until we know it's safe. She's very strong, and she's probably not used to lots of different people leading her.'

But Caroline behaved perfectly once again, and the sight of the huge dog, walking sedately behind the small boy, was extremely sweet.

The other two boys then both wanted a turn and she behaved just as well for them. Then Anna spotted an old lady with a Yorkshire terrier getting out of her car, and took over the lead.

'It's another SFC – small furry creature,' she said. 'Caroline might think she has to chase that, too.'

Much to everyone's relief Caroline merely glanced at the small dog, and continued on her stately way.

'You see, she's really well behaved,' said Chloe smugly. 'You'll have no trouble with her.'

'No, I suppose not. But the rehoming officer might not like her having to live in a house with no staircase.'

'I wouldn't worry about it. Most of the greyhounds I know aren't allowed to go upstairs anyway. But what are you going to do about the staircase? I happen to know they're awfully expensive.'

Anna knew this too. 'I rather thought I might build it myself,' she said cautiously.

'Oh my goodness!' Chloe looked at Anna with awe.

'It will be difficult, but you're right, they are fantastically expensive.' She paused to allow Caroline a good sniff at a tree.

'But don't you have to be trained to do that sort of thing?' Chloe watched as her boys ran towards the swings, glad of an opportunity for some uninterrupted adult conversation.

'Well, it would help. Shall we follow the boys? You could have a turn holding Caroline while I push them.'

'They'll be all right by themselves for a few minutes; we can see them. I want to know more about you.'

'Well, when I was working, saving to buy this house, it was what I did.'

'What do you mean?'

'I worked as a chippy, a carpenter.'

Chloe looked even more amazed. 'I thought you said you worked in bars.'

'Well, I did. But not always as a barmaid. And I worked on other people's renovation projects.'

'But I thought you did that as an interior designer.'

'Only when I could. Mostly I fitted skirting boards, rebuilt windows and shutters, put up shelves, made wardrobes under stairs, stuff like that.' By now, all three boys had negotiated their way on to a swing and were pumping their legs back and forth, hoping for forward momentum. Anna took pity on them and handed Caroline to Chloe.

'But where do you start with a staircase?' asked Chloe, while Anna ran between children, like a juggler with a line of plates.

'I've got a book,' Anna panted. 'It does involve a lot of sums.'

'I like sums,' said Bruno. 'Can you push me higher?'

'I was hopeless at maths at school,' said Chloe, looping Caroline's lead round her wrist and pushing another of her sons. 'Still am.'

'Practice does help,' said Anna, going to the youngest. 'I thought you weren't supposed to put dogs' leads round your wrist in case they ran off and broke it.'

'I suppose you're right,' said Chloe, putting her foot on the lead instead. 'But Caroline doesn't seem to be going anywhere.' In fact, she had sunk on to her haunches and seemed quite happy to stay where she was. 'How do you know so much about dogs, anyway? I thought you told me you'd never had one.'

'I watched quite a bit of afternoon television when I was a student. They had loads of animal programmes.'

'So tell me how you make a staircase, then.'

Anna wasn't sure she wanted to talk about her staircase as she wasn't sure she could do it, but it was too late to be coy about it now. 'It'll take masses of drawing and measuring and calculating. Making it and fitting it comes later.'

Chloe was persistent. 'So how did you find out you could do carpentry?'

Anna sighed, giving in to the inevitable. 'Well, as a student I'd made furniture out of pallets and stuff, but I learnt to do it properly when I was a designer. I did know I had a knack for it, but on practically my first assignment, this chippy refused to put in a cupboard where I knew a cupboard could go. He resented taking instructions from a woman, especially one hardly out of college, and he said there wasn't room, and if I was so sure there was, I could bloody well put it in myself. Only he didn't say "bloody".' She laughed at the memory of herself: hugely lacking in confidence, but stubborn as all-get-out.

Chloe laughed, too. 'I can imagine. So what did you do?'

'I stayed in the house all night, doing the cupboard. Well, not all night, but it was tricky.'

'And what did the chippy say in the morning?'

'He was impressed. In fact, he became my best friend.

It changed his mind about women in general and interior designers in particular. He made me his unofficial apprentice. I used to go to the job in my spare time and he taught me how to look after tools, dovetail joints, all sorts of things.'

'That's so romantic! You learning your love of woodwork from a gruff old carpenter, spending every spare minute ingesting his wisdom until now you're thinking about building a staircase.'

Anna laughed. 'It wasn't like that. He was quite young – the young ones are always the worst when it comes to being anti-women, or at least they are in my experience – but he did teach me a huge amount. And it was through him that I got the timber to make the staircase.'

'You've got the timber already?'

'In a storage facility in London. Fortunately, it's mostly my sister's stuff, so she pays.'

'So you knew you were going to make a staircase all those years ago?'

'Oh no. But Jeff told me that they were ripping the floors out of this old house and dumping them in a skip, and when would be a good time to . . .' Anna hesitated, 'er, relocate them.' It was stealing, there were no two ways about it, but the thought of those lovely wide boards being burnt was a worse sin, she thought. And as Jeff pointed out at the time, if she didn't take them some other yuppy designer would. 'I had to do it on my bicycle, at night. It took about three nights, but I knew they would come in useful sometime.'

'And weren't you worried that someone might take them during the day?'

'Absolutely! But Jeff made a bed in the skip for his little Jack Russell, who barked like mad if anyone went near it. It meant the lads couldn't put stuff in the skip, either, but they were very good about it. I bought them a few pints.'

Chloe sighed. 'You have had an exciting life, Anna. I just fell in love and got married at a horribly early age. But at least I found True Love.'

Anna laughed, although not feeling as merry as she sounded. She'd found True Love too, and True Love Unrequited was a very painful state.

'Shall we take the products of your True Love back to mine for hot chocolate? I bought some flakes; we could dip them in.'

'Terribly bad for them, all that milk, plus chocolate, but as long as it's at your house, it's all right,' said Chloe. 'Come on, boys! We're going to Auntie Anna's for hot choc.'

'Oh, please don't make them call me Auntie Anna! Anna is fine. Oh my goodness, there's a cat!'

After her exemplary behaviour on their first and subsequent walks, Anna became confident that Caroline wouldn't let her down and decided to take her when she visited the small market the next Saturday morning. It was not a farmers' market, but according to Chloe it not only had a very good fruit and veg stall, a county-famous fish stall and a van that sold wonderful cheeses that you couldn't usually get outside France, but it also had a WI stall that made the best cakes for miles.

It was a beautiful day and, feeling pleasantly rural, Anna collected some carrier bags and set off with Caroline. As she walked she peeped into the cottage gardens outside the stone houses along the road and wondered if she'd have time to do much to her own long garden. But it was the large area of allotments that caused her to stop and gaze. Not, Anna realised, because she particularly wanted to have one herself – she would never have the time – but because they were so aesthetically pleasing. She was leaning over the wall, taking in the scene, when she realised she recognised the man busy digging as the owner of the village shop. He saw her at the same time.

'Morning!' he called. 'Thinking of having an allotment, are you?'

'Not really. I just love looking at them.'

The shopkeeper looked about him. 'Well, some of these have been let go a bit, but we're well represented at the flower and produce show at the back end of the year. My onions win, sometimes.'

'Goodness me. I don't know how you have time, with the shop and everything.'

'Well, there are lots of people wanting Saturday jobs, and there're the evenings. I find it relaxing, getting in among the soil.'

They chatted for a bit longer while Anna admired the patchwork effect of the different plots. There were quite a few little sheds dotted about, and she could just imagine one or other member of a couple saying they were 'popping down to the allotment' and having a sneaky read of the paper in the shed instead of digging.

'I'd better press on, I suppose,' she said. 'My neighbour told me that if you're not at the market in good time, the WI stall won't have any cakes left.'

As she walked on down the slight incline, Anna met a woman pushing a bicycle. The basket was full of carrots with their tops still on. Several more bags were hung off the handlebars and riding the bike was no longer an option. A cyclist herself, Anna smiled in greeting and the woman stopped, panting slightly. 'That's a lovely dog,' she said.

'Yes. I haven't had her long, but she's very good company.'

'So, are you new to the village?'

Anna nodded. 'I live in Brick Row. I'm doing up my house.'

The woman nodded. 'Oh, I know. They're tiny, those cottages, but very picturesque.'

'That's what I thought.'

'I did a watercolour of them last year. You should come and see it. I live in the little house behind the conifers at the crossroads.'

'Oh yes.' She didn't really know where the woman meant, but she didn't want to spend hours having it explained when she knew she'd never visit unless she was given a proper invitation.

'So do pop in!' the woman called, pushing her bicycle back up the hill again. 'Any time!'

How friendly everyone was!

The village was heaving and Anna got the feeling that people came here as much to catch up with their friends as to do their shopping. Although Caroline was being very good, and was getting lots of approving glances, Anna did wonder if bringing her somewhere so crowded had been a good idea.

The old butter market, with its columns of stone supporting an ancient meeting room above and with a covered area beneath, had provided shelter for market traders for centuries, Anna had gathered from Chloe. The continuity was very pleasing and Anna loved the thought that people had brought their produce here, year after year, decade after decade. There seemed to be dozens of stalls crammed under the supported building, although none of them apparently sold butter. Lots of the people pushing through the crowds smiled at her and it made Anna feel she was part of a community in a way she never had in London. Downshifting was such a good idea! She must ring Laura and tell her about this market – she'd love it.

Even Caroline seemed a good idea, judging by the number of people who stopped to talk to her. Animals were a channel of communication, Anna realised, and began to feel slightly less foolish for having taken Caroline on.

'Is it good with children?' asked one woman carrying

a wicker basket full of interestingly shaped brown paper parcels, and surrounded by little ones. 'Can they pat her?'

'If they're gentle,' said Anna, having checked that the children in question did not look like miniature psychopaths. 'And go one at a time.'

Caroline stood patiently while each child stroked her head and murmured, 'Nice doggy!'

'I haven't had her long, but she's very good,' said Anna to their mother.

'She's gorgeous.' The woman sighed. 'We can't have a dog. My husband has allergies.'

After another smile and pat from the children, they moved on, and Anna felt it was time to get down to her shopping. What a contrast this jolly scene was to the heaving aisles of a supermarket on a Saturday morning.

The smell of samosas being freshly made floated across to her, giving the quintessentially English scene a mouth-watering touch of the exotic. She paused, wondering where to go first.

Across the way, Anna could see a stall selling rustic benches, unusual boxes and a chest of drawers big enough for only very small items. A stall with second-hand clothes on a rail and boxes of china and kitchen utensils could prove useful, and a large banner advertising home-made organic dog biscuits seemed a 'must visit' for Caroline and Anna.

'We'll go there later, darling,' Anna whispered to Caroline, 'but I need some fruit and veg first.'

'Good morning!' said the stallholder, a man in his fifties with a serious expression. 'Looking for apples? Wrong time of year, really, but there are some New Zealand Coxes if you must have apples.'

Anna smiled shyly. In the part of London where she had lived there'd been no neighbourhood market and she wasn't used to banter. 'Yes, please. About five.'

'It's about half-ten, actually, my love, but we won't split

43

hairs.' Seeing him put five apples into a bag told Anna that beneath his lugubrious expression the man actually had a very dry sense of humour. 'Now, what else can I sell you? Got some lovely grapes? Spuds?'

With Caroline taking up one hand, Anna didn't let herself get too carried away but moved on to the fish stall. Here every sort of fish seemed to be on sale and judging by the queue of people, it was obviously extremely popular. She overheard the pretty girl scooping up mussels and putting them into a bag saying that the stallholder had been up at three in the morning to get the fish from Brixham. When her turn came, she bought two fillets of sole and put them on top of the apples.

While she was moving away a man with a child on his shoulders stepped on her foot. He had a huge black beard and a hand-knitted jumper that nearly reached his knees. The child, his fingers entwined in the man's dark curls, wore a hat made up of concentric circles of startling bright colours and wailed loudly as his father nearly toppled over Anna.

'Sorry, mate! Must mind me big feet. I never saw you!' The man was mortified. The child was lifted off his shoulders so he could apologise properly, and then the little boy had to pat Caroline.

'I'm Aidan,' the man introduced himself. 'You're new here, aren't you? Thought so. We would have recognised you by the dog.'

Anna laughed. 'I am new, but I'm beginning to feel I've lived here long enough to know a few people.'

'That's what's good about this area. Now, if you fancy circle dancing, or Five Rhythms dancing, it's on at the Institute on Wednesdays, during termtime.'

'It does sound . . . fascinating, but I'm a bit busy just now.' What on earth was circle dancing? She must ask Chloe.

'Well, the new term starts in just over a fortnight's time.

44

It's very good exercise, although you probably don't need help getting that with her.' He smiled down at Caroline. 'I make musical instruments, by the way.'

'If ever I need a lute, I'll get in touch,' Anna promised solemnly and the man laughed.

'Come on, Ocean.' He heaved the little boy back on to his shoulders and went striding off through the crowds.

Anna watched him fondly before moving on to the cheese counter, which did, she was pleased to note for the sake of the continuity of the ages, sell butter.

Accustomed as she was to London supermarkets, with, she thought, every possible cheese, Anna found herself mystified. There were cheeses here that she had never heard of. The man behind the counter, wearing a white coat and hat, smiled helpfully.

Anna drew a deep breath. 'I'd like something soft but strong.'

The man laughed. 'Right, what about this camembert? Have a taste?'

By the time Anna had tasted quite a few cheeses, and filled her bags with rather more than was possibly wise, the fact that she hadn't had breakfast was no longer a problem.

She was just on her way to the WI stall, to see whether (if she balanced her shopping carefully) she could manage to fit a small carrot cake on top of everything else, when a car backfired.

It took several seconds for Anna to work out what had happened. At first she thought her wrist was being wrenched from her arm and then suddenly it was released as Caroline reversed out of her beautiful wide collar and set off for home. Anna's carrier bags slipped out of her hands, sending everything to the ground. Apples bounced behind peaches, grapes were crushed by potatoes and a grapefruit, going for a strike, landed in the gutter. For a second she dithered: should she pick up her things or go after Caroline? One glance in Caroline's direction made up her mind. Small children, most of whom had probably tried to pat her, were sitting in the road, howling; a woman with a wicker basket, loaded and dressed like Little Red Riding Hood, fell back as if the wolf himself had gone rushing past; and a group of teenagers lounging against the wall shouted in glee: 'Look at that dog go! Fast or what?'

Anna, struggling to catch up with her, fought her way through the mêlée, ignoring the fallen children and over-turned shopping trolleys alike. She had just come across a small roundabout and was wondering if she could clamber over it, or go round, when she spotted a man holding Caroline.

Relief flooded over her along with perspiration. Her mouth was so dry she could hardly speak. 'Thank you,' she rasped out, seeing that he had Caroline on a blue nylon lead.

She wasn't expecting him to be angry. 'What do you think you're doing having a dog you have no control over?' he stormed at her.

Anna opened and closed her mouth, still finding speech difficult. Behind her she was aware of Aidan of the bushy beard and his son Ocean gathering up her belongings.

'Now hang on,' Aidan said, handing Anna most of her shopping. 'It wasn't her fault!'

'Well it's not the dog's!' said Caroline's rescuer.

'No, but . . .' agreed Aidan, and helped his son hand Anna her bowling-ball grapefruit.

Anna took it gratefully. She was painfully aware that she was in for an earful and although she felt it was not undeserved, she was putting off the moment of hearing it.

'Will you be all right, love?' asked Aidan.

'Oh yes. Thank you so much for rescuing my shopping.'

Aidan's teeth appeared for a moment amid the forest of his beard and then he swung his son back up on to his shoulders. They strode off into the crowd, the size of a giant. Anna watched them go regretfully, then turned reluctantly to her accuser.

'Don't you realise that these dogs are very sensitive?' Caroline's rescuer, free of the inhibiting presence of a tall man and a small child, got into his stride. 'A lot of them are terrified of bangs. You should never have taken her out among all these crowds on that bloody ridiculous collar!'

Anna was already upset. Caroline getting away from her like that had been a dreadful shock, but she also felt guilty and certainly didn't want to have a row with a complete stranger in such crowded circumstances.

'Thank you very much for catching my dog,' she said with as much dignity as she could manage, given that she was surrounded by carrier bags and people. 'It was very lucky you had a spare lead on you, but if you could just let me have her, we'll get off home now.'

The man took her arm, then dropped it. He picked up the bag full of cheese and the fruit one and then took hold of her again. He didn't let her have Caroline, but more or less frog-marched her out of the crowd and beyond the village.

Anna protested as much as she could. She wasn't being kidnapped, obviously – in fact, she was being helped – but she didn't like it.

'I can manage!' she insisted crossly. 'You don't have to come home with me. Caroline's fine now.'

The man halted and looked down at her. 'Maybe, but by the looks of you, you need a cup of coffee. So do I. You owe me,' he added less fiercely.

Anna chose to ignore the twinkle that had appeared in the corner of his eyes, which, now she came to look at him, obviously twinkled often.

47

'You can't just invite yourself for coffee!' She said indignantly.

'I just did. Where do you live?'

'I'm not telling you! It's nothing whatever to do with you! I'm not giving you coffee!' Anna couldn't quite work this man out. One minute he had been furious, now he was intent on becoming her second ever visitor.

'I'll pay for it then,' he retorted. 'Just tell me where you live.'

'No!' Anna bit her lip hard so she couldn't smile by mistake and stopped dead. The whole situation was ridiculous. She wasn't going a step further with him.

The man discovered that it's quite difficult to drag someone who's reluctant to be dragged, especially if they're weighed down by bags of potatoes. He let go of her arm.

'Look, I realise you don't want to go telling strangers where you live,' he said reasonably, 'that's understandable, and I could survive without a cup of coffee, though not well. But there's the welfare of a dog at stake.' The twinkle had faded somewhat which made it easier for Anna to stick to her guns.

'Listen, I can look after Caroline perfectly well, I don't need you—'

'Yes you do! Trust me! I'm the rehoming officer for the local greyhound rescue centre.'

Anna, who was already quite hot, got even hotter, then she went cold. 'They told me there wasn't one.'

'They lied. Or at least, they were mistaken. I've recently taken it on. Now, tell me where you live,' he added more gently.

Anna took her time. The man, though fairly tall and wide, did not look like an axe murderer, though she realised she didn't know what an axe murderer did look like. It was unlikely that he'd been hanging round the market looking for a victim, and if he was, would he choose someone with a large dog? No, reluctant as she was to acknowledge it, the rehoming officer profile fitted better.

'It's really not a good idea for single women—' she began.

'—to announce the fact to complete strangers,' he finished for her.

The twinkle was back but Anna resolutely ignored it. 'But if they've done it by mistake, it's even more stupid to let that complete stranger into their house!'

At first glance people sometimes thought Anna was a shy and mousy creature; if this man had made the same mistake he was disabused of it now.

His expression became quizzical. 'My name is Rob Hunter. Why don't you check with whoever let you have that dog that I'm a bona-fide member of the Greyhound Trust?'

This, annoyingly, was a perfectly reasonable solution. Anna could take the man as far as Chloe's, and if Chloe knew him, OK, but if she didn't – well, with luck, it wouldn't be blatantly obvious that Anna lived next door.

Given her day so far, Anna wasn't surprised when Chloe, the one person who could say whether or not this man was an opportunist axe murderer, proved to be out. She banged on the door again, but the house felt empty and no one answered.

Rob Hunter regarded her with one raised eyebrow. It was all very well for him to find the situation potentially amusing, she was the one possibly taking her life in her hands. Hoping her sister would never learn of her complete and utter folly, she decided to take a chance. She unlocked her front door.

Chapter Four

'You'll have to excuse the—,' she began, on autopilot, and then stopped.

'Oh my God!' His cry of horror was out even before Anna had got to the word 'mess'.

She was indignant. 'Look! I'm still building it! There's no need to have such a fit.'

'There's every need, I'm afraid.' He walked into the room as well as he could, given how few floorboards there were.

'Why? And would you mind not talking so loudly. Caroline's very nervous.'

The man's glance would have withered a mature oak tree. Anna turned away. Caroline went to her bed. 'She hates men,' said Anna, having regrouped her nerves.

He regarded her, his gaze making her feel like a ten-year-old caught doing something extremely naughty. He really was a strange man, given to quick bursts of temper one minute, humour the next and back again to temper. He obviously had a short fuse, but she wasn't standing for it.

'You can see!' went on Anna, in a sort of shouted whisper. 'She's hiding!'

Caroline had indeed buried her head in Anna's sleeping bag and Rob Hunter, momentarily so angry, was transformed. He walked over to where Caroline's back end could be seen. 'Hello, darling.'

Something happened. Caroline's head emerged and she regarded the man. He went towards her, murmuring sweet nothings, and she rolled over and lay on her back with her legs in the air in an attitude of complete submission. When he started rubbing her chest and throat, she went into a state of bliss. She let her legs swing down and when the man began to caress her throat, she stretched her neck to give him greater access. It was a miracle. 'Well, she doesn't appear to hate me.'

'She knows you a bit by now, since you dragged her home,' said Anna crossly, refusing to notice that he'd stopped being angry and was twinkling again.

'Look,' he said, his words honeyed with sweet reason, 'why don't you make us a cup of coffee? We both need one.'

She was indeed desperately in need of something – even a glass of water – but should she give in to this man's demands? As he wasn't paying her any attention, concentrating his social skills on the dog instead, she decided that she could put the kettle on without appearing to capitulate. Caroline was now sitting up, giving him a paw. Anna suspected that if she'd had any furniture beyond a kitchen chair, and he had sat in it, Caroline would have jumped on his lap in an instant.

When Caroline stood up, so did her uninvited guest, and he ran his hands all over her.

'What are you doing now?' demanded Anna, affronted and amazed at the same time. 'It looks as if you're checking for broken bones.'

'I am.' He continued to pull Caroline's silken ears through his fingers, over and over, while she leant against him, gaga with adoration.

'Oh,' said Anna, less amazed and more affronted. 'Did you find any?'

'No.'

Now he opened her mouth and inspected Caroline's teeth. 'These need a bit of attention. Have you taken her to the vet since you've had her?'

'No.' She tried not to sound defiant, and failed. 'I haven't had her long. I thought she should get used to me before I dragged her off to the vet.'

'But you were quite happy to drag her off to the market and let her get traumatised by a backfiring car?' His reproach was accompanied by a half-smile, but it was still a reproach.

'Listen, she was fine until that happened! And how could I have known a bloody car would make a noise like a gun going off? You're being totally unreasonable.' And Anna felt totally wrong-footed.

He sat back on his heels and looked up at her. 'I'm sorry if I seem like that, but it's my job to check out your house to see if it's suitable. And quite obviously, it's not. And if I may say so, I'm not convinced you're a responsible-enough person to have charge of her, either.'

'Well, it's bit late to find that out! I've had Caroline for a . . .' She hesitated. She had actually had Caroline for a week, but did he need to know that? 'For quite a bit. And I'm not giving her up!' It was only now that Anna realised how important the dog was to her. Up until then, she'd thought that if Chloe said she and the family were moving to a bigger house and wanted to take Caroline with them, she'd have been delighted. Now she suddenly knew that she and Caroline were a team, and inseparable. 'And if you really want coffee as badly as you said you did, you'd better stop treating me as if I'm a dog-molester!'

He chuckled but went on seriously, 'None of the proper procedures can have been gone through when you took Caroline,' he said, rather too patiently for Anna's liking. 'And you probably don't know the first thing about how to look after a rescue greyhound.'

'I didn't take her! You make it sound as if I stole her.' Anna knew she was getting more het up than was sensible, but couldn't help herself. 'A woman called Star

52

came, just for a visit, and left her with me, without us even knowing.'

'Us?'

'My neighbour was with me. She's very big in grey-hound rescue.'

He coughed, possibly concealing a laugh Anna chose not to notice. Instead she scowled. No way in the world was Caroline going to be wrested from her, but she was only too aware of how unorthodox their union had been. 'Well, you're not having Caroline back. She's mine now; that's all there is to it. Do you take sugar?'

'Just a splash of milk, if you've got it.'

Anna moved back to the kettle, the mugs and the instant coffee.

'Did you go through all the paperwork? Does the Trust know where she came from? That she's not stolen?'

Anna poured boiling water into the mugs. 'That was all organised for me.'

She carried a mug of coffee over to him and put it down so it was within reach. She planned to lure Caroline away from this man, for, however much Caroline loved him, he was not having her! Anna was in a custody battle, and she was going to win. She pulled out Caroline's collar, which she had stuffed into her pocket, and put it on. It was a badge of ownership.

Rob Hunter raised the coffee mug. 'Cheers!' he said.

Anna went back to where she'd left her own mug and took a much-needed sip.

Rob Hunter sighed. 'Well, you're obviously very fond of her but letting her get away from you in the market could have had fatal consequences. You'll have to be much more careful in future. Taking a dog you don't know very well into such a crowded situation—'

'Oh, do be quiet! I know she slipped her collar, but that won't happen again now I know about it! And she was fine with all those people.'

He looked at her, apparently doubtful. 'I'd better have a proper look round and see if it is possible for you to keep her.'

Anna became defensive again. 'Absolutely not! This is my home!'

He sighed again. 'I realise that this has come as a shock to you – and to me if it's any consolation – but the Trust should never have let you have a dog on a permanent basis without giving you a home check. I might as well do it now, while I'm here.' He almost smiled. 'It would save you having to have me here again.'

Anna almost smiled back. 'In which case, help yourself.'

After all, she reasoned, righteous indignation could only sustain you so long, and as most of the house was visible from where he was, and Caroline couldn't get up the ladder, making the upstairs irrelevant, there seemed no point in flinging herself across the boarded-up windows.

He strode to the back of the house. Had he been anyone else in the world, Anna would have explained how she hoped to have double doors out to the garden, but she said nothing.

'Is there a garden out there?' he asked, turning to look at her.

'Yes. It's not very big, but there's a common not far away where we go for exercise.'

'Is the garden secure? They can jump quite high, although not as high as lurchers, thank goodness.'

Anna opened the back door so he could see into the small, square space that would one day be a charming, secluded courtyard garden. The fence round it was higher than Anna could look over without getting out the ladder.

'That seems secure enough. And you've been clearing up the mess. Very important to keep their living conditions clean.'

'Who'd have thought it?' Anna murmured. He had put his officious hat on again.

54

'And how is Caroline with other animals?' Rob Hunter went on, ignoring Anna's sarcasm. He had taken over Caroline's ears again. Anna gave up her custody battle, but only temporarily.

'She's hopeless with cats, but she doesn't chase small dogs. I haven't let her off the lead, though. Chloe told me that lots of greyhounds can never be let off the lead unless they're in an enclosed field.' Anna felt it was important to show she had some knowledge of the dog-adoption business.

'Well, that's sensible. Now, her collar. It is very smart and I see you've got lots of contact telephone numbers on her medal, but as you've discovered, she only has to turn round and she's out of it.'

Anna sighed. There was nothing she could say in her defence.

'This collar is fine for inside use, but when you're out you need a slip collar as well.'

'OK. I'll get one.'

'And does she suffer from separation anxiety?'

'What?' This man really was the limit.

'Does she destroy the place when you leave her?'

'No. I haven't ever left her for very long, but she's fine when I go to town for a couple of hours or so.' She didn't tell him that she'd bought her an electric blanket to sleep on. He would think this totally overindulgent.

'And although you might not like the idea, an indoor kennel is a very good idea. It makes a den, a place of safety for them.' He looked around. 'You put something over the end so it's like a tent, and apart from anything else, it keeps them free from draughts.'

'I don't like the idea,' she said stubbornly.

'I thought you wouldn't, although they are good, really.' Seeing he wasn't getting anywhere he went on, 'What are you feeding her?'

'A complete food, as recommended by the Trust.'

'And she likes it?'

'Most of the time. Sometimes she doesn't seem hungry.'

'And what do you do about that?'

Anna shrugged. She considered herself good at second-guessing – she could always get top marks in multiple-choice quizzes to test your personality. But this time she had no idea what the right answer was. She fell back on the truth. 'I chuck it out for the birds. I assume she'll eat all her food next time.'

He nodded in reluctant approval. 'Most women tempt them with other food, tinned dog food that will give them the runs.' He paused for the full horror of this to sink in. 'Another alternative is raw tripe. It's cheap, very nutritious, and excellent for their teeth. But it does smell rather.'

However keen Anna was to avoid being classed with 'most women', she didn't think she wanted to feed Caroline on raw tripe. 'She's perfectly happy with the dried stuff.'

'Can I see where you feed her?'

Anna led him to where the two buckets held the two washing-up bowls up off the ground. One was full of water; the other was empty. Now she no longer felt he was accusing her of dog abuse, she felt less defensive.

'Good. That's fine,' he said.

'I do realise it's important to feed the dogs off the ground and everything.'

'So that's all right then,' he said and suddenly Anna was exhausted by the entire inquisition.

'Look, Mr . . .'

'Hunter, Rob Hunter, but you can call me Rob.'

Anna ignored this friendly invitation. 'Mr Hunter, I do appreciate that if you're from the Greyhound Trust you have to make sure that the dogs are rehomed properly. But if you're satisfied that Caroline is being looked after properly, could you please go? I've got lots to do, and

I'm sure there's some other innocent dog-owner you could be harassing.'

'I am satisfied that you're looking after Caroline properly, but I should warn you that she'll find a nearly spiral staircase very difficult. She may never be able to get upstairs.'

'I'm not planning to have a nearly spiral staircase,' Anna said firmly.

He frowned. 'Aren't you? Isn't that what the rest of the row have?'

'Maybe,' Anna said a bit less firmly.

'Then you should have the same.'

'Mr Hunter, what sort of staircase I have is absolutely nothing to do with you! I plan for Caroline to sleep on my bed, so I will have a staircase that's easy for her to manage!' This wasn't remotely true, but she knew it would annoy him. 'Now, will you please leave!'

He raised an sceptical eyebrow and let himself out of the front door.

Busy or not, Anna had to abandon Caroline for a few moments and storm round to Chloe's in order to rail about Rob Hunter's awfulness. If Chloe hadn't come back from wherever she had been, she would die of frustration. Fortunately for her blood pressure, Chloe was unpacking shopping and opening tins of baked beans. Although, as the boys were all home, Anna had to limit her language rather.

'Bastard!' she mouthed at Chloe, who seemed a bit taken aback. 'Not you,' she said aloud. 'That pooey man who came to check on Caroline.'

'Anna said pooey,' said Tom.

'Sorry,' said Anna, 'but he was! He asked all sorts of dreadfully impertinent questions.'

'But that's his job!' Chloe pointed out rashly. 'When did he come? And what did you say his name was?'

'Rob . . . Barbour? Harvester? I can't remember although he's only just gone.'

'His name wasn't Hunter, was it?' Chloe became thoughtful.

'That's it! I knew it was something to do with wellington boots. But, honestly, he was so objectionable.' Although, Anna privately acknowledged, it was the fact that he was right that was most enraging her. Chloe found a saucepan and tipped in the beans, letting Anna rave on. 'I suppose we did meet in rather difficult circumstances but he was dreadfully . . . arrogant, although I don't suppose that's quite what I mean.'

'That can make men more attractive. Like Mr Darcy.' The beans got a cursory stir.

'He was just – I don't know – overbearing,' said Anna determinedly, although as she thought briefly about the man who'd filled all her romantic consciousness for the last three years, she acknowledged that he was a bit arrogant too.

'So what were the difficult circumstances?'

'I went to the market this morning.'

'Oh, it's great, isn't it? We went really early, which is the best time really, before it gets busy, then did the supermarket shop. So what happened?' Without looking at what she was doing, Chloe extracted two slices of bread and put them in the toaster.

'A car backfired and Caroline slipped her lead.'

'What! That's terrible!' At last the horror of the situation penetrated Chloe's maternal bubble. 'You mean you took Caroline to the market?'

'Well, yes. Is that a bad thing?'

'Not necessarily, but you haven't had her very long, she might not have liked all those people.'

'She was fine with all the people,' said Anna, feeling betrayed. 'It was the car backfiring. And you bought her the collar!'

'What was wrong with the collar? It's beautiful and it had her telephone numbers on the medal.'

'Yes but they can slip out of them really easily! As I have just found out!'

'Oh, Anna, I am sorry.' Chloe was horrified. 'I had no idea. Sit down. Let me make you a cup of coffee. Or I think there might be a beer in the fridge somewhere.'

'I'd better get on.'

'Go on, sit down and have a beer.' Not taking no for an answer, Chloe produced a cold can from the fridge and a glass. 'At the risk of seeming unsympathetic and changing the subject' – Chloe smiled – 'I've got some good news!'

'Oh? What?'

'Mike's coming home. Next Thursday. And so I've arranged that dinner party I promised you. Just some local friends.' An expression Anna couldn't interpret crossed her face – it was mischievous, almost. 'On Friday.'

Anna was so touched and quite glad to think about something other than the horror of Caroline and Rob Hunter that she didn't comment on the expression. It was such a sweet thought and she was looking forward to meeting Mike. 'But will you want to go to all that trouble when Mike's just got back? Won't you want to be just family?'

'God no, and as for all that trouble, people will bring things, different courses.' Chloe paused. 'No need to look so stricken. I only ask people to do that if they've got kitchens.'

Chapter Five

✦

Chloe's dinner party shone temptingly at Anna all through the hectic week that ran up to it. She was determined, for that evening, to throw off her Girl-with-drill image and be pretty and feminine. She would arrange to have a bath at Chloe's the night before, as there would be too much pressure on the bathroom for her to have it on the night. She would get it right!

But before she could panic at the state of her nails she had a lot to do. First thing on Monday morning she bought Caroline a very beautiful slip-collar-and-lead-combined in bright blue. As it was made of soft rope, it didn't look as if it would hurt Caroline if she pulled at it, and everyone agreed it enhanced her already lovely appearance. She and Chloe's boys took it for a test-run to the park in the evening, while Chloe made supper.

'She likes it,' announced Bruno.

'She couldn't tell us if she didn't,' said Tom, precociously.

'I think we'd be able to guess,' said Anna, keeping the peace.

She had had a good week with the house, too. Chloe had recommended a good electrician and on Wednesday, he came round to check the wiring.

When she opened the door to him, he was so young and fit that Anna suspected Chloe of matchmaking. Chloe was very like Laura in some ways, and this was just the sort of thing Laura might have done.

'Hi, I'm Colin, the sparky,' said this vision in ripped jeans and tight T-shirt. 'My dad sent me.'

'Your dad?'

He nodded. 'You spoke to him on the phone but he had a job to finish over at Miserden so he asked me to come instead. We work together,' he added, possibly noticing Anna's misgivings. 'I'm qualified.'

Anna opened the door wider. 'I'm so sorry. I was just expecting an older man. Chloe – she lives next door – said she knew this wonderful electrician and . . .' She faltered. She had been going to say that Chloe would have mentioned it if the wonderful electrician had also been gorgeous. Now she felt rather embarrassed. 'I don't know, I just thought he was . . .'

'I've only joined up with Dad quite recently,' said Colin reassuringly. 'Now, shall I have a look at what's needed?'

Later he announced, 'This has all been done quite recently,' to Anna's immense relief. 'I'll just check everything, but whoever did it seems to have known what they were doing.'

'Well, that's a start. I thought it looked OK, but although I know a bit, I wasn't quite sure about current regulations.'

'Current regulations? I like that! A good joke for a sparky.'

Anna smiled because he was friendly, not because she thought much of his puns. 'Would you like a coffee? Or tea? I've got biscuits. I bought them specially.'

'Tea, please. Nice place you've got here. Bit of a mess now, obviously, but it's going to be really great. And you can put the floorboards down now.'

'I hope I can. The previous owners ripped them all up and I found them propped up outside against the fence. I hope they're not too badly rotted.'

'Left out in the open, were they?'

'Not quite. Someone had put some tarpaulin over them. I'll have a look when you've gone.'

Colin insisted on having a look with her. 'They're OK,' he said.

'They do seem to be,' she agreed, pleased and surprised. The bottom of that one has rotted a bit, but I can easily sort that out.'

'I know a very good chippy if you need one,' said Colin. 'And it looks as if you might.'

Anna smiled again. 'I am hoping to do most of the work myself, but if I should need some help, I'll get back to you.'

When he'd gone, and Caroline had emerged from Anna's sleeping bag, she started fitting the floorboards. She took up the square of plasterboard, and laid the boards in place. She didn't mean actually to do it, she just wanted to work out where they fitted and whether they were all there, but by the time the light was gone and she couldn't work any more, a good half of them were down.

'The hard part is going to be the sanding,' Anna told Caroline as she ate her cheese on toast, feeding the dog the crusts in a way not approved of in the Greyhound Trust handbook. 'The machine is bloody heavy. I'll have to ask Chloe to get it from the hire shop for me. It's really hard work. Like putting down the floorboards. Goodness, I need a bath!' But although Chloe was very generous with her hot water, Anna didn't like to presume and just brushed her teeth and washed her feet.

'Now if I'd washed my hair as well,' she told Caroline, who was developing her listening skills, 'I'd really feel clean.'

On Thursday, Anna got Chloe to drop her off at the hire shop while she went to Waitrose, and then pick her up afterwards. It took two hefty men to get the machine into the back of Chloe's car but Anna was confident she and Chloe would manage to get it out again, and down the lane.

'We can always get someone to help,' said Chloe as they drove off.

'We won't need it. Laura and I discovered there's nothing two really determined women can't do if they set their minds to it.'

'Huh,' grunted Chloe, not as averse to borrowing muscle if required as Anna seemed to be. 'And put our backs out doing it.'

In fact, they got the machine along to Anna's house without too much difficulty.

'Are you sure you'll manage that beast?' asked Chloe.

'Of course!' Anna laughed. 'You go and make your melba toast or whatever. I'll be fine.'

'Darling, melba toast is so seventies! But if you're sure you can manage, I'll go. It's not the cooking that takes the time, it's the cleaning up.'

The machine was incredibly heavy to use, but seeing the dirt of ages being whirred away was hugely satisfying. Caroline hated it, and Anna put her bed in the little garden so she'd avoid the worst of the dust. Luckily it was a sunny, relatively warm day, and she needn't be out there for long.

'I don't think you'd like wearing a mask, would you, sweetie?' Anna said to Caroline, stroking her silky ears. 'Although you should have one really.'

Thursday passed. Anna was absorbed in getting her floor perfect, and it was only when she heard Mike, or so she presumed, arriving home next door that she realised another bath opportunity had slipped by. She couldn't ask now.

'Still,' said Anna brightly to Caroline. Her hands and arms were still vibrating from the sander, although she had finished a while ago. 'It'll be better to have one tomorrow, after the boys have had theirs, then I'll be really clean. Chloe and Mike won't feel so intruded upon then.'

Caroline listened to this with an expression that said her mistress was a complete idiot, but utterly adorable. Anna was quite happy with this opinion.

To Anna's eternal gratitude, on Friday morning, Chloe, Mike and the children took the sander back to the shop. They collected it while Anna was out with Caroline and although sad that she'd missed an opportunity to meet Mike before the dinner she was very relieved to get the machine out of her tiny house.

When she'd settled Caroline she got out her own domestic sander and started on the edges.

The day passed happily, and after the electric sander could do no more, Anna got out sandpaper and a block. She couldn't stop. Every pass made the floor look more beautiful.

Eventually the signature tune of the *Archers* penetrated her obsession. 'Oh my God! It's after seven o'clock! The dinner party! Oh, Caroline, I've done it now. No bath. No time. And I haven't even thought about what to wear!'

Anna, feeling like an expectant father, boiled a large saucepan of water on her little stove as well as putting the kettle on. She wasn't exactly panicking, and hot water was essential for washing, but she did feel a bit like a headless chicken, not knowing what to do first.

'I can't believe this, Caroline,' she said, tipping water into the washing-up bowl that currently doubled as a sink. 'I've spent all week looking forward to this, and then I nearly forget to go!'

In retrospect, washing her hair had probably been a mistake, but it had been horribly full of dust and Anna was the sort of girl who felt clean hair was the most important thing. The fact that she would arrive with it still wet was just too bad.

'At least washing your hair gets your hands clean,' she said, inspecting her nails. Her hands were in a terrible state, but there was nothing much she could do about that.

She found her least scruffy jeans, her cleanest top and a scarf that Laura had given her, now rather crumpled. It wasn't haute couture but Chloe had assured her the meal wasn't going to be haute cuisine either, so she hoped she'd get away with it.

'I may have awful hands and slightly dusty clothes,' Anna told Caroline as she tucked her up, 'but my hair is at least clean and my floor is going to be fabulous!'

'It's always the people who are closest to school who come late,' said an attractive dark-haired woman as Anna came in through the door. She had never seen Chloe's house so crowded and admired the heroic furniture moving that must have gone on in order to fit in so many people.

'Anna, darling!' called Chloe from the stove. 'Mike, say hello, get her a drink and do the introductions!'

Mike identified himself by getting up from the row of people who were squashed on to a small sofa by the fire. He was tall and gangly with an open, friendly face. Anna warmed to him immediately.

He stepped over several sets of legs and took her in his arms and gave her a hug. 'I've heard so much about you, I feel I know you already. What would you like to drink? Red or white – and don't tell me you want something soft because you don't have to drive home.'

Anna, still a bit breathless from her dash to get ready, handed him the bottle of red wine she was clutching. 'Red, please.'

'Can you pour Anna a glass of red, Ted?' Mike said. 'The bottle's by you and there's a glass on the table. Now, introductions.'

Once she had had a chance to get her breath Anna realised there weren't that many people there really, it's just they were all so squashed.

'OK, from the right,' said Mike. 'Dorothy – she was the

one who was rude about you being late. Ted is her husband.' Dorothy and Ted both waved in a friendly way.

'We're always late,' said Dorothy, 'so I'm always thrilled when we're not the last.'

'This is Sue.' A pretty blonde-haired woman nodded. 'And Ivan, her husband. He's Welsh.' Ivan had thick curly black hair and looked as if he might play rugby. Although it meant stepping over everyone else, he insisted on getting up and giving Anna a hug too.

'Must make sure you get a proper welcome,' he said.

Anna smiled. Everyone was being so wonderfully friendly.

'Right,' said Mike, 'now you squash yourself down there. You can't move but you don't have to until dinner's ready and heaven knows when that will be.'

He cast a calculating eye at Chloe who was beating a sauce with vigour. She appeared not to have been listening but a moment later she said, 'If you hadn't let the boys get overexcited, I could have got this in the oven hours ago. You'd think, wouldn't you' – she addressed the company – 'that with Sue bringing a pudding and Dorothy the starter, I could have managed a main course.'

'It's so difficult with children,' said Dorothy, sympathetically. 'We haven't had people round for ages. It's just too much hard work to get the house tidy, cook the meal and get rid of the children. I always forget I have to cook for them, too.'

'No change there then,' said her husband.

Dorothy dug him in the ribs.

'Well.' Chloe clambered over people's legs until she could perch on a little three-legged stool that was the only place left. 'That shouldn't take more than half an hour to brown. The oven's turned right up. We've got to eat our starters – looks fab, by the way, Dor – and we're still waiting for our mystery guest.' She winked at Anna.

Anna felt suddenly tired. She didn't want a man found for her; she had her man, locked in her heart.

'So, who is he?' demanded Dorothy and Sue together.

'Honestly! He wouldn't be a mystery guest if I told you, now would he?' Chloe laughed.

'Well, do we know him?' Sue persisted.

'Don't think so. He's newish to the area, which is why I wanted him to meet Anna. They'll have things in common.'

'Not necessarily,' said Dorothy, earning Anna's gratitude.

'Oh, it'll be fine.' Chloe drained her glass. 'Any more wine in that bottle?'

Anna had drunk two glasses of red wine and was fast feeling the effects by the time there was a knock at the door and the mystery guest appeared.

'I am so sorry,' he said. 'I ran out of petrol, then I got lost. Although I shouldn't have, I've been here before.' One look around the room stopped him in his tracks. 'Oh. You're here.'

He and Anna looked at each other and Anna's head swam. For a moment he seemed as confused and surprised as she was and then he grinned apologetically. Anna did her best to smile back but she was so cross! Rob Hunter! How could Chloe have done this to her? And without warning! Why hadn't she told her? Some friend she was. Anna wondered if she could get up and walk out, or if it would be just too rude. It would, she decided, but also she was too squashed in.

Fortunately attention was taken away from her while bottles and flowers were handed over. He was obviously as astonished as she was and this made her feel a bit better disposed towards him. If it had been obvious he'd known she was going to be there she would have left, squashed or not.

There being nowhere else to sit, he perched on the arm of the sofa and twinkled down at Anna, his eyes full of apology. 'I expect I'm the last person you want to see.'

'Why's that?' asked Sue.

'We've met,' said Anna, because everyone was looking at her and she felt she had to, not because she particularly wanted to. It was going to be a long night.

Chloe, who knew they'd met, kept her face turned away guiltily. Rob and Anna both started to speak at once and then stopped.

'You go,' he said gallantly.

Anna sighed. 'Well, I was at the market with my dog and a car backfired. She ran away and . . . Rob' – although she privately thought of him as the Bastard Dog Man she couldn't call him this in public, – 'rescued her.'

'So he's your hero?' asked Dorothy. 'Rescuing your dog from certain death on the road?'

'Not exactly,' said Rob, a little ruefully.

'But why on earth not?' went on Dorothy, mystified. 'I always fall in love with my vet!'

'I don't think Anna's met her vet yet,' said Rob infuriatingly. 'And I was probably a bit too bossy and overbearing to fall in love with.'

Anna was scarlet in the face by now. 'Yes, definitely,' she agreed, wishing she could melt into the sofa and disappear.

Dorothy took another long look at Rob and sighed deeply. 'Well, I just don't understand.'

Had Anna had an opportunity she might well have explained that she was already deeply in love with someone else, but the moment was lost as Mike came to her rescue.

'Well, now we've got that clear,' he said, 'fill your glasses, everyone. Ted, do the honours, would you? I can't reach over there.'

'Yes, then it's time to eat,' said Chloe still not quite daring even to look in Anna's direction. 'I haven't worked out where everyone should sit because it never works with eight.'

Anna felt certain that with so many people she could avoid sitting next to Rob Hunter but her certainty was misplaced. She took the last place at the table and had to squeeze in next to him. She glanced at Chloe to see if she could have possibly engineered the *placement* as well as inviting Rob without warning her, but realised even she couldn't have managed that.

'Well,' said Chloe when everyone was sitting down, contemplating the plate of smoked salmon, blinis and crème fraîche on their plates, 'before we start, I'll re-do the introductions for Rob. Oh hell!' She jumped up. 'I've forgotten the caviar garnish!'

'It's lumpfish, actually,' said Dorothy, while Chloe burrowed in the kitchen.

'I'll introduce people, then,' said Mike, obviously used to his wife's forgetfulness.

Anna was trying to keep a gap between her arm and Rob Hunter's. It was not easy. The table was so crowded.

'. . . and this is Rob Hunter, whom we met through greyhound rescue.'

'Yes, I'm the rehoming officer,' he said, looking down at Anna, who ignored him. 'For my sins,' he added.

'And obviously mine,' muttered Anna, who was disconcerted to find she had lost too many of her inhibitions.

'And have you lived here long?' asked Dorothy who, fortunately for Anna, hadn't heard. Dorothy took the garnish from Chloe and began sprinkling it over the plates.

'A couple of years. I've only got involved in the Greyhound Trust quite recently.'

'Why?' asked Sue, and was nudged by her husband, who was sitting next to her.

'So nosy!' Ivan muttered.

'Well, when I first came down here from London I was with someone. We were downshifting. She worked in London and did a weekly commute, and I had a new job here.'

'So what happened to your partner?' Sue persisted.

'Sue!' Ivan was mortified. 'It's all right, mate, you don't have to answer.'

'Yes he does,' said Chloe and Dorothy in unison.

'You women!' complained Ivan. 'Can't let a man eat his dinner before he's completed a questionnaire on his private life.'

Rob laughed. 'It's OK, I don't mind the Spanish Inquisition.' Ivan raised an eyebrow. 'She stayed in London more and more,' Rob went on. 'She didn't really like country life. And she didn't like dogs at all.'

'How did you get together with her, then?' asked Sue.

'Let's change the subject,' said Chloe who, having got all the information she needed, was willing to let Rob Hunter off the hook. 'More wine, everyone?'

'But we don't know why he got involved with grey-hounds yet,' objected Sue.

'Because I love dogs and wanted to do something in the community,' said Rob quickly, as if he'd said it many times before.

'Well, that's all explained then. Now, more wine, everyone?' Chloe repeated.

'I really shouldn't,' said Anna, covering her glass.

'Oh, go on,' said Rob, taking her hand away and giving her more. 'I've gone through my torture, you have to go through yours. It's not as if you have to drive home.' He whispered this last bit and, in spite of her resolution to hate him, Anna giggled.

'I think I've already had too much,' she said.

'I'll get a jug of water,' said Chloe. 'I meant to buy some but I forgot.'

'Not top of your shopping list?' asked Ivan.

'No, I was thinking of you, Ivan, and that made me buy wine.' Chloe dealt with this teasing easily.

'So, Anna,' said Sue, 'we've heard how Rob got down here, what's your story?'

'Well, I bought the house next door. I'm doing it up. I hope to sell it,' Anna replied; it was obviously her turn to be interrogated.

'Oh, so what do you do?' asked Ted.

'I'm an interior designer.'

'What, like Linda Barker?' asked Sue.

'I'm not sure what Linda Barker does, to be honest, but it doesn't mean just choosing paint colours and fabrics, although that comes into it,' she said. 'It's much more about soil pipes.'

She had hoped that this would end the conversation, but they were a robust lot, not to be put off by the mere mention of sewage arrangements.

There followed several minutes of questioning until Chloe called time. 'Golly, I think even I've grasped that Anna is practically an architect,' she said. 'Can we gather the plates? I think the main course must be brown by now.'

'Bet you're glad that's over,' Rob whispered in her ear under the guise of taking her plate.

Anna chuckled. 'Kind of.'

'OK, everyone!' announced Chloe, pulling a large dish out of the oven. 'Here it is. Cannelloni stuffed with ricotta and spinach. Ted, can you reach into the fridge and get out some more white? Angel! Oh, and the parmesan. It's got it on already, but in case you want some more. Mike! The salad.'

No party with Chloe as the hostess could be dull, and now the interrogation was over, Anna really began to enjoy herself. Rob made little asides to her from time to time that made her feel part of things, and as people were genuinely interested in her as a person, it wasn't hard to tell them about what she did.

71

Pudding was rich and chocolatey, served with cream and raspberries, and after it Anna felt thoroughly stuffed. She had been doing hard physical work and not sleeping as well as she might, owing to the hardness of the floor and Caroline's nocturnal attentions, and was getting sleepier and sleepier. She refused coffee or tea, feeling too tired to drink it.

'I'm going to take Anna home,' Rob announced. 'She's turning into a dormouse before our very eyes.'

'Well, you haven't got far to take her,' said Mike. 'And you can come back and have a brandy.'

'I won't have brandy, but a cup of coffee would be nice.'

'You don't need to take me home,' said Anna, indignation waking her up somewhat. What did he want from her now?

'Yes I do. Trust me.' He looked a little anxiously at her.

When all the goodbyes had been said, and anyone who could reach had kissed Anna, she and Rob fought their way into the path. It was a clear night and the stars shone brightly.

'I love the stars,' said Anna, suddenly overcome with red wine and a balmy evening. 'They're so much brighter down here than they ever were in London.'

'Less light pollution,' said Rob. 'I love them, too. Now,' he went on briskly, rather to Anna's relief, 'the reason I wanted to walk you home was that there's something I've got to tell you.'

'Oh, what?' Anna shivered; all her fuzzy romantic feelings about stars dissipated.

'You're going to get a letter tomorrow.'

'How do you know? Have you been reading teacups or something?'

'No. It's from my office.'

'Why?' She fought to remember if she knew what he did, but it seemed most of their conversation had been about his interest in dogs.

72

'I work for the listed buildings department.'

'So?'

'Yours is a listed building.'

'I know, but how . . .' Her mouth grew dry. He had been all over her house when he was checking it for Caroline. He must have seen something terrible. She suddenly felt wide awake.

He watched the pennies that were dropping like hailstones. 'And none of the work that was done on it before you bought it had permission,' he went on softly. 'You'll have to come in so we can look at your plans.'

All the goodwill towards him that she'd built up during the evening vanished. Not only had this man bullied her about how she should look after her dog, now he was bullying her about her house. He was Bastard House Man as well as Bastard Dog Man.

'Well, that's . . . terrible.'

'Try not to worry too much. But I felt I had to tell you. It would have been a bit of a shock if you'd come into the office and saw me when you weren't expecting to.'

'This is just an outrage. I don't know what to say.' Rationally she knew he was trying to break it to her gently, but why on earth hadn't he mentioned it earlier? Did he take pleasure in the art of surprise?

'Don't say anything. Just go to bed and put it out of your mind until you get the letter. You can't do anything until we've seen the plans. Have you got your key?' he added.

Anna despised the sort of woman who allowed men to unlock their front doors for them but as in this case it meant she didn't have to speak to the man involved, she handed it over.

'Goodnight, Anna.' He kissed both her cheeks while she held open the door and couldn't duck. 'I had a lovely

73

evening. And I'm really sorry I'm the listed buildings officer as well as the rehoming officer.'

She went into the house without saying anything, too angry and confused to speak. She felt so betrayed.

Chapter Six

Caroline's cold nose nudged Anna's cheek and she woke up. She felt thirsty, a little muzzy but happy.

'Hello, darling,' she said, rubbing her eyes and yawning. 'Sorry I overslept.' She hauled herself out of her sleeping bag and padded to the back door to let Caroline out, admiring the beauty of the floor as she went.

'It'll look fab when it's treated,' she told Caroline through the open door. She poured herself a glass of water and stared out at the little overgrown patch. 'I had a lovely evening. Rob wasn't too bad as I got to know him a bit so your taste wasn't completely off when you liked him so much.' She put the kettle on and then remembered. 'Oh my God! The letter! He wasn't nice at all – he's the listed buildings inspector! Ergh!'

She ran to the front door to see if the post had come. It had, and in amongst a lot of junk mail for the previous owners was a long white envelope. It looked very official and she didn't want to open it. She had always been a bit of a coward about opening her post.

She made herself a cup of tea first. After all, a few minutes' delay wouldn't matter.

The letter, when she did get to it, having read through the junk mail first (just in case there really was a massive cheque in any of it), didn't say much. It just requested her to ring the office to make an appointment to visit them at her earliest opportunity. But it still made her feel slightly sick. She made and drank another cup of tea and then telephoned her sister.

Anna didn't like asking for help – she had struggled so hard to get out from under her sister's blanket of advice – but this time, she felt she had to confer with someone, and Laura was the obvious choice. For once, Laura didn't inundate Anna with 'I told you so's'.

'You can definitely get retrospective planning permission,' Laura said, 'and I expect it's the same for listed buildings. I didn't know your house was listed.' She sounded impressed.

'Actually, life would be much easier if it weren't, then I could just do what I liked.' Anna paused. 'If only I hadn't got Caroline I would never have met that horrible man and he would never have come into my house.'

'You might have met him through Chloe,' said Laura reasonably.

'But I wouldn't have had him in my house!'

'You might have done! You might have liked him and had him over for coffee!'

Anna was just about to deny this but realised it might involve her explaining about Max. Anna had never told Laura, and now was not the time to enlighten her. 'Well, anyway, I have got Caroline, and wouldn't be without her.' She sighed.

'Don't worry too much, love,' her sister reassured her. 'Take along your plans to show them what you intend to do, and I'm sure they'll be fine.'

'You think so? I have got some quite detailed drawings.'

'And your drawing was always lovely. Oh!' said Laura suddenly. 'I was going to ring you only you rang me first. There was an email for you!'

'What? How could there be?'

'It's from your old college. They're organising a reunion and they managed to track you down through me. It's because I kept my own name for my business, I suppose. Anyway, you must get in touch if you want to go. They're organising something in London. Quite soon, I think. When are you going to get a computer, by the way? They're not that expensive.'

'London,' said Anna, ignoring this oft-repeated question, her heart beating faster with hope. 'I'm not sure I could leave Caroline and go to London.'

'Shall I read you the email?' Laura read it out, ending: '"We've managed to get in touch with lots of our tutors including some of the guest lecturers – Max Gordon, Eric State and others."'

The moisture fled from Anna's mouth. Just hearing his name was enough to send her into a flutter. 'Um, it would be nice to see everyone again.' She tried to sound casual.

'Perhaps Chloe could look after the dog? Or if not, perhaps I could come down and stay the night. You'll want to stay over in London, won't you?'

'I suppose so. I haven't had time to think about it, really.'

'I could come down and stay the weekend with you, and look after the dog on the Saturday night,' Laura offered.

'Is it on a Saturday night?'

'Bound to be.'

Anna hesitated. 'I couldn't put you to all that trouble, Laura, and this house isn't fit for guests yet.'

'I'm not a guest, I'm your sister! And I'm used to building sites.'

'It's a very kind offer,' said Anna. 'I'll find out more about it, and what Chloe says and everything.'

'I'd really love a weekend away from the boys.'

Anna heard the wistfulness in her sister's voice. 'You could come down anyway.'

'No, I couldn't justify abandoning everyone up here unless I was on a mission of mercy.'

They continued to argue gently about this until one of

Anna's nephews ended the call for them by pulling the phone out of its socket. Then Anna cleared the floor so she could seal it.

Anna managed to get an appointment with Rob Hunter the day after she rang the office, so on Tuesday, she put on the same jeans she had worn for the dinner party and her most entire jumper – one without huge holes under the arms, or with the welt hanging off the end of her sleeve. She put her plans in her drawings tube, and, having left Caroline in Chloe's house watching the morning chat shows, set off to town on her bicycle. As she cycled, she thought about her beautiful floor, protected by three coats of wax and looking like an ice-rink.

The building was imposing and, having found a place to park and lock her bike, Anna went nervously up the steps, her plans under her arm. She was sweating slightly, from nerves and from the bike ride, but she was determined not to be bullied by officialdom, particularly in the form of Bastard Dog Man.

'Come and sit down,' he said eventually when he opened the door. He smiled. 'I'm sorry to do this to you.'

Anna went into his office and sat on the chair opposite the desk. 'Then why do it?' She didn't return the smile. She was not going to forgive him.

'It's my job. I really am sorry.' His ruefulness would have made her mouth twitch under normal circumstances, but these were not normal.

'You came into my house under false pretences to spy on me,' she accused before remembering her determination to behave in a calm and professional manner.

'No I didn't! I came in because of Caroline. How is she, by the way?'

'Fine. Chloe's got her.'

'And have you taken her to the vet yet?'

'No! Now can we get to the point?' She realised that

she shouldn't have been so belligerent but she couldn't help herself, she felt so wrong-footed. She should have realised when she first saw the house that what had happened to it wouldn't have conformed to regulations, but she'd been blinded by the potential, the views and the price.

'OK.' He looked down at his papers and then up at her. 'Obviously, I've seen your house. I know what desecrations— Sorry?'

'I thought for a minute you'd said decorations,' said Anna, thinking she should open her mouth before it welded itself shut for ever.

'I'm aware you didn't eviscerate—'

A stifled whimper emerged from between Anna's tightly closed lips.

'I beg your pardon? Did I forget to put my teeth in this morning?'

Anna refused to allow the laugh to escape. 'No,' she said solemnly. 'I just don't know what you mean.'

'Eviscerate? I mean rip the guts and heart and lungs out of your house.'

'Oh. Nothing too emotional then.'

He regarded her quizzically and a little sadly. 'I'm afraid it's all going to have to go back.'

'Well, obviously, I've put the floorboards back now.'

'And the staircase?'

'Well, hardly! I only got the floor done last week! And have you any idea how difficult—'

'Staircases are to make? Well, you'll have to get your cabinetmaker to copy the one in the house next door.'

'I've got my drawings. Of the staircase I planned. It's very tasteful, and won't look out of place.'

He shook his head. 'It's got to be as near to the one that was taken out as possible. You'll have to use new timber, I suppose.'

Now she felt a small buzz of superority. 'Possibly not,'

she said, hiding her new smugness. 'I'm hoping to use reclaimed timber.'

'It's unlikely you'll be able to get boards wide enough. Those treads are very wide at the end.'

Anna nodded non-committally.

'And I'm afraid any ideas you might have had about having patio doors into the garden are a non-starter, too.'

'I was going to have French doors. Much more tasteful.'

'I'm sorry, Anna, that's just a matter of semantics. That's a study of the meaning of words . . .' he explained, inviting her to share the joke. When she didn't, he went on, 'We just want the house restored to how it should be. That's a very special row of houses and it's vital we keep them as near to how they originally were as possible.'

Anna inhaled and exhaled, slowly, to give herself thinking time. It was a shame that she'd got off on the wrong foot with this man, then got back on the right one, and then wrong again. Nor could she respond to his attempts at humour, even if they were quite funny. She was too nervous; he had too much power. She made an attempt at a smile.

'So what do you want me to have, then?' She tried not to sound petulant, but feared she'd failed.

'A plain window out to the backyard, so you can keep an eye on the children playing in the smuts from the ash-pit.'

He'd made another joke, but only his eyes were smiling. It was very unnerving. 'I haven't got children,' she said.

'But you have got a dog.'

'I know.'

'You should take her to the vet to have her checked over. It could prevent any problems she might have getting worse.'

'I know that, too.'

He sighed, as if despairing of her ever relaxing. 'What about that indoor kennel? They are a very good idea. Especially if Chloe's boys ever visit.'

'They do visit. They're very good with Caroline—'

'I've got a kennel I can lend you. I'll drop it round some time.'

'And will you take the opportunity to check what's going on in my house?' The words were spoken before she'd thought properly and Anna realised she'd been terribly rude. 'I'm so sorry. I should never have said that. You're only doing your job. I'm just so anxious . . .'

'There's no need to be anxious. On the whole we're reasonable people who want the best result for everyone.' He paused, apparently relieved that she'd softened a little. 'What those other people did to your house really was dreadful.'

'And how do you know it wasn't me who ripped everything out?' She smiled, making an attempt at light-heartedness.

His smile was wider and more genuine than hers. 'Gut instinct. Very useful in my job. Or jobs.'

Now she did feel a bit more relaxed. 'So, what do you want me to do about the staircase? Do some drawings and show them to you?'

'That's the best thing. You don't want to spend a fortune on having it built and then have to alter it all.'

Anna felt her mood shift slightly. 'How do you know I haven't got a fortune?'

'As I said before, gut instinct.'

Anna smiled, not quite ready to laugh, and got to her feet. 'I'll start drawing, then.'

'Who are you going to get to build it?'

She tried to sidestep the question. 'I haven't decided yet.'

'I could recommend some people who are used to conforming to our requirements, but you'd have to get on to them soon. They've got a long waiting list.'

'I said, I haven't decided—'

'Let me give you their name. And do get on to them quickly.'

'Isn't it unethical to give out names of joinery firms to people? In your job?'

'Only if I get a backhander out of it.'

Anna was tempted to smile again so she picked up her tube of drawings, none of which were relevant now, and her bag and got up. 'Thank you for your help,' she said formally.

Rob Hunter rose to his feet and came round the desk to open the door for her. Anna wasn't used to having doors opened for her and this was the second time in less than a week. 'I'll be seeing you,' he said.

'Not if I see you first,' muttered Anna, inaudibly, knowing it was a cliché and relieved to have got through a meeting with Rob Hunter without a fight.

When Anna got home, she called on Chloe before she went into her own house, nominally to collect Caroline, but actually with another motive in mind.

'Give me coffee and let me look at your staircase!' She accepted Caroline's greeting while she said this, and got her to sit down again.

Chloe, who was a very satisfactory friend, put the kettle on. 'Why do you want to measure my staircase? Do you need them both? Or just the first one?'

Anna sank down into the chair, having removed a universe worth of Superheroes from it first. Caroline wandered over so that Anna could stroke her ears. 'I've got to make my staircase exactly the same as yours,' Anna announced, sounding exhausted. She looked across to where the stairs were revealed behind the half-open door. The treads resembled slices of pie.

'Oh my goodness,' said Chloe, diplomatically.

'And it's your friend Rob Hunter that's making me do it,' said Anna, remembering to be indignant.

'What on earth are you talking about? Do you want me to whisk the milk and make a proper cappuccino?'

'Oh, yes please. And I wouldn't say no to a chocolate biscuit.'

Chloe got out the tin in which all treats were hidden. 'So what's Rob making you do? I thought Friday night went very well, didn't you? Rob obviously liked you a lot.'

'I don't think so. He was quite friendly and chatty but that must have been because he felt guilty. He knew he was about to turn my life upside down.'

'How do you feel about him?' Chloe fished.

Anna considered. She had liked him, he did make her laugh and she had thought that maybe they could become friends. But the fact that he was the listed buildings officer made it all seem so complicated.

'Well?' Chloe persisted.

'He's nice, it's just . . .'

'What?'

'Nothing.' One day she might tell Chloe all about Max, but not now. 'Anyway, it was he who said I've got to make my staircase exactly like yours. It does tend to put you off a bloke, that sort of thing.'

'Oh my God!'

Anna nodded, finding Chloe's reaction entirely appropriate. She sipped at the chocolate-powdered froth. 'I've got every right to hate him, really. He used one job to further the interests of his other one, which I'm sure is immoral, if not illegal.'

'But you don't?' Chloe, having made sure Anna found the biscuit she wanted, helped herself. 'Hate him, I mean?'

'Well, no, not really. I agree that these are very special houses—'

'Very small houses.'

'And they should be done properly. I just feel a bit daunted about doing it.'

'I have huge faith in you, Anna. Think what you've

done already. Even your sister would be proud of you. The floor is lovely.'

'Yes, it has worked OK, hasn't it? I might ring my sister. If I'm going to make this darn staircase, I'd better get my boards. Oh, where are the boys?'

'Bruno and Tom are playing with Alistair, a friend of Bruno's from school. Harry's having a nap. I wondered why you said darn.'

Anna drained her cup. 'Thank you so much, Chloe. I feel revived now. You're such a good friend, even if you didn't tell me Rob was coming to dinner.'

Chloe laughed and patted Anna's arm. 'Yes, well, a good friend who wants an en suite in her garret,' she said. 'When you've got a moment.'

'I'll do it as light relief from the damn staircase. Come on, Caroline, time to go home.'

Once she'd let Caroline out into the garden and back in again, Anna telephoned her sister. Laura was pleased to hear how Anna had got on, though also worried. 'Oh my God!' she said. 'Are you sure you can do it yourself? I mean a plain staircase is one thing, but one that's practically spiral is something else.'

'I know. But the listed buildings man – Rob Hunter – said that was what I had to have.'

'Can't you appeal? You mustn't let these people bully you, you know.'

'I don't know if I could appeal, but my heart tells me he's right.'

'You and your heart, Anna.'

Anna chuckled. 'I was wondering about how to get my boards, Laura.'

'What, in the storage place? It's funny you should say that, but the bill came the other day, and I was thinking it's fearfully expensive, and if we haven't missed the stuff, and I haven't, we should get rid of it.'

Anna instantly felt guilty. 'I should pay you something towards the cost of the storage unit.'

'Nonsense,' Laura replied resolutely, 'but if you want your boards and we want to get rid of most of the stuff, we'll have to come down with a van and collect it.'

'It's an awfully long way.'

'We wouldn't do it in a day.' Laura had obviously been thinking about it. 'We'd stay the night with Sally in London, and drive back the next day, dropping your boards off with you.'

'Would you want to stay?' Anna tried not to sound alarmed at the prospect.

Laura laughed. 'Don't worry. I'm dying to see how you're getting on, but one night on a floor will be enough for me. I'm not as young as I was.'

'What about the boys?'

'Will's mother will have them, I hope. I need a night away so badly! You've no idea!'

Anna realised her sister did sound rather exhausted. 'Laura, if ever you want me to come up and stay for a weekend so you can go away, I will.'

'Sweetie, that's lovely, but you've got enough on your plate at the moment. I'll ring Will and see what he thinks about the van.'

When Laura got going, the tough lay down and did as she wanted. Within twenty-four hours she had organised time off for Will, a weekend with their grandparents for her sons, and a bed for the night in London for just over a week's time.

'Your sister is amazing,' said Chloe, watching Anna measure her stairs for seemingly the nineteenth time. 'I can't wait to meet her. You mustn't let her come here though, unless you give me plenty of warning.'

'You could come over and have coffee when she and Will come then,' Anna suggested.

'Won't that be a bit much for Caroline? If I've got the boys with me?'

'Well, it will be a bit. We'll have to think. Now I must go and make a start on these drawings. I want to have something substantial to show Laura.'

At midnight that night Anna was still sitting at her drawing board, inspection lamps supplementing her old Anglepoise, until Caroline's whimperings at the foot of the ladder forced her to stop.

'Poor darling,' she said, stroking the dog's ears, 'you suffer from separation anxiety even while I'm in the house! It's just those drawings are very difficult to do, and I haven't made a staircase before. It's going to take me ages, but I'm going to do it, and it's going to be beautiful.' That would show Rob Hunter and his 'I could recommend some people', she thought determinedly.

Chapter Seven

Anna had mixed feelings about her sister and brother-in-law's impending visit. On the one hand, she loved them both and hadn't seen her sister for ages. On the other, she wanted her little house to look its best for them and that was quite difficult to arrange. The floor was still looking wonderful but it was difficult to make the boarded-up end wall look good. Anna was not planning to do the brickwork herself, or the plastering. While she could make some sort of a fist of it, if all her work now had to be inspected by the Dog and Building Police, she wanted it to be right. (This far from snappy but appropriate soubriquet had taken root in her mind and she found it hard to remember that Rob Hunter had a name apart from the DABP.)

'But they're not staying the night, are they?' asked Chloe, giving Anna the coffee she craved. It was the day before they were due to come, and Anna was fussing.

'No, they'll probably be rushing back to Yorkshire, but I will give them lunch.'

'What? Salad?'

'It's too cold for salad. Soup, I thought.'

'You're going to make soup, with an electric kettle? That'll be Soup in a Cup, I presume?'

Anna saw her point. 'I've been meaning to buy one of those tabletop stoves. I need something to cook on, anyway, but I just haven't got round to it. Laura won't be impressed when I tell her I mostly cook at your house.'

'She will be if she knows you do it while you babysit,

and let me get out a bit. Why don't you take them to the pub?'

'I might well do that,' said Anna, 'but we couldn't be long because of Caroline.'

'Caroline's all right, isn't she?'

'Well, yes, but when I was with you for longer than usual the other day, I came back to find she'd wee'd on the floor. And I know she couldn't really have needed to go because I took her out before I went. It must have been psychological.'

'Oh. And you wouldn't want to come back from the pub with your sister and find a huge pool on the floor.'

'No.'

Chloe thought for a moment. 'I know. I'll pop in and take her out while you're at the pub.'

God, Chloe, that would be brilliant. Could you really?'

'Of course.'

'You're a star!'

Chloe was also a star when, the following morning, just before the visitation, she bought Anna two huge bunches of daffodils and vases to put them in. So, when Anna waited at the end of the row for Laura and Will to arrive, having been warned by mobile phone, she knew her little house was looking charming. Even if it was mostly a building site.

Laura hardly waited until the van was stationary before she jumped out and embraced Anna, who was just as thrilled to see her. They hugged and laughed and talked over each other while Will observed them with his usual patience.

'Where do you want these boards then?' he asked eventually.

'Oh, sorry, Will!' Anna hugged him. 'Let's get them out, but I should warn you that Caroline, that's my dog, is frightened of men. You have to speak very quietly. In fact,

I may put her in the garden while we unload.'

'I can't wait to see her,' said Laura.

'Well, grab hold of the end of this plank and your wish will be granted,' said her husband.

Anna darted down the path and put Caroline into the garden, explaining there would be a certain amount of noise but then she could come in again. There would be a man, she said, but he was very nice.

'You may not like him quite as much as you liked the DABP, but actually he's nicer.'

Caroline, apparently understanding every word, looked over her shoulder at Anna, squatted down and produced a puddle the size of the Serpentine.

'Oh, Anna! It's to die for!' Laura squealed as she saw the outside of the house. 'No wonder you fell in love with it!'

'I didn't fall in love . . . Oh, OK, I did, but you do see why.'

'I do! Now let's go inside. This plank weighs a ton.'

Anna opened the door. 'You go in and wait while I help Will unload the others.'

'No, no, I'll come and help. Oh! This is going to be wonderful!' Then Laura peered through the glass window that was at the top of the current back door. 'Oh, is that Caroline? She's enormous!'

'She's only the usual greyhound size,' Anna said protectively. 'You'll meet her in a minute. Let's just get the stuff unloaded.'

'And while we're about it,' said Will, 'there's some furniture Laura thought you ought to have.'

Half an hour later, Anna's house had taken on the appearance of a rather small junk shop.

'It's awfully kind of you,' she said, not sure if she was grateful or annoyed.

'Getting the bed up the ladder will be a bit tricky,' Laura acknowledged, 'but you do need one.'

'Yes I do.'

'And that little cooker is perfect.'

'I was thinking of buying one,' Anna admitted.

'How have you been cooking up to now?' Laura enquired curiously.

'Look, let's all sit down on those super armchairs,' Anna cried, 'and I'll get Caroline. Then we can go to the pub.'

Caroline came in from the back garden. 'Now, Will,' said Anna. 'Offer this biscuit. I'm trying to get her happier around men. She won't hurt you.'

Will offered the biscuit, and Caroline, after a few moments' thought, delicately took it from his fingers.

'Well done, darling!' said Anna.

'I did think I did rather well,' admitted Will.

Anna gave him a withering look and Caroline carried her biscuit over to the newly arrived sofa and climbed up.

There was a small, eloquent silence. 'Oh, Anna! You're not going to let her get on the furniture, are you?'

Anna took her sister's arm, burrowed for her keys in her pocket, and escorted her family out of her house, leaving Caroline in possession of the sofa and the biscuit.

'I'll sort it out later,' she said as they went down the lane, 'and I must admit, if I scrape my leg on the corner of Caroline's bed again, I'll take to wearing puttees. At least the sofa won't attack me.'

A couple of hours later, Anna, Laura and Will came back from the pub and edged their way in. What had seemed to Laura and Will to be a few bits and pieces had eaten up all the floor space in Anna's cottage like a power-hungry monster. Caroline was treating the sofa like a life-raft, and so far no one had had the heart to make her give it up. There was also no room for her on the floor.

'Right,' said Will, taking charge in a manly way that

was half irritating and half wonderful, 'we need some muscle.'

Anna thought for a minute. 'Mike's home, Chloe's husband. I could ask him.'

'It'll take more than two of us to get that double bed up the ladder,' said Will. 'Even though it does come apart.'

'I'm sure there's another neighbour Mike can ask,' said Laura. 'Come on, let's go and see Chloe. I want a look at her staircase.'

'She's probably terribly busy,' said Anna, protective of her friend's lazy Saturday. 'It's the weekend, she'll have the boys home—'

'Don't be silly! She's a good friend of yours.'

Anna knocked tentatively on Chloe's door. Chloe had expressed a desire to meet Laura, but she had also made it clear that she didn't want her coming round without plenty of warning.

'Hi, Chloe.' Anna spoke quickly and apologetically. 'I know you haven't got time for visitors, but I was just wondering if Mike was available to give Will a hand with some furniture? There's a double bed to go up my ladder.'

Anna was standing firmly in front of the crack of the door that Chloe had opened, so Laura couldn't see if the house was untidy.

'We're painting,' said Chloe firmly, 'but you can come in if you don't mind the mess.'

'Gosh no,' said Laura, following Anna into the house. 'I've got boys of my own. But only two,' she added, impressed at the sight of Bruno, Tom and Harry, all sitting at the kitchen table, wearing plastic aprons, with paint-brushes in their hands. They were decorating models made of plaster of Paris. Several sets of dwarves sat around dolefully, looking for Snow White, who had not been made, being female and thus uninteresting.

'I'm sure Mike would love to heft furniture about,' said Chloe, pleased that Laura had found her being so creative, and such a good mother. 'He's been getting restive – he's not usually at home so long.' She called up the stairs: 'Mike! We need muscle!'

Mike thundered down. He always made Anna think of the wrong-sized doll in the doll's house: he was too big. But he was a very kind man, and agreed to help immediately.

'We might need an extra bod,' said Laura, smiling up at him.

It occurred to Anna that Laura had inherited all their mother's famed ability to get people to do things for her. Either that or she hadn't rejected the use of feminine wiles in the way that Anna had.

'I'll ask Bill from two doors down. He's a big lad,' said Mike, eager to help. 'I'll go and see if he's out of bed yet.'

'It's three o'clock in the afternoon!' said Chloe.

'Yes, but he likes his kip.'

Anna and Laura didn't follow Mike. Chloe put the kettle on, Anna joined in the painting, and Laura inspected the staircase. When Laura had perched at the bit of the table not covered with Disney characters, Chloe got out the chocolate-biscuit tin.

The boys, seeing this, eyed Laura anxiously, recognising an authority figure, even if she was dressed in jeans and a sweater.

Chloe selected a biscuit each for them, and then handed the tin to Laura, who took the smallest biscuit and said, 'My favourite! I wonder what my two are up to?'

Anna took a larger one. 'What do they do when they're with their granny?'

'Cooking, mostly.'

'I like cooking,' said the largest boy. 'We do it at school sometimes.'

'Yes, but only sweet stuff,' said Chloe, her mouth full of chocolate. 'When are they going to learn how to do a Sunday roast, or a nice pasta sauce?'

'That's up to us, I'm afraid,' said Laura. 'I reckon most education goes on in the home.'

There was a loud crash from next door. Anna winced, thinking of her newly waxed floorboards.

'They'll be saying bad words,' said Tom sagely.

'Yes,' agreed Laura, 'that's why we're over here and not helping. We wouldn't want to be hearing bad words.'

'I like bad words,' said Bruno. 'But Mummy doesn't,' he added quickly.

'That's right!' said Chloe. 'Now, are you going to give Anna that model of Caroline?'

'When it's finished. I haven't done her tail yet. And it's not really of Caroline.'

Anna inspected the model, which had the long droopy ears and slightly poppy eyes of a King Charles spaniel. 'It's got her loving expression, though.'

'Are you going to curse me for dumping all that furniture on you?' asked Laura. 'I knew you hadn't any, and it didn't seem much in the van. Now it looks as if you should open a junk shop.'

'It will look less overcrowded when the bed's upstairs,' said Anna cautiously. 'But as long as you don't mind me getting rid of anything I haven't room for.'

'Of course I don't mind! I just feel silly for storing it all that time, but you know how it is, you learn to live without things and then you wonder why you ever hung on to them.'

'You were storing my boards for me,' Anna said gratefully. 'I wouldn't have wanted to get rid of them. They're like solid gold.'

'There are plenty of women at the mother-and-toddler group who haven't got much furniture,' said Chloe. 'And I'm sure they'll be happy to take anything off your hands that you don't want. And you did need some things, Anna.'

'You did,' agreed Laura, and the two of them united in

looking at Anna somewhat reproachfully, as if she were about to shun all worldly possessions and live in a cave.

'I know!' Anna felt ganged up on. 'And I never look a gift horse in the mouth. The furniture that I need will be really useful. Just not quite as useful as my boards,' she added more quietly.

'I just hope you can make the staircase,' said Laura, looking at Chloe's again. 'It's very complicated.'

'It'll be fine,' Anna insisted. 'I'm very lucky I've got one to copy. It would be much harder working it all out from scratch.'

To Anna's relief (she was suffering rather under the strain of two surrogate mothers), the men came back shortly afterwards.

'Well,' said Bill. 'The bed's upstairs now. Although how you manage with that ladder, I don't know.'

'She's going to build a staircase,' said Laura.

'She's very good at DIY,' said Chloe.

'You couldn't really describe making a staircase as DIY, love,' said Mike.

'You know what I mean,' said Chloe, looking anxiously at Anna to see if she'd caused offence.

'Well, I will be doing it myself,' said Anna, sounding more cheerful at the prospect than she felt. 'Shall we go and see what it all looks like?'

Anna's heart sank, rather, when she walked through the front door and realised how difficult it would be to move about.

Chloe was more positive. 'Ooh, lots of good stuff here, Anna,' she said, 'but you're not to get rid of anything until you've checked with me you don't really need it. I know your minimalist tendencies.'

'We put the boards over there,' said Mike proudly. 'Like a sort of table. I think they look rather nice.'

When everyone had finished ogling the furniture, and all three boys had been accompanied upstairs to inspect

Anna's new bed, (which conveniently came with a duvet and bedding), Laura declared it was time to go home.

'I'm sorry to leave you in such chaos, but we don't want to stretch Granny's patience too much, or she won't let me come again.' Laura hugged Anna. 'It's been such fun! And it's going to be dreamy when you've finished it. You won't want to sell it.'

'I'll need to pay you back, Lo – and it'll still be very small,' she said.

'We manage!' said Chloe defensively.

'But we haven't got room for a dog,' said Bruno, eyeing Caroline, who was staring in through the window as if the woes of world were her personal responsibility.

'It's bound to feel a bit crowded now we're all in it,' said Will. 'And once you've got the furniture arranged, it'll be much more spacious.'

'We should stay and help—' began Laura.

'No, no! I'll be fine on my own,' said Anna, feeling suddenly a bit forlorn. 'You must go back to your boys, but just come and see me again soon.'

'Come on, you lot,' said Chloe, gathering up her boys, hoping her husband would follow, 'so Anna can say goodbye to Laura and Will.'

Anna made her way up the path to where Laura and Will's hired van was parked. 'Thank you for bringing my staircase, and all that lovely furniture.'

'It was a pleasure. We had such fun, didn't we, Will?'

Will nodded good-naturedly.

'It was possibly a bit more fun for us than it was for you,' said Anna. 'We drank coffee and chatted while you heaved furniture about. Thank you so much, Will.'

'I've got something for you in the van.' Laura opened the back and rummaged under a pile of blankets that the furniture had been wrapped in. She pulled out a black case and handed it to Anna. 'It's my old laptop. I want you to have it. I can't be forever printing out your emails.'

'But, Laura—'

'I've got a new one, and I just can't be bothered to sell it, not when it would be useful to you.'

'I can't—'

'Nonsense!' Laura said in a tone that left no room for debate. 'You'll be able to email Mum. Save you having to talk for hours on the phone. Now we must fly.' She hugged her sister hard. 'And I'm going to come down again as soon as I can.'

Anna felt a combination of relief and loneliness when she got back to her house. She let Caroline in, who immediately got up on to the sofa, and Anna regarded her with a sigh. It was a question of discipline versus gashed ankles. Gashed ankles won and Caroline remained in possession of the sofa. The camp bed could be put out of the way somewhere, for when the DABP came.

She was in the middle of trying to impose some sort of order on the furniture, and had carried a couple of dining chairs and a bedside table up the ladder already, when there was a knock at the door.

Caroline started, fearing another invasion, and Anna wondered what her sister could have possibly left behind. She opened the door.

It was the Dog and Building Police. 'Oh,' she said, and added a tentative, 'Hello.' She couldn't decide if he was the man who was so helpful with Chloe, or the monster who was bullying her about her house. He probably wasn't a monster, but could he be just a friend?

'I've brought that indoor kennel round,' he said. He smiled, the ruefulness of his expression telling her he was sorry about having to lay down the law about her house. 'Can I come in?'

Anna smiled back, making an effort, and opened the door. 'I really don't think I've got room for an indoor kennel.'

'Oh, I see what you mean.' He stood in the doorway,

contemplating the furniture that took up all the floor space for a few moments. He gave her a quick grin that Anna couldn't help responding to.

Caroline, who had been hiding her head under a cushion, heard his voice and pushed her way through the furniture to him, knocking over a reading lamp, a small table and the kitchen stool that Chloe already had her eye on as she did so. She pressed her face into his stomach and swooned as he stroked her neck and ears.

'Well, someone's pleased to see you!' said Anna.

'I'll take a welcome wherever I find it,' he said, and then turned his full attention to Caroline. 'And how are you, my darling?' he crooned. 'You're looking very well, I must say.'

For a moment, Anna wondered what it would be like to be talked to in that caressing way by the right person, or, in her case, the wrong person. Then she cleared her throat.

'Would you like some tea, or something, um . . .' That was the trouble with nicknames. They made you forget people's real names.

'Rob. Rob Hunter. I could write it down for you, to help you to remember,' he added, looking at her sideways.

Oh, why did he keep twinkling at her? Anna felt herself blushing. It was so distracting. 'That's fine, I'll remember it OK now. So, would you like a cup of tea, Rob?' She gave him a proper smile this time, to prove she had some social skills.

'Yes, please.' He sat on the sofa, and Caroline got on top of him. He moved her hindquarters over so it was only her front paws and head restricting his breathing.

Anna opened the box of biscuits that she'd bought for Laura and Will's visit. 'You can see, I really haven't got room for an indoor kennel.'

He looked confused for a moment. 'But surely this isn't how you're going to have your furniture, is it?'

'No, of course not. I only got it today. My sister gave it to me, and she's only just gone. But I still don't think—'

'I'll give you a hand with it if you like and then set up the kennel.'

Anna had had more than her usual dose of manly help already that day and wasn't sure she could take any more. Especially not from this man. 'If you'd rung to say you were coming . . .'

'Sorry, I left your telephone number in the office.'

She handed him the box of biscuits. 'Don't give one to Caroline, will you? She's very persuasive.'

'Oh, I'm a man of steel. She's got no chance of getting round me.'

Anna smiled politely but she wondered if there was a hidden message here. Was he trying to tell her that she wouldn't persuade him to let her do anything that wasn't absolutely by the book? It was so hard to tell with him!

'Do you take milk and sugar?' Anna hoped very much he took milk because she'd already put it in.

'Just milk, please.'

She handed him a mug, wishing she'd washed up the better mugs that she'd used for Will and Laura. The one he had was chipped and had a rather vulgar cartoon on it.

She perched on the edge of a chest of drawers, sipping tea she didn't really want. If I was more assertive, she thought, I could have just explained I didn't have room and sent him away. Now he's on my sofa, cuddling my dog, and I don't know what to do with him.

'Where is the indoor kennel?' she asked.

'I left it in the car, in case you didn't want it.' His smile was rather attractive, but Anna made a mental note never to let Chloe know she thought this. Matchmaking wouldn't cover the shenanigans she would get up to if she thought Anna liked Rob at all. Which she didn't, really.

'I'm afraid I don't want it. Honestly, Caroline's fine without it, as you see. And anyway, there's not an inch to spare.'

'Let me help you with the furniture, and then you can decide. They really are useful,' he persisted.

Anna allowed herself to wonder if, when the boys came over, it would be nice for Caroline to have somewhere to retreat to, should they get too much for her.

Rob got to his feet. 'Come on. Let's get this lot sorted out.'

Anna hadn't planned for an assortment of furniture to be delivered to her house without notice. She had no idea where she wanted everything – anything – to go.

'I want as much of it as possible upstairs. Anything I know I don't want to keep, I'll put in the garden. Chloe's going to help me get rid of it.'

'Right. What about this piece?' Rob gestured to a large sideboard with a carved back and inset mirrors. 'It's nice but it's quite large and the wrong period for this house.'

In spite of his best efforts Anna couldn't quite stop seeing him as the Dog and Building Police and panicked. 'Goodness, I don't have to furnish it in period, do I?' She was aghast.

He laughed at her. How dare he!

'Of course not! Whatever gave you that idea? I just thought that might help you decide what to keep and what to get rid of.' He chuckled on, obviously relishing her mistake.

'Well, for all I know . . .' she said, feeling incredibly silly.

'You're perfectly right. Some of the things we get people to do could appear ridiculous – let's face it, *are* ridiculous – but we don't quite go that far.'

She decided to forgive him for laughing. After all, it was quite funny, in retrospect. 'OK,' she said slowly, not sure if she was going to let him know he was forgiven,

'I'll get rid of that sideboard, although it would swallow up a lot of stuff.'

'It would swallow you up, if it was hungry,' said Rob seriously.

Anna stifled a laugh. 'No it wouldn't, it's a vegetarian, I happen to know.'

'It might make an exception for listed buildings officers who laugh at people.'

Anna nodded. 'It might. Let's get it outside quickly.'

A hour or so later, Anna made more tea and got out the now diminished box of biscuits. But she was really hungry, and a Viennese Whirl wouldn't do it. When Rob came back with the kennel, she surprised herself by saying, 'There's a very good Chinese round the corner. Do you fancy a takeaway? You've been so helpful, I feel I should repay you in some way.'

He regarded her, one eyebrow slightly raised and a half-smile on his lips. 'Now, how am I to take that? At first I thought you were suggesting we had a meal together, and then you wanted it to be like payment?'

For a moment Anna wished she could read his mind. Was he really offended? And why did she ask him anyway? Possibly because the thought of being alone, even with Caroline, was not what she wanted just now. And she was genuinely hungry.

'I just meant,' she said, realising she sounded a bit flustered, 'you've worked really hard to help me, and deserve a meal.' She took a deep breath and smiled, feeling a little more in control. 'It's not that I want to bribe you into letting me do something against the listings law, or anything. Perish the thought.'

He smiled properly this time. 'Well, that's very kind of you, but I should be getting back. I've dogs of my own to see to.'

'Oh my goodness, Caroline! I should have fed her hours ago. What time do you usually feed yours?'

'I like to keep it flexible, then they don't fret if I'm not there to feed them for whatever reason. It's just some-time in the evening. Now, shall I set up the kennel over there?' He pointed to the only space big enough to take it and Anna nodded.

'So you could stay and have a meal?' Anna smiled, wishing she had picked up just a few of her mother's winning ways. At times like this, they would have been very useful. She had enjoyed his company and, although she didn't really want to admit it, now everyone had gone back to their respective homes, she couldn't quite face supper for one.

'I could,' Rob said.

'Good. Right, well, here's the menu, choose what you want while I feed Caroline, and then I'll go and get it.'

'I could go,' he offered.

'No.' Anna was very firm. 'I'll go.'

Chapter Eight

Anna dragged the door of the Chinese takeaway open and fell inside. The restaurant had a very powerful extractor fan and the door was always difficult and although she knew this, she always arrived feeling faintly surprised, as if she'd been dropped there by aliens.

She was confused for other reasons, too. As she gazed at the list of meals on the wall, referring occasionally to the bit of paper in her hand, she wondered about Rob. He would be much easier to deal with if he was just a friend or just a listed buildings officer. The crossover made it tricky and so did Chloe's attempts at match-making.

Maybe that was why she felt so awkward about making a perfectly ordinary offer. Her sister, when she was single, would have had no qualms about offering a man who had helped her a meal. But while Anna had wanted to make this normal and friendly gesture, she had felt very uncomfortable. It was because she couldn't quite reconcile in her mind the strict Dog and Building Police, who had told her off about Caroline and subsequently her plans for the house, with the man who had teased her and made her laugh, and who had helped her move furniture. Her feelings would be less muddled, she thought, if she didn't keep thinking about Max.

'Next!' The pretty Chinese girl behind the counter broke into her thoughts.

'Er – yes – I'll have two portions of prawn toast . . .'

* * *

She found Rob and Caroline on the sofa together. They were both asleep. She nodded to Caroline, who raised her head as she came in, but said nothing. Rob had worked hard and deserved a bit of a doze. He also looked rather endearing with his eyes closed. His lashes formed shadows on the side of his nose and the bit of stubble that was now evident shaded his jaw in quite an attractive way.

She arranged the plates on top of the Calor gas heater, wishing she'd got round to having the chimney sorted out. A fire, or a wood burner, would be so much cosier. Then she found some tea lights which had come down with the furniture, and arranged them about the place. She could now turn off the inspection lamps that were her usual form of illumination. It wasn't that she wanted to create a romantic atmosphere, more one where conversation could take place without every nuance of expression being visible. Anna found Rob difficult to read but suspected he didn't have the same trouble with her. She didn't want him to have any advantage over her.

When the meal was as ready as she could make it, she said, 'Um – hello. I'm back.' She suddenly felt nervous, as if they had not shared a lot of silliness just over an hour ago.

Rob opened his eyes, and Caroline got off the sofa to investigate the foil dishes.

'Get your nose out. It's not for you. Go and sit down,' said Anna, aware for the first time that entertaining with a large dog was not straightforward.

'Let's try her in the kennel,' said Rob. He unfolded himself from the sofa and went to the corner where the kennel was set up. He'd put all Caroline's bedding in it, and her toys. 'Come along, girl,' he said to her, in the voice he used for no one else. 'Come and see how you like this.'

To Anna's surprise, and slight irritation, Caroline walked into the kennel and sat down.

'Good girl,' said Rob. 'Have a biscuit.' He produced one from his pocket and she took it delicately, and then held it between her paws. 'We'll leave the door open. It's as much a place for her to retreat to, as somewhere to put her out of the way. No, stay there, my darling.'

To stop herself asking if he ever spoke to his girlfriend like that, Anna said, 'So what about your dogs? They'll be starving by now.'

He shook his head. 'After you'd gone I rang my neighbour. She quite often sees to the dogs for me. Although it's perfectly possible to have dogs and work full time if you take them out early, and again when you get back, I like to have someone who can let them out, feed them, give them a bit of company when I'm not around.'

There was something rather nice about a man who was so fond of his animals, Anna decided, and wondered again if Max liked them. 'Well, if Caroline's settled in her cage—'

'Kennel,' he corrected her, his expression maddeningly quizzical.

'Kennel,' she repeated obligingly. 'We can eat. Shall we just have a bit of everything? The prawn toast is delicious.' She handed him the container so he could help himself.

'You were a long time,' Rob said, taking one.

'It's in the next village.'

'Was there a queue?'

'Not really. Well, a bit of one,' she added quickly. She didn't want to explain to him that the reason it took so long was that she went there on her bike. In London lots of people only had bicycles, but in the country it seemed more eccentric. Anna handed him a loaded plate. 'Here you are. And a fork. What would you like to drink? I bought some lagers, or would you prefer tea or something?'

'A can of lager would be great. Don't bother with a glass. I can manage.'

Anna perched on a stool opposite him. She didn't want to share the sofa with him. She wasn't Caroline, who was just too easy, in her opinion. They ate in silence for a few minutes, both hungry.

'I see you've got some lovely boards there,' said Rob, chewing. 'Are they for the staircase?'

'Yes. I rescued them from a skip in London, with the help of a builder friend.' She related the story of the Jack Russell defending her ill-gotten gains. 'I just couldn't bear for anyone else to have them.'

'I'm surprised the builder didn't sell them on.'

'I was, too, but he was a friend of mine. My sister brought them down today, along with all this furniture.' They both looked round at the furniture while crunching prawn toasts amicably.

'So, have you decided who you're going to get to make the staircase?' Rob asked finally. 'You don't want to be climbing up and down that ladder for too much longer.'

'Well, it's a big decision,' Anna hedged. 'I haven't got all the quotes in yet.'

'You haven't asked for any quotes, have you?' Rob said with a smile.

'How on earth—'

'I asked around. No one's been asked to quote for anything remotely like a staircase that's nearly spiral.'

'I really don't think—'

'You're planning to do it yourself, aren't you?'

Anna opened her mouth to deny this. It sounded so foolish, such a silly idea, she couldn't bear to admit to it. But then she thought: What is there to be ashamed of? 'Yes.'

There was a long silence. The tea lights flickered; the gas stove popped and murmured. Caroline suddenly gave a little yip that made them jump.

Rob broke the silence. 'Well done. That's a brave decision.'

For a moment, Anna teetered on a fulcrum of emotion and then thoughts of Max flooded in and she landed back where she'd been since she left college. It wasn't a particularly happy place, but it was familiar and therefore safe.

When Chloe called round to look at the furniture the following day, she was surprised to find everything in such good order.

'Golly, you must have been up all night getting this lot sorted,' she said. 'Oh, and you've got a cage.' She said this with a mixture of reproach and query.

'Rob Hunter came over yesterday, after Laura and Will had gone. He brought the cage – kennel, I mean – and helped me move the furniture.'

Chloe's eyes widened. 'Are you and he . . . er, you know?'

Anna realised how important it was to disabuse Chloe of her romantic notions or her, Anna's, life would become a misery. 'Goodness me, no! Honestly, Chloe, excuse me for laughing but that's such a ridiculous idea!'

'Why?' demanded Chloe, offended.

'Because! He's the listed buildings officer! He's the Dog Police, and, well, he's just not my type.'

Chloe sighed. Like many happily married people, she didn't like single people to roam around loose like odd socks. 'At least you like dogs.'

Anna grinned. 'Let's face it, I've looked like a dog most of the times I've seen him – all the times, really, except when I met him at your house and went to his office, when I was reasonably tidy. And I am not looking for a relationship,' she added firmly.

'Why not? You do like men, don't you?'

'Well, yes, sometimes, it's just . . .'

'So why don't you want a boyfriend, then?' Chloe demanded.

'I just don't! I haven't time for a boyfriend!' And the

term seemed rather childish to Anna, as the man in her head was so definitely not a boy. She sighed, seeing Chloe was not satisfied with this answer. She really didn't want to explain to Chloe about Max – her friend might think it was silly. It probably was. 'I've got no time for a relationship when I'm still building my house, not to mention my staircase!' But mentioning the staircase reminded her of Rob's reaction. He hadn't said it would be difficult, impossible, or even against listed building regulations, he had just said, 'Well done.' No, the man wasn't all bad.

'I think it's a shame. Two nice single people, who both love dogs, not getting together.'

'Chloe, both loving dogs and being single isn't quite enough to base a relationship on. Last night when we were eating Chinese—'

'You had Chinese? And you say you're not interested?'

'No! We were hungry! He helped me organise all the furniture, and so I went and got some Chinese.'

'On your bike?'

'Yes, on my bike, but my point was, we found conversation really difficult. We sat in silence most of the evening, sipping lager from cans and saying, "Pass the rice, please," every so often.'

'It sounds really coupley.'

'I'm sure that's not a word.'

'Don't change the subject. It sounds as if you were really comfortable with each other. Usually on first dates – sorry, I know it wasn't a date – it's really awkward and you have to keep talking rubbish to avoid the silence.'

'We were too tired for that,' Anna explained. 'We'd been moving furniture all day. And I was tired because of Laura and Will coming, although I really enjoyed their visit. Did you like Laura?'

'Yes, when I stopped thinking of her as Supermum. You're changing the subject again.'

'Yes! It's perfectly reasonable when one subject is exhausted to think of another one. Really, Chloe, where did you learn your social skills?'

Chloe laughed. 'All right. I won't say any more about you and Rob.' She lowered her volume: 'But I do think you'd make a lovely couple,' she murmured, almost inaudibly.

Anna laughed. 'Lovely couple or not, you're not going to get us together. Let's go and look at furniture.'

'Before we do that, can I see what you've done with the upstairs?'

'Sure.' Anna followed Chloe up the ladder to her bedroom, which now looked like a bedroom. 'Of course, I'm still planning to make a big bedroom, with en suite and clothes storage, upstairs. The views from there really are something, but I'll have to see if I can get the listed buildings department to agree.'

'Have you asked Rob?'

'I had the plans with me when I went to his office, but as none of the ones for downstairs were relevant, I didn't show him the others.' Anna suddenly had a thought. 'Of course, we couldn't have a relationship because it would be terribly unethical.'

'You're using that as an excuse,' said Chloe.

'No! I just didn't think of it before. So no more match-making.'

'OK,' she said resignedly. Chloe moved to the window. 'Gosh, I hope he does let you have a suite up here. We're so lucky to live in such a beautiful place. Did your sister like it?'

'Loved it. I knew she would.'

'Oh, and you've got a laptop!' Chloe exclaimed. 'I didn't know you had one of those. You're not very high-tech on the whole, are you?'

Anna laughed again. 'No, but I do live in the twenty-first century. Mind you, I probably wouldn't have got one, but Laura gave it to me. It's her old one. She said she couldn't be bothered to sell it.'

'Does it work?'

'Oh yes, it's fine.'

'I'll send Mike round to set it up for you when he comes back with the boys. He's taken them to play football. I think he thinks if he starts them young, they'll turn into David Beckhams.'

'That'll make him a very popular man, but don't worry about asking him to set up my computer, I've done it. I sent my first email this morning.'

Chloe was amazed. 'You set up your computer? Anna, you are clever.'

'Not particularly, I learnt about computers at college and I just hate asking for help. My mother was always getting neighbours to do things for her. I hated being the one to go round and ask. It's made me very self-sufficient, I'm afraid.'

'No, I think it's brilliant! I can do a lot on a computer, but I can't set one up.'

Anna smiled. 'It's probably more useful for you to know how to mend toys and bake cakes and read aloud, all at the same time. Which I have seen you do.'

'Oh yes, being a mum is all about multi-tasking, that's for sure. Now if you're certain you don't want that little desk . . .'

When Anna finally got to her computer a while later, there was an email forwarded to her by Laura, as well as a long one from Laura herself.

Clever you to sort out an email address so quickly. We had a brilliant time, she wrote, when she'd finished telling Anna everything the boys had done in her absence. *Don't forget my offer to come down and look after Caroline if you decide you do want to go to your reunion. Will and I would love a weekend down there, especially now you've got a double bed! I think it would be good for you to get in touch with your old college friends because although Chloe is a darling and a wonderful friend for you, she's not likely to know any single men.*

Laura had obviously read the email she'd forwarded, and if it hadn't been for the fact that Max was definitely going to be there (she gathered when she read it herself), Anna would have declined immediately. Heaven help her if Chloe and Laura both decided to try and find her a boyfriend at the same time. She shivered at the thought.

But Max was going to be at the reunion and, therefore, so was she. After all, if she'd spent so many hours and days and weeks thinking about him, she couldn't let an occasion where he was going to be present pass her by. Not now that Laura had been so definite about wanting to come down.

She emailed the organiser, saying that yes, she would be interested in taking advantage of the 'great deal' that still had 'had a few places available' at a hotel near the venue where 'several of us' would be staying. It was all horribly short notice and she was lucky to be able to squeeze in, but the woman who was organising it had been so thrilled at the prospect of nailing down another old college chum that it hadn't been a problem. Anna's finger hovered over the 'send' button for a few seconds, wondering if seeing Max again would be a mistake. After all, since she'd had the house, Caroline, her staircase and everything else, she hadn't been thinking about him nearly so much. Perhaps she should move on, find a new love.

But she pressed the key before she could think any more. He'd been the focus of her imagination for so long that it would be crazy not to see him again. The only problem was, what the hell was she to wear? She'd have to tell Chloe. After all, if Laura and Will were going to come and stay in her house, Chloe would have to know. She'd need to advise them about Caroline if there were any problems. She had two weeks to organise herself.

*   *   *

Chloe, of course, was delighted to help when, a few days later, Anna brought the subject up. The boys were at school or playgroup, and Mike was out. Chloe was thrilled to have an opportunity to talk about something infinitely girly.

'So, what sort of a do is it? Black tie?'

'Yup. Though the thought of some of that lot in dinner jackets is quite funny.'

'It's fun to dress up,' Chloe said excitedly. 'There aren't enough opportunities for it these days. Have you got anything long?'

'I haven't got a dress at all,' Anna confessed. 'Let alone a long one.'

'That's OK, we'll look in my wardrobe and then trawl the charity shops. What size are you?'

'I've no idea. I was wondering if I should go on a diet. What do you think?'

'For goodness' sake, Anna! I was wondering if you were a ten or a twelve! You certainly don't need to lose weight. Although you might need a padded bra. It's hard to tell under those dungarees. Shall we go upstairs now and have a look at what I've got? You could try on a couple of things and get a sense of what you like and what you don't.'

Upstairs, Chloe opened a wardrobe that was somewhat smaller than it needed to be, given the amount of clothes it had in it. 'You can't go wrong with classic black,' she said, extracting an example with great difficulty. 'On the other hand it's rather a cliché. Try this.' 'This' was a sequinned scarlet sheath. 'Let's give it a go.'

Feeling rather embarrassed, Anna started to get undressed. There was a long silence while they both looked at Anna's reflection. Anna saw a very white figure in bra and pants that were both grey, but somehow not the same grey.

'Well,' said Chloe bluntly, 'you'll definitely need new

underwear, even if you don't need a padded bra. And the armpit hair has to go, I'm afraid. I don't care if it's a feminist—'

'It's not! I've just lost my razor.'

'And you need a leg wax and a pedicure. I'll do it for you if you like.'

'It's OK, I can paint my own toenails.'

'All right, as long as you do do it. You might want to wear strappy sandals, and painted toenails are a must.'

Anna looked at her toes. The nails did look a bit gnarly at the moment.

'Right, let's get this over your head.'

The scarlet sequins moulded themselves to Anna's figure except when they got to her breasts. There the dress flapped about in a disheartening way.

'Now I come to think of it, I was breastfeeding when I bought that. I have got some of those chicken fillet things somewhere.' Chloe started rummaging about in her drawers.

'Don't bother,' Anna mumbled, struggling out of the dress. 'I don't quite see myself in scarlet sequins, sadly. Have you got anything else a bit . . . quieter?'

'There's this skirt and camisole. You could either wear it with a pashmina or a shrug.'

'What on earth is a shrug?'

'Oh, Anna! Don't you watch any normal television? No, I forgot, you haven't got one.' Chloe gabbled happily. 'It's like a cardigan that just covers your arms. No, on second thoughts, you've got great arms. You should show them off.'

Anna looked at one arm. 'Is it great?'

'Yes! Toned but not stringy. It looks as if you work out, but carefully.'

'Hmm, to think I got great arms by hulking timber about. Perhaps I could market the idea and get people to pay me to come and shift stuff.'

'Great idea,' said Chloe, who wasn't listening, but instead was trying to prise her clothes apart so she could see what was what. They were packed so tightly it was a hard job. 'The good thing about having so many clothes,' she said, at last pulling something out, 'is that they stay in place just by themselves, without hangers. Now, what about this? This is what I wear when I want to feel sexy.'

'I don't want to feel sexy. I want to feel safe,' Anna objected.

'Rubbish! Where's your feminine pride? You've got to show all those old college friends that you've turned into a wonderful woman.'

'They won't care!' Anna spoke defiantly but took the garment that Chloe held out to her. It was black and made out of a soft stretchy material She did want to look sexy, but she didn't want to admit it to Chloe and risk having to tell her why.

It seemed to take a while to get the dress on because it kept snagging on Anna's bra and knickers but at last she got it pulled into place.

Chloe looked critically at her. 'Wow! You'll need your hair up.' She found a clip and twisted it on top of Anna's head. 'Or cut. And you need proper shoes and some jewellery, but basically it's a wow!'

Anna gazed at herself. She was almost unrecognisable. With her hair back from her face she looked entirely unlike herself. She stood on tiptoe to get the effect of high heels. 'Gosh, I look almost feminine.'

'You need a smaller size, really, to show off your fabulous waist,' said Chloe. 'I bought that soon after I'd had Harry when I hadn't lost all my baby weight.'

Anna kept turning this way and that in astonishment. She looked so different. 'Do you think I look sexy in this dress?'

'Mm. Definitely.' Chloe paused. 'So you *do* want to look sexy.'

'Of course. It's a party.'

Chloe gave her a suspicious look and Anna wondered how on earth she'd explain Max away if, by any wonderful chance, he did more than glance at her. 'I want a good night out, with my old friends. And you're right, I don't want them all to think that I've lost interest in my appearance completely.'

'OK,' Chloe said after a considered pause. 'Now, what are you going to do about your hands?'

'What do you mean?' Anna regarded them. 'Wash them? Paint my nails?'

'Definitely paint your nails, and wash them, and have a manicure, but they're still a bit . . .'

'What?'

They both considered Anna's outstretched fingers.

'Well, let's put it this way,' said Chloe. 'You can tell you're a dab hand with the hammer and nails.'

Anna inspected her hands more closely. She'd never given them much thought, really. She didn't wear rings: they didn't fit in with carpentry and the other things she found herself doing each day; and she could see that the nails, all different lengths, with a fair amount of paint under them, and an old cut across the thumb where a saw had leapt out of her control, did make her look more like a workman than a femme fatale. 'They do rather spoil the effect.'

'Well, don't despair, there's quite a lot we can do before the party. When is it?'

'About ten days – the Saturday after next.'

'Well, if you slather on the hand cream, wear rubber gloves, let me give you a manicure—'

'Chloe, I have loads to do. I can't work in rubber gloves or hand cream. I can do what I can about my nails, but—'

'I know!' said Chloe gleefully. 'Gloves!'

'I've just said, I can't—'

'Not rubber gloves, idiot! Long, sexy black ones. Velvet, if we can't get glacé kid.'

'Which we won't be able to, which is just as well, as I don't approve.'

'Velvet then. I'll scour the charity shops, and if we can't find any there, we'll go to Cheltenham. I know a shop that sells that sort of thing. We might go there for jewellery. Oh, this is so much fun! I wish I'd had a girl, really.'

'You're better off with boys. Girls won't wear the pretty little smocked dresses with itchy collars their mothers try and force them into. Take it from me, I know.'

Chloe laughed. 'I bet Laura wore them.'

'Not for long. After she'd stopped conforming, she rebelled, only she did it in such a way that our mother thought that what Laura wanted was her idea. Laura's a genius at getting her own way. It's surprising she's so nice.'

'So what about your father?' Chloe asked.

'Mum was widowed very young. I think that was when she started becoming dependent on friends and neighbours. She's got a husband now.'

'And don't you like him?'

Anna thought for a moment. 'He's OK. Mum adores him and that's the important thing. He just seems a bit of a . . . I don't know. I wouldn't say scoundrel, or bounder, exactly . . .' She paused. 'I expect it's the permatan that makes him look a bit dodgy.'

'But handsome?'

'If you like that sort of thing. Now, I'd better get my own clothes back on. Do you need me to come and buy long black gloves?'

Chloe looked at her in amazement. 'I don't understand you! You're turning down a lovely bit of retail therapy, for what?'

'A lovely bit of plumbing. If my sister's coming down, I've got work to do.'

* * *

Will drove Anna – all kitted out with Laura's smart little silver case on wheels – to the station on the Saturday morning. They had arrived the night before, so Anna had given them the double bed and returned to her sleeping bag. Caroline started the night in her cage (which she loved), for Laura and Will's sake, but everyone knew she'd creep back on to the sofa later.

It had been such a jolly evening. Chloe and Mike had got a babysitter, and they had all gone to the Chinese for a meal. Now, on the forecourt of the station, queuing for her ticket, Anna wished she wasn't going to a nerve-racking college reunion, but was staying at home to have a nice, relaxing time with her sister and brother-in-law and her friends.

Laura had insisted on packing her bag, since she didn't trust Anna not to just stuff everything in. Fortunately, Chloe's dress was made out of some obliging sort of crepe that didn't crease. The gloves, bought from the little shop in the back streets of Cheltenham known only to the cognoscenti, who fortunately included Chloe, didn't crease either. And nor did the beautiful jet necklace that Laura had brought down for Anna to borrow. It was choker length, with strings of beads hanging from it, and it was real Whitby jet. It made the dress, the gloves and the shoes (Chloe's, elegant but hideously uncomfortable) look supremely classy.

Neither Laura or Chloe knew exactly why Anna was so intent on looking fabulous, seeming to accept that wanting to look your best when you're going to see old friends was entirely normal.

Once on the train, cup of coffee in hand, a book, a magazine and an A–Z in a little shopper lent by Chloe, Anna sat back, sipped her drink and looked out of the window at where the Cotswold stone buildings clung picturesquely to the hillside. When she'd first seen the view, coming down from London to look at what was to become her house, she'd known it was a good place to move to. Nowhere so divinely pretty could possibly be a mistake.

Now she felt a little proprietorial as she admired the golden stone and the quirky building styles; it was where she lived, or very near. She decided to enjoy herself.

'For the duration of this train journey, and for a little while afterwards, my dream is still intact,' she told herself. 'It may all shatter dreadfully later, but just for now, I can indulge it.'

When the pretty bit of the journey was over, instead of reading the book or the magazine, or even checking how to get from Paddington to the hotel, she closed her eyes and daydreamed until she fell asleep.

Chapter Nine

At Paddington, Anna was surprised at how quickly she got into the rhythm and swing of London, and found she was excited to be back. Perhaps she wasn't a country girl, after all. Perhaps she was a city slicker. The thought was so amusing she found herself smiling into the mirror in the Ladies. She'd put make-up on that morning for the first time in ages. Laura and Chloe had convinced her to have a practice at wearing it before the party that night. Now, as she regarded her features, pleased she hadn't rubbed her eyes, she realised they did seem more defined with the bit of kohl that Laura had chivvied her into putting on, and the few tentative swipes of Laura's eye-shadow. These two were now in Anna's sponge bag, along with Laura's concealer, which Anna was very dubious about knowing how to use, and various other aids to beauty.

Yes, make-up did have a purpose, the most valid one being to make Anna feel different – and different, in her case, meant more confident.

Laura and Chloe had nearly despaired of her that morning. Chloe had come round, ostensibly to lend Anna some spare tights but in fact so she could join in the make-up process, which she thoroughly enjoyed. Anna enjoyed her trips to the dentist marginally more.

'I don't understand you!' said Chloe. 'You happily pick up an electric saw and cut into some precious boards—'

'Not happily! I'd measured them about twenty times, and made a cardboard template!'

'And yet you go all girly and pathetic when confronted with a make-up brush,' Chloe finished.

'It's different,' muttered Anna.

'It washes off!' declared Laura. 'Now close your eyes.'

But Anna didn't wash it off in the Ladies, as she'd promised herself she would, because she liked feeling different. Instead, she headed for the tube.

It was only when she came across a group of her college friends in the foyer of the hotel that she realised how competitive reunions could be. There were various ways of acquiring status and Anna doubted if she had mastered any of them. She didn't have a stunning job, wasn't studying for a further degree, and wasn't married.

Crystal, whom Anna had never been close to, was showing off a huge sapphire engagement ring that linked with a platinum wedding band. 'He does something with property, I'm not sure what. Here's a picture.' She produced a wedding photo of herself looking suave and slinky, showing off her perfectly formed and tanned arms, and her husband, who was equally perfect if you over-looked the lack of chin.

'Wow,' exclaimed Anna, not knowing what else to say.

'And what about you, Anna?' said Crystal, stowing the photo in her limited edition Chanel bag. 'Have you got a husband, a partner?'

'I've got a dog,' she said, suddenly missing her.

'Have you?' said another friend, who didn't seem to like Crystal much either, 'I love dogs.'

'So, are you married, Zara?' asked Anna, hoping she wasn't the only singleton in the group, although they were all still young.

'Oh, God no! I'm disastrous with relationships. I'm hoping to find an old flame tonight. I always had the hots for Max Gordon.'

Anna tried to smile. 'Not sure I remember him.'

'He was only a guest lecturer, you may not have come

across him.' She frowned. 'Though wasn't it you who had the last dance with him at the Grad Ball?' Anna gulped. 'Perhaps it was someone else.'

Anna relaxed a little. Being wrapped up in Max's arms had made her oblivious to who might have been watching them. She had no idea if their dance had been witnessed or not.

'God, he was gorgeous. He just had to open his mouth and I practically had an orgasm,' said Zara. 'He had the most wonderfully sexy voice.'

Anna couldn't openly agree because she'd pretended not to know him, but inside she nodded. 'I'd better check in,' she said out loud. 'What's the plan?'

'Well, we thought we'd get ready quite early and go out for a few drinks beforehand, in case there isn't anything much to drink when we get there,' said Zara, who was obviously up for a night of uproarious fun.

'But we'll be in posh dresses!' said Crystal.

'I know, but we'll go to a nice cocktail bar or some-where,' said Zara. 'Meet some nice men.'

'I thought you fancied Max Gordon,' said a girl whose name Anna couldn't remember.

'Well, yes, but he might have got fat and old. You know how men do. I'd like a fall-back position.'

'So, what did you say you were up to, Anna?' said Crystal, sensing a person less successful than she was.

'I'm doing up a house in the Cotswolds,' Anna said.

'Oh my God! You must be practically the only one who's actually doing what we trained for,' said the girl-whose-name-Anna-couldn't-remember.

'I'm terribly sorry,' Anna said boldly, 'but I've forgotten your name.'

'Amanda. I'm in IT now.'

'So you're not doing anything to do with design, then?'

'Well, I do make the websites appealing, but it's not really what I do.'

'Well,' said Anna after a pause for more conversation that didn't happen. 'I really had better check in now.' She was feeling a bit depressed. 'I'll see you all down here – when?'

'About six,' said Crystal, 'that should give you plenty of time to shower and change.' The look she gave Anna implied that she sorely needed to do both.

But I had a shower at Chloe's this morning, she thought indignantly as she went up in the lift to her room, and I've got make-up on.

Her room was small but cosy, and Anna unpacked her bag, as per Laura's strict instructions. Chloe's dress, which looked fine to Anna, was to be hung in the bathroom while Anna had a bath or shower and she might as well make the most of the hot water. She could lie back and read the magazine, with cream on her face, like a proper girl.

She enjoyed her bath. It had been nice to feel that no one was likely to want to come in, or talk to her through the door about a really cool new game. However, now came the time for the nerve-racking business of getting ready.

On Laura's advice, she'd started with the dress, in case putting it on disrupted her hair. Putting it on was not as much fun on her own as it had been in Chloe's bedroom, and then again, at home, for Laura. But she was determined to hold her own among her friends, even if she wouldn't have much of a chance with Max if Zara – confident, attractive, and very sexy – also wanted him. At least the dress still fitted. She hadn't suddenly sprouted love-handles because of the crisps she'd eaten on the train, or because she'd had more of her share of prawn crackers the night before. And the new black bra she wore underneath it definitely gave her more bosom.

'Right,' she said to the mirror, which was quite flattering, because the light wasn't very good, 'my hair.'

They'd had a trial run with that, too. Laura had wailed that Anna shouldn't have washed it, because it made it far too slippery to put up easily. Having said this, she had twisted it up into a neat French pleat with no trouble at all. 'There you are, Audrey Hepburn to the life. Why haven't I got cheekbones?'

'Who?' said Anna, who was hypnotised by the sight of herself looking so different.

'Never mind. You look gorgeous.' Brutally, Laura pulled out the pins. 'Now you try.'

The effect had been definitely more bird's nest than Audrey Hepburn. Even Anna, who wasn't completely sure which Hollywood star Audrey Hepburn was, could tell that. They had just pulled all the grips out again (and Anna had used the whole packet), when Chloe and Mike came to collect them, to take them to the Chinese.

Will had given Mike a beer while Chloe had a go with Anna's hair. Her efforts resulted in something more relaxed and modern and, for Anna, more achievable.

'You've got very nice hair,' Chloe had said as Anna brushed it. 'It's so shiny, and a lovely colour.'

'My mother calls it Rich Mouse,' said Anna. 'So let's go, I'm starving.'

Now, alone in her hotel room without her assistants, Anna twisted up the bundle of hair, which had got quite long without her noticing. It took about three attempts, but at last it looked more or less as Chloe had had it. She was reluctant to spray it because she knew that when she pulled out the pins and let it loose, in the middle of the party, it would look odd. She'd said as much to Laura, who had told her that she mustn't pull out the pins until she went to bed. Anna, suspecting this was a counsel of perfection, didn't use the travel-sized can of spray that Laura had so thoughtfully bought for her. She now had to put on her make-up, and just the thought was making her hands sweat.

'What you really should have done,' she told her reflection as she leant into the mirror in the hope that would make it all easier, 'was to have a practice night out. All this dressing up, added to the whole Max thing, is just too much.'

But she knew she wouldn't have arranged it. She couldn't have explained to anyone that she needed to rehearse wearing elegant clothes and make-up. 'You've only got one shot, girl,' she said, and opened the tube of special cream guaranteed to make her look fresh as a daisy.

She might have had only one shot, but she took several. After the third time she found that the amount of kohl left round her eyes was just right, without putting any more on.

'Right, now eye-shadow.' She opened the little box and noticed the brand name for the first time. 'Golly, Laura, you've got expensive tastes.' It did glide on in a satisfactory manner, though, more easily than it had done that morning, with Laura breathing over her shoulder, giving instructions.

'OK, now the eyebrows.' She always talked to herself when she was doing something difficult; she found it helped her to concentrate. 'Laura said not to leave them out, but to make sure you didn't put on too much and look fierce.' The surplus hairs had been plucked the night before; Anna had not enjoyed it.

'Now lipstick.' This was to be put on with a brush, too, when Anna had outlined her mouth with the pencil. For someone who could draw, Anna found this surprisingly difficult, and wiping off lip-liner did not have the same beneficial effect that wiping off the kohl pencil had had. Still, her mouth only looked a little smudged by the time she had finished.

Then the powder. It was only after she had put it all over her face that she remembered Laura's instructions about powdering her lips and then putting on another coat of lipstick. 'It's like preparing a surface for painting,' she'd said, using a language she hoped Anna would understand. 'The final layer of gloss will only stay on and look good if you've got a really smooth base.'

Remembering this, Anna dabbed some powder on her mouth and put another layer of lip-gloss on, convinced that whatever she did, it would all come off after the first drink. 'Oh, to hell with it!' she said fiercely, and then remembered not to look scary.

'You're a pretty girl when you're all scrubbed up!' Laura had said. 'Remember that, tell yourself it, and everyone else will see it too!'

Eventually, when Anna could no longer bear to stare at her reflection and she was sure that she'd followed Laura's and Chloe's long menu of orders, she finally got out the gloves and put them on.

There was no doubt about it, they looked wonderful. Seeing herself in them did remind Anna of an old film, *Breakfast at Somewhere*, that might well have had Audrey Hepburn in it. But she just couldn't go down in the lift, her coat over her arm, wearing them. She'd put them on later, after the cocktails, when she'd got used to the dress, the hair and the make-up.

She placed her gloves in Chloe's evening bag and, a couple of twenty-pound notes in her bra, in case she lost the evening bag. Then she hid her return ticket, one credit card and anything else she'd really miss if she was robbed in her room, taking only her spare credit card and the rest of her money with her. She also had a plastic bag with the party shoes in it. She wouldn't put them on until the last minute, either: sufficient unto the day was the pain thereof. Then she opened the door of her hotel room, which had become her home and her sanctuary over the past couple of hours, and went downstairs. She couldn't tell if she was shivering with excitement or cold.

She wasn't the last; they were all waiting for Crystal, but the girls who were there (the male alumni were staying at some club or other) were satisfyingly impressed by Anna's appearance.

'Great dress!' said Zara.

'It's my neighbour's. I've been living in dungarees or jeans ever since I started doing up my house and didn't have anything remotely suitable. Fortunately my neighbour fancies herself as Trinny and Susannah and lent me the dress. And the shoes.' She offered up the carrier bag. 'But they kill me. I'm only going to put them on when I don't have to walk anywhere.' She was currently wearing Laura's suede loafers, and if Laura had known about it, she would have arranged for them to spontaneously combust.

'Well, let's just see the effect with heels,' said Zara, who probably had a lot in common with Laura. 'Oh, fab! You have got a lovely figure. Has anyone ever told you you look like Audrey Hepburn?'

'Only since I borrowed the dress.'

'And that's a gorgeous necklace. Is it real jet?'

Anna nodded. 'My sister's. But you look wonderful, too. In fact we all do.'

Zara was wearing a short scarlet dress with a plunging neckline, which somehow looked endearing, not predatory. Amanda was in pale blue with bugle beads, and Crystal, when she appeared, was in Armani. The classic black did put Anna's less classic – or certainly less expensive – black into the shade a bit, but Anna didn't mind. She wasn't expecting to be the belle of the ball. She just didn't want to be the stick insect among a flock of butterflies.

'Right, girls,' said Zara, 'let's get a taxi. I've found a nice-sounding bar quite near the venue. The chaps are meeting up with us there later, if they're not too stuck into drinking themselves stupid.'

'I thought that was what you had in mind,' said Crystal.

'No, no! Just a couple of shots to get us in the mood! Do lighten up, Crys, you're only young once.'

'I am a married woman.'

'Then put your rock in your handbag and have a good time!' Zara was not going to let Crystal spoil the evening.

She's so nice, thought Anna, sipping her margarita and looking at Zara's bubbly, friendly face – she'd already convinced the barman that they were a hen party, and therefore should be given cheap drinks. If Max fancies her even remotely, I haven't got a chance. Unless, of course, Max Gordon's got fat and old. That would put Zara off him. It wouldn't affect her feelings, she knew that, but it would knock out the competition.

'Cheer up, Anna!' said Amanda. 'Have another drink! We're here to enjoy ourselves!'

'I am cheerful,' said Anna, trying to look it, in spite of her nerves. 'I'm just a slow drinker.'

'Well, thank goodness you're not all intent on drinking yourselves silly,' said Crystal, who was nursing a spritzer. 'Apart from anything else, alcohol is so bad for your skin.'

Anna drained her glass. 'On the other hand, another drink might be a good idea.'

She put her bag on the bar and tried to attract the attention of the waiter. 'Do we all want another?' she asked.

'My dear girl,' said Crystal, in a low voice. 'Look at your hands!'

To her credit, Crystal had tried to be discreet, but her words had fallen into a brief silence, and the whole group now looked at Anna's hands. Crystal took hold of one and opened out Anna's fingers.

'I've got nail varnish on,' said Anna, defensively.

'On what nails you've got left!' Crystal was appalled.

'I told you, I'm doing up a house. It does ruin your nails, rather.'

'When you said doing up a house,' said Amanda, 'I

thought you meant getting builders in. I didn't think you meant you were doing it up personally, your own self.'

'That is impressive,' said Zara. 'You mean you wield hammer and nails, stuff like that?'

'Yup.'

'But, sweetie, your hands!' said Crystal. 'They look like you've been clawing stone out of the cliff face with them.'

Anna regarded them once more. They didn't look too bad to her, but then she was used to them. Hands were for doing things with, after all. 'I have got gloves,' she said.

'Gloves?' said Amanda. 'What kind of gloves?'

'This kind.' Anna retrieved them from her bag and put them on, smoothing them up her arms until they covered her elbows.

'Oh wow,' said Zara. 'They're fab. They make the rest of us – well, except Crystal, of course – look so damned dull.'

'Won't you find them difficult to eat in?' said Crystal.

'I'll probably take them off quite soon,' said Anna, embarrassed by the attention her accessories were receiving. 'Isn't it time we were going?'

'Didn't you want another drink first?' said Zara.

'Darling, she can hardly walk in those heels sober. She won't have a cat in hell's chance drunk,' said Crystal.

Zara frowned. 'Shall we go, then?'

Anna recognised Max Gordon's back the moment they got in the door. He was surrounded by young men, Anna's contemporaries, and yet he stood out as being more attractive than them, even before she'd heard his voice, or seen his sexy eyes, or anything. He happened to turn as the girls came in. 'Wow!' murmured Zara. 'He hasn't got old and fat, then.'

Anna wished he had. In fact, he seemed to have got even more attractive in the three years since she'd last seen him.

'He might have turned into a prune close to,' said Amanda.

'Rubbish! He's heaven on legs. Let's go over.'

Anna didn't dare take off on her own, so she followed the girls up to the boys, beginning to wish she hadn't come. She hadn't been thinking about him so much since she'd been so busy, but here he was, in the flesh, just as sensational as before. Now she would have to concentrate really, really hard on getting her house done, because her brain was going to wander off the point at every chance she gave it.

There were a few of the boys they'd known at college there, too, and Zara, who had a good memory, introduced everyone. 'And this is Anna,' she said. 'Interior Design, same year as me. I don't think you ever taught her,' she added, to Max Gordon.

'Oh yes I did,' he said softly. 'She was the one who got away.' And looked at her with something that even she had no trouble in recognising as approval.

Zara regarded Anna with her head on her side, silently accusing her of being a dark horse. Anna looked down. Actually being in Max's presence after dreaming about him for so long was almost too heady for her.

The exchanges of achievements took up most of the conversation. Anna didn't join in. If anyone asked her directly what she was up to, she would tell them. For now she was just happy to be in the orbit of Max Gordon. He had always been smart, but in a dinner jacket he was stunning – even more so now, she thought, than he had done at their Graduation Ball.

'I want to dance!' said Zara. 'Come on, Max.' Gaily, she dragged him on to the floor. He didn't seem exactly reluctant.

Following Zara's example, the others paired off and headed for the area set aside for dancing. Anna and a couple of the other boys stayed sitting at the bar. While she did manage to keep up a reasonable flow of conversation, Anna's mind was dizzy with thoughts of Max. She could ask him to dance, of course. It wouldn't look strange, forward, or presumptuous. They were equals now. He had remembered her. But it had all gone so wrong the last time. It would probably go wrong again! Yet she knew she had had to come, no matter how the evening turned out.

Couples drifted to and from the dance floor, but still Anna sat, wishing she did have the nerve to drag someone off to dance, if only to stop herself looking such a wallflower. It was quite hard to keep an expression of polite enjoyment fixed on her face.

Max and Zara came back, Zara looking very cheerful. Anna wondered if she'd done more than dance with him, and knew that if she had, they'd all hear about it in the taxi back. Anna couldn't look at her watch without taking her gloves off, and that would be a bit of a palaver. How soon could she go home without looking like a party pooper?

'Come on, you.' Max's voice jerked her out of her daydream. 'You haven't danced yet.'

He took her hand and she trotted after him, wondering if one could actually die of ecstasy. By the time they'd got to the square of parquet she'd decided he was only asking to dance with her out of kindness, and she shouldn't regard it.

He didn't bop about like most men, he took her into his arms in the old-fashioned way and, somehow, she managed to follow his lead. She thanked the gods for making her watch that series about ballroom dancing – at least she could make the top half of her look right, even if her feet were all over the place.

'Right,' he said, when the track came to an end. 'That's the formalities over, let's go where we can talk. Why didn't you ring me?'

Chapter Ten

❧

Max led Anna to a part of the hotel she hadn't been to before. The music was still audible, but not so loud as to preclude conversation. There were sofas and chairs set around a low table, but no one else was there.

'Would you like a drink?' Max asked.

'Mm. Sparkling water please. I'm quite thirsty.' She was also determined not to drink any more alcohol. She didn't want her senses remotely befuddled: this was her moment, the one she'd been dreaming of for so long. He *had* remembered her; he'd asked her to dance; and then he'd taken her somewhere away from the others so they could talk. She could be in the portal of heaven. She settled back in her chair, trying to prevent a blissful smile from creeping over her face.

He came back with her water and something short in a glass for himself. 'Here you are. I hope you like it. It's the best brand they had.'

'I'm sure it's fine,' she said, and took a sip. Now she would have to make conversation. She took a breath to do this but he interrupted her.

'Now, tell me why you didn't ring me.'

Although she'd rehearsed this explanation in her head a million times, she hadn't expected to have to deliver it. She took another breath.

'I was devastated,' he went on, before she could speak. 'I really thought we had a connection.' He looked into her eyes. 'We did, didn't we?'

'Er – yes! I thought so. But I got flu and – er – lost your

number. I was devastated, too. I thought about you for months.' She smiled, pleased with this little lie. It made her sound so grown up and normal.

'You didn't go out of my head for years.'

She took a sip of her drink, not sure if she believed him but pleased all the same.

'So,' he said. 'What happened to you after you walked out of my life?'

She giggled a little, feeling more relaxed. 'I didn't walk out of your life. As I recall, I was in a taxi.'

His smile gave her butterflies. 'You walked to get into the taxi.'

'But you were with me! You put me in the taxi!' She remembered having to rip herself away from him, like Velcro. She had so wanted to follow her instincts and desires and go to bed with him. Leaving him had taken real moral effort. At that second she resolved she wouldn't make the same choice again. If he asked her to go to bed with him tonight, she'd go.

'So what have been doing with your life without me? You didn't carry on and do architecture, did you? As I remember, you had real potential.'

'No, I didn't.'

'You stayed with Interior Design.' He glanced at her sideways, his smile more noticeable in his eyes than on his mouth. 'Cop-out.'

She sat up straighter, her own smile tugging hard at the corners of her mouth. 'Did you bring me all the way over here to insult me?'

'Not necessarily, but if it seems appropriate . . .'

The twinkle in his eyes made it almost impossible not to respond but she was determined not to let him off.

'Why would it be? Interior Design is a perfectly respectable profession. It's not lap dancing, you know.' Not all her indignation was fake; she'd had this conversation before.

131

'Let's face it, it's thinking up colour schemes for rich women who are too idle to do it themselves. They need you to arrange the scatter cushions.'

Usually these sorts of remarks infuriated her. Now they made her want to giggle helplessly. 'Rubbish! I don't arrange scatter cushions! I haven't even got any scatter cushions!'

He put his head on one side and looked intently into her eyes. 'So what do you do, then? Don't tell me you're actually in IT, or Sales, or something entirely unconnected with your expensive education.'

She swallowed, biting her lip to stop herself laughing. Flirting with an expert was such glorious fun. 'Not at all. I'm doing up a house, which I shall sell at a vast profit.'

'Oh, really? You must have a lot of money, then. If you come from a rich family, why didn't you carry on and get qualified as an architect?'

'I don't come from a rich family!' Her hand flew out to touch him reproachfully but she snatched it back. 'My sister and I did inherit a bit of money. We bought a flat and sold it at a profit, but that's all the money I'll ever inherit.'

'So how did you get the money to buy a house, then?'

He was being appallingly rude. Why did she find it so attractive? 'I got a mortgage, like everyone else. And a bit of a loan from my sister.'

'And have you got good builders?'

'I'm doing most of it myself.'

The smile danced between his eyes and his mouth. It might have been in both places but she could only look at one at a time; both places were utterly fascinating. 'Nonsense, you're telling the builders where to put the scatter cushions.'

This time she allowed herself to put her hand on his sleeve. 'What is it with you and scatter cushions?'

He put his hand on top of hers. 'I like to see you

animated. The colour in your cheeks really suits you. But why won't you tell me what you really do?'

She sighed, frustrated but enjoying herself enormously. 'I told you, I've bought a house in the Cotswolds, and I'm doing it up.'

'My mother lives in Gloucestershire. Where is your house?' Max asked.

'Amberford. Near Stroud.'

'Oh, but that's where my mother lives!'

The words 'I know' were bitten back just in time. Anna drank more water, so glad she'd declined alcohol.

He leant forward, very interested now, keeping hold of her hand. She wished she wasn't wearing gloves so she could feel the heat of his fingers properly. He was probably planning to ask her to design an en suite for his mother, she told herself, fighting to keep her imagination from going into orbit. Or an airing cupboard.

'So who are your builders?' he said, almost serious now. 'I'm looking for someone reliable to work on my mother's house.'

I knew it, she thought. He's not remotely interested in me, he just thinks I might be useful. 'I haven't got builders! I told you, I'm doing it myself!'

'Oh, come on!'

Anna regarded him, more confident now and exhilarated by their argument. 'You don't believe me?'

'Frankly, no.'

Some memory of an old film, watched aeons ago by her and her sister one wet Sunday afternoon when they were little girls, flitted into her mind. For all she knew it had Audrey Hepburn in it. She withdrew her hand and sat up straight. Then she started to take off one of her gloves, slowly, fingertip by fingertip, until her hand was free, then she pulled off the rest of it in one moderately graceful movement. 'Look!' she said.

He took hold of her hand and held it, inspecting her

fingers, her varnished but sorely mistreated fingernails, the scars and scabs and smears of paint.

'Wow,' he breathed. 'You really are doing it yourself.'

Suddenly losing confidence, she snatched her hand away and started to put on her glove again. The touch of his fingers on hers was making her visibly shake. 'So, what are *you* doing these days?' she asked, wishing she really was in an old film and had her lines written for her.

'I have my own architectural practice. We're very busy.'

'That's nice for you.'

'There's no need to be so prickly, although' – he smiled down at her – 'there is something very attractive about it. I am genuinely impressed by what you're doing. Tell me about your house.'

At last Anna let herself relax. She pulled off the glove that she'd only half got on and sat back in her chair. Asking her to talk about her house was like asking a new mother to talk about her baby. 'The staircase is going to be really tricky,' she finished.

'And it's listed?'

She nodded.

'That's a bit of a pain, isn't it.' It was a statement, not a question. 'And is the listed buildings officer an officious bastard?'

Anna thought carefully. At the outset she had certainly been thinking of Rob Hunter along those lines, but now she wondered if that was fair. 'Well, no, he's been very helpful actually, although admittedly he wouldn't have known about my original plans for the staircase if he hadn't been in my house for some other reason.'

'They're all jobsworths. I would never buy a listed building,' Max went on. 'I really cannot stand my aesthetic taste being criticised by people who aren't even properly qualified.'

'It's not quite like that,' said Anna carefully, 'and my

house is lovely. It would be criminal to put in patio doors, really.'

His lazy smile penetrated deep into her stomach and caused havoc. 'Oh well, it's probably a good idea for your aesthetic taste to be criticised.'

Anna touched her top lip with her tongue. 'There's nothing wrong with my aesthetic taste, I assure you.'

'Sorry, I was forgetting, you're qualified to arrange scatter cushions.'

She threw a beer mat at him and he got to his feet, pulling her to hers at the same time. 'Let's dance some more,' he murmured.

Anna felt like Bambi on ice. It was partly her natural gangliness and partly the effect Max had on her knees. Eventually Max just put his arms round her and she put hers round his neck.

'That's better,' he whispered into her ear. 'I didn't wear my steel-toecapped boots this evening.'

'Nor did I,' muttered Anna, wishing she could control her limbs a bit better.

Eventually, the music stopped; the evening was over. He led her to the door and the butterflies in Anna's stomach made a bid for freedom.

'Sweetheart,' he said softly, having steered her to a little lobby away from the main foyer. 'I've got an old friend staying so I won't ask you back for a drink. We'd just have to talk to him and he's terribly boring. Besides . . .'

'What?'

'I don't think I could stand spending the rest of the evening looking at you and not . . .' His eyes narrowed in a lazy smile.

'What?' asked Anna, more insistently this time.

'I'm sure you know.' He brushed a lock of hair off her face and behind her ear, then he let his finger trail along the line of her jaw. It stopped at her chin, which he raised slightly, then he outlined her mouth in a way that made

Anna's breath become very short. 'I really want to see you again. Would that be possible?'

'Er, yes, I think so.' Anna felt almost too flustered to speak.

'Have you got your phone on you?'

'Yes.' She found her bag, which had slipped round, and scrabbled for her phone. 'Here it is.'

He took it from her, pressed some buttons and then handed it back. 'I'm not taking any chances with you losing my number again. And I'm going to take yours.'

Anna knew perfectly well how to use her mobile phone, but seeing him tapping in numbers made her feel incredibly inept. Unusually for her, it wasn't unpleasant.

'I'll ring you,' he said. 'We'll meet again. Soon.'

While she was putting Laura's suede loafers back on in the Ladies, some hours later, Anna considered the fact that if Max Gordon had suggested she went back to his flat, she'd have gone. She wouldn't have cared about the inevitable consequences, she'd have just gone.

Zara was being sick in the loo. Crystal was redoing her eye make-up for the taxi ride home. Amanda was gleefully counting how many new telephone numbers she'd collected.

'I think that was a jolly good evening, don't you?' she asked the room in general.

The lavatory flushed and Zara emerged. 'Next time we do this, can one of you remind me not to mix my drinks? Hey, Anna, what about you? Dark horse, or what? I didn't think you even remembered Max Gordon.'

'He sort of – came back to me,' said Anna, trying to keep a smile of pure smugness under control.

'I'll say. You were practically glued together on the dance floor, you lucky cow.' Zara turned on the tap and stuck her mouth under it. 'I really had planned to have him myself, you know.'

'I know, I'm sorry,' said Anna, who did feel a bit rueful under her ecstatic happiness.

'So why didn't you go home with him?' asked Zara, who was showing no bitterness about Anna's success.

'He didn't ask me,' she said simply.

'You wouldn't have slept with him on the first date!' said Crystal. 'That's so against *The Rules*.'

'We're not at school, Crystal, there are no rules,' said Amanda.

'I meant the book,' said Crystal in a quiet voice, suddenly aware that only she had heard of it.

'So, have you got his number?' asked Zara.

Anna nodded. 'More to the point, he's got mine.' However much she loved him, fancied him, wanted him, all the possessive, passionate sort of words in the dictionary, she would never ring him up, not if her life depended on it. It was something to do with having not done it before. He had her number; he had to make the running.

Fortunately, she was, at this moment, fairly optimistic that he would ring her. Tomorrow she knew she'd doubt it, but tonight, she had faith.

'Are we all ready, then?' said Crystal, satisfied with her appearance at last.

'I think so,' said Anna, swinging the bag with the black high-heeled shoes in it.

'Have we all said goodbye to all the people we should say goodbye to?' asked Amanda.

'Think so.' Zara sighed. 'It was a good night. We must do it more often.'

'What about you, Anna?' asked Crystal. 'Have you said goodbye to Max?'

'Oh yes, we said our goodbyes in the foyer.'

'And he didn't take you with him? I think that's almost insulting.' Zara was still miffed about this.

'Not at all, he's showing respect,' said Crystal. 'Now come on.'

Although Anna had seen Max leave the hotel, he must have come back specially, for he was waiting in the shadows by the door as they left. He didn't say anything, he just raised his fingers to Anna in greeting. No one else noticed him, but it made Anna's heart leap.

Her mobile rang just as she was settling into bed. Her heart leapt again, but this time in panic. What could possibly have happened for her sister to ring her at this time of night? Caroline, their mother, her house, all suffered various terrible fates in her imagination in the few moments it took her to get to her phone.

'I was ringing to make sure you'd got back safely,' said a low voice that didn't say whom it belonged to.

Anna sighed ecstatically, not for the first time that evening. 'Of course I did. What could possibly happen to me?'

'Nothing. I suppose I just wanted to hear your voice again. I'll say goodnight now.'

'Goodnight,' breathed Anna.

It took her ages to get to sleep. Every word, every bit of dialogue had to be replayed in her mind, analysed, dissected, inspected for double meanings. She couldn't believe such an attractive man fancied her, done up like Cinderella in borrowed finery.

On the other hand, he would never have fancied the girl in dungarees, her hair stuffed into a scarf to keep it out of the machinery, who kept just about clean, but who didn't wear make-up and quite often shared her bed with a dog.

But why worry about that? She could keep that girl a secret, and always be soignée and elegant. She might even learn to put her hair into a French pleat.

Her ecstasy continued for the entire journey home. Inevitably, she suffered moments of doubt: he only wanted her for her body – except if that were the case, he could have had it, if he'd only asked! He only wanted her to design an en suite for his mother – that didn't quite fit, either, because he'd cut her out from the crowd before he knew what she did, because he'd remembered her. The most realistic fear was that he wanted a short affair and would leave her more broken-hearted, more obsessed, more useless than ever. And that was what would happen. At Didcot, as the train passed the cooling towers, she came to this realisation. And yet, somehow, it didn't bother her. She would have had the rapture, the seventh-heaven experience. So what if it came to an end? In real life, men like Max Gordon didn't marry and live happily ever after with girls like her.

Laura and Will were there to meet her train, as arranged. As soon as she got on to the platform and walked towards Laura's open arms, she knew something was wrong.

'What's happened? It's Caroline, she's got out and been run over, hasn't she?'

'Oh, for goodness' sake!' Laura hugged Anna hard. 'If she did get out, she'd hardly get run over trotting along the lane.'

'If she saw a cat, she might chase it across the main road,' said Anna, confident now that this had not happened.

'Honestly! Did you have a nice time?'

Anna was faintly surprised that the sort of time she had had was not inscribed on her forehead. 'Wonderful, thanks, now tell me what's wrong.'

'It's nothing that bad,' said Laura, frowning. 'How did you know anything is?'

'I could tell by your expression.'

'Oh, Anna,' snapped Laura, 'you always did have that sixth-sense thing.'

Anna smiled up at Will, who had taken her case. She didn't think she had a sixth-sense thing, she just thought Laura was a bit lacking in feminine intuition.

'So, what is it, then?' Anna asked when they were in the car. 'If it's not Caroline, it must be Mum.'

'No, she's fine,' said Laura.

'And it's not anything really terrible,' said Will over his shoulder to Anna, who was sitting in the back seat. 'We could have a cup of tea at home before we discuss it. No need to make a drama out of a crisis,' he muttered to Laura.

'So,' said Laura, falsely bright. 'How was the party? Did you meet up with anyone nice?'

'Nice' didn't quite describe Max Gordon but Anna said, 'Yes,' anyway. Zara and Amanda had been nice.

'What sort of nice? Friendly nice or romantic nice?'

'I just meant I met up with old friends who were nice,' said Anna, who didn't feel anything like ready to tell her sister about Max. 'We had cocktails and a lot of fun.'

'And nothing bad happened to Chloe's dress?'

Was this code for: 'Did Chloe's dress get thrown up on, or torn to shreds by a passionate old flame?'

'No. What could happen to it? It's very "easy-care". She told me.'

'So, no more goss?'

'How much do you want? It was a college reunion, not speed-dating.'

'OK.' Laura sighed and then brightened up. 'I bought a cake at the market yesterday. You didn't tell me about that!'

'Didn't I? Sorry!'

'It was wonderful! Do you know, there's a man there who sells local champagne? We had a bottle last night, didn't we, Will?'

'Sure did.'

'That bed's really very comfortable, and the bedroom is going to be heavenly.'

At last, after Caroline had greeted Anna, giving her a nasty scratch in her excitement while she did it, and everyone had been settled with cups of tea and cake from the WI stall, Anna felt able to say, 'So what's the drama then?'

Laura exchanged glances with her husband. 'You don't need to worry about it, really.'

'And maybe you won't need to worry about it at all,' said Will firmly.

'The thing is,' said Laura, 'we heard yesterday from a colleague. Will's been made redundant.'

'Oh my God!' Anna exclaimed.

'If we hadn't been here, Will would have got the news on Friday. His friend rang him on his mobile. But it's been on the cards for some time.'

'That's awful!' Anna, still buzzing from the party, tried to take it in. The thought of her sister's family, which had always seemed so perfect, with Will out of a job, was such a shock.

'I'm quite likely to get a job soon, or consultancy,' said Will confidently. 'There *are* other jobs.'

Anna glanced at Laura and saw that she wasn't quite as relaxed about it as her husband. 'Well, you are good at what you do,' she said.

'Exactly! I probably won't be unemployed long enough to finish the decorating.' Will laughed, but Laura still looked rather anxious.

'I thought you were a specialist,' said Anna. 'Are there lots of jobs in your field?'

Will grinned. 'Well, not in the field, because mostly I work in an office, but—'

'Oh, Will!' Laura snapped. 'You know perfectly well that Anna is right! It's very unlikely you'll get a job doing what you've been doing. You'll have to downgrade.'

'Well, that won't kill me. It'll be a nice change.'

'So what would your perfect job be?' asked Anna. 'If you wrote your own job description?'

Will decided to take the matter seriously for a moment.

'I'd set up on my own, not work for anyone else, and then if I didn't make it, it would be my fault, not anyone else's. I want to be in charge of my own destiny.'

The two sisters regarded him, considering this rather grandiose statement.

'Then I must sell the house,' said Anna rather shakily. 'You'll need all the capital you can get.' Although she knew it was the only decision she could make, it wasn't an easy one.

'Oh, it's all right, Anna,' said Laura quickly. 'Will won't actually do that. It would be far too risky.'

'Not as risky as all that. I've got enough good clients to start off with if I had a bit of money to tide us over,' said Will.

'And you must follow your dream!' Anna was suddenly aware of sounding like an old film. 'I mean, if that's what you've always wanted to do, and think you can make it, you must do it. I'll sell the house. It's what I always planned, after all.' But it still hurt to say it.

'Don't over-react, Anna,' said Laura. 'You must take your time to do up the house. It would be silly to rush and spoil it. We've got some savings.'

'Yes, but weren't you going to use them to put on an extension? The boys are getting bigger by the second!'

'We've still got more room than Chloe's got, and only two boys,' said Laura.

'You'll need every penny you can get. I'm going to sell the house as soon as possible, and that's final.'

'You may not find it that easy,' said Laura, shaking her head. 'The market's very slack at the moment.'

'I'll put it on the market now then, which will give me time to finish it.'

'You love this house!' Laura protested.

'I know but it always was an investment. You were the one who told me I mustn't fall in love with it.' Thank

God Laura didn't know whom else she'd fallen in love with! If she told Laura about Max now, she'd die from anxiety.

'I know, but it's such a perfect little house. We've loved staying here and were having a brilliant time until we got the news. I don't think you should rush into selling this. We can manage for a while. There'll be redundancy money, though not much,' Laura conceded.

'Well, I'm selling,' Anna insisted. 'This house was bought as an investment. I'm not changing my plans, I'm just bringing them forward by a few months. I'll have to get builders in to help me, but I budgeted for that anyway.' She frowned, wondering if her design for the bathroom would be passed.

'Oh, Anna! This is such a pretty area.'

'I can buy again in the same area!' Privately she doubted this as her house had been such a bargain. 'Maybe I could get something at auction.'

'That would be exciting,' said Will.

Laura sighed deeply. 'To hell with tea, let's have a proper drink.'

Will produced a bottle of whisky. 'I didn't buy this at the market.'

Chapter Eleven

❧

Laura and Will left the following morning. While they were collecting their belongings – and there were a great many of them – Anna began to feel flat, and decided she should give Chloe back her clothes as soon as possible. She had left her phone turned off all Sunday, in case Max rang and she couldn't speak to him because she was with her sister, but when she went to bed, there were no missed calls. She tried hard not to feel disappointed – after all, he was a busy man, and although he'd seemed very keen yesterday, she couldn't expect him to be so keen that he'd want to ring her the very next day. So after she'd waved Laura and Will off, she settled Caroline and then found her borrowed finery.

'Hi, Chloe! I've brought your dress back, or should I get it dry-cleaned?' She had put her phone in the pocket of her jeans, so she would feel it if it rang. She had nearly decided to leave it at home, but then thought that Laura would want to ring and tell her they'd got back safely. The fact that this was unlikely to happen for at least a couple of hours didn't seem relevant.

Chloe took the bag that Anna was holding out to her. 'No, it washes like a rag. Now come in, sit down and tell me everything.'

Anna decided not to fob Chloe off with the nice time she'd had with her old college chums. She felt a strong need to talk about Max and if Laura weren't likely to worry herself silly, she'd have told her. Chloe would be just as satisfactory a confidante. Anna allowed a smile to lift the corner of her mouth.

'Don't tell me! You met someone!' said Chloe gleefully.

'OK then, I won't tell you.'

Chloe checked automatically for small ears although the sound of fast motorbikes from upstairs should have set her mind at rest. 'You cow! Now you tell Momma everything, yo' hear?'

Anna stretched luxuriously. In Chloe's sunny kitchen, drinking coffee, it seemed perfectly reasonable for Max not to have rung on Sunday. He'd rung to say goodnight on Saturday night, just over an hour after they'd said goodnight. 'Well, I didn't mention it before—'

'Why not?'

'Because I didn't know if it would come to anything. In fact, I was sure it wouldn't.'

'What "it"?'

'If you let me get a word in edgeways, I'll tell you.'

Chloe got down the tin of chocolate biscuits and opened it. 'Go on. From the beginning.'

'Well, years ago, when I was at college' – Anna rummaged in the tin until she found something with a bit of caramel in it – 'there was a guest lecturer who came to talk to us about being architects. The course we were doing was the first part of the qualification and he was supposed to encourage us to carry on. Anyway, I fell in love with him.'

'You mean, you had a crush,' said Chloe, her mouth full of chocolate.

'No,' said Anna rather ruefully, 'it was love. If it had just been a crush I wouldn't have been still holding a torch for him all these years later, would I?'

'Oh my goodness, you haven't?'

'Yup. We did get together, sort of, at our Grad Ball, but I lost – no, that was what I told him – I destroyed his number and never rang him.'

'Oh!'

'The taxi came sooner than we thought and there was

only time for him to give me his number. I never got to give him mine. And then I got flu and didn't phone. When I was a bit better, about three days later, I staggered out for some tomato soup—'

'Very comforting, tomato soup.'

'– and I saw him with a woman.'

'But she could have been anyone!'

'Of course when my brain came back I realised that. She was probably a colleague or something, but at the time I over-reacted and burnt the bit of cardboard – it was the back of someone's cigarette packet.' Anna still had pangs of remorse whenever she saw that particular brand, but she didn't think Chloe needed to know quite how doolally she'd been. 'The strange thing is, his mother lives here, in the village.'

'Really? What's her name?'

Anna shrugged. 'Mrs Gordon, I suppose.'

'Does she live in that big house at the end of the lane? The one that leads on to the common?'

'I don't know! She could do.'

'Well, for your sake, I really hope that's not her. She's an old dragon! She shouted at the children because they tricycled – tricycled, mind you, they were still on three wheels – a titchy way into her drive.'

'Oh . . . well, I hope that's not her, then.' Anna felt faintly irritated by these diversions. She wanted to tell Chloe about her fabulous evening, not be regaled with stories about some woman who might not even be her potential mother-in-law.

'So go on, then,' said Chloe.

'Well, when I heard there was going to be a reunion, and that he was going, I knew I had to go, too.'

'I did wonder a bit about that. It didn't seem a very "you" thing to do, getting all dressed up to go to a party in London.' She sighed. 'It's a very me thing, though.'

Anna ignored this. 'So I went, as you know, in your

dress – oh, and the gloves! The gloves were wonderful!'

'They did look good, I must say. And did you manage your hair?'

'More or less, the way you did it. I couldn't do it like Laura did.'

'Not surprised, it's quite thick. Anyway, I know what you looked like, so tell me what happened.'

'Well, we all – all the girls I knew, that is – met up in a hotel where we'd got this cheap deal. One girl, Zara,' – Anna was hurrying on, trying not to give Chloe time to interrupt – 'said she really fancied Max Gordon—'

'Is that his name, then?'

'Yes.' Anna paused for a moment. 'Don't tell me you know he's married, that he got married in the local church, and his mother wouldn't let your boys be page-boys?'

'No! I don't know anything about him! What are you on about?'

'Just being neurotic. Anyway, Zara said she really fancied him, and aimed to get off with him. Zara, I should tell you, is gorgeous, and she's really bubbly and outgoing. I knew I didn't have a chance.'

'But?'

'But I did have a chance! When he first saw me he murmured, "The one that got away."' Anna sighed deeply. 'I thought I'd die on the spot from sheer . . . I don't know: happiness? Desire? Something like that. Then he cut me out from the crowd and took me to a little table where we could talk, and he asked me what I did. I told him I was doing up a house and he didn't believe me – or at least, he didn't believe I was doing it myself.' Anna's smile came dangerously close to a smirk. 'So I proved it!'

'How?'

'I took off a glove! Really slowly, like Audrey Hepburn did in that film.'

'I don't think that was Audrey Hepburn. That was in *Gypsy*. It was about a stripper.'

'Oh well, never mind. But it worked! He took my hand in his and examined it. It was so romantic!'

'And quite sexy, too,' said Chloe, grinning. 'Sort of masterful.'

'Yes it was. And after that, he took me off to dance and—'

'Did you kiss?'

Anna shook her head, a little smile tweaking at the corners of her mouth. She sighed with remembered lust. 'No.'

'No! And you've gone all – unnecessary, my mother would have said.'

'Well, yes. It was a very – promising – non-kiss.'

'And he didn't ask you back to his flat?' Chloe asked carefully.

'No. He had a friend staying.' Anna remembered her frustration.

'I must say, restraint is very attractive.'

Anna chuckled. 'And unexpected!'

'So, would you have gone back with him? If he hadn't had a friend staying with him?'

Anna could tell that Chloe was trying very hard to sound non-committal, but she couldn't keep the anxiety out of her voice.

'He didn't ask me, but I do have to tell you that if he had, I'd have gone.'

'Yikes,' said Chloe.

'But he didn't, so you don't have to look so worried. But what he did do – so sweet – was to ring me when I was in my hotel room, just to say goodnight.'

'Wow,' said Chloe slowly. 'He sounds a real ladies' man. Let's have some more coffee. I need something to take away the taste of all that chocolate.'

Anna decided to ignore the remark about Max being

a ladies' man. 'So do you think he sounds keen?'

'I should think so!'

'So why didn't he ring me yesterday then?'

'Because he has a life? Have you got his number?' Chloe asked.

'Yes, but I wouldn't use it unless his mother was in a fire and he had to come down and rescue her. Even then I'd ring the fire brigade first.'

'Much more sensible. But you could ring him, you know. People do.'

Anna shook her head. 'I really don't like ringing people I don't know well.'

'Oh, come on! Are you a man or a mouse?'

'Well, neither, actually.' She stopped for a moment. 'Oh, and there's been some bad news.'

'What?' Chloe looked anxious. 'It's a roller-coaster ride with you, Anna.'

'It's Will. He's been made redundant. It means I've got to get the house on the market asap. I must pay them back. Oh, hi, guys!'

Chloe's boys trooped down the stairs. 'You've been up there a long time,' Anna said. What have you been doing?'

'But the house is nowhere near ready!' Chloe looked more than anxious now.

'Playing cars,' said Harry.

'That sounds fun. Do you want to go and fetch your favourite one so I can see it?' When Harry had run off, Anna turned back to Chloe, 'I know. I must really hurry up. I'll have to get the plans passed and get on with the brickwork and plastering. There's loads to do.'

As she didn't appear too disheartened by this Chloe said, 'Being in love helps everything, doesn't it?'

Anna nodded. 'But I will need some help to get the house done. You don't know any wonderful craftsmen with time on their hands, do you?'

Chloe opened her mouth as if to speak, then, after a second's pause, she said, 'Rob does.'

'Oh? I've got to ring him anyway, to see how long it's going to take his office to look at the plans.'

'Good. He'll sort you out. Oh, and, Anna, I've just had a brilliant thought! While you're all gooey and on cloud nine . . .'

'Yes,' said Anna slowly, wondering what her state of bliss was about to let her in for.

'Well, you know I raise funds for Greyhound Rescue.'

Anna smiled. 'To my cost – but also my eternal gratitude – I do.'

'Well, there was a joint fundraising effort with another charity and we sold raffle tickets.'

'If you've sold the tickets, you obviously don't want me to do that.' Anna was confused.

'No,' cried Chloe, 'I want you to be the prize!'

'What?'

'Well, you and me both. But don't start to get all het up! We're labour.'

'Chloe, this is no time to talk about politics!' The conversation was getting more mystifying by the second. 'What on earth have you done?'

'The prize, or at least one of them, is an afternoon's work: gardening, cleaning out attics, stuff like that.'

'Oh.' Anna wasn't sure quite how she felt about that. 'I do think if you were going to offer me as a raffle prize you should have asked me first. I am dreadfully busy, what with the house and—'

'Honestly, Anna, you're being so dense! The prize – the whole raffle – was ages ago! The person who won two people to do an afternoon's work has only just decided what she wants done. And the people who were going to do it have since moved away. We have to stand in. I thought you wouldn't mind, when I told you that we've got to clean out a greenhouse for . . . guess who?'

150

'Chloe! How can I possibly guess! I don't know anyone round here except for you.' Then she bit her lip. 'Oh no – you mean it's for Max's mother?'

'If she's the woman who lives in that house I told you about.'

'Well I never! Who'd have thought it?' She considered for a moment. If they were working outside it would give her a chance to give the formidable Mrs Gordon a look-over without getting close enough to be recognisable. Chloe could do all the talking. 'Yes, of course I'll do it,' she said, realising it wasn't perhaps her most sensible decision.

'Is next weekend OK? Mike'll be home to look after the boys.'

'Should think so.' After all, Max, if he contacted her, was unlikely to want to see her during the day.

When Anna got home she found that a bouquet of lilies and roses that was almost too big for her to lift had been delivered while she'd been out. The message read: *To the one who got away, love, M.* Anna had to sit down for several minutes before she could do anything useful.

The following morning, still on a cloud of happiness that made her love all the world, even the Dog and Building Police, Anna dialled Rob's office number and happily listened to 'Greensleeves' until she was put through to him.

'Rob? It's Anna. With Caroline? You know?'

'Of course I know.' Rob sounded mildly amused. 'What can I do for you?'

'Well, you can tell me my plans have been passed and I can crack on with them. I have to put the house on the market more or less straightaway.'

There was a pause. 'Oh. Well, I can't quite manage that, I'm afraid, but I can tell you that I've looked at your plans, and I think, as long as you get a structural engineer to check the joists – they're often very suspect in houses of that age – they should be OK.'

'Are you saying I can go ahead? That's wonderful! Thank you so much,' Anna gabbled.

'Hold your horses. I'm afraid I'm not saying quite that. I'm saying when you've given me a report from a structural engineer, I'll submit the plans to the next planning meeting. I'm afraid that's the best I can do.'

Anna came down off her cloud a few notches. 'Oh. That sounds time-consuming and very expensive.'

'It is, but necessary. And surely you've got lots to get on with?'

'Oh yes, loads.' She fell silent, thinking about just how much she did have to do.

'Anna, is there anything else I can do for you?' Rob broke into her thoughts. 'I know I'm at work, but I can spend a couple of minutes on the phone.'

Anna laughed with relief. 'That's terribly kind. I really hate asking people for favours.'

'You shouldn't; people like being asked. What is it?'

'Well, I was going ask you if you knew any good tradesmen. I need a brickie and a plasterer.'

'I know someone who does both. That do?'

'That would be perfect! I am quite good at bricklaying,' she went on, 'but my plastering is not perfect. This house has to be perfect.'

'You know you have to use Cotswold stone for the outside wall, don't you? You can get away with blockwork and plaster on the inside.'

As the previous owners appeared to have sold all the better bits of dressed stone that must have come out of the wall, this was good news. 'Fine. I'll do that.'

'And get in touch with Eric. I don't know how busy he is at the moment but he's done work for me and I was very pleased.'

She took down the number he gave her. 'You're a star!

Thank you so much. If ever there's anything I can do for you,' Anna offered, still loving all the world, 'just say the word.'

'Well, since you've offered,' said Rob, to Anna's complete surprise, 'I've promised my sister to help at her Country Fair and Novelty Dog Show, over at the other end of the county.'

'That sounds fun! What are you doing?'

'That's why I need support. She hasn't told me. It could be anything from judging the novelty dogs to selling ice creams. She's in charge of everything. I'll get the job no one else will agree to do. Last time she had me shinning up trees with bottles of whisky.'

'Why?' Anna's mind reeled with possibilities.

'It's to do with . . . Oh, never mind. It would take too long to explain. But you don't mind coming along?'

'Of course not! It sounds a blast. When is it?'

'I'm still not sure of the date. Can I let you know nearer the time?'

'Sure thing.' She hesitated. 'I may not be able to manage the date, of course.' If she had a date with Max, for example. 'But if I'm free, I'll certainly come.'

'I'll keep my fingers crossed that you're free then.' She could hear the smile in his voice. Chloe was right, he was a nice man and could maybe become a real friend.

As she was still waiting for permission to build the bathroom and Eric, the brickie/plasterer whom Rob had told her about, couldn't come for a few days, Anna decided to concentrate on rebuilding the fireplace – but the first thing she had to do was get the chimney swept. While a man draped her house in dust sheets and prepared to fire up an industrial-sized vacuum cleaner, Anna decided to take Caroline for a walk. It was partly for the sake of Caroline, who was nervous of the sweep, and partly for the sweep, who was nervous of Caroline.

While she was making the circuit, she felt her mobile

153

phone vibrate in her pocket. It was Max. Instantly she heard his deep, cultured voice she felt like a teenage girl talking to her boyfriend, instead of a young woman who in some ways was really quite old for her age.

'Hello,' she said, trying to keep the smile out of her voice.

'Hello, you,' he said. 'Thank you for your nice text.'

'Thank you for the flowers! They were stunning.' So stunning, in fact, that she had given half of them to Chloe. This had served the double purpose of allowing her to actually move around her cottage without knocking over yet another bucket of lilies, and proving to Chloe, who seemed dubious, that Max was a Good Thing.

Now he said, 'What are you up to?'

'I'm just walking Caroline to the common. I've left the sweep at home. It's a glorious day. What are you doing?'

'Well, among other things, there's a small chance I might be in your area next weekend. It's only a very small chance but I wanted to see if you're free before I go on making arrangements. No point in coming all the way down there if you're not free to come out to dinner with me.'

Anna blushed with pleasure. 'But you'd be seeing your mother, presumably.'

'Well, yes, but doesn't a dutiful son deserve some reward? So, are you free or not?'

Of course she was free! And if she wasn't, she would be immediately! But something, possibly some gene she had in common with Laura, made her say, 'Obviously I haven't got my diary with me.'

'Why obviously?'

'Because I'm taking Caroline for a walk. I've got things to carry. The lead, my phone if it rings . . .' She was about to add kitchen towel and plastic bags to the list but decided that the etiquette and technique of cleaning up after your dog might be lost on him.

'Well, let me know as soon as you can. I'll be very disappointed if I can't see you.' His disappointment would be nothing on hers, she suspected.

'I will.'

All in all it was a very satisfactory phone call and she would confront the problem of what to wear when and if the date was confirmed. For the first time it occurred to her that if she and Max were to start going out properly, she'd have to have a few more clothes. Her wardrobe was not so much limited as non-existent. Although there was Chloe of course; her wardrobe might have been very cramped, but there was plenty of it. Just as well they were more or less the same size.

Having paid the sweep and cleaned up what little soot he left behind him, Anna started on the fireplace. She had already picked out the best dressed stone for the outside, and was hoping she had enough left for the fireplace. But what was a very small stone for a wall, might do well for a fireplace. She put on Radio 4, mixed some lime and mortar, and began. She hummed as she worked, high on love and the scent of lilies. To complete her happiness, Max telephoned later to tell her that dinner the following Saturday night was definitely on if she was free, which she most certainly was. The fact that she would have spent all day helping Chloe clean his mother's greenhouse caused her wry amusement. She didn't say anything – let him find out!

Chapter Twelve

❧

Anna and Chloe turned up at the appointed time on Saturday morning. Mike was at home and when he had taken Caroline and the boys for a long walk, they were going to spend the rest of the day watching boys' television. Fortunately, Caroline hadn't yet learnt to express a preference for cookery and make-over programmes over sport.

Anna and Chloe were wearing old, working clothes, which in Anna's case meant her usual attire. She'd tied a scarf round her hair, because she'd just washed it, and Chloe was looking businesslike in an old boiler suit of Mike's, cinched in with a tight belt, so she wouldn't fall over it.

Mrs Gordon did not look impressed when she opened the door. All ideas about introducing herself as a friend of Max's vanished off Anna's agenda in a blink. Her look could have curdled milk.

'Oh, are you the people who've come to clean out my greenhouse?' she said haughtily.

'If that's what you'd like us to do, Mrs Gordon,' said Chloe. 'We are the very people.' She smiled in a friendly, efficient way. She was not going to be put off by Mrs Gordon's officious manner, even if Anna was just standing meekly behind her.

'Good, well I'm glad to see that you're on time. No, don't come in, if you don't mind.' Mrs Gordon looked them both up and down and frowned. 'Could you go round the side and in through the back door?'

It was not unreasonable not to want heavy working boots tramping over antique Persian rugs, but both Chloe and Anna felt like second-class citizens as they went round the back. 'Don't say anything about Max! I don't want her to know I know him!' Anna whispered.

'Don't blame you! I'm surprised she didn't have a tradesmen's entrance.' Chloe muttered back.

'She probably did, only we didn't see it,' said Anna.

They knocked again, at the back door this time, and Mrs Gordon opened it. 'Now, you see that greenhouse?'

A long, traditional wooden glasshouse stood at the bottom of quite a long garden. They nodded.

'Well, it's fallen into disuse and needs a thoroughly good clean, as do all the pots and bits and pieces.' Mrs Gordon sighed, as if it was in some way Chloe and Anna's fault that things had got so bad. 'My son thinks I should pull it down, but there's a man locally who wants to rent it, to raise bedding plants.'

'Bedding plants,' said Chloe, for want of something better.

'There's hot water in the scullery,' Mrs Gordon went on bossily. 'And buckets and brushes. You'll have to carry the water down to the greenhouse, of course, but you look like good strong girls.'

'We are,' said Anna, scanning the handsome, unbending face for similarities to Max. There were plenty. She smiled. 'We like a challenge.'

'Have you got rubber gloves?'

They shook their heads, feeling ashamed and belligerent at the same time.

'Well, I suggest you go to the shop and get some. You'll need really hot water for the glass and soda crystals are very harsh on the hands.' She glanced down at Anna's, which were looking particularly battle-scarred. 'Even if you don't take care of them as a rule.'

'Remind me to wear mittens if ever I'm invited for tea,'

muttered Anna as they went to investigate their task. They'd told Mrs Gordon that they were going to make sure there was nothing else they needed before they went to the shop.

'I'm not paying for fancy sprays and polishes,' Mrs Gordon had said firmly. 'Hot water, soda crystals and elbow grease are all you require. And there's no need for both of you to go to the shop.'

Chloe, determined that she would find something else she needed apart from gloves, bought a roll of stockinet and some sugar soap.

'I'm not sure what you do with it,' she told Anna when she came back, 'but it looked suitably old-fashioned.'

'I'm surprised she didn't expect you to pay for the materials,' said Anna, who had made a start by moving as many piles of pots as she could out of the greenhouse.

'Well, she might yet. I didn't like to disturb her to say I was back. Ugh – how are you with spiders?'

'Not bad, thank goodness, seeing how many there are here. Just don't ask me to touch them.'

'I think I'm going to get some plastic buckets and just pay for them myself,' said Chloe later. 'These old metal ones are so bloody heavy!'

'I know what you mean.' Anna wiped her face with her sleeve, adding another layer of dirt as she did so. 'Shall I go?'

'No! It was my idea, I get to escape!'

'You went last time!'

'I know, but I'm desperate for a wee and daren't ask her. I could go at the shop. I will buy chocolate,' she added temptingly.

Anna sighed. She was beginning to feel tired and thirsty. 'You'd think she'd give us a cup of coffee, a drink of water – something!'

'I'll get some caffeine-filled fizzy drinks while I'm about

it. As long as you promise to brush your teeth really well later.' Chloe grinned.

Anna stuck her tongue out and went back to her task of washing a very fragile pane of glass without breaking it. There were lots of missing panes, and one more wouldn't make much difference, but she liked to do a job well if she was doing it at all, even though half her mind was on her date with Max that evening. It was only fair to let Chloe get away to the shop; Anna was in love, and things were a lot more tolerable when you had a wonderful man to think about. Even if his mother was a bit of a battleaxe.

Chloe came back having been away mere moments. She was rolling her eyes and giggling. 'I had to come back and tell you! A very smart car has just drawn up and the most gorgeous man got out! I saw it just as I got round the corner into the drive. I don't think he saw me. Do you want to see if it's Max? But you'd better run!'

Anna ran and was just in time to see Max's back disappearing behind the huge front door. She came back to report. 'It's him! Oh my God! What shall I do? I can't let him see me like this!'

Chloe, obviously about to tell Anna not to be so silly, took another look at her. 'Fair enough. You go back.'

'But supposing he goes into the scullery and looks out of the window at me?' Anna was feeling decidedly panicky.

'Unless you want him to, he's unlikely to recognise you.' Chole said, trying to calm Anna down. 'You don't look quite so much like Audrey Hepburn now. More Doris Day in one of those movies when she dresses like a boy.'

'Thanks very much!' Anna stifled a giggle.

'Not to say that's not a very good look for you,' Chloe went on hurriedly. 'But it's not the same as the slinky black dress and the gloves.'

'I'll just stay hidden then. He might be awfully cross,

though, when he discovers I was actually in his mother's garden and didn't say hello,' Anna said tentatively.

'You don't have to tell him, and anyway, he'd understand. He must know his mother is a harridan and would be furious if her afternoon's labour, which she got for the price of a raffle ticket, was interrupted by social niceties.'

Anna giggled. 'I don't think there's much danger of that. Even if we took our shoes and socks off, she wouldn't let us into the main part of the house.' She chuckled again. 'I suppose it is quite funny, though.'

Chloe nodded. 'I'll go and get supplies and if anyone sees me, I'll break into broad Gloucestershire,' she said, having done just that.

Chloe stole back past the house with plastic buckets and chocolate. They both felt they were at boarding school, or summer camp, sneaking in and out. 'Which is ridiculous,' said Chloe, chomping down on a Mars bar and tucking her hair behind her ear. 'We're adults – I'm a mother and you've got a career – doing charitable works. We shouldn't be feeling furtive and giggling.'

'No,' agreed Anna, giggling again.

Although it was early May, the weather was still chilly. Chloe and Anna had put on lots of protective clothing and so got into quite a sweat as they washed windows and flowerpots, weeded the stretch of earth, and did their best to get rid of all pests and diseases that lurk in disused greenhouses, using only what Mrs Gordon had given them and their own limited extra supplies.

'I'm not sure elbow grease will get rid of all the bugs,' said Chloe. 'But it does seem to have sorted out the mould. I'd have put a bit of bleach on it, myself.'

'I'm sure we need Jeyes Fluid,' said Anna. 'Or something to get rid of red spider mite.'

'What do you know about red spider mite?'

'Nothing. I've heard of it though. Oh!' Her mobile phone vibrated in the pocket of her boiler suit.

'Hello,' said Max in a low voice. 'I'm at Mother's. I've just popped into the garden to phone you, to confirm you can still make it.'

Anna suppressed a scream as she glanced round and saw Max. He was standing outside the back door and could have seen her if he had just turned round a bit. She sank into a crouch, convinced that if he did see her in her current state embarrassment would make her explode.

'Hi,' she whispered.

'Are you are all right? You sound rather muffled.'

'I'm fine.' She glanced at Chloe, who had stuffed a very dirty rag in her mouth to stop her giggles becoming audible. 'Just a bit busy.'

'What are you up to, then?'

'Oh – er – cleaning.' That was true, at least.

'So you'll have dishpan hands when I see you?'

'Probably!' Definitely would have been more accurate.

'But you still want to come?' He laughed teasingly. 'You won't be too tired?'

'Of course not. I have lots of stamina.'

He chuckled. 'Fortunately for you, so have I.'

Anna swallowed. 'I have to go. I'm really looking forward to tonight.'

'So am I.' And she saw him disappear safely back inside the house.

Anna wiped her brow, mingling dirt with sweat and creating yet another very dirty mark.

'That was Max,' she explained to Chloe who was now tackling a stubborn clump of mould on a window pane.

'I gathered. What did he want?'

'I think he was just bored, actually.' Anna sighed and leant against one of the benches lining the greenhouse walls.

'I must say he's keen. He rings you a lot.'

Anna smiled, the release of tension making her even more gooey than usual. 'Yes!' she breathed.

Chloe, keen to get Anna back into work mode said, 'So did the man Rob told you about come last week?'

Anna snapped out of her reverie and retied her scarf that was coming loose after all their exertions.

'Oh yes! Didn't I tell you? He did a great job on the blockwork and plastering. I got the fireplace finished too.' She glanced down at her hands. 'It really does for your hands, lime, even though I wore gloves. I did the pointing with a spoon. It's the perfect thing.'

'I don't suppose that did much for the spoon, though,' Chloe chuckled.

'No, but the fireplace looks wonderful, though I say it myself. I'll be getting on to the staircase soon.'

'You're amazing, Anna, really you are,' Chloe said.

'The structural engineer came too. He seemed fairly satisfied.'

'That's a relief.'

'I know! I was dreading being told to put in more steels.' Anna had been convinced he'd find some extra problem for her to worry about, but his visit had gone remarkably smoothly.

Chloe, who didn't want an explanation of this statement just then, nodded in agreement.

Eventually they declared the greenhouse finished. And it was only now that Anna realised there could be genuine embarrassment in going up to the house, rather than just the suppressed giggling sort. 'You go and say we've done it,' she said to Chloe. 'I'll stay here until you tell me the coast is clear.'

'She'll want to see both of us,' Chloe insisted. 'You can't hide here and just scuttle out. It'll look so childish.'

'That's how I feel!' Anna said petulantly. 'It was bad

enough when it was just his mother, but now Max is here . . .'

'He might have gone.'

'Be a love and go and check. I'd feel so much better if he was off the premises. We're supposed to be meeting for dinner in a couple of hours.'

'All right,' Chloe said. 'You wait here.' And she strode off towards the house, leaving Anna lurking in the greenhouse. A little while later, Chloe reappeared and reported that the car was still in the driveway. She glanced at her watch. 'I do hope Mike has remembered to feed the boys.'

'And Caroline, although she will be all right until I get home.'

They regarded each other, both aware that they were just putting off the evil moment. Mrs Gordon had to be faced.

They removed their boots on the back step, which took a long time in Anna's case because they had laces and reinforced toecaps, then went into the scullery and knocked on the door that connected with the rest of the house. They could hear voices. For a moment Anna wanted to rush to Max and throw herself into his arms, but it was only for a moment. She would make this a funny story later this evening, but she did not want to meet him now.

They had to bang quite hard before Mrs Gordon heard them. She appeared in the scullery, seeming annoyed.

'Oh, it's you, she said in the abrupt manner she obviously reserved for 'Staff'. 'Have you finished? I'll come down and see if you've done a good job.'

'Mrs Gordon,' said Chloe, suddenly finding the dignity she'd misplaced earlier. 'We have worked very hard all day for nothing. You were charged only the price of a raffle ticket. We are also adults, not boy scouts. I don't think checking that we've done a good job is really appropriate, do you?' She didn't give Mrs Gordon a chance to answer before ploughing on. 'However, if you would like to offer us some appreciation for our efforts, I would be glad to show you what your greenhouse looks like now.'

'Oh.' Mrs Gordon was not accustomed to being spoken to like this and she frowned, but possibly more because she'd been caught out being ungracious than because Chloe had stood up to her. 'Yes, I do see what you mean. It's because you both look so young that I made that mistake.' She gave a politician's fake smile.

Wily old boot, thought Anna. She thinks slipping in a compliment like that will make us like her. It was sort of flattering.

Chloe inclined her head.

'I would offer you both a cup of tea,' went on Mrs Gordon, taking the high ground again, 'but my son is with me.'

'That's perfectly all right,' said Chloe, 'we came to work, not to socialise, and I have sons of my own to see to.' She looked at Anna and then realised her friend wasn't going to say a word. It would be too embarrassing if Anna ever did meet Mrs Gordon socially. She had to keep up her disguise.

Chloe valiantly went on, 'I think you'll find that we've done the best we could with the materials available. I dare say you'll need some sort of disinfectant or fungicide to make sure the greenhouse is sterile.'

At the sight of Mrs Gordon's face, Anna turned away. Mrs Gordon was obviously furious about being put in her place by a mere girl, but she couldn't – politely – do a thing about it. Anna had thought that the desire to giggle had left her, but, at this very awkward moment, it came back. She coughed to hide the noise that escaped and nudged Chloe's leg with her foot, catching sight of a bundle of sweet wrappers that was sticking out of Chloe's pocket.

'Well, thank you for supporting Greyhound Rescue,'

said Chloe, who was holding up against the giggles marginally better than Anna. 'We must be getting home now.'

Both women bent to put on their boots, fighting laughter. Anna pulled a handkerchief out of her pocket and held her nose with it. Too late she realised it was a filthy duster and was probably full of spiders. Her boots took for ever to do up, although she was doing them as fast as she could. Mrs Gordon stood over them until they were safely off the premises.

'God! I thought we'd never get out of there without me bursting out laughing, wetting myself, or both!' declared Chloe as they walked through the series of footpaths that eventually led to their own row of little cottages.

'I must say, things are much funnier when you can't laugh. I haven't had so much fun for ages.' Anna blew her nose on the duster she found in her pocket. 'Oh no, I've stolen her duster! I suppose I should wash it and give it back.'

Chloe snorted 'It's not a lace handkerchief! Just forget about it! But you have now got cobwebs on your face as well as everything else.'

'Oh well,' Anna laughed,' as long as I can pop in the bath later, I don't mind.'

Chloe grasped Anna's hands. 'A bath, my whole wardrobe: you're welcome to both. Lots of people wouldn't have done the greenhouse if they were going out with Mr Sex-on-a-Stick in the evening.' She glanced at her watch. 'You'd better hurry!'

'I could pop in the bath after the boys, if you like. I'm so filthy you wouldn't want them popping in after me.'

'You can have all the hot water you need. You have been a total star. I had no idea what a lot there'd be to do when I volunteered us both. Mike will definitely give you a hand with your house to make up for it.'

Anna grinned. 'You'll volunteer him, you mean.'

Chloe shrugged, her hands in her pockets. 'I sleep with him. That gives me power and influence.'

'And babies.'

'I think we've worked out what was causing that by now. But seriously, I know how busy you are with the house, and you had to give up a whole day. Mike's going to be home for at least another two weeks. I'm sure he'd willingly help you.'

Anna considered how reluctant she was to accept help, and then pondered how she would manage with some of the very large upright timbers she would need for her staircase. 'That could be very useful,' she said. 'Although I hate to admit it.'

They arrived back at Chloe's cottage and were greeted with cries of: 'Don't disturb us, we're watching a really good film,' from the sofa.

Chloe smiled and gestured for Anna to follow her upstairs. 'Let's look at clothes while we run the bath,' she said.

'I should get some of my own, really,' Anna said as she padded up behind Chloe.

'Rubbish! No point in spending money on things you're only going to wear once.'

'I don't see why she shouldn't,' Mike shouted up the stairs. 'You seem to do it all the time.'

Chloe gave Anna a lift to the gastro-pub that Max had selected for their evening. To be fair, he had offered to pick her up, but Anna felt shy about showing him her house just yet. He was an architect who built very cutting-edge buildings (Anna had looked him up on the Internet); hers was an old cottage being done up by a one-woman band and a few helpers, to listed building regulations. He was bound to see it when he took her back (she hoped), but she wanted to have had a lovely evening before she exposed her home to his critical gaze. After all, if she invited him in for coffee, he might have other things on his mind apart from the fact there was no staircase. His faintly suggestive remarks on the phone had given her a pang of desire that was unexpected. He was so gorgeous, he could be quite sleazy and still be the sexiest man on the planet! Her heart gave a little skip at the thought.

She wasn't wearing the long black gloves, although after today her hands were in an even worse state than they had been when he last saw them. She thought about his reference to dishpan hands and rubbed in more hand cream. She was wearing a knee-length skirt (Chloe's), long boots (also Chloe's), and a fitted V-necked cardigan that they'd found at a charity shop Chloe had taken her to in town a few days ago. Chloe had managed to darn the little hole they'd discovered later. She'd also insisted that Anna wore her best black jacket. 'You deserve it,' she had insisted when Anna had protested. 'I hardly get to wear it anyway.'

Mike had grunted.

The whole effect was, Chloe declared, an understated look that would take Anna anywhere. 'As long as it takes me to the Grey Mare,' Anna had said, fighting down the butterflies that were making it difficult to speak, 'although I thought you'd said you'd give me a lift.'

Chloe had raised her eyes to heaven, sprayed Anna heavily with scent, making her sneeze, and told her if she didn't get into the car now she'd be late, and then what would happen?

Aware that Chloe, like Laura, did sometimes think of her as another of her children, Anna didn't take offence, and got into the car. She had the number of a local taxi firm, in case, for the return journey, and a wad of cash, ditto.

'Anyone would think I was a sixteen-year-old going out for my first date with an older man,' she said mildly.

'Well, you practically are!' declared Chloe, starting the

engine. 'You're a child in the clutches of a wolf!'

'I like wolves. And anyway, he's not that much older than me. I'll have a lovely time.'

'Well, I hope you do,' said Chloe, abandoning her role of parent for a second. 'But just—'

'Be careful. I know. Honestly, Chloe, this isn't the back streets of Brixton, you know. This is the posh end of rural Gloucestershire. What can possibly happen to me?'

As they had at last arrived, Chloe didn't have to answer that particular question. 'Do you want me to wait?' she asked Anna, as she unbuckled her seat belt. 'Then if he's not there, I can come in with you and have a drink so you don't have to wait on your own?'

Anna didn't like the idea of sitting at the bar waiting for her date, but the thought of trying to explain away Chloe's presence was worse. 'No thank you, I'll be fine,' she said, trying to sound more confident than she felt. 'And as it's a quarter to eight already, he might be waiting for me.'

'Fine.' Chloe kissed Anna's cheek, probably because she always kissed Mike when she dropped him off anywhere, and Anna made her way into the pub.

The boots took a bit of getting used to, but they made her legs look longer, and although Anna was normally quite happy with her shape, going out with Max was rather nerve-racking. And the fact that she had been so dressed up when he'd last seen her didn't help. He hadn't even recognised her when she'd been in an extreme version of her normal clothes, although to be fair to him, she hadn't allowed him to see her face.

All these thoughts flashed through her mind as she made her way to the bar. She wondered why on earth she had let herself in for such a terrifying experience before she remembered she was doing it for Max. She'd have walked over broken glass for him, and shouldn't baulk against walking over a carpet in high-heeled boots!

Chapter Thirteen

Max was sitting at the bar and got up the moment she walked through the door. He'd obviously been watching for her, and came to meet her, looking very handsome and gratifyingly pleased to see her.

'Sorry I'm late,' she said as he put his arm on her back and kissed her cheek. 'I got a lift with Chloe and she had to do something with the children.' Now was not the moment to tell him the reason she'd had so little time to get ready. That would come later, should she need to entertain him. It was nice to think that she had an amusing story up her sleeve, just in case.

'You're not all that late and you look – beautiful. What would you like to drink? Wine? Gin and tonic? Or what about a glass of champagne?'

His smooth sophistication made her feel suddenly gauche, as if he could tell most of her clothes were borrowed. 'A glass of champagne,' said Anna without thinking. 'Thank you so much.'

It was only when she saw a bottle being opened that she realised this was probably not a cheap option. It wasn't that she didn't think Max had plenty of money, but she didn't want to appear greedy. This was so important to her: she had to do everything right.

Max, who had been drinking mineral water at the bar, fetched his glass and led her to a table. 'You can have some red later if you'd prefer. It rather depends on what you want to eat.' He looked at her as if what she wanted to eat was the most important thing in the world.

'What about you?' she asked, suddenly daunted. 'Will you have red and champagne?'

'Certainly not! I'm driving. I'll just have one glass of champagne.' He smiled into her eyes.

Chloe's mention of wolves flashed through her mind. Was he planning to get her drunk so he could have his evil way with her? Then she remembered that it was Max, and his way would not be evil, it would be what she'd been dreaming of for years.

The first sip of champagne went to her head and she relaxed a little and smiled back at Max. The thought that she might have lipstick on her teeth flashed through her mind. She didn't wear lipstick often. She was surreptitiously running her tongue over her teeth when Max leant forward.

'Do you mind if I say something?' he asked gently.

'No!' She sounded startled in spite of trying not to.

'You have not got lipstick on your teeth.' He was smiling at her and she found his reassurance rather endearing.

Anna laughed and leant back in her chair, feeling much more relaxed.

'How did you know I was worrying about that?' she asked.

'Experience.'

Oh my goodness, thought Anna, he must know a lot about women. But then, of course, someone as good-looking and self-assured as he was would undoubtedly be very experienced. She was about to express this thought when he said, 'So, Anna, what have you been up to?'

She was quite glad of the change of subject and to be able to talk about something she was knowledgeable about. 'Well, I've finished the fireplace and the end wall looks wonderful,' she said, warming to her favourite topic. 'Eric, who did the blockwork and plastering for me, did a wonderful job. I could have done the bricklaying OK, but my plastering's not all it might be . . .' She realised that she'd lost his attention somewhat. 'What about you? Did you get the contract for the shopping precinct?' In Anna's, albeit rather limited, experience of men, she felt sure this would be a safe conversational gambit.

'We did,' he said proudly.

'Wow.' Anna was impressed although personally she couldn't imagine anything worse than having to spend a year at least designing a shopping mall and multi-storey car park.

'Yes, lots of excuses to celebrate. Shall we think about ordering? The chef here is very good.'

The menu, when it came, was full of items she didn't understand or couldn't pronounce. 'What are you going to have?' she asked, to give herself time to decipher the menu.

'I'll have the calamari to start with, and then the sea bass. The fish is very good here.'

Anna didn't like fish very much and had finally spotted something she recognised as steak. Would he think her dreadfully unsophisticated if she chose that? Unsophisticated *and* greedy? She decided to go for it anyway. Better safe than sorry.

'I'll have the steak, I think. My mother reckons women need red meat.' Then she wished she hadn't mentioned this in case he asked her why her mother thought that, and the reason was too feminine and intimate. What was it about Max that made her so gauche? Why couldn't she just keep quiet and at least give the impression of sophistication, even if she wasn't likely to fool him?

'And to start?'

'Prawn cocktail. I love this retro-food, don't you?' she suggested.

He smiled. 'No, actually, crustaceans covered in pink sauce have never appealed to me.'

'But I expect here the sauce will be really delicious and prawns are very good for you.'

'Do you eat everything because it's good for you?' His raised eyebrow told her he found this faintly amusing.

'Well, I try to eat healthily, when I'm not eating junk.' She sighed. 'I do eat rather a lot of biscuits.'

He gave her a long look that made her blush. 'It doesn't seem to have affected you in any adverse way.'

A wave of desire washed over her. This was Max, whom she had fixated on for years and years, whom she loved, and he was about to be hers. She smiled again, no longer worried about lipstick on her teeth or choosing the wrong things on the menu, and said flirtatiously, 'Oh good. I'd hate to think it had made me come out in spots.'

'You know perfectly well that it hasn't.' He flicked her nose with the tip of his finger. 'Even someone as lacking in vanity as you would have noticed that.'

She chuckled at the compliment, although she had indulged in her fair share of vanity that evening. She and Chloe had worked very hard to make her look her best. 'I suppose so, even though I haven't got a mirror.'

'You haven't got a mirror? You are a one-off, Anna!'

Anna accepted this gracefully but luckily didn't have to reply because at that moment the waitress appeared to take their order.

Anna declined a glass of red wine with her steak, preferring to stick with champagne – that did seem to have an emboldening effect and she was rather enjoying her new-found confidence.

Max joined her in finishing the rest of the bottle, as he was having fish. Anna smiled at him again over a forkful of prawn cocktail, which was indeed delicious. She was ecstatic with happiness. She was with Max, flirting with him, eating delicious food, and afterwards, when he took her home, she would invite him in. She had spent precious moments making the bed look tempting and had hidden all her dirty clothes.

'So, how long will it be before the house is finished?' he asked, smiling across the candlelight at her.

'Ages, really, but I'm going to put it on the market the moment the staircase is finished. Things are a bit slack at the moment, everyone keeps saying, but I need to sell as soon as possible.'

'How much are you hoping to get?'

Anna named a figure that wouldn't have bought a two-bedroom flat in London, but was still an awful lot of money for a very small cottage. 'Mind you, that will be my starting price. I'll probably have to come down from there. If it's all looking wonderful, which I hope it will be, I'll ask even more.'

'Hmm, greedy!' he said.

Anna knew she shouldn't have had champagne *and* steak.

'I like that,' he went on.

Anna smiled, heartily relieved.

'Actually, I've got a friend who's looking to buy in this area,' he said. 'Perhaps I could bring him over to have a look next time I come down to stay with my mother?'

'Er . . . of course,' she said brightly, thinking about her still-very-much-a-work-in-progress cottage. 'As long as it's not next week or anything. It won't be nearly ready. And it is very tiny. He might want something bigger.'

'I'm sure it'll be fine. He just wants a little love nest in the country, for weekends. And as an investment, of course.'

'I had wanted to sell it to someone who'd live there all the time, a couple and a baby, perhaps,' Anna said quietly.

'Darling, if it's as small as you say it is, that doesn't sound very likely.'

She cherished the endearment for a moment before saying defensively, 'Chloe manages, although they are very cramped.' She thought about the happy, noisy chaos where Chloe's family lived on top of one another, but hard to admit not everyone would want to live in a doll's house, however charming.

'Anyway, can I bring him round to look?' He seemed very determined.

'As I said, as long as it's not too soon.' She smiled at him, hoping he'd move on to a less daunting topic of conversation.

'I was thinking more the week after next.'

Anna gulped. 'That is a bit soon,' she squeaked. 'I mean, It hasn't got a bathroom or a staircase yet.'

'How much longer do you want?' he persisted.

'I really have no idea – a month?' she said hopefully.

'Make it three weeks and we've got a deal. He only wants to view, remember. He's got enough imagination to fill in the gaps. Even if he bought it on the spot, you'd still have time to finish before he could move in.'

Anna was flattered he had so much confidence in her project but then again, he hadn't seen it yet. Still, he was probably right. 'You're right,' she said. 'I suppose I just panicked. I'm doing as much as I can myself.'

'You got someone in to do the plastering. Provided you're not totally under-funded . . .'

'Of course I'm not! I planned it all very carefully.'

'No need to get offended. Most people have absolutely no idea bout how much money alterations and improvements are going to cost.'

As this was true, and she had under-budgeted a little, she sighed and said, 'So, tell me about your friend. What sort of man is he?'

He laughed. 'I promise you he'd be a perfectly good incumbent of your beloved house. I knew him at school. He used to come and stay. He was one of the few friends my mother approved of.' Anna could well believe few people came up to her exacting standards. 'He can be guaranteed not to smoke in the house, or put his feet on the furniture.' He paused while she replaced her glass. 'I might ask you to tea, too. You could meet Mother.'

She smiled, ready to regale him with her funny story now she'd had a few drinks. 'Actually, I've already met her.'

'Oh? She didn't say anything. But it's hardly surprising, considering how near to each other you live. How did you meet?'

She giggled. 'I cleaned out her greenhouse with Chloe. Today! While you and your mother were inside, Chloe and I were scrubbing away with our hair tied up in scarves like old-fashioned cleaning ladies.' Somehow the story didn't seem so funny, now. 'She won us in a raffle in aid of Greyhound Rescue.'

He frowned slightly. 'So that was you? Two women, both covered in dust and cobwebs. You were filthy. I saw you out of the window.'

'I know. And you phoned me! I was terrified you'd spot me. But you should have seen the greenhouse. Spiders as big as mice; cobwebs like camouflage nets; enough creepy-crawlies to colonise another planet.'

He was smiling politely, but he wasn't rolling on the floor laughing. But then Max wasn't the sort who'd do that. She pressed on. 'Anyway, it was quite funny, really: I was so dirty, I didn't want you to recognise me. And you didn't.' She twinkled up at him, willing him to share the joke, which at the time had seemed so hilarious.

His lips flickered slightly. 'I doubt if my mother would find it all that funny. And let's hope she doesn't recognise you, either. She wouldn't be remotely amused to be entertaining someone as a guest who's been a sort of – servant.'

Anna realised she'd made the most ghastly mistake. 'You probably had to be there, but it was funny at the time, honestly,' she said to the tablecloth.

'I hope I'm not coming across as pompous,' he said.

Anna looked up. 'Oh no!' she said insistently.

'That's good, but I'd like to think I know when to take life seriously.' He laughed gently.

'Well, so do I, obviously, and I'd never do anything to upset your mother.'

'Of course not. You'd never upset anybody.'

He probably meant it as a compliment, but Anna decided this made her sound pathetically bland, someone she was determined not to be. 'Excuse me, I must just go to the Ladies,' she said.

Once there she gave herself a sharp talking to about not being too flippant. She couldn't expect a man like Max to be amused at the childish things that made her and Chloe fall about. They may have found it funny that she had spent all day cleaning out his mother's greenhouse and then been too shy to say hello but it wasn't really, and she probably hadn't told the story very well. He was possibly a bit touchy about his mother, but then, lots of men were. She resolved to make Mrs Gordon love her when they met properly. Suitably braced up, she went back.

'I assumed you didn't want a pudding,' said Max when she returned to the table. 'I just ordered you an espresso and a Cognac. Is that OK?'

If Anna had been with anyone other than Max, she might have gone for the exuberant chocolate creation she had seen go past earlier, but he was not the sort of man to eat chocolate with, unless it was that wincingly black sort that was so bitter it made your mouth curl.

'That's perfect. I may not sleep if I drink the espresso, though.'

'Then stick with the brandy.' He smiled at her. It was such a sexy smile – more a slight closing of the eyes and lifting of one corner of the mouth than a toothpaste beam – and Anna's stomach contracted with longing. As just seeing his name had caused this to happen for years, it was hardly surprising it happened now. But was she having the same effect on him?

She smiled back with, she sincerely hoped, the right mixture of mystery and enthusiasm. She'd be all right when she'd had the brandy. Alcohol always made her feel relaxed and affectionate and she'd stop feeling she'd put her foot in at any moment. When the drinks came, she scrutinised him over the top of her brandy glass. He was very handsome; even Chloe acknowledged that. She suppressed a sigh.

'Now little one, I'm going to have to take you home.'

'It's been a lovely evening.'

'And it's not over yet.' He smiled and her stomach flipped with a mixture of desire and, she realised, nervousness.

'I hope you like my dog,' she said.

He chuckled. 'So do I.'

'Um – I'll just pop to the Ladies again before we go,' she said. She couldn't explain that she'd have no opportunity to check on her make-up or comb her hair when she got back and not just because she was hoping they'd be in each other's arms the moment they had got through the door and said hello to Caroline.

She didn't keep him waiting long and he steered her to his car.

'So,' he said, when they were strapped in and about to set off, 'How soon will your house be ready for sale, did you say?'

Oh heavens, he was back on that subject again. 'I've already told you, not for ages. It's not nearly ready!'

'That could be a good thing. I've been thinking, we could make any necessary alterations before he moves in.'

'All the plans have already been submitted. It would be terribly time-consuming to change them now. It is a listed building,' she added, feeling a bit panicky. He was soon going to see exactly how much work needed to be done.

He reached out and took her cheek in his hand. 'I don't think we need to bother ourselves with a little thing like that. Anyway, I'm working forward to seeing it myself.'

'I did explain that the house isn't nearly finished,' she whispered, after they'd parked at the end and she led Max along the lane, past the sleeping houses.

'Only about a thousand times,' he said, taking her arm.

She leant into him: not that she'd drunk that much but these boots were a little awkward to walk in.

'I just didn't want you to be shocked,' she said. 'I mean, there isn't anything that makes it comfortable, not yet, and Caroline is huge . . .'

She apologised all the way. When they got to her front door, he said. 'Do shut up, darling!'

Anna found this strangely sexy and giggled. She looked up at him, unsure how to proceed.

He took the decision out of her hands. He put his hand under her chin, and lowered his mouth to hers.

He really was a fantastic kisser, she thought as she felt his tongue explore her mouth with delicate intensity. He finished with a peck right on her mouth, sealing the kiss with a full stop. It was, she decided, technically perfect.

She smiled up at him, confident now that shared passion would over-ride any shortcomings of the house. 'Do let's go in. I'll make you some instant coffee.'

He winced. 'Wish I could, darling, but actually, I've got to get back to London tonight.'

She couldn't believe it. 'What? Surely not?'

'Surely, yes!'

'But it's miles! You'll be exhausted!'

'It's not a bad journey at all at this time of night. It's why I think Julian might well be interested in your little house. Now –' he patted her cheek – 'be a good girl, and I'll be in touch.'

She let herself in, reeling from surprise and disappointment. Caroline got up from the sofa and Anna took her silky ears in her hands and gently pulled them. 'You don't have to worry,' she said to her flatly, 'he didn't come in.'

Although she was very tired she felt too jittery just to go to bed, so she made herself some hot chocolate and shared the sofa with Caroline while she drank it. She replayed the evening in her head, wondering why there was a niggling sense of doubt in among the blissfulness. Later, as she lay in the bed she had thought would be for both of them, she decided it was because she hadn't played her part perfectly. She'd meant to make him laugh and hadn't quite done it. It would be better next time, she was sure of it.

Chapter Fourteen

On Monday Anna was up early. She'd spent most of Sunday pottering round, barely having a moment to think about her evening with Max, as she finished off her fireplace and put the final touches to her plans for her staircase. Today she was going to start.

After she'd walked Caroline she got on her bike and set off to the builders' merchants. There was really no time to hang around – if Max's friend might consider buying her house, she must make sure it had a staircase when he came to see it. Besides, Chloe had kindly offered her the loan of Mike. If he was willing to be loaned, she must take advantage of it.

She ordered her timber, took her ticket round the outside of the premises to where the payments were made, had the amount added to her account, and then asked them to deliver it.

'I'm afraid the van driver's off this week. Broken his ankle. If you want it delivered it'll have to be next week, when we've got someone else coming.'

This was awful news. 'Surely you'll be getting someone else sooner than next week?'

The kindly man in the brown overall shook his head. 'Most people collect their own stuff.'

'Is there a problem?'

Rob Hunter's deep voice from behind her made her jump. 'Oh! Hello! What are you doing here on a Monday morning?'

He smiled. 'Much the same as you are, I assume. I work

flexitime,' he explained, answering the question in her eyes. 'So, is there a problem?' he asked again.

'The young lady was wanting us to deliver her timber, but our van driver's off.'

He looked at Anna quizzically. 'Why do you need it delivered?'

'Well, because . . .' Anna suddenly felt awkward. She'd dodged the car issue with Rob once before and she didn't really feel up to explaining it now. 'I just do!' she said defensively.

'Why don't you take it yourself? How much of it is there?'

'Just a couple of long ones,' said the man.

'Only a couple? You could probably manage them in the car if you thought about it. I could give you a hand working out how to fit them in.'

'I don't think so,' said Anna, beginning to laugh with embarrassment.

'Why? What sort of a car have you got?'

This really was silly. 'A bicycle,' she said in a small voice.

'Excuse me?'

'I haven't got a car! I've got a bicycle. Does that explain why I can't fit the timber in?' There, it was out. He could laugh at it if he wanted to, and he did.

It was a low, attractive laugh. Max's laugh was slightly higher-pitched.

'You mean you've been managing all this time, doing up your house, without a car?' Rob asked, raising an eyebrow.

'Yup. Chloe gives me lifts or I take taxis if there isn't another way round.'

'Goodness me. Just as well I have a lumbering great Volvo, and can probably take it for you.'

'Oh no, I couldn't put you to all that trouble.' The words were out of Anna's mouth before she could check with her brain.

'Why?' He was looking puzzled.

'Why what?'

'Why don't you want me to take your timber home?'

'Yes, why don't you?' asked the man in the brown coat.

'Because – because I like to be independent.' She didn't need to look at them to know that both men were exchanging exasperated looks.

'Listen, love,' said the man behind the counter patiently. 'You need your timber delivered, this man says he'll do it for you. Now I know it's not a good idea for young ladies to get into cars with men they don't know, but I can vouch for him.' He leant in confidingly. 'He's the listed buildings officer.'

'I know that,' Anna felt herself being backed into a corner but still felt she ought to put up a fight. 'It isn't a question of me getting into a car with him. I have my bike.'

'So, you're just worried about me running off with your four-by-fours.' Rob's mouth twitched and his eyes had that disconcerting twinkle in them again.

'No, but . . .' Anna wasn't prepared to give up just yet.

Deciding that they could sort it out between them, the man in the brown overall moved off, muttering under his breath.

'We'll put the bike on the roof and fit the timber in where we can.' He looked down at her teasingly. 'What's the problem? You don't want me to see that you've put in the patio doors after all?'

Now she let herself laugh. 'No! I just don't like to be beholden. And if this is your day off – your flexitime,' she said, returning the tease, 'you don't want to spend it shifting timber for me.'

'I can't imagine a more entertaining way of spending my time. Come on, let's get this timber loaded.'

It fitted in his Volvo quite easily, the ends of the beams

182

sticking out of the back, with a rag – Mrs Gordon's duster – tied on to them.

'Now,' said Rob, considering the car, which was now quite heavily loaded. 'Where are we going to put you?'

'Um, I could sit on the bike on the roof, I suppose.' She grinned at him.

He grinned back. 'Don't be silly. We just need to think.'

In the end Anna sat with a bag of cement between her knees, clutching another of fire cement.

'I've just got to call in at the Green Shop for some recycled loo paper and some kitchen towel,' he said, as they set off.

'Er!'

'Only joking.'

Anna chuckled. 'This really is very kind of you.'

'It's a pleasure. Besides, it'll give me a chance to catch up with Caroline.'

When Anna opened her cottage door Caroline leapt at Rob as if she loved him most in all the world. She said hello to Anna, too, but it was Rob she jumped up at.

'I'm trying to train her not to do that,' said Anna, exasperated, as Rob put her paws back on the floor. 'Supposing she did it to a small child? Or an old lady?'

'It's a dreadful habit,' he teased.

Anna felt a little uncomfortable. 'Shall we get the timber unloaded?' she said quickly. 'Or do you need a cup of coffee or something first?' She felt she ought to be hospitable, especially as he'd put himself out for her.

'I'd really like to have a look round first.'

Anna stiffened slightly, losing some of the goodwill she felt towards him.

'Don't worry, I'm not here to spy,' he explained when he saw the look on her face. 'But if I could have a peek it would save some time.'

'In which case I'll just put the kettle on,' she said in a

more businesslike manner. 'We can have coffee after-wards. What do you want to see?'

'I wanted to see the bathroom, or rather the potential bathroom.'

'Right, follow me.' Anna led the way.

'You'll be glad when you've got a proper staircase,' he said, coming up behind her, rather too close for her comfort. 'How are you getting on with it?'

'I've made cardboard templates, copying Chloe's, and I've cut the first tread, just to get used to the idea of having to, but I hope to press on this week, while I'm waiting for you lot to decide about the bathroom.' She stopped and turned round. 'I'm in a bit of a hurry. I've got to put the house on the market as soon as possible.'

He frowned. 'Why? It isn't nearly finished.'

'I know, but it's a very slack market just now and it might take a while to sell. I can finish it in the interim.'

'So you don't want to live in it yourself for a while?'

'I do. I love this house and this area, but . . .'

'What?' He was staring at her expectantly.

She found his gaze rather unsettling and took a deep breath. 'As I said on the phone the other day, I need the money rather quicker than I thought,' she replied.

He nodded, seeming satisfied with her answer. 'Let's have a look at this bathroom, then.

'Well, what's there seems to coincide with the draw-ings,' he said when he got there.

'No need to sound so surprised – it's my job!' Why did everyone think she wasn't up to it?

'We quite often get drawings that bear no relation to what is actually there. It's no reflection on you, just house-improvers in general. They push the regulations to the limit.'

'Oh.' She frowned, thinking of Max's comments. 'I'm depressingly law-abiding, I'm afraid.'

'Don't apologise! It's a good thing. In this instance, anyway.'

'Sometimes it's just stupid.' She turned away from him to gaze out of the window. It was what often happened to her up here; she got distracted by the beauty of the countryside. The view was so stunning, out over the village, to fields and hills beyond. She would be desperately sorry to leave it.

'So why have you got to sell the house so quickly? I can see you really want to live in it.' He came up behind her and she didn't turn round.

Anna realised she might as well tell him the truth. 'I could never have afforded to live here anyway except while I was doing it up. But I need to pay my sister some money, quite quickly. I'll have to take less for the house with it not being decorated but I'm doing all the building work, of course.'

He paused for a moment. 'I see. Well, these houses usually sell very easily. They're the perfect second home,' he went on.

Anna tutted and turned to face him. 'I can't help thinking of who lived in them when they were built, growing their own vegetables, walking to work down the lanes. I don't really want someone from the city who complains about the village shop and puts decking where there should be a veg. patch.' Aware that she'd been caught out being romantic, she bit her lip. 'Of course I know you don't have any control who buys it really, or what they do with the garden, but I would prefer it to go to someone who's going to live here.' She thought of Max's friend Julian and half hoped he'd lose interest before he'd even seen the cottage.

'They are quite small for families,' Rob said.

'I know.' Anna sighed. 'I don't know how Chloe manages. Three children! Just as well they're close. My house is quite crowded enough and it's just me and Caroline.'

'And quite a lot of furniture.' He chuckled. 'Talking of

Caroline, have you found anywhere where you can let her off the lead to have a really good run yet?'

'Chloe did mention somewhere, once, but quite honestly, I haven't had much time to explore.'

'And it's hard to explore on a bicycle, with a dog.'

'Don't knock bicycles. They keep you fit!'

'Of course they do, but you can't go more than a certain distance on them when you've got a dog to consider.'

Was he being Bastard Dog Man again? She couldn't quite tell with him. 'I wouldn't dream of taking Caroline with me on my bike,' she said, horrified. 'Think of the traffic!'

'It might strain her heart, too.'

Anna considered. He was twinkling at her. Well, two could play at that game. 'I could fix up some sort of child seat, so she could go on the back.'

He shook his head seriously. 'You'd never get a helmet to fit her.'

'I bet they sell them in those catalogues that sell coats and leads, stuff like that.' She tried not to smile.

'Except I think they call them Dogalogues.'

'Idiot!' Anna pushed at him playfully.

He smiled back. 'Tell you what, why don't you take a day off for flexitime?'

'What on earth . . . ?'

'Let me take you and Caroline to a field near me that's totally secure, and where there are usually a few rabbits to chase, to get her going.'

'I don't want Caroline to chase rabbits!' Anna said rather loudly.

'She'll chase them whether you want her to or not, but she won't necessarily catch them. She'd appreciate a good run. It's probably been a while.'

The thought of a proper outing, with Caroline, was very tempting. 'I really mustn't. I was going to start my staircase.'

He didn't speak and she looked at him. The thought of some time off too was equally tempting. 'Oh the other hand . . .'

'What?'

'I meant to buy a new saw today and forgot. It's amazing how many of them you get through.'

'And no one sharpens them these days.'

She laughed. She was enjoying their easy banter.

'It would be better to start when you're really fresh. You've earned some time off. I'd like to see Caroline really move, to make sure she doesn't need a vet for any reason.' He grinned. 'Now I know why you haven't taken her to be checked up.'

'Well, she wouldn't have a "backy" and we've discussed the helmet issue.'

He grinned, and his teeth looked very white in the darkness of his emerging beard. 'Come on.'

Anna considered.

'I won't press you if you'd really rather get on, but I genuinely feel you'll work better if you've had a bit of time off. I know that from my experience.'

As this tied in with her own she made her decision. 'OK.'

'Great. Right, get your coat, and Caroline's, and we'll go for a run.'

'Will you bring your dogs?' Anna said as they went downstairs.

'Next time, when we can introduce them properly. Now I just want to see how Caroline gets on.'

Caroline jumped up into the back of Rob's Volvo as if she'd been doing it all her life. Anna said as much.

'They're very agile, as a rule, they can leap huge distances,' said Rob.

Anna got into the front seat. 'I should get a car, really.'

'Can you drive?' Rob asked as he started the engine.

'Sort of,' Anna replied, adjusting her seatbelt. 'I passed

my test, but then never drove. What with the house and everything, getting a car never seemed a priority. But that was before I had Caroline.'

It wasn't a long journey, but surprisingly pleasant. The hedgerows and trees were in their freshest greens, the summer waiting for the moment to arrive. Anna gazed out of the window, melancholy at the thought that she might not be here to see summer at its height.

They parked the car and headed for the field, Caroline on her lead.

'That's not a field, it's a precipice,' said Anna, as she looked over the gate.

Rob laughed. 'It is a bit steep. It belongs to a friend of mine. He lets me run my dogs in it whenever I want to as long as there's no stock in it. Luckily, they must be in the other field today.'

There were a couple of fields before a stream separated them from a small wood. It was extremely pretty. 'Perfect for a picnic when the weather's warmer,' said Anna. 'I wonder if Chloe knows about this place.'

'You'll be able to tell her.'

Just inside the gate Anna unclipped Caroline's lead.

'You'd better take her coat off,' said Rob.

'Why? She feels the cold terribly.'

'If she really goes for it, she could get her paws caught,' explained Rob patiently. 'But if she just stands around shivering, we'll put it back on and walk sedately about.'

Walking sedately about wasn't really an option. Caroline stood and sniffed for a few seconds, then spotted a rabbit and was off. It was a thrilling sight: her legs curling under her and out again, so fast all her feet were off the ground at the same time. It didn't last for long, though. The rabbit was used to being chased by greyhounds and wheeled away, down a hole, before Caroline was even close. Caroline came bounding back up to them, panting hard, demanding congratulations, which Rob and Anna gave lavishly.

'Wow,' said Anna. 'That was utterly amazing. Now I understand what they mean by poetry in motion, although it was very fast poetry. I hope she hasn't pulled a muscle or something, taking off like that.'

'She looks fine,' said Rob, running professional hands down Caroline's legs. 'And yes, it is wonderful seeing them run. I have to say, it's even more exciting when they're racing. I'd ban it tomorrow, but you can see why people like it, apart from the betting angle, I mean. Now, do you want a hand going down the field?'

'Of course not! I've been walking on my own for years,' said Anna glibly, and then set off.

It was far harder than she had imagined, and her boots were not as grippy as she'd thought they were. To take the attention away from her stumbling progress she said, 'Can you train greyhounds to retrieve? It would save me having to lay on rabbits, if I did find a good place for her to run in a bit more locally.'

'Not very satisfactorily. They might do it a couple of times, to please you, but they're hounds, they've got minds of their own.' He was obviously accustomed to walking down cliff faces and strode ahead without having to look at his feet.

Anna, feeling terribly citified and inept, was making for a patch of brambles that marked the bottom of the gradient. She stumbled and he took her arm. Her instinct was to shrug it off, but she thought better of it. After all, it was easier with two of them and she'd look so silly if she fell over.

Max flashed into her mind – which was odd because he usually lived there – and Anna wondered how he would cope with this steep field. No, Max was not one for long country walks with dogs. Or even short ones. He was strictly urban. Or at least, as far as she knew he was. Could she go back to London, having lived here? But somehow she felt that although she loved him so much, and would do anything for him, he wouldn't ask her to marry him, or even live with him. His interest in her was surely only passing – after all, why should someone as sophisticated as him be attracted to a slightly gauche young woman who did up houses for a living? It could only end in her tears – her tears – and this insight made her all the more determined to enjoy him while she could.

When they reached the bottom, Anna let go of Rob. She didn't want to look clingy; she was an independent woman. Caroline was loping along, her nose to the ground, her energy momentarily spent. Rob seemed lost in his own thoughts too.

Anna walked on, along the bottom of the field, wondering what on earth she'd do with Caroline if Max really surprised her, and did want her to live with him in London. There were the parks, of course, but they were always full of small dogs and squirrels: things dogs shouldn't chase. Still, Caroline hadn't seem to miss running. But having seen her do it, she didn't want to deprive her of the opportunity for ever.

She was just considering this when she tripped over a tuffet of grass and fell headlong into the mud.

'Are you all right?' Rob, who had gone off to inspect a potential gap in the hedge, came running up.

'I'll be fine,' said Anna, 'if you don't laugh.' She knew this was a tall order, because she was beginning to laugh herself, but she felt she should set boundaries. He put out a hand to help her up. She could tell he was fighting laughter, but took it gratefully. As her own hand was covered in mud, it slipped out, causing Anna to fall back into the mud again. This time her face got it, too. She tried to get up and couldn't. Her legs kept slipping from under her. Although shock was still making her laugh, she began to think she'd never get out.

'Come on,' he said, his eyes still narrowed with merriment, and gripped her under her armpits and hauled her upright. Her muddy front collided with him, covering his fleece with mud.

'Oh, look what I've done. I am sorry.' She tried to break free and her feet slipped again. 'I seem to have lost the ability to stand up unaided.'

'Those aren't the best footwear for walking. You need proper boots or wellingtons. Townie,' he added.

'I'm all right usually!' she said indignantly. 'I don't often walk in places like this. How dare you call me a townie!'

He shook his head wisely, still trying to keep a straight face, 'If you're going to be a country-dweller, you'll have to get used to a bit of mud.'

She smiled back at him and then said, 'I may not be a country-dweller for much longer.' She suddenly felt a bit melancholy.

'You can buy another house in the country, even if you have to leave that one.' He caught hold of her again and pulled her firmly towards him. Then he put his arm round her, holding her up. They walked together, as if tied up for a three-legged race.

When they had safely reached the top of the field he released her. 'There you go. You should be all right now,' he said.

'Except I'm covered in mud. And so are you.' She chuckled. 'I'm such a nana.'

'A what?'

'It's what Chloe's children say. It's short for banana.'

He laughed. 'Come on. Let's get you home. You need to change.'

They rounded up Caroline, who was surprisingly biddable, and put her coat back on. That too was fairly muddy, but mud, Anna decided, looked OK on a dog. Just as well I have no idea how it looks on me, she decided. The thought of Max seeing her covered in mud was on a par with him seeing her covered with cobwebs: just not an option.

They had gone a fair distance in the car before Anna realised that they were not going in the right direction. 'Is this another way back?' she asked. 'I don't know my way round here at all.'

'We're not going to your home, we're going to mine. Let's hope the dogs get on,' Rob replied as they turned into a narrow lane.

'But I can't . . .' began Anna, before she realised she didn't quite know what excuse she could give, without sounding rude.

'Have you got a washing machine at your house?' he said, as if anticipating her objections. 'I have. And I've got clothes you could borrow. Anyway we're here now. I'll let Caroline out, then my dogs. If they meet out here, they should be fine. They're not particularly territorial.'

His house had obviously once belonged to a farm, although it was almost surrounded by a small wood. It had good proportions, but was in a bad state of repair. She realised he couldn't have lived in it long. He wouldn't have let the guttering drop off, the window frames begin to rot, and the outbuildings fall apart.

He opened the front door and called. Three huge greyhounds came milling out. They saw Caroline, sniffed her, and then turned all their attention to Rob. Anna was accorded the most cursory sniff.

'Will they let her in the house? I don't want her staying in the car for long. She'll get cold,' she said anxiously.

'It should be fine. If there's any trouble, I've got a room I can shut them in, and she can stay in the kitchen with us.'

Anna started to take her boots off.

'Don't worry about that,' said Rob. 'It's all flags and rugs downstairs. The mud won't matter and your feet'll freeze if you walk about in your socks.'

He ushered her into a small, square hall, with doors opening off it. 'Come in.'

'It doesn't seem right bringing all this mud in, somehow,' said Anna, following him into the kitchen.

'It'll dry and then I'll just sweep it up. Don't worry. Come in and get warm.'

The kitchen was an interior designer's dream. Anna couldn't help sighing. It was full of original features and a long refectory table stood in front of a bright red Aga. Rob peered inside a saucepan that was on the top. 'It's all right. It hasn't boiled dry yet,' he said.

'Oh good. What is it?' It did smell delicious.

'Soup. Would you like some?'

The thought of hot, tasty soup filling her body with warmth was magical and she realised she was hungry after all that exercise. 'Oh yes. Soup would be marvellous. If you've got enough.'

He nodded and she pulled out one of the chairs and sat down. Caroline came and sat by her, resting her head on her knee, pretending to be a small dog and not a long-legged speed fiend. 'That's a wonderful Aga,' she said.

'Yes,' he said, leaning against it for warmth. 'But after I'd bought it, I didn't have much money left for anything else.'

'The house is a work in progress, I assume?' Too late she realised she shouldn't have assumed, but in her mind she was already demolishing a dilapidated tin lean-to she could see in the garden and replacing it with a proper wooden shed, seeing if there were original shutters in the window embrasure, and scrubbing the stone flags with something to get the grease off. There also seemed to be some sort of extension that was cutting off half the light.

'You would know. Actually, it's a money pit, but I fell in love. What could I do?' he stated.

'I fell in love with my house, too. I knew there was too

much for me to do on my own, but I just couldn't help buying it. It was fairly cheap.'

'How much was it?' he asked and she told him. Instead of him exclaiming at the bargain price, he was horrified. 'My goodness, that's extortionate!'

Anna shook her head. 'Not really, compared to London prices. And it's commutting distance to London. But I wonder if I am asking too much . . . I suppose I was used to London prices. It's such a gem.'

'Don't worry, some other fool who is used to London prices is bound to come along,' he said, laughing.

'Well, I hope they hurry up,' said Anna crisply.

'Come on, take your coat off and I'll hang it over the Aga to dry. Then would you like soup first? Or a hot bath and a change of clothes?' he asked, taking her coat from her.

The thought of hot water on her muddy, clammy flesh was very appealing.

'I can lend you some clothes. You'll have to roll the trousers up a bit, but I'm sure you'll manage.'

'I don't need to change, I could put these back on.' Suddenly the idea of wearing his clothes seemed too intimate, even if he was just being kind.

'Don't be silly. I can put yours in the wash and then bring them round to you another day, when they're dry.'

'I can't have you doing my washing for me!'

'How else will you get them clean?'

'Um – Chloe lets me use her washing machine from time to time.'

'Use mine. There's only one of me and, after all, I do feel faintly responsible for you getting so muddy in the first place.'

'You didn't push me over!'

He smiled. 'No, but I should have held on to you firmly all the way and not let go once we got to the bottom.'

'I'm not an old lady with dodgy knees!'

He laughed. 'No, but nor are you a mountain goat with proper boots on.'

Anna had to smile. 'I should get some proper walking boots I suppose, or at least wellingtons with grips. I tend to wear those working boots for everything.'

He twinkled. 'No, I can't quite see you in high heels, somehow.'

Anna laughed. 'You'd be surprised. Now, if that offer of a bath and some clean clothes is still on, I'd love to take off some of this mud.'

Chapter Fifteen

Anna sank back in the bath with guilty pleasure. It was a much longer bath than Chloe's, in which you had to wet yourself in two halves. This bath was almost too long, Anna's feet only just touched the end. She got her hair wet, and then decided to go the whole hog and wash it. There was a bottle of baby shampoo on the side of the bath and she used it. She also found it rather touching that this should be the chosen brand of Rob Hunter, Dog and Building Police.

He was a bit of a softy, really. He pretended to be firm with his dogs, keeping them in their place, not spoiling them, but while Anna had been standing in the doorway of his bedroom, waiting while he found dry clothes for her, she'd seen dog-shaped indentations on the bed, and footprints on the duvet cover.

He'd handed her a pair of old corduroys, a shirt that was soft from years of washing, and a jumper. The jumper was cashmere, but it had a hole in it. Sartorially, she and Rob Hunter were perfectly suited, Anna had reflected, unlike her and Max. She'd brushed that thought away and taken the bundle and the clean towel.

'I'm impressed you've got a clean towel,' she'd said, during the rather awkward pause.

'I have a cleaning lady. She despairs of ever getting rid of the dog hair, so she consoles herself with keeping my linen cupboard in order. It's a great luxury.'

Anna had smiled. That would be a luxury. Her clean clothes and towels were currently kept in one black plastic sack and her dirty ones in another. She had a perfect design for a fitted wardrobe, but she hadn't got round to building it yet. 'I'll go and have my bath then.'

When she came down she found him in the kitchen. Her hair was tied up in the towel and the trousers were rolled up several times round the waist and several more times round her ankles. Her feet were bare.

He looked at them. They did look rather small and defenceless, Anna realised, curling up her toes.

'I'll get you some socks,' he said.

Anna noticed her coat on the back of a chair – it was obviously dry by now. She went to the Aga and leant on it, looking out of the window, wondering why Rob hadn't cut back the plant that was almost totally obscuring it. She asked him when he came back with the socks.

'It's more than just a matter of cutting it,' he said. 'It's actually got inside the brickwork. It's on my list.'

'There's so much to do on an old house, isn't there?' Anna said, putting on a pair of thick woollen socks, perfectly suited to padding about on cold floors. 'But I'd always have old rather than new if I possibly could.'

'Would you like a look round?' Rob asked.

Anna nodded vigorously. She'd been dying to ask but hadn't wanted to seem too nosy.

'Well, this is the kitchen, obviously,' he said. 'I'll keep the flags. They're cold and things break if dropped them on them, but they're part of the house.'

'Anyway, wouldn't it be against your own rules to change them?' she enquired.

Rob shook his head. 'This house isn't listed. It should be, but it isn't. It's one of the reasons I bought it.' He gave her a lopsided smile. 'It's a terrible nuisance, trying to do up a listed building.'

'Tell me about it!'

'Of course I do plan to have everything totally in keeping, in the best possible taste, as they say. But not having a listing does give me a bit more freedom.'

Anna sighed, resigned to the restrictions of her own house. 'Well, come on, let's see the rest of it.'

'I'll just move the soup over. We really don't want it to boil dry.'

There was a generous hall, which Anna had already seen. There was an ancient sofa that now had a dog on it, and three doors opening off.

The first was a little sitting room. The sunshine was forcing its way in past the creeper, through the sash windows. 'The sun pours in here in the morning. It would make an ideal kitchen really. There's not much sun in there until the evening.'

Anna looked around the room longingly – what a project this would be. 'Even without a listing, you wouldn't want to move it though,' she said. 'This would make a lovely little breakfast room.'

'Except you're not likely to take your eggs and bacon across the hall, are you?' He had wandered over to look out of the window.

'If you had guests, or ran a B&B, this would be the perfect spot for people to have their breakfast. You could fit three or four tables in, and they could look out of the window into the garden while you're struggling to fry eggs without breaking them.'

He turned and laughed. 'You've never run a bed and breakfast, have you?'

She shook her head. 'No, but I helped out in one as a holiday job once. It was fun, actually.' She grinned a little ruefully. 'I think that B&B was one of the reasons I wanted to become an interior designer. The food was lovely, really well cooked, with lovely ingredients, but the decor was eye-watering. Now where?'

'This is the formal drawing room,' he announced, opening a door across the hall. 'More creeper – I think it's jasmine this time – but I'm sure it's going to be super.'

Anna took in the room's generous proportions, the double aspect, the stone fireplace, the mouldings. 'Oh yes! And look at that floor. Is it original, do you think?' she said excitedly.

'I don't think it can be. Parquet didn't come in until a bit later, but it's nice. Of course it's in very poor shape in parts, but it can be repaired.'

Anna looked at him sideways. 'Wouldn't it be cheaper just to pull it all up and replace it with new, laminate flooring?' She teased.

He frowned at her. 'Hm, probably, especially when I could sell this floor to a reclamation yard, but no, I'm not going to do that.'

She walked across to where French windows formed a bay. 'I expect this is a later addition,' she said.

'Definitely, but it makes this room, don't you agree?' he said, coming over to join her.

'Oh, absolutely. It's gorgeous.' Anna looked around thoughtfully. It was fairly large and square, apart from the bay that was big enough to house another dog-filled sofa, a desk and two deep, old leather armchairs. A couple of freestanding bookcases leant slightly forward under the weight of the books. 'A built-in bookcase would look nice there. The floor is pretty uneven, and fitted would be better.'

'I'm not sure I like built-in furniture. It cuts down your flexibility.'

'But if you had the floor repaired, and matched the timber, they'd disappear into the walls.' She smoothed her hand over the plaster that was flaking badly. 'This isn't a particularly nice wall.'

'It's perfectly pleasant, thank you! But you may be right. I do have an awful lot of books.' He ran his hands along one shelf of them.

'It would look brilliant. I'd do it for you – when I've finished my own house, of course, and only if you wanted me too,' she added, not wanting to seem too keen. 'I really enjoy doing that sort of cabinetmaking. Are you planning to do most of the work yourself?'

He nodded. 'I'll get things like the wiring done by professionals, but it would cost the proverbial arm and leg to get it all done by builders. I shall do it bit by bit. It's a lifetime's project.'

She nodded slowly as they walked back into the centre of the room. 'So, what were you going to do with your day off – sorry – flexitime-day or whatever you call it?' She bit her lip in sudden realisation. 'We met at the builders' merchants – you were going to do your house, and you took me and Caroline for a walk, and now we've taken up all your morning and' – she glanced at her watch – 'quite a lot of your afternoon as well.'

'It was a conscious decision.' He smiled at her. 'And unlike you, I don't have any pressing deadlines.'

'Still, it was very kind. Caroline and I really appreciated it. Especially Caroline.'

'She had the advantage of not falling full length into the mud,' he said with mock solemnity.

Anna adopted his twinkle: 'Indeed!'

He grinned. 'Now, let's go and have the soup. You can see the rest of the house another time.'

'You must be starving. I didn't think.'

'Stop apologising. And you're not hungry yourself?'

'Mm, now I think about it,' she said, following him back to the kitchen.

They ate their soup in silence. Unwillingly, she thought about Max. It was so easy to be relaxed and giggly with Rob, whereas with Max, it was much harder work. But surely all relationships took a bit of effort? Anna put her spoon down. 'That was brilliant soup.'

'My wonderful cleaning lady told me how to make it,' 'Rob said. You just put some pulses in a pan with some water, an onion, carrot, celery, any of that sort of thing you've got in the fridge, and cook it slowly. You need a good dollop of vegetable stock powder, of course. She starts it for me, leaves it off the hot plate but just on the top, and when I get home, it doesn't take long to finish cooking it.'

Anna opened her mouth and shut it again, remembering that he'd had a partner, who didn't like the country and who didn't like dogs. She wondered briefly if she was in danger of having the same thing, and if it would end the same way. 'Did you have this house with your . . . ? Sorry to be nosy, it's just . . .' she tailed off, wishing she hadn't asked.

'My partner didn't come here very often,' he said. 'She doesn't much like living in building sites.'

'Don't blame her! I don't much like it either, but I've got no choice. And actually,' she went on pensively, 'I suppose I don't mind. As long as I see a bit of progress each day, and the work goes OK. It's quite rewarding. But I do crave a properly finished and furnished house sometimes.' She grinned. 'But if I want to make my fortune by developing property, I probably won't get that often.'

Rob leant back in his chair. 'So, what about you? Have you got a partner or anything? Tit for tat in nosiness.'

Anna laughed awkwardly. She really wished she hadn't started this whole conversation. 'Well, not a partner. A sort of boyfriend – man-friend even. He lives in London.'

He raised an eyebrow. 'And you think he might not like the country?

'I don't know about that, exactly,' Well, it was the truth. 'His mother lives in Amberford.'

'You've met his mother? It must be serious.' He spoke lightly, but he didn't seem all that amused.

'Well, I have, but not with Max! It was hilarious, really. Me and Chloe were the raffle prize. We cleaned out Mrs

Gordon's greenhouse. It was utterly filthy, and while we were there, Max arrived! I didn't let him see me.'

'Why not?' He took another mouthful of soup, looking across at her.

'I was covered in cobwebs, filthy dirty and besides . . .' She paused and made a face, 'Mrs Gordon was so stuffy, and when I told Max about us being there, in the evening when we went out to dinner—' She stopped. Rob was not the person to tell that Max hadn't found it funny when she had regaled him with the tale of the spiders. 'Oh, never mind.'

'Have some more bread.' He seemed as anxious as she was to change the subject.

Anna took another thick slice of brown bread that he'd cut up rather roughly. 'Don't tell me you made the bread too,' she said, pleased to be on safer ground.

'I can make bread, but haven't for a while. This comes from a local bakery. It's very good.'

When they had both finished, Anna gathered the bowls and plates and took them over to the sink.

'It's all right; I've got a dishwasher. Priorities,' he added, seeing her look of surprise.

'I'd be grateful for a proper kitchen sink,' she said. 'Well, that was a delicious lunch, but I think I should go now.'

'OK. I'll just feed the dogs then I'll drop you back,' he said, getting up from his chair.

She looked at her watch. 'This early? I don't usually feed Caroline until later.'

'I'll do it now and then I don't have to remember to do it when I come back.'

Anna laughed. 'I don't imagine they let you forget.' She followed him into the little scullery that seemed to be the designated dog room. 'Or do they?'

He was measuring biscuit into bowls. 'No, but they will lie to me and tell me they haven't been fed when my neighbour has come in and done it.'

At last they were ready, and loaded Caroline, who seemed to have fitted into Rob's pack quite easily, into the Volvo.

'I've had a lovely day,' said Anna. 'I feel awfully guilty when I'm not working on my house, but I've really enjoyed myself.' She hadn't quite realised this was true until she said it. 'It was so relaxing.'

'Do you think you'd be able to steer Chloe in the direction of the field?' he asked. 'It would be OK to use it if there's no stock in it.'

'Not a cat in hell's chance. I've got no sense of direction. It's why I like cycling. I make mistakes, but I can stop a lot and get my bearings.'

He laughed and they drove the rest of the way in companionable silence.

'Well, thank you for today, Anna. I enjoyed it,' Rob said as he dropped her off.

'Oh so did I! You've been so kind to me and Caroline, Rob.'

'And you're still willing to help at my sister's fête? It's at the end of the month, I think.'

Anna had the impression that he was giving her an opportunity to back out but found she didn't want to. 'Oh yes! If I possibly can do it, I certainly will. It sounds wonderful fun.'

Chapter Sixteen

Anna's day with Rob had been good for her, she decided. When, on Tuesday, she braced herself to make the first cut into her lovely reclaimed boards, she felt clear-headed and confident. It was because she was happy, she realised. Yes, she had to rush doing up her house and might have to miss the bit she liked best – choosing colours, textures and finishes – but the work was going well, she had good friends in Chloe and Rob, good tradesmen she could call on, and, of course, lovely Max.

She put all this out of her mind as she set everything up to make the first mark. She had braced the board so it couldn't shift, and marked where she was to cut with a pencil. Mike had lent her his table saw: this was something she had intended to buy for herself but she knew it would save her having to take yet more time off to go and buy one, so she had been delighted. She took a deep breath and went for it.

There was a feeling of exhilaration that lasted quite a long time. Each piece she cut fitted the template, and when offered up to the central column, still fitted. When she finally decided it was time for breakfast, she found it was nearly twelve.

For days she concentrated on her staircase, hardly doing anything else except care for Caroline and snatch the odd meal. She spoke to Laura on the phone from time to time, but there were still no jobs in the offing for Will. Her almost nightly calls from Max were the highlight of her day although she'd learnt that telling him exactly what she'd done with her staircase that day was not the way to keep his attention.

'It's just as well you've got Caroline,' said Chloe, after the fourth day. She cared for Anna by bringing her cups of good coffee. 'Otherwise you'd never go out!'

'Thank you so much for this!' Anna sipped at the foam that Chloe had dusted with chocolate powder. 'But I'm getting on very well. I've nearly finished! Apart from the sanding and varnishing, of course.'

'That's amazing,' Chloe said, examining Anna's handi-work. 'This is extremely professional. But you need a day out, when it's done, to celebrate.'

'Oh yes. That would be marvellous.' Anna ran a fingertip over the end of a mitred board.

'Heard from Max lately?' Chloe asked nonchalantly.

Anna smiled. 'Oh yes. He phones most days.'

'Something not right between you? You don't seem to be talking about him so much recently,' Chloe fished.

'Oh no! We're absolutely fine.' Anna laughed. 'He's not exactly fascinated by the tread-by-tread account of my staircase, but it doesn't stop him ringing.' She took another sip of coffee, relishing its hot strength. 'In fact, I may ask you to babysit Caroline for a night. He's invited me to a gallery opening!'

'Lovely! And of course I'll babysit. When is it?'

'I'll have to check, and if it's not convenient—'

'Of course it'll be convenient! Now, what shall we do for our day out?'

Anna regarded her friend speculatively. 'Something tells me that you know what you want to do.' She realised Chloe had a plan.

Chloe jumped up and down. 'Yes I do! And I'm sure you'll want to do it too! Mike says he'll have the boys.'

'So what is it you have in mind?'

'It's called a Home Decorators' Fayre and it's at Horsecombe House.'

205

'Which is?' Anna asked, finishing her coffee.

'Oh, it's a stately home, not far from here.'

Anna sighed. 'I hardly know any of the area really. I do hope I can buy another property near here. I would like to get to know it better.'

'And stay living near your friend Chloe,' said Chloe.

Anna draped her arm over Chloe's shoulder. 'That goes without saying. Now when do you want to go to this fair?'

'Sunday. Suit you?'

'I'm fairly sure, but I promised I'd help Rob out at a local show his sister helps run. I'll just have to check it isn't this Sunday, although I'm sure he'd have told me by now if it were.'

'Ring him then.' Chloe picked up Anna's mobile and handed it to her.

'Do I have to do it now?'

'Yes! I need to know about Sunday,' Chloe insisted.

Anna scrolled through until she found Rob's work number. She suspected Chloe of wanting to eavesdrop on the conversation because she still had her heart set on pairing her up with Rob.

Anna found herself surprisingly excited at the prospect of a day away from her little house, much as she loved it. She had made good progress and as she'd found the other day, she did seem to work better after a proper break. Chloe, too, was relishing the thought of time away from her boys.

'I've dragged the poor things round these sorts of things before,' she told Anna as they settled themselves in the car. 'They get terribly bored and nag me for money.'

'And that's just Mike?'

Chloe nodded. 'And the toys he buys are really expensive. It'll be terribly crowded, it being a Sunday, but who cares? I feel all wind-in-my-hair, day-off-school-ish.'

'We're going to a cut-down Ideal Home Exhibition,' said Anna. 'It's hardly *Thelma and Louise.*'

Chloe laughed. 'When you've got children you'll realise that however much you love them, a little time away makes you love them even more. Let's hope they've laid on plenty of parking.'

There were several marquees leading one from another and they were all heaving with people. 'Thank God for mobiles,' said Chloe. 'If we lose each other we can get back together. When I take the boys to anything like this, I stick labels on their clothes with my mobile number on them.'

'I can see you wouldn't want little ones with you in this crush,' said Anna, trying to see past the stall selling pigs made from MDF which were supposed to hide your milk bottles. 'What do you want to look at?'

'I need a new wallet,' said Chloe, her eyes shining at the prospect of some retail therapy. 'And a loft ladder, and possibly a new bed. What about you?'

'I don't think I want to buy anything, but I would like to get some ideas.' Anna looked round. 'Shall we split up or – Oh, Chlo, over there. Now that's what I call a bed.'

'For old people!' said Chloe indignantly.

'Not at all. Yes, my friend would like to try it,' Anna said to a besuited young man. 'You go on, Chloe. Have a nice lie-down.'

It was a little cruel, Anna accepted, as she watched Chloe being taken through the motions, her legs going up and down, her back going down and up, both going together and then, by mistake, both going in opposite directions.

'Actually it was lucky that happened,' said Chloe, after she had been rescued from a position she was familiar with from yoga and was stuffing a business card into her bag. 'It meant I didn't have to buy one. It was quite good though. The boys would love it!'

'I know you promised you'd bring them something back but I think that's going too far. Oh look!' She pointed. 'A jacuzzi bath.'

Chloe spotted her chance for revenge. 'Yes!' She marched purposefully towards the stand and smiled broadly at the slim blonde woman who was calling out to the crowd with very little hope of being answered. 'My friend would love to borrow a swimming costume and have a go.'

'No I wouldn't! Don't be silly.' Anna tried to walk on but Chloe took her arm and pulled her back.

'When was the last time you had a bath?' she said, just loud enough for the woman in charge to hear.

'Yesterday, as you very well know!'

'Hi! I'm Tina,' said the woman, who had looked at Anna and decided that although her hands were in a terrible state, she was clean. 'If you demonstrate it for us, we'll give you all these lovely products free.' She made a sweeping gesture with her hand, that appeared to Anna to have Tipp-ex on the ends of the fingernails. But there was an impressive array of products that included a foot spa.

'Go on!' urged Chloe. 'Those are nice things. I love that brand! I've always wanted a foot spa.'

'You do it then,' muttered Anna inaudibly. Out loud she said, 'Why didn't you hire a model if you wanted your jacuzzi demonstrated?' She was heaving with suspicion.

'We much prefer to save the money and pass the saving on to our customer,' said Tina, looking expectantly at Anna.

'But I'm not a customer!' Anna protested.

'You might be,' said Chloe. 'You have got to put a bathroom in, after all.'

'I'm not going to supply whoever buys my house with bath foam, honestly, Chloe. Come on, let's look over there,

208

I see some rather nice baskets.' Anna tried to move away, but Chloe kept a firm hand on her arm.

'We might be able to do a bit better than that,' said the saleswoman quickly. 'I promise you and your friend will do very well out of it.'

'Oh go on!' Chloe pressed her.

'You do it!' insisted Anna, feeling increasingly trapped.

'Can't.' She leant in confidentially and whispered, 'I've got my period.'

Anna sighed. The saleswoman saw the chink of Anna's weakness widening and pounced. 'Just slip this on.' She handed Anna a swimsuit. 'And then come and try it.'

'Do I have to keep my knickers on? If so, I'm not doing it. I'm not going round in wet knickers all day for a bottle of bubble bath and a foot spa.'

'We're offering you much more than that – and your friend. And take these.' Tina was a professional and thrust a pair of paper knickers into Anna's hand before she could get out of reach. 'In there. There's a lovely little cubicle.'

Deciding that the person who put the word 'slip' in conjunction with a swimming costume had never worn one, Anna took off her clothes as fast as she could in the cubicle, which may indeed have been lovely, but was hardly bigger than a coffin. Eventually she emerged, grateful that her reunion dinner meant that her legs and armpits were moderately hair free. If she kept her arms clamped to her sides the regrowth shouldn't show too much.

'Lovely!' said Tina, beaming at Anna, relieved to have found a volunteer – albeit such reluctant one – at last. 'That fuchsia really suits you. Now come this way and step into the tub.'

Anna regarded Chloe, who looked as if she was giggling already. 'I'm doing this for you! I don't even want a foot spa!'

The water in the tub was just slightly cooler than was

comfortable. Anna sat down nobly. 'Right, well, it seems – just like sitting in a bath, really.'

'You haven't got the bubbles on!' Tina pressed a button and instantly the water bubbled.

It was quite pleasant and would have been more so had the water been hot enough. Anna lay back and pretended to relax. To her horror she noticed a crowd had started to form. Chloe gave her a little wave from the front. Anna scowled back.

'Er, would you mind if we took a photo?' said someone.

Anna sat up immediately, water sloshing about her. 'No, really, I don't think so.'

'It's for the local paper,' said the man to Tina, ignoring Anna.

Tina was ecstatic. 'Oh great! A bit of free publicity. The office will be thrilled!'

'Then you get in here and be photographed in the bath!' wailed Anna, knowing no one would listen.

'You look wonderful,' said Chloe, openly amused now. 'Really, that colour does do something for you.'

The photographer, who seemed to be about ten years old, took on the mantle of Mario Testino and began asking Anna to do things with her arms and legs that she was highly reluctant to do, scared as she was of exposing her excess body hair. She stuck a foot over the side and a hand on her ear.

'No! You look like you've got earache! Put it behind your head . . . Oh, don't do that then,' he went on impatiently. 'How can we make this exciting? I know! More bubbles!'

'The bath is on its highest setting,' said Tina. 'There's a lovely rolling bubble going on there.'

'I'm getting cold,' said Anna grumpily. 'Can I get out now?'

'Not till you've had your photograph taken,' said Tina firmly.

'I'm going to want more than a bloody foot spa,' muttered Anna. 'I'm turning into a prune.'

'Ah! This'll do the trick!' said the photographer, picking up one of the luxury bath items that were to be Anna's reward. He took off the lid and poured a generous quantity into the spa.

'No!' shrieked Tina. 'You're not supposed to do that!'

The small, energetic bubbles caused by the jacuzzi began to grow and grow. Anna, who felt more covered up now, and was at last used to the cold water, began to feel more relaxed.

The photographer started snapping away enthusiastically. Tina, torn between the profanity of having bubble bath in a jacuzzi and the joy of having such dramatic pictures being taken, which would not only go in the local paper, but might go into the brochure, started to field the bubbles as they came over the side. The crowd was increasing at the same terrifying rate as the bubbles.

'Perhaps you should turn the machine off,' called Chloe to Tina, who was still baling the bubbles back into the bath.

'That's a good idea,' said Anna, and then changed her mind. Suddenly she wanted the mountain of foam to become a Himalaya so she was entirely hidden: in the crowd she had spotted Mrs Gordon and an equally Gorgon-like friend. Their expressions of disdain could have frozen the Atlantic – they had obviously never seen anything so vulgar in their lives before. Anna shrank down so she was almost entirely hidden.

'No, no, you'll have to sit up a bit,' said the photographer. 'I just want one last shot of you, smiling happily in the bath. Think luxury, think – think Kylie Minogue. Stick your leg out.'

Anna couldn't think Kylie Minogue, she could only think Mrs Gordon, and it didn't have the right effect on her facial expression. She poked a dubious toe over the side. The nail varnish that had enhanced her strappy shoes was now very chipped.

'Come on, love, smile!'

Anna did her best. She forced Mrs Gordon out of her head and out of her line of vision and smiled. She put her leg further out; she waved. At least if she recognises me now, she thought, I'm doing something clean.

At last the photographer was happy. Anna was allowed to get out of the bath and be wrapped shivering in a very large bath towel.

Chloe hurried over. 'I think she deserves lots more presents than that,' she said, indicating the box. 'After all, she's free advertising.'

Anna was still shivering. She returned to the coffin and forced her clothes over her damp limbs. At least her knickers were dry although the ones Tina had given her came off in pellets of disintegrated paper. She went to join Chloe.

'Well,' said Tina, hesitating, 'you do get all these bath products, a luxury brand, a foot spa and half the price off a jacuzzi, if you buy one.'

'I don't want a jacuzzi!' said Anna.

'Oh, go on!' said Chloe. 'It wouldn't make any difference to the plans, and you've got to buy some sort of bath, haven't you?'

'Yes, but this one will be probably be more expensive than an ordinary bath would be full price.'

'If you have this one,' said Tina, spotting a potential sale, 'you could have it for less than a third of the original price. We'd sell it cheaper anyway, but as it's you and because you've been such a good sport – well, we'll practically give it to you.'

'Oh, that's a good offer,' said Chloe. 'Go on, Anna, you'd be mad not to.'

'It is a good offer,' Anna acknowledged. It would save her hunting round for a bath, and having done some quick sums she decided it should fit the intended space very nicely. 'Are you sure? I could pay for it now.'

While Tina was filling in the paperwork, Anna and Chloe couldn't help noticing that the bubbles had travelled quite a long way. The plastic sheeting that had been spread to prevent the floor of the marquee getting wet was soaked. There was a mop propped up against a partition and Anna picked it up. Chloe gathered up the soggy newspapers that someone had put down to sop up some of the moisture. Anna was squeezing her mop into a washing-up bowl while Chloe was scooping up water with a dustpan when something made them both look up at the same time. It was Mrs Gordon. She had come back with her friend and was looking over at them, a peculiar expression on her face.

'Please don't say anything,' Anna murmured out of the corner of her mouth. 'I really don't want her to recognise us.'

Just as she said this, the demonstrator, who had finally worked out how much the jacuzzi bath was going to cost, said in a loud and jubilant voice: 'Here you are, Anna. This is what you have to pay. Now, you couldn't get a bath in a local DIY store for as cheap as that.'

Mrs Gordon's head turned, like a hound scenting its prey. Anna kept her head well down as she went to the desk and fumbled in her bag for her purse but she thought it was unlikely that Mrs Gordon wouldn't recognise her if she turned up for tea and cakes. And if she did, Anna was done for. Not only had she been caught being utterly ridiculous in public, but she'd bought a very vulgar item, too.

'Yikes!' she said to Chloe as at last they could escape. 'Max's mother. What will she think of me? Cleaning windows one minute, frolicking in a bubble bath the next!'

'She may not recognise—'

'Just take me to the bar!' Anna exclaimed.

'But, darling, it's only eleven-thirty.'

'I don't care!' Anna was already striding purposefully towards the refreshment tent.

As they came out of the bar a little later, they saw Mrs Gordon (who was now indelibly etched in Anna's mind as Mrs Gorgon) and her friend leave. The elation and the spritzers kicked in at the same time.

'Come on, Thelma,' said Anna to Chloe, 'let's shop!'

They arrived back at Chloe's house with enough plastic bags and bits and pieces to satisfy even Chloe's boys and Mike, who spent a happy time burrowing through them.

'Do you realise that wallet has fourteen different pockets for you to lose your credit card in?' Mike said accusingly to Chloe.

'Yes but it was only a fiver and it's real leather!' she protested.

'And do you really need shoe balm? What's shoe balm when it's at home?'

'You put it on your shoes instead of cleaning them. Look!' Chloe smeared her husband's feet with stuff that smelt deliciously of honey. 'Look how shiny!'

Mike snorted and picked up another bag. 'What's this?'

'A cute little cover for the hoover. It looks like a little mouse in a mob cap.'

'What? Have you gone mad? When have you ever had time to put a cover on the hoover?'

Chloe bit her lip. 'I'll try and give it to someone. I just felt so sorry for the woman selling them. She'd made them and her stall wasn't exactly thronging with buyers.'

Mike rolled his eyes at Anna who grinned back.

'Dad,' asked Tom, regarding his parents. 'Do you think Mummy's a nana?'

'Yes,' he said definitely, 'but a kind nana.'

'And that's a very good sort of nana to be,' said Anna. 'Did you take Caroline out for me?'

'Yes. We went round and round the common and then to the swings,' said Mike.

Harry came up to Anna and whispered in her ear. 'I held her!'

Anna put her arm round him. 'I expect she liked that very much,' she whispered back.

Harry ran away again, to play with the toy his mother had brought for him from the fair.

'Well, I suppose I'd better drag myself away,' said Anna, an hour or so later. 'It's been a great day, Chlo, thank you for taking me.'

'Thank you for being such a good sport about the jacuzzi.'

'Well, I might just forgive you,' Anna said. 'And I got a spa bath practically for nothing, so I think it was worth it in the end.'

Mike and the boys, who'd been told in lurid and exaggerated detail of what had gone on all felt miffed for having missed it. 'I'd have done a lot to see Anna in the bath, with bubbles, being lucky, like Kylie Minogue.'

'I don't think it was generally so well appreciated,' said Anna, thinking of the Gorgons – Max's mother and her evil twin.

'Well, at least you won't be round ours wanting a bath,' said Mike, faking grumpiness fairly convincingly.

'No.' Anna kissed his cheek. 'I'm so clean I probably won't need another bath for days.'

'Mum,' Anna heard one of the children say as she went out of the door, 'if we stay in the bath a really, really long time, does it mean we don't need another one the next day?'

Caroline, though very pleased to see her, didn't need any attention, as she had been exercised and fed by Mike and the boys. Anna gave her a biscuit, mentally apologising to Rob as she did so. She knew titbits were bad for dogs, but she was a novice, she had a right to feign ignorance.

Her phone rang as she was taking a cup of tea up to bed. It was Max. Hearing his voice made a happy day perfect.

'Hello,' she breathed ecstatically.

'Hello. I've got the date for that private view, if you still fancy it. Otherwise we could do something else.'

Her first thought was that she couldn't take any more time off, but then she decided she couldn't turn down a date from Max. 'I'd love to. When is it?'

'Thursday week. Will you be able to make arrangements for your dog?'

'I should think so.'

'We can make more detailed plans nearer the time but I suggest I meet your train at Paddington and, depending on what time that is, we can either go straight to the gallery, or for a quick drink first.' He paused. 'Dinner afterwards.'

'I'd better book a hotel room. That one we stayed at for the reunion was nice.'

'My guest room would be much more comfortable, not to mention free.'

Anna chuckled. 'Well, I'll check it out and then decide. A girl likes to have alternatives.'

He had a very sexy laugh. 'It'll be so nice for me to have you all to myself for once.'

Anna felt a frisson of excitement. She hoped she wouldn't be needing the guest room. 'You won't have me all to yourself at the gallery,' she said. 'What's showing?'

'A new young Brit artist I'm interested in. He's very good, although I'm not sure he's to my personal taste. Anything I bought would be more of an investment than something to put on my wall.'

Privately Anna thought it strange to buy pictures you didn't like just because they'd be valuable one day.

'Couldn't you buy something you liked that would be an investment?'

'To be honest I've got no more room for pictures at my flat. You'll see when you come.'

'I'm looking forward to it.'

'So am I, Anna.'

Chapter Seventeen

Chloe drove Anna to the station. They spent most of the journey talking about Caroline.

'Don't worry, Anna,' Chloe said for what seemed like the fiftieth time, 'Mike will take her out last thing, and I'll have the baby alarm on all night. I'll hear if anything happens to her.'

'It's very kind of you, and I must say I wouldn't have thought of the baby alarm. Are you sure it's a good idea?'

'Absolutely. I'll know instantly she develops any kind of problem. I'll probably hear her fart.'

'Chloe! I know the boys aren't with you, but there's no need to let yourself go completely.'

Chloe ignored this. 'And we'll take them all out together before school and playgroup tomorrow, probably. It does the boys good to have a run around. Mike will take them.'

'It's such a relief Mike is home,' said Anna, not for the first time. 'It would be too much to ask otherwise. And I couldn't have asked Laura during the week.'

'Most people have parties at the weekend,' said Chloe.

'Darling, this isn't a party! It's a private view and they're always during the week. Don't you know anything?'

'By the sounds of it, you didn't know all that much until quite recently.'

Anna laughed. 'Well, I did know because we used to go to private views when we were at college. Lots of us had art student friends. They always wanted to go to try and get talking to an agent.'

'But you won't be doing that this time?'

'I didn't ever do it before, but no, I expect I will be concentrating on Max.'

The question, 'Will you sleep with him?' hung unasked between them.

'Excited?' asked Chloe as they pulled into the station car park.

'Mm. A bit worried too. I mean, what do you wear to the opening of a cutting-edge art show?' Anna asked anxiously.

'I told you, what you are wearing: black trousers and a little sparkly top. Now, have you got everything? Reading book? Packed lunch? Spellings?'

Anna smiled fondly at Chloe. She really was like Laura but it was nice to be looked after once in a while, however bossily. She kissed Chloe on the cheek, rescued her case from the back seat and walked on to the platform. She was going to enjoy this visit. And this time she would definitely sleep with Max and it would be perfect.

As she wandered down the platform, she found herself worrying about her house as much as Caroline, whom she knew would be all right. It was as if she was worried that the fairies would undo all her hard work in the night, as in 'The Elves and the Shoemaker', only in reverse. She decided she was spending far too much time reading Chloe's children bedtime stories. For the past week, that had been her only entertainment. Almost every other hour had been spent working on her house.

She went into the waiting room to check her appearance from behind a row of people doing the same thing. She looked OK, she thought as she peered at herself. Her hair was freshly washed and she wore it in what Chloe described as a ponytail with the ends sticking out. She was more practised at putting make-up on now and had decided she needed to buy her own black trousers.

'They'll take you everywhere,' Chloe had declared while Anna was modelling them for her.

'You mean like a sort of taxi service?'

'Don't be flippant. If you're going to go out with Max, you'll need some decent clothes.'

This was a bit of a problem, but Anna refused to worry about it. When the house was done she'd have more time for shopping. Now Anna wondered if she looked sufficiently smart and sophisticated to be Max's girlfriend. He had warned her – told her – that his friends would be there. She wanted to do him proud.

At least I haven't got spots, or my period, she thought, inspecting herself. She had refused Chloe's suggestion of false nails. She knew one would flip off at an awkward moment and that she would giggle and Max might not. Her own nails were short but, thanks to the fact that she'd washed her hair, for the moment scrupulously clean. She was wearing a neat little leather jacket, borrowed from Chloe, who had bought it at a charity shop, possibly with Anna in mind. She looked . . . well, if not cool, at least not a complete dog.

'You've got cheekbones, and you're not fat!' Chloe had wailed in envy. 'And you're really pretty! What more can any girl want?'

At last the train pulled into the station, and Anna turned away from the mirror and made her way towards it. She had to stop vacillating between a reluctant admiration that she looked remotely presentable, and the belief that Max would take one look at her and leave her at the station. The almost certain knowledge that tonight they would really become lovers was making her veer between blissful anticipation and fear that she might have forgotten what to do. He was a sophisticated man-about-town and she – well, she was just a girl in love. It should be enough, she thought. Passion would take her through any initial awkwardness.

She clambered on to the train, placed her overnight bag above her seat and sat down. She felt exhausted already and closed her eyes, hoping to dream of Max. Instead, a kaleidoscope of risers and goings and nosings – all the parts of her staircase – intruded until at last she slept.

Max was looking very sophisticated in crushed linen. Anna longed to ask him if he had come out of the door looking crushed or it had happened on the journey over. You could never quite tell with designer labels.

'There's not much queue for taxis just now,' he said, when he had kissed her cheek and given her an approving once-over. 'It's this way.'

It was pleasant being in the charge of a tall, confident man-about-town, Anna decided as he took her overnight bag and put his hand in the small of her back to steer her in the right direction. She began to look forward to the evening ahead.

The gallery was white, all white; everything was white. The only non-white items were the pictures, which, Anna was forced to concede (having taken against the all-white theme) looked fabulous. Except that you couldn't really see them, there were so many people, all of them talking at the tops of their voices. Most of them were wearing black.

'Wow,' she said, taking a glass of white wine from a tray that held an array of all white drinks. The girl holding the tray was wearing a clinging white sheath that went from barely over her bust to just over her hips. 'This is amazing.' She smiled at the girl who smiled back and moved on – an art student, if ever Anna had seen one.

'Have you not been here before? I'm surprised,' said

Max. 'Oh look, there's Andreas. Come and meet him. I'm hoping Julian, who might buy your house, will be here.'

Anna followed Max as he forged a path through the people and reflected that everyone seemed to be there for social reasons, to be seen rather than to look at the work. This was no place for a bit of reflection on a work of art.

All the women seemed to be tall, skeletal and wearing Armani. Some of the men were the same, but others were older, ugly and much more interesting-looking. Anna felt flattered that she'd been allowed in wearing her plain black trousers and Chloe's leather jacket over a sparkly top from a high-street store.

Andreas and Max hugged in a way that Anna found rather surprising. She wondered if Rob would have embraced another man like that, doubted it, and then congratulated herself on being with a man who was more open to such things.

'Andreas, meet Anna. Darling, this is Andreas Bugatti – no relation to the car. He's a collector.'

'Oh, that sounds sinister!' said Anna gaily and then realised she shouldn't have. 'I mean, interesting.'

'And what do you do?' asked Andreas, obviously not expecting her to do anything at all.

'I'm an interior designer. I'm doing up a house in the Cotswolds. I finished the staircase yesterday.' She smiled in a way designed to end the conversation. It did.

'There's Julian,' said Max. 'Now he's the one you ought to talk about your house to. Sorry, Andreas, we must circulate,' But Andreas had already moved on. 'Julian! Over here!' Max waved at a pleasant, well-dressed man who dutifully came over.

'Hello, Max. Who's this?' He smiled at Anna with just the right amount of interest.

'This is Anna, she's the one doing up the house I was telling you about. Could be just what you want.'

'But, Max, you haven't seen what I've done yet!' Anna

protested. 'You shouldn't go telling your friends about it when I might have made an awful mess of it.'

'Oh, that's OK, Julian's got plenty of money. He could always get me in to sort things out.' Max smiled, a little superciliously, Anna thought. 'In fact, he'll probably need to do just that.'

Anna took a breath, to calm herself down and so she could make a short speech defending her house and her abilities. Julian caught her eye and she exhaled again. He was smiling in a friendly, reassuring way.

'I'm sure you've done a very good job on it,' he said. 'And if the house is listed, you're quite restricted anyway.'

Sensing that of all the people in the room Julian might actually be interested in her staircase, she said, 'I've just finished making a staircase. I copied it from my neighbour. I put a coat of water-based varnish on it before I got ready.'

'You didn't want to use oil or wax?' he asked.

'I did, but it takes so long to dry. The varnish works very well,' Anna explained.

'So what's the rest of it like?'

'Well . . .'

As Julian seemed genuinely interested and Max, satisfied that he'd set up the conversation, was talking to Andreas again, she started.

'Well, it's got beautiful wood floors, all sanded and sealed. Keeping the dog off them was a real problem.'

'What sort of dog?'

'A rescue greyhound, but you don't want to hear about all that.'

'I definitely do. Besides, if your cottage is big enough for a greyhound, it's probably big enough for me.'

'It's not really big enough for a greyhound, but she and I manage very well,' Anna said, relaxing properly for the first time that evening.

They continued to chat about the house until Max

touched her arm. 'Time for dinner, darling. I've got a table booked.'

'But I haven't seen a single picture close to!'

Max laughed. 'Come back another time, sweetie.'

Anna felt fleeting regret at leaving Julian's easy, interested company, but then realised that a dinner à *deux* with Max, at what was probably a very good restaurant, was the stuff of dreams, her dreams.

The quality of the restaurant was evident the moment they got through the door. Max was obviously a regular as the maître d' and the waiters addressed him by name. They were ushered to a table in a discreet but comfortable corner. Bread, menus and doll-sized circles of toast with something delicious on them appeared almost immediately.

'Well now, what shall we have?'

Max's expert knowledge of food was obvious and while he didn't exactly order for her, he talked her through the menu. Anna wasn't sure if she was grateful for this or not. Whilst she looked around at the other diners in their identikit his-and-hers designer suits, Max and the sommelier discussed the wine at length.

Anna, who'd had two glasses of white wine at the gallery, felt she shouldn't really have too much more, but Max wanted them to have white wine with the starter, and a very exclusive bottle of Rioja with their main course. She decided that this was her dream date. She shouldn't worry about units of alcohol. After all, she was going home with Max! Her heart gave a skip that was half excitement and half nerves.

'So, tell me about your flat,' she said when a plate of oysters had been put on the table in front of them.

'What do you want to know? You'll see it soon.' His laughing, mocking expression was very sexy, Anna decided.

'I want to know if I'll like it.'

'You'll certainly like the view. Now open your mouth.' He tipped her first ever oyster into it. It tasted, as everyone had always told her it would, of the sea.

'Mm,' she said. 'Quite nice. But if I lived near the coast I'd just have a sip of sea water instead.'

'Philistine! Have another.'

'Perhaps I could get used to them,' she admitted a little later.

'We've eaten them now. I hope you're happy to eat foie gras? There's a very lightly cooked cushion of it served on the fillet.'

Anna was not at all happy about eating foie gras but she couldn't bring herself to say so. He was going to a lot of trouble and expense to give her the very best dinner possible; she couldn't spoil it by talking about animal rights. Besides, he'd never understand.

A tiny nest of grated fried potato sat opposite the steak. A matching nest of courgette was opposite. In between were spears of baby asparagus and something very pretty that Anna didn't recognise.

'That's a courgette flower,' said Max. 'Now dig in.'

Anna regarded him quizzically. 'I don't think "dig in" is what your mother would say at a time like this.'

His mouth twitched. 'Certainly not, but do it anyway.'

Anna addressed her steak, wondering if they'd both had enough to drink for her to tell him about the jacuzzi incident. She might have done had his mother not been a crucial part of the story. As he hadn't found the first incident very funny, she doubted she'd even raise a smile with this one. If Mrs Gordon had recognised her as the woman who cleaned her greenhouse, and Anna subsequently turned up on Max's arm for tea, it would be better for Anna to deny all knowledge. For a moment Anna prayed that Max would never introduce her to his mother, but then she realised that meant she was now in danger of seeing their relationship as only temporary. Surely she couldn't think that about a man she'd loved for so long?

'Ah, an intercourse,' said Max challengingly.

'I'm not going to respond to that,' said Anna, inspecting the tiny frosted glass containing grapefruit sorbet.

'How wise.'

Later, when they'd eaten rare steak and fois gras, he said, 'Now what about pudding? They do a delicious little champagne soufflé that you might like.'

'Haven't we just had pudding?'

'No, that was the intercourse.'

Anna chuckled obligingly. 'Well, it will do for me. I've eaten far too much already.'

'Coffee then? The petits fours they serve are exquisite.'

'Not unless you'd like some, in which case I'll have tea. If I have coffee I won't go to sleep at all.'

'We'll go then. Fabulous as this place is, I don't think they quite understand tea.'

Somehow Anna felt she'd made yet another social gaffe.

'There.'

Max had led her out of the vast glass wall on to the balcony. Anna felt that all London was laid out before her. The Thames, the first and ancient artery of England snaking past towards the estuary, was like a gilded pathway. It was not yet dark but the streetlights and illuminated buildings made the city, always glamorous to Anna's eyes, seem spectacular.

Appropriately enough, his flat was right at the top of an old building practically next to Tate Modern.

'You can see nearly all the newer buildings, except the Eye, which you can just about see the top of.'

'It's fantastic,' said Anna in awe. 'And there's St Paul's. I can understand why you wanted this flat, Max.'

'A lot of the more Brutalistic buildings went up while I was training. Marvellous, exciting stuff. Have you seen the Trellick Tower? Brutal indeed, but with, I think, a sort of savage beauty.'

Anna took a breath. 'I don't think I have. I'm afraid any school of architecture that calls itself Brutalistic is a shade too modern for me. Not that I don't like modern buildings,' she hurried on, possibly digging the hole she was in even deeper, 'but something a bit softer is more to my taste.'

He laughed indulgently. 'Well, I'll leave you to enjoy the view for a bit longer while I do something inside. You can see the Gherkin. You probably like that.'

Anna, who did like the Gherkin building twisting its way into the sky, ignored this dig and indulged in the view. Tucked in among a plethora of innovative vibrant buildings that had gone up during the last century, Anna found herself gazing at St Paul's. For so long it would have been the tallest building, a landmark for the whole of London. It wasn't that she didn't appreciate the new as well as the ancient, but it was the ancient that made her think of London's long and beleaguered history.

'So, are you ready for a tour?' Max came out and touched her arm.

Obligingly, Anna went in with him, although for preference she'd have stayed in the summer air and gazed at the view for quite a bit longer.

'This is the living room,' he gestured. 'Only one, but as you can see it divides up quite nicely into an eating and living space.'

The floors were polished wood, far finer and deeper in colour that Anna's were. 'What sort of wood is this?' she asked.

'Cherry. Expensive, but the best always works out cheaper in the end.'

Anna kept to herself the thought that only rich people could afford to make statements like that.

'And the walls?'

'Polished plaster. I like the rawness. It's white, but not just the ordinary white. It was hand done.' Of course.

227

He took her to the achingly extravagant kitchen with polished granite surfaces and appliances that gleamed with quality. Her professional eye told her that the range cooker probably cost more than she planned to spend on her entire kitchen. Doubt touched at her; could Julian, who was Max's friend, possibly like her old, simply designed house with original features that belonged in a workman's cottage?

The bathroom had a walk-in shower with a head the size of a football. There was also a semi-sunken bath.

'It's carved out of a single piece of limestone,' said Max. 'Again, expensive but worth it.'

'Lovely,' said Anna, feeling a little overwhelmed.

'Now tell me, would you like some champagne?' He turned her so that she faced him and lifted her chin with his finger.

Anna blinked. 'Yes, I rather think I would.' It might help her relax.

'Then come with me.'

He led her, not to the kitchen or sitting room, but to the bedroom.

The bed was enormous, with a bedspread that looked suspiciously like fur and seemed to take up most of the space. Opposite was a wall of mirrors that were probably wardrobes. Two ebony side tables were set into the wall, one on either side of the bed. On one of these was an ice bucket with a bottle of champagne in it. On the bed and round it were scarlet rose petals.

'My goodness,' said Anna, her heart pounding. 'When did you do all this?'

'While you were looking at the view.'

Anna sighed, and watched him open the bottle and half fill two glasses.

'To you, Anna.' He raised his glass to her, smiling seductively.

Anna sipped her champagne. This was her perfect

moment – her perfect evening: the private view, the restaurant, the perfect city apartment. What could be better?

When Anna had finished her champagne he gently took the glass from her and enfolded her in his arms.

I've dreamt of this for years, she reminded herself, and returned his embrace.

Chapter Eighteen

'These are the nicest croissants I've had since I was in France,' said Anna, who still felt tired. 'And I can't remember when I last had oranges squeezed before my very eyes.'

'It's a shame you have to rush off,' said Max. 'We could have taken in an exhibition and gone out for lunch, possibly on the river.'

Anna sighed. 'That would have been lovely, but unfortunately I can't leave my dog on Chloe's hands for too long. Next time,' she added, not wanting him to think she was too eager to escape, 'I could get my sister and brother-in-law to stay. Then I could stay for longer.'

'Unless you've sold by then. Julian's very keen.'

'Well, that's good news.' Anna looked at her watch. 'I really should be going or I'll miss my train.'

'I'll come down and get you a taxi.'

It went against the grain with Anna to take a taxi when she could perfectly well have managed on the tube, but she was in a hurry, and she thought she'd cut it a bit fine to do that.

'You're all right, love,' said the taxi driver when she asked him if she was likely to catch the ten o'clock train. 'Traffic's not too bad this morning. I'll get you there.'

Anna wondered at her anxiety to get away from her lover. He'd been so attentive, so skilled, she might even have said loving, but for her the earth hadn't moved. And surely it should have been the culmination of all her dreams? It was probably because she'd been dreaming about it for so long, it was bound to be a disappointment. Or possibly it was because whenever she closed her eyes she saw bits of staircase. She'd spent too long on her knees sanding it; she couldn't get it out of her head. The last time she came back from London she could have floated down the railway lines without the train. This time she felt edgy and disconcerted.

The next time she and Max were together would be better, she thought, gazing blindly out of the window. Next time she'd be really into it.

She telephoned Chloe to tell her that she had managed to catch the ten o'clock train. It was good to hear her friend's voice.

'I told you it was fine if you caught a later one!' said Chloe. 'We're loving looking after Caroline.'

'I'm sure she's loving it, too,' Anna said, thinking of little Harry's tender ministrations.

'So, did you . . . ?'

'What?'

'You know!'

'I am not talking about things like that!' Anna whispered vehemently into her phone. 'I'm on a train, Chloe!'

'People don't care what they say on trains these days,' Chloe said dismissively.

'Well, I do! I'm going to be with you in less than an hour. I'll tell you everything then.'

Sighing, Chloe ended the call. No sooner had she done so than Anna's phone rang again.

As Anna registered who it was, she thought how nice it was to hear from someone who wanted nothing from her. 'Hello, Rob.'

'Hi! Good time to call?' he asked.

'It's fine. I'm on a train.'

'Oh! Been anywhere nice?'

'London. A private view. With Max,' she added after a moment's hesitation.

'Ah.' He paused, too. 'So, are you still OK for Sunday? The Country Fair and Novelty Dog Show?'

'Oh, is it this Sunday? Yes, I'm certainly still on for it.' She found herself smiling at the thought of a novelty dog show – a bit different from a sophisticated private view, but so much less stressful! Max had murmured about taking her to have tea with his mother sometime soon. If it was this Sunday, she had a perfect excuse to refuse. 'Do you know what we're doing to help?'

'It could be selling raffle tickets, or ice cream. My sister isn't sure. Apparently the committee members are still fighting it out.'

'Well, I don't mind what I do.'

'Great. Can I pick you up on Sunday at about eleven? We can have a bite to eat in the pub before the show.'

'I really should work in the morning but if you wanted to come at about twelve you could see what I've done to the house.'

'I'll make it twelve then. I'm looking forward to seeing it.'

Anna smiled to herself as she dropped her phone back in her bag.

'So?' asked Chloe, the moment Anna's bag was tossed into the back of the car, nudging aside a couple of booster seats as it went.

'What?'

'You know what I mean!' Chloe was beside herself. 'I know I shouldn't ask, but I'm desperate to know.'

'To know what? Did I buy a picture? Is Max's flat wonderful? Definitely, if you like that sort of thing. Not sure I do, actually.'

'Not that! Although you can tell me afterwards, but, come on, tell me, did you and Max fall on each other like rabbits?'

'In a manner of speaking. I'm not terribly up on the mating habits of rabbits.'

'Ah . . . it wasn't good, was it?' Chloe said as they drove away from the station.

'It wasn't bad! Max is very attentive, and all that. And he'd gone to a lot of trouble to make it romantic. He'd put rose petals all round the bed.'

'That's lovely,' Chloe said brightly. She glanced at Anna. 'Oh well, first times never are all that good, in my experience.'

'No,' agreed Anna, not saying that there had been a second time and that hadn't been very inspiring, either. Then, to change the subject as much as anything, Anna said, 'I'm going to a novelty dog show with Rob on Sunday.'

'Oh, that's nice!' said Chloe.

'Why don't you and Mike and the boys come? It should be a great day out for a family. Novelty dogs! How sweet is that?'

'Very sweet,' agreed Chloe, 'but we've got something else on.'

For some reason Anna didn't quite believe her. 'What?'

'Lunch with friends,' said Chloe glibly. 'Now, do you need anything in town or shall we go straight home?'

'If we could call in at the paint shop, I need some charts.'

'My goodness, you're not at the decorating stage already, are you?'

'Not really, but it'll take me ages to decide.'

Anna found herself surprisingly excited at the thought of seeing Rob. It was, she realised, because she wanted to show off her house to someone who was likely to appreciate the work that had gone into it. She put on her black trousers, having gone to some trouble to remove Caroline's hairs from them with parcel tape, only for her to put more back on again.

He was very prompt. Anna opened the door with a smile and an appeal to Caroline not to jump up. Rob accepted Caroline's welcoming paws with equanimity and returned the smile. He didn't come in, but he kissed her cheek. Anna's heart fluttered; this was the first time anyone but Chloe or Mike had seen her staircase and her floor, which had had a final coat of varnish.

'Well,' he said, and then paused for a very long time. 'This is fantastic.'

Anna let herself breathe again. 'Well, come in and see it properly.'

'I hardly like to walk on the floor,' he flashed a smile at her.

'Don't worry I am trying not to move furniture or anything, but it seems fairly tough. Keeping Caroline off it while it dried was a nightmare.'

'How did you do it?'

'Chloe had her while I actually put the stuff on, then we went for a very long walk. Then camped at Chloe's for a while. The boys love her.'

He stepped into the cottage and went to the staircase. Anna's breathing pattern was suspended while he inspected it but then, when he said, 'You really have done an amazing job,' she put her arms around him and hugged him.

He hugged her back rather awkwardly.

'Thank you very much for approving of it!' she said, almost tearful. 'I worked so hard. I think if you hadn't liked it my heart would have broken.' She paused, frowning a little. This mention of hearts was a little excessive, wasn't it? After all, her heart was in good hands with Max. He and she were definitely an item now, even if she hadn't officially met his mother.

Rob smiled down at her, a little amused. 'One does get very emotionally involved with projects like that.'

'Yes. Sorry! Now do you want to see anything else?'

'I would like a good look round. It will save an official visit later.'

'That sounds highly illegal,' said Anna, cheerfully. 'Come upstairs.'

Eventually Rob looked at his watch. 'We'd better be going. What's happening with Caroline?'

'Mike and the boys will take her out.' She frowned. 'I suggested we all went to this fair. I thought it would be a nice day out for the family, but Chloe said they were having lunch with friends.'

'Well, they might be.'

'Hm. Anyway, it means we don't have to rush back for Caroline.'

'Let's go then.'

The Turrellford Country Fair and Novelty Dog show was the other side of the county, where the terrain was less hilly and the villages far more prosperous. This was evident in the perfectly maintained stone walls, the clematis and the well-pruned roses that were just about to burst into flower.

'My sister's married to "something in the City",' explained Rob, amused and slightly apologetic at the same time. 'Salt of the earth: I love her dearly, but I wouldn't want to live any nearer to her than I do.'

'I would like to live a bit nearer to my sister,' said Anna, looking out of the window at the picturesque scenes. 'She's a real rock and support to me. But I wouldn't want her next door. Chloe's enough of a surrogate mother as it is.'

'What about your own mother?'

Anna turned to look at him. 'Oh, she's alive and well, but she's got a new husband, and Laura, that's my sister, thinks she doesn't keep enough of an eye on me. Why should she? I'm an adult, after all.'

'I'll always be my sister's kid brother. It's just the way it is,' he said as they arrived at their destination. 'Right, parking. In this field, obviously.' He followed the waving arms of a young man in a yellow jacket who was playing cars for real and having a lovely time.

The car disposed of, they joined the throng of people on their way to the field where most of the activities were taking place.

'It's busy,' said Anna, surprised.

'It's always very well attended. As you'll notice, it isn't only the commuters and their house guests, there are real locals here.'

Anna had noticed a few flat caps and hairy tweeds in among the linen jackets, brightly coloured corduroy trousers and cut-glass accents. The Boden catalogue was well represented as were those catalogues attached to old-fashioned men's outfitters that sold red socks, pink shirts and very expensive brogues. She looked up at Rob, her eyes sparkling with enjoyment. He smiled back and then said, 'Let's have a whiz round the stalls before we find Cassie. There's always an amazing tombola with fantastic prizes, but if we don't get there early, we'll only win a scented candle.'

'A scented candle is a very nice prize,' said Anna, following him through the crowd.

'But not as good as an antique gilded cherub, worth two hundred pounds.'

'Oh, I don't know, I'm not sure a cherub would fit into my house,' she said quickly.

The man running the stall was flamboyant, dashing and extremely amusing. He sold Rob ten pounds' worth of tickets, convincing him he was getting a bargain. He won, not a scented candle, but a curtain tie-back that wouldn't have looked out of place at Buckingham Palace. 'I think Cassie would like this,' he said, having seen Anna's expression of shock and awe at the thought she might find a home for it in her cottage. 'We'd better find her now or she'll think we haven't bothered to come.'

His sister looked very like him. She was tall and handsome, wearing a linen skirt with roses on it and a cash-mere cardigan with a V-neck. Round her neck she wore a very beautiful silver necklace. 'Something in the City' possibly gave good presents.

'Hi, Rob, and you must be Anna.' She pecked them both on the cheek. 'I'm Cassie. So glad you could come, Anna. I want you both to sell ice cream. Definitely a two-man job.'

'I love ice cream,' said Anna.

'Good. I'll lend you a tabard. We've got some some-where. Otherwise you'll get covered in the stuff. Here's a price list.' She was obviously well practised at this. 'It's only one scoop or two, so not complicated. I'm off to do teas in the house.' And she hurried away.

'The house' was a heavenly Cotswold vicarage, big enough for several curates and dozens of children. It was just visible through a stand of cedars and could have starred in any costume drama for its timeless beauty.

'Cassie and Marcus don't live there,' said Rob, some-what to Anna's relief. 'They have something a bit smaller a little way out of the village.'

'Oh good,' said Anna without thinking.

'They do have an indoor swimming pool though,' he added.

'Ah!'

Rob dealt with the money and Anna did the ice cream. It was difficult but satisfying trying to make the blobs completely round. She chatted to the children as she gave them their cones, adding a bit here and there when she thought they were being short-changed.

'Hurry up, there's a queue,' said Rob, as Anna tenderly smoothed off a perfect sphere for a little girl who defi-nitely appreciated it. She had a puppy with her, all legs and tongue and, pound for pound, about the same size as the child.

'We're going in for Best Mixed Breed Handled by a Child,' said the girl. 'Mummy's helping.'

Given that the puppy in question seemed to have a lot of greyhound in him, and was extremely boisterous, Anna thought this just as well. 'Oh well, I must try and watch you. When is that class on?'

'In about ten minutes, Mummy says.' The little girl indicated her mother, who, in tight pony-skin trousers and a very revealing top, was one of the many women present definable as a yummy mummy.

The child had long fair hair, curled for the occasion, and the puppy had a ribbon round his neck. Anna wisely refused Rob's bet on the chances of this ribbon staying on long enough for it to appear in the show ring. It was, she declared, too long and too silky to stay. Rob, who had hoped to win ten pence from her, was disappointed.

'I can manage on my own now,' said Rob, when they seemed to have sold ice cream to absolutely everyone. 'You have a look round. It's a lovely event.'

It was, Anna decided; a mixture of the immensely wealthy, who leant over the rope watching the puppies, discussing the virtues or otherwise of their new stable girls, and the true country people, who had leather gaiters, hair springing from every orifice and the sort of terriers that made one feel sorry for rats. They mingled happily, admiring each other's dogs. Were all these animals – the stately lurchers, pure-bred Labradors, springers and field spaniels, cockers and cavaliers, the latter as dumb as they were beautiful – going to enter for something? It was possible. A glance at the programme told her that Veterans, Novices, Mixed Breed and Pedigree all had classes. She watched the Best Mixed Breed Handled by a Child and noticed her ex-customer with the puppy who gambolled along like a young lamb. He was very good and, given the cute factor, which was less apparent in the other competitors, Anna felt she had a good chance. One puppy wearing a Little Bo Peep outfit trotted behind a little girl with plaits, but most of the other puppies were in charge, and led their owners round the ring at a cracking pace. Mothers occasionally rushed into the ring to rescue a child from being dragged along on the grass, or admonish the dogs, but mostly the children managed on their own. Fathers followed the scene through the lenses of video cameras, and proud grannies held babies and begged them to 'Look at Lulu with Andromeda – isn't she good?'

Rob joined her while she watched the Dog with the Waggiest Tail competition, which was straight after the child and puppy event. Lots of the entrants were the same, and Anna had high hopes for the lurcher whose rope-like tail had already caused visible bruising on the legs of its diminutive handler, and that was before he had been called on to really perform.

'I've sold out of ice cream,' he said. 'I won't tell Cassie until I've had a chance to look round. I fancy guessing how high the bottle of whisky is.'

Anna turned round. 'What?'

'See over there?' He pointed. 'There's a bottle of whisky hanging from a rope on a tree. Well, I did that stall last year and I know how high the branch is.'

'That's cheating!' protested Anna, following him in the direction of the stall.

'I know. I will share.' He smiled and Anna laughed back. She didn't have to think about what she was saying with Rob. Being with him was so easy somehow, possibly because she could just be herself and not feel she had to compete with Max's urbane and worldly-wise friends.

When Rob had made his guess he took Anna to the cake stall. 'Hooray! They've got fudge again. It is fantastic. Worth having all your teeth drop out for.'

'It's not hard fudge,' said the woman selling it, affronted. 'I made it myself.'

'It is delicious,' said Rob consolingly. 'Just too wicked. Here, Anna, open wide.'

As he put a square of fudge into her mouth she had a sudden flashback to Max and the oyster. In theory oysters were much sexier than fudge, given their reputation as an aphrodisiac, but she decided she preferred the fudge.

'It's wonderful! I'll buy Chloe some,' she said, digging out her purse.

They both ate another piece, then said, more or less together: 'Time for a cup of tea.'

The teas were excellent: Home-made cakes and scones; tea made fresh every few moments. Anna and Rob took theirs to a bench under an enormous cedar tree. 'I feel I should be wearing a long white lacy dress and a picture hat,' said Anna dreamily. 'It's that sort of place.'

'You look fine to me just as you are,' said Rob. His eyes were half closed against the sun and Anna couldn't tell if he was smiling, or just warding off the dazzle. He did have rather good eyelashes, she noticed.

'Oh my goodness, look what we're missing!' he suddenly exclaimed.

'What?' Anna sat up straight and looked around.

'Over there. My favourite thing. The best bow-front!'

Anna stared at him, uncomprehending. 'Rob, you're not telling me they get out their chests of drawers and commodes, stuff like that, and compare them, are you? I suppose there are some jolly nice antiques in some of these houses but—'

Rob was laughing so hard he couldn't speak. He just shook his head weakly. 'They're dogs!'

'Dogs? How can furniture be dogs?'

'Bow-fronts: dogs with bow legs, like corgis, some terriers, dogs that dig. Sorry to laugh, but the idea of dragging the Sheraton on to the lawn is quite funny.'

Anna thought it was quite funny too but was determined not to laugh.

'You'd have men off the *Antiques Roadshow* wearing long white coats, looking at them,' he said.

'And then getting the very posh owners to drag some of them to the front,' said Anna, joining in with the spirit of things.

'And then –' Rob could hardly speak – 'the winner would have to do a lap of honour.'

Anna couldn't hold it back any longer. She laughed until she felt weak.

Cassie found them before the last smear of jam had been licked off their fingers.

'Just the people I need!' she declared. 'I've got Smalls running all over the garden collecting dirty crockery and no one to wash it up. Into the kitchen with you both!'

Rob looked doubtfully at Anna. 'But Anna's hardly had time to finish—'

Cassie fielded Anna's cup before she could put it down. 'You don't mind donning the Marigolds, do you?' She smiled sweetly, obviously used to getting her own way.

'Of course not! It's all right, Rob,' Anna said reassuringly. 'We are here to help.'

Anna enjoyed the washing up mostly because of the cheerful flutter Rob's presence in the kitchen caused. As the only man he was the object of a lot of light-hearted joshing, which he handled with great good humour. The final cup had finally been dried and put in its plastic box, and the helpers were just finishing off the last crumbs of cake and scones, when Anna heard her mobile.

'Oh, sorry!' she said to the room in general and hoiked it out of the bag that she'd left in a corner. It was Mike.

'It's Chloe,' he said. 'She's in hospital.'

'Oh my God!' said Anna, sitting down on a chair and feeling suddenly sick.

'What is it?' said Rob, and everyone else in the room too.

Anna shook her head and signalled for them all to be quiet.

'What's the matter?' She demanded, fearing the worst.

'They don't know.' Mike sounded close to tears. 'It's just some unspecified pain, really, really bad. Could you get here as soon as you can to look after the boys while I go to Chloe? We've rung both sets of grandparents and another friend of Chloe's, but no one can get here until six. I thought you might be nearer.'

'Yes of course, I'll come immediately.'

'Thank you, thank you, Anna. I'll tell the others.' Anna heard the relief in his voice and, disconnecting, turned to Rob. 'We have to go, Chloe's in hospital,' she said, her voice shaking.

'God, what's wrong . . . ?' he asked.

'I'll tell you in the car, we need to go now. How long will it take us to get home?'

'About forty minutes, less if we don't get caught behind anything.' And he was already heading for the door.

Rob sped along the lanes at a speed that was terrifying. Anna's heart was racing, her feelings divided between sympathy for Chloe, her little boys and Mike.

'We'll be there in less than half an hour now,' Rob said, his steady gaze not wavering from the road ahead. Although he was driving very fast, she had got used to the speed and felt perfectly safe. Supposing she'd been with Max when that call had come? Would he have reacted like Rob had? She could almost hear him say, 'Darling, she's only a neighbour. There must be someone else she can ask.'

Anna watched the passing scenery and decided it was unfair to make that assumption. Max might have been just as supportive and heroic as Rob.

Anna ran down the lane while Rob parked the car. Mike was on the doorstep, jigging from foot to foot, beside himself with anxiety.

'Thank God you're here!' he said. 'I must go to her. I've

tried to keep calm in front of the boys, but it's not easy.'

Anna touched his arm. 'What have you told them?' she asked.

'I said that Mummy had bad tummy-ache – which they saw for themselves – but that the doctor will make her better. They seem quite satisfied with that but I'm not sure they really understand.' He looked stricken.

'We'll explain again,' said Rob, who had joined them. 'We'll have a great time together.'

Anna turned to him. 'There's no need for you to stay, Rob. I can manage.' She said the words because she felt she ought to, but really hoped he wouldn't believe them.

'Nonsense,' he said after a quick glance. 'We're in this together.'

'I'm terribly grateful to you both,' said Mike. 'I suppose I'd better organise some things for Chloe.' He attempted a smile. 'I don't suppose I'll need her birth plan and music-to-give-birth-by tape.'

'I'll just quickly check on Caroline and come and help you,' said Anna.

'I'll see to the boys,' said Rob. 'They're a bit too young for poker, I suppose?'

Mike nodded. 'But they'll have the shirt off your back at snap.'

If Mike felt able to joke then perhaps Chloe wasn't as seriously ill as they feared, Anna thought as she hurried next door.

When Anna had seen to Caroline she ran straight back. 'Hi, guys! It looks like we'll be looking after you for now,' she said brightly.

The three little boys, who had been staring up at Rob with round and anxious eyes, relaxed when they saw Anna. She always let them do things their mother wouldn't allow, and would probably let Caroline come over. Harry came up and put his arms round her legs. She picked him up, and he buried his face in her neck.

'Can we make fudge again?' asked Bruno, who was better at making a positive out of a negative than his brothers.

Anna glanced at Mike. The fudge-making episode was the sort of thing that made anxious parents doubt she was capable of looking after children. He shrugged and headed for the stairs.

Anna looked down at three expectant little faces. 'Possibly,' she said. 'But we'd have to do extra good tooth-brushing afterwards.' Then, hearing sounds of cupboard doors being opened and shut, she said, 'Right, I'll go up and see how Daddy's getting on. Why don't you boys show Mr Hunter – Rob – where the snakes and ladders is and we can play?'

As she climbed up the stairs, she heard someone wail that they didn't like snakes and ladders, it was scary!

Mike had a small bag open and seemed to be putting things into it without much thought as to their useful-ness.

'What do they think is wrong with Chloe?' asked Anna, checking the bag for a nightie and some underwear and not finding any. She took out two sweaters and a knot of tights.

'They didn't know last time I rang her but it might be a kidney stone,' Mike said, his voice edged with fear.

'Oh, that doesn't sound too bad!' Anna said as cheer-fully as she could. She found a clean nightdress and unhooked Chloe's light cotton wrap from the back of the door. 'I think it hurts like hell but doesn't kill you.'

'Are you sure?' asked Mike.

'Well, not absolutely, but I think so.' Anna tried to sound light-hearted. Mike was so worried and seeing such a large man white with anxiety was distressing. 'I'll just find Chloe some make-up. She'll be furious if there's a dishy young doctor and she hasn't got mascara.'

Mike smiled with relief. 'Thank you.' He squeezed her

arm with painful gratitude. 'I don't know what we'd do without you.'

Anna patted him. 'It's the least I can do after all you've done for me. Right, I hope that's all she'll need. Moisturiser, cleansing lotion, make-up, deodorant. Here's a bottle of lavender oil, that's very comforting.' She glanced at him. 'Maybe you should have that.'

'It was so awful, seeing her in pain like that. Worse than when she was having the boys. At least then I knew why she was in agony.'

'I'm sure she'll be all right, Mike,' she soothed. 'She's young, she's healthy, she's fit. I'm certain it can't be anything too dreadful.'

'Do you really think so?'

'Yes! Now, you go to her. We'll see to the boys.'

After Mike had hugged his sons, he said, 'Chloe's friend Susannah will come as soon as she can but just in case she can't, my parents live the nearest. I'll try them again from the hospital. They're rather strict, I'm afraid. It would be good if you could have the boys ready for bed. They have a no-splashing-in-the-bath policy.'

Anna nodded. 'That's the fudge-making idea out of the window, then.'

Mike smiled, as if he hadn't smiled for ages. 'It's such a relief you're here, Anna. We'll make it up to you, I promise.'

'Don't worry about that! You go to Chloe, and give her lots of love.' And she gently propelled him towards the stairs.

When Mike had gone, Anna said, 'I think we could get Caroline in now.' Although she had tried to hide it from Mike, she was really worried about Chloe, too. She bit her lip.

'Right.' Rob, who had organised the snakes and ladders very efficiently, got up and went over to Anna. 'You take over my counter and I'll fetch her. It's the red one. I'm not doing very well.' He put one arm round her shoulder and gave her a gentle squeeze. He murmured, 'Try not to worry too much. It's probably something quite minor, but if it isn't, she's in the right place.'

She threw him a grateful glance before taking her place at the table. 'That's why you want to fetch Caroline, is it? My go?' She shook the dice. 'Whoops. Straight down the anaconda. You're in a worse position now, Rob.'

'I like Ludo,' said Tom. 'No snakes.'

When Rob came back with Caroline the game was suspended so the boys could cuddle her and be licked in exchange. Then she was settled down on the hearthrug, as near to being out of the way as was possible for her.

'I'm just going to pop next door for a cardy,' Anna said. 'It's suddenly gone a bit chilly.' She didn't feel she could borrow one of Chloe's, somehow.

She realised it was worry that was making her cold, and found an old cardigan that Laura had discarded because it had a hole in the sleeve. It was very comforting, Anna decided.

She was about to go back again when her phone rang. It was Max.

'Hello, you,' he said. 'I was going to try and get down today, but something cropped up.'

'I couldn't have seen you anyway,' said Anna, forgetting to say hello. 'And now my friend, Chloe?' she rushed on, 'I've told you about her, is in hospital. I'm looking after her little boys.'

'Oh. That's very good of you. Isn't there anyone else?'

'Not at the moment, no. I don't mind doing it. They're great kids. I just popped back to my house for a cardigan. There's – someone else with them at the moment.'

'Well, can't they look after them, then?'

'No! They don't really know him.'

'It's a him, is it? How come he happens to be there?'

Anna heard the tension in his voice but decided she

had no time or emotional energy to explain Rob. 'He was just passing. He's holding the fort until I get back.'

'Oh. Well, give me a ring when you're free, then.'

Anna frowned as she put the phone down. She didn't want to analyse why she hadn't been more pleased to hear from him, she wanted to get back next door as quickly as she could.

Chapter Nineteen

❦

'Hi, guys!' Anna said as she walked through the front door. She'd brought back with her some tiny brass cup hooks that she'd fallen in love with, and bought for no other reason. 'I thought we might think up a game with these.'

'You were a long time,' said Bruno.

'Yes, sorry, the phone rang. You know how it is.'

Bruno nodded solemnly. 'Sometimes Mummy asks me to answer the phone and say she's out.'

'Does she?'

'Yes. 'Specially if she thinks it's Grandy.'

'Grandy? Is that Mummy's mummy, or Daddy's?'

'Daddy's.' Bruno sighed. 'They might be coming to look after us if Alistair's mummy can't. I wish you could stay and look after us.'

'The trouble is, I've got Caroline to look after, and I'm not sure I could manage all of you. And it's nice having your grandparents to stay, isn't it? Do they give you treats?'

'No. They say children have far too many toys these days.'

'Oh.'

'Do they take you to museums and things like that?' asked Rob.

Bruno nodded. 'And they only let us have ice cream if we've been good. And sometimes we've been good and they don't let us have ice cream. We haven't been good enough.'

'Oh,' said Anna, who felt this was very unfair. 'Well, I tell you what, let's have tea, and then a nice long bath, so you're all clean and in your pyjamas, with your teeth brushed, before whoever it is gets here. Then they'll read you a story.'

'Not if it's Grandy-pa,' said Bruno. 'He'll look in the cupboards for whisky and find Mummy's mess and then say that the chairs are uncomfortable, and Grandy will say the stairs are too steep.'

Rob and Anna exchanged glances. 'They are very steep,' said Anna.

'Yes,' agreed Rob firmly, 'but you couldn't have any other kind of stairs.'

'Can we have psgetti?' asked Tom, who'd been very quiet. 'And suck up the ends so it hits our nose? The Grandies never let us do that.'

'Oh, definitely,' said Anna. 'I like to do that too. Though not in public, of course.'

'What's public?' asked Tom.

'People you don't know,' said Rob. 'Anna wouldn't suck up her spaghetti like that if she was in a café or anything because that would be in public. Or at least, I hope she wouldn't.'

Anna laughed. 'Let's get cooking! Who's going to grate the cheese?'

The telephone rang and Anna ran to it. It was Mike. They had a brief conversation, then Anna hung up and turned to Rob. 'He says Chloe's had major painkillers and is asleep. He sounded a bit less worried but terribly tired. I bet Chloe tried to make him come home and he wouldn't.'

'He wouldn't want to leave Chloe before they knew what was wrong. That's most unreasonable.' Rob frowned, as if putting himself in that position. 'Besides, if he had to rush off again, it would be really unsettling for the boys, him being here and going away again.'

'Although, in a way, they're used to it.' She smiled. 'He also said that there's a bottle of wine in the cupboard under the window.'

'Good!' said Rob. 'Where's the corkscrew, Bruno?'

There was another call from Mike a short time later.

'They're going to keep Chloe in until they've done some more tests but they're going to let her sleep for a bit now.' His voice was rather strained.' 'I've rung my parents and they going to break their journey at a hotel as it seems likely that Chloe will be back home tomorrow. God, I'm going to have to keep them away somehow, Chloe has a real problem with them.'

As they went through her cupboards looking for strong drink and then complained at what they did find, Anna wasn't surprised.

'So, do you want us – me – to stay the night then?' she asked. This would make the sleeping arrangements interesting.

'Oh no. Susannah, Alistair's mother, is definitely going to come and stay, but she's got to get her own family settled first. She'll be over at about ten, if you can hang on until then.'

'Of course I can. Mike, are you all right?'

'Yes, I'm fine. I'm just worried. Chloe's never ill. Even when she had the boys she was up and about bossing everyone around about five minutes later. She looks so little somehow, now she's asleep.'

'If it's a kidney stone, I really don't think it's serious.' Anna tried to sound reassuring, but, like Mike, couldn't help being worried.

'I suppose you're right. They haven't rushed her off to theatre or anything like that. Are you guys all right?'

'Oh yes. We're having a great time.'

'And is Rob Hunter still there?'

Anna glanced across. 'He's helping Bruno crush garlic.

We're making spaghetti. In fact, I'd better go. I'm worried they'll get cloves of garlic muddled up with bulbs of garlic and we'll be ostracised from society for weeks. Give Chloe lots of love when she wakes up.' She disconnected. 'Hey, guys, that might be enough now. No, I don't think you're old enough to chop onions, but you could grate a carrot if you're very, very careful.'

While she supervised this activity, she said quietly to Rob, 'I can't help being worried because Mike is. I don't think he's a fusser, usually but that's the second time he's called.'

Rob put his arms round Anna and gave her a hug. It felt perfectly natural, and for a few seconds she hugged him back, finding comfort in the strength of his arms around her. Then he released her. 'She'll be all right. I'm sure of it.'

Anna, suddenly aware of the boys who were watching them with a mixture of revulsion and childish cynicism, said, 'How's the dinner getting on? It won't make itself, you know.'

'Are you getting married?' asked Bruno.

Anna turned away so that Rob couldn't see her blushing.

'No!' said Rob, with a laugh. 'I'm only giving an Anna a hug because she's a bit worried. Like Mummy hugs you if you fall over.'

'Why are you worried, Anna? Is it Mummy?' Bruno looked anxious.

'No,' she said hurriedly, 'it's the thought that your grandparents might come in the morning and find spaghetti all over the floor.'

'They don't like us,' said Bruno, nodding. 'We're too noisy.'

'You're not noisy,' said Anna, 'just a little loud. Sometimes.'

'I think that means noisy,' murmured Rob who had gone back to the tiny kitchen and was rummaging in

251

the fridge. 'I've found a stick of celery, shall we put it in?'

'Oh, good idea. But, Rob, if you want to go, so you can see to your dogs, you don't have to stay.'

He was indignant. 'I'm not spending all this time making psgetti—'

'Spaghetti,' corrected Bruno.

'– and not getting to eat it. My sister's got kids,' he added, 'I quite like them.'

'My sister's got them too. That makes us expert aunts and uncles, but what will we be like as parents? I mean, I wonder how I'd be as a mother,' Anna quickly added, realising what she'd just said. 'I think I might be a bit lax.' She thought of Laura, who had routines and star charts and chores for everyone.

'I'm sure you'd be fine,' Rob said – a little bleakly, Anna thought.

She swiftly changed the subject. 'But I can certainly manage as a solo aunt, so if you want to go . . .'

'I told you, I want to stay! It's fun with you guys.'

'What about your dogs?'

'I rang my neighbour. She's going to pop over and feed them and let them out. They've got each other. I'll go back later, when this lot are fed and in bed.'

Anna found herself unexpectedly pleased – he was such good company. She went back to the stove and concentrated on cooking the mince so it was all brown, and not just a solid mass of grey, the boys milling around her. For the second time she wondered how it would have been with Max. But the thought of Max in this merry mayhem didn't quite fit; she couldn't picture him happily cooking, assisted by three little helpers who relied more on enthusiasm than ability. Just as well she didn't see Max as husband and father material, although the fact that she didn't came as a slight shock. She carried on turning over the mince with a thoughtful frown.

'Penny for them,' said Rob, making her jump.

'I was just wondering if we should get them all bathed and then feed them, or feed them first and wash off the tomato sauce afterwards.' She smiled, pleased with her quick improvisation.

'Feed them first, definitely. There's no point in washing them twice.'

'True,' Anna agreed, 'but I think it might make them a bit late for bed.'

'It won't matter, I don't suppose. Hey, guys,' he said louder, and the boys, who'd lost interest in cooking and were now playing with their cars with ear-splittingly realistic sound effects, all looked up. 'Have you got school, playgroup, nursery, anything like that, tomorrow? It'll be Monday.'

'I hope not,' muttered Anna, 'because if I had to take you, we'd have to walk.'

'No,' Bruno piped up, beaming. 'It's half-term!'

'And Mummy was going to take us swimming,' Tom added hopefully.

'Well, there's no way I'd manage that on a bicycle,' said Anna. 'Perhaps Alistair's mummy could take you. If Alistair wanted to go.'

Caroline chose this moment to get up from her place on the hearthrug.

'Oh no, now she wants to go out!' Suddenly Anna understood why Chloe said she couldn't manage a dog and children.

'I'll take her round the block,' said Rob. 'It's my turn for a few adult moments.'

She smiled warmly at him. He was so good at being an uncle and she realised, worry about Chloe apart, she was enjoying this.

When he came back he gathered the children on to the sofa and read them a story, with all the voices.

Anna did a bit of washing up. How would it be to be

part of a couple, who lived and had children together? She was happy in her life – she had everything anyone could need: a career, a dog, friends, family who loved her, a glamorous lover. Why was she hankering after mundane domesticity? She stifled a sigh that was nearly audible. It was hard to admit it, but being a proper couple would be lovely.

'Hey ho,' she said out loud. 'I think the sauce is nearly ready. I'll just put the spaghetti on. I don't suppose any of you lot want to set the table?'

The boys regarded her indignantly. 'But we're having a story!'

'Of course. Sorry.' She'd heard Mike read the boys stories, but although he tried hard, he didn't do it quite as well as Rob did.

Bathtime was noisy and meant that all the towels had to go into the washing machine after they had mopped up the large amount of water on the floor. Rob and Anna were both soaked.

'I could probably rummage around and find a jumper of Mike's,' she said, looking at Rob's shirt, which was clinging to him in rather a revealing way. It reminded her of the scene in the television adaptation of *Pride and Prejudice* when Mr Darcy threw himself into the lake for no apparent reason.

'My sweater's downstairs. I'll be fine. There's a good heater in the car.'

'Are you going?' asked Bruno, although Anna wanted to know too.

'I'll wait until you lot are all tucked up and asleep, and then go. Anna will be here. Possibly for breakfast,' he added. 'Which makes you very lucky.'

'Why?' asked Tom.

'Because people like having breakfast with Anna, at least I assume they do.'

Anna laughed. 'Actually Alistair's mummy will be here for breakfast.'

The boys, bored with breakfast when they were still full of spaghetti, started turning their duvets into tents.

'None of that,' said Rob firmly, 'or there'll be no story.'

'But we've had a story,' said Bruno. 'Downstairs.'

'I'll read you another one,' said Rob, 'if you're all in your beds before I can count five.'

'Three! That was very good,' said Anna. 'Do you mind if I leave you to it and clear up?'

'But you'll miss the story!' said Tom.

'I'll read it to her later,' said Rob.

'Oh goody!' said Anna. She kissed all three boys good-night, and went downstairs.

She had found an old newspaper and was doing the crossword when Rob came down. He sat next to her on the sofa so he could read over her shoulder.

'Is that the cryptic one, or the quick?' he asked her.

'The quick one. We can do the cryptic if you like. This is last week's paper so I don't suppose anyone would mind.'

'One across. "In favour of very old, good man becoming college head",' Rob read out loud.

They chewed this over in silence. '"In favour of . . ." Pro?' said Anna.

'OK, what's a college head – provost! Well done!'

'Well, you got the clue,' said Anna.

'Yes, but I wouldn't have done if you hadn't got the first bit,' said Rob, taking the paper. 'Let's do another one.'

They had done a couple more clues when there was a knock on the door. Rob got up from the sofa and Anna was aware of a sense of loss. Doing the crossword together had been fun: cosy yet stimulating. She followed him to the door.

'Sorry I'm so late!' said a young woman of about

Chloe's age. 'I'm Alistair's mother, Susannah. Is there any news from the hospital?'

Realising that the relief babysitter had arrived, Anna passed on all the information she had about Chloe's condition.

'I don't think kidney stones are fatal,' said Susannah. 'Just painful.'

Eventually the handover was complete and Anna, Rob and Caroline found themselves outside under the night sky.

'You've been a real hero, Rob,' said Anna. 'The boys think you're top banana.'

'What?' he asked.

'It's a family expression. It means good.'

'That's all right then.' He peered down at her. 'I enjoyed doing the crossword.'

'Mm, so did I! I don't often get very far on my own, but with the two of us – I mean, doing it with someone else—'

'Two heads are better than one?'

Anna nodded solemnly. 'In this instance, yes, but mostly, two heads are just freaky.'

He laughed. 'You are funny.'

Anna chuckled. 'As long as that's not code for freaky, that's fine.' She paused, suddenly feeling awkward, unsure how to end a surprisingly enjoyable and intimate day. 'I'll walk down the lane to your car with you, give Caroline a chance to have a wee,' she said at last.

'Have you always used expressions like that or is living next door to small children having a bad effect on you?'

Anna smiled. 'No, I think I've always been like it. Now come on, it's way past Caroline's bedtime.'

He pulled her into his arms and ruffled her hair. 'Come on then, Bossy Boots.' He kissed her cheek and then pushed her away from him. 'Walk me to my car.'

* * *

Chloe returned at lunchtime the following day. 'I feel such a fraud,' she said, recumbent on the sofa, covered with the boys' teddies. The boys themselves were with Alistair and his hardy and stoical mother. 'It was such awful bloody agony, worse than labour, and then it went away. It came back from time to time, but I've got mega-strength painkillers if I get a twinge.'

'You're still supposed to take it easy,' said Mike, standing over her.

'I'm fine! Lapping up the attention and all the better for knowing your parents aren't coming to stay after all. Now be a dear and make us a cup of coffee. I want to know how Anna got on with the boys.'

'The boys were great! We had a super time.'

'And you had Rob Hunter with you?' Chloe's expression took on the gleam of a true matchmaker.

'Yes,' said Anna cautiously. 'We'd been to the country fair together and he stayed and helped me look after the boys.'

'Oh?'

'He's very good with children,' said Anna, trying to make Rob sound more like Mrs Doubtfire than Mr Darcy. 'He's got nieces and nephews. I met his sister.'

This sort of detail was meat and drink to Chloe. 'Oh, what's she like?'

'Scary but nice. She's very elegant and organised; everything I'm not, really. A bit bossy.'

'Sounds like you, darling,' said Mike, handing his wife a cup of coffee.

'I'm not bossy!' she said indignantly.

'Of course not,' said Anna, taking her cup. 'But we love you, even if you are.'

'So did anything happen between you and Rob?' asked Chloe when Mike had gone off to collect the boys.

'What would happen? I have a boyfriend, as you well know.'

257

Chloe snorted dismissively through her chocolate biscuit. 'But you do like Rob, don't you?'

'Of course I like Rob, he's a really nice guy, it's just not like that. We're friends, that's all.' She spoke firmly but wondered if this statement was as true as it had been.

'But are you friends with Max?'

'We're lovers, what more do you want?' Anna made a carefree gesture, hoping Chloe would stop her interrogation.

'Being friends is important, too. Almost more important in some ways. You want a man who'll be there for you in a crisis. Like Mike.'

'You've got a diamond in Mike, Chlo, I'll give you that.'

'But have you got a diamond in Max?' she persisted.

'I don't know! I expect so.' Although Anna really wasn't sure if this was the case. 'He gave me oysters, and scattered the bed with rose petals.'

Chloe snorted again and started to choke on biscuit crumbs.

Anna wasn't surprised to hear from Max the following day, especially since he'd known she'd been in the company of another man when he'd called on Sunday evening. But she was more shocked than surprised when she heard what he had to say.

'Darling, I'm bringing Julian down next weekend. He's very keen to see the house.'

'Oh God, it's not ready yet!'

He chuckled warmly. 'I'll give you until Sunday. We had a deal, remember? And afterwards, I want you to come and have tea with my mother.'

'Oh?' Her voice caught in her throat and came out as a squeak.

'It's ridiculous you and she living in the same village and not knowing each other properly.'

'I have met—'

'If you dress nicely and are very polite she won't connect you with the greenhouse-cleaning incident.'

Anna hadn't mentioned the jacuzzi incident, but at least for tea she wouldn't be wearing a bikini, not if she 'dressed nicely'.

'So that's settled then?'

'Yes.'

'Darling, you should sound a bit happier. I'm possibly selling your house for you and introducing you to my mother. It's not everyone I do that for you know.'

'Thank you, Max,' said Anna, hoping she sounded suitably grateful, dying to get off the phone so she could do something, make some sort of plan.

She walked round her house, trying to see it as a buyer would. There was a staircase. There were floors. The attic was going to be a fabulous space, large for such a small cottage because it went from the front to the back of the house. The space for the bathroom was there, and the jacuzzi bath that Anna had suffered so much to buy was waiting for her in a warehouse. All she had to do was to make a phone call, and it would be delivered. She really had done a great deal in a very short time. She was proud of herself.

Then she realised how much there was still to do and went round to Chloe's for proper coffee and comfort.

Chloe reacted with frightening calm. 'OK, we'll make a list of everything that needs doing.'

'Well, there's the decorating for a start. The end wall hasn't even had an undercoat on it. It makes the room look so much smaller pink.'

Chloe shot her an uncomprehending glance and found a pad of paper that was only half drawn on. She selected a red felt-tip pen from those on the table and started a new page.

'Decorate sitting room,' she said, writing it down. 'Though in my opinion it's important to divide it up into smaller jobs, or you never get to cross anything off.' She looked at Anna a little ruefully. 'I always write "brush teeth" on my list so I've got a chance of doing at least one thing on it.'

'Then there's the bathroom. That jacuzzi is ready and waiting, although how we'll get it up the stairs, God alone knows.'

'It's quite short, which is why you bought it,' said Chloe, chewing the end of the pen.

'I bought it because otherwise I'd have gone through all that torture for nothing!' said Anna indignantly. 'I'm not sure I approve of jacuzzi baths!'

'Oh, don't be so po-faced. It'll be fab, add thousands to the value. Now what else?'

'Curtains and carpets, where I haven't got polished boards.' She frowned. 'Although I can't possibly do that in the time. I'll leave that. Then there's the family bathroom.'

'You wouldn't have to plumb it in would you? Just put in the bath and stuff?'

Anna shook her head. 'It won't take long to do the plumbing, I've got the soil pipes.'

They discussed what else had to be done and then Chloe put the top back on the pen. 'So that's it then!'

'No! Then there's snagging!' Anna was beginning to see Chloe's point. There was no good writing 'decorate house' on the list or there'd never be a point when she could say she'd done it, not before Sunday anyway.

'What's snagging?' Chloe asked, taking the top off her pen again.

'It's all the little things, like bits of skirting that haven't ever been put on, bits that need fixing,' Anna explained. 'That usually has a list of its own.'

Make snagging list, wrote Chloe.

'It's no good, Chlo. I can't do it!'

'Yes you can. We have the Sisterhood to help us.'

'Who are the Sisterhood?' Anna looked at her friend in bewilderment. 'Chloe, if you're a member of a secret sect or a coven, I really wish you'd told me. A little witchcraft could have come in very handy.'

Chloe made a gesture with her hand that indicated Anna was an idiot. 'I don't mean anything like that! I just mean I have lots of friends who would absolutely love to come and help.'

'But why should they? Why would they want to work on someone else's house? I can't afford to pay very much.'

'Oh, it's not about the money! It's the fun! They won't want money. A few bottles of wine and some fish and chips or a Chinese will be more than enough payment.'

Anna didn't want to offend Chloe but she was doubtful about the thought of drunken amateurs splashing paint about her perfect house. 'But Chloe, the details are very important. It would be better for the job to be unfinished than finished badly, really.'

'Trust me! I'll only ask careful women who do their own decorating.'

'But where do they come from?' Anna was imagining an army of women with their heads tied up in scarves, wielding mops and buckets like something out of an Ealing comedy.

'Don't worry. I have friends in high places.' Chloe ticked off her fingers. 'Playgroup, mother-and-toddler group, swimming club, Junior Gym. Believe me, these are high-powered women with creativity on their hands.'

'Won't it wash off?' suggested Anna wickedly.

'Silly. I mean they all used to have high-powered jobs but now mostly just look after children. It would be a treat for them.'

Anna sighed. 'If you really think that you can get some of them to give me a hand—'

'Trust me, Anna.'

Anna frowned, not at all sure that, in this instance, she

did. 'I'd have to go home and make a snagging list,' she said.

'When the kids are in bed I'll come over and help you.'

'Where are they now?'

'Swimming again. It's brilliant. It really tires them out and cleans them at the same time. I don't usually take them at this time of day but Mike and a couple of his mates are all taking their kids swimming. Male bonding. It's great.'

Anna went home still feeling rather doubtful. She had very high standards. She didn't want unknown women slopping coats of emulsion about as if they were on reality TV.

Her worries weren't laid to rest when the following day a now fully recovered Chloe brought with her two women, even though they were both looking very businesslike.

'I worked in the theatre in my previous life,' said one, called Maddy. 'I can paint. And I don't just mean so it looks good from the back of the stalls.'

'I was in events management,' said the other, who was called Betsy. 'I can make a beside table out of an orange box quicker than you can say knife.'

'And anyone with in-laws like mine,' said Chloe, 'can make a place look good very quickly.'

Anna was dubious but didn't like to say so. 'And who's looking after your children?'

'Mike, mostly, although he's offered to come later to do any heavy stuff if we need him,' said Chloe. 'I'm the co-ordinator,' she added. 'The link woman, who runs between the two teams, seeing how you're getting on. Don't look so worried,' she went on, 'it'll be fine.'

'The finish is very important,' said Anna. 'It's better to leave a room undecorated than done badly,' she repeated, hoping she was getting her point across, without sounding too rude. She was the only qualified designer in the room, after all.

'We know that,' said Chloe. 'We all watch those property programmes.'

'OK then,' said Anna meekly. 'Who fancies their hand at tiling? That'll be my job then.'

'My brother's a tiler,' said Maddy. 'He's very good.'

'Then he'll want proper money,' said Anna, 'and I'm not sure—'

'It's all right, I'll tell him Betsy's here. He fancies her rotten.'

'Oh my goodness! I thought all my fanciability went when I had babies!' Betsy went into a minor swoon of happiness. Then she said, 'Have I met your brother, Madds? Are you sure he hasn't muddled me up with someone else?'

'Well, it doesn't matter,' said Chloe brutally, 'as long as he comes. They are lovely tiles,' she went on, looking at them.

'I've had them ages,' said Anna. 'I bought them from a friend who went to art school so they're all individual.'

'It would be a shame not to put them on properly,' said Chloe.

'I'm good at tiling, too,' said Anna firmly, 'but as I'm good at lots of things, I'd better delegate. Oh, I didn't mean that quite how it sounded.'

'It's OK,' said Betsy, still high on being fancied by a younger man now she was in her mid-thirties. 'We know what you mean. Now get on the phone to that brother of yours, Maddy, I want a look at him.'

Obligingly he came. He was young, shy and very sweet. All the women except Anna wanted to mother him. He was soon happily applying the hand-made tiles in the bathroom and round the kitchen sink. To begin with, Anna hovered over him, but then realised that he knew what he was doing and left him to it.

The decorating went well too. It was a cottage and the walls were uneven so the glassy finish achieved in Max's flat wasn't necessary. Anna covered every inch of the floor with dust sheets and taped them in place. Then she sanded the walls. It was one of those jobs that no one could think of as fun but was so important. While she was doing this, Betsy and Maddy went to buy brushes, rollers and everything else they could think of from the local builders' merchant where Anna had an account. When they got back, Anna was ready for them to start.

'We'll only do the walls,' she said. 'There just isn't time to do the woodwork, but having the walls done will make a big impression.'

'Hm,' said Maddy. 'I think we could get one coat on, if we tried. I do really understand about sanding the wood really well, and then filling,' she insisted.

'Let's get the walls finished first,' said Anna, not convinced.

As the sitting room was too small for more than two people to work in at once, Chloe took charge of the vacuum cleaner. She had a previously unsuspected eye for dust.

'If we keep cleaning up behind us,' she said, pointing her nozzle at where Maddy was drilling holes so that they could hang a small cupboard in the kitchen, 'it means we can stop at any time. It won't look finished, but it won't look a shambles, either.'

'Quite right,' said Maddy. 'It'll keep the dust out of the paint, too. But would you like to go upstairs now?' Chloe had become rather over-enthusiastic with the hoover.

Anna turned her specialist attention to filling the gaps in the skirtings and staircase. Some needed little fillets of wood, measured with infinite precision and slotted into place. Others just needed filler, applied with the delicacy of a make-up artist. It was exacting work and she loved it.

Chloe was an excellent motivator. If ever a tea break became too long, she chivvied them back to work like an over-zealous sheepdog. They might have all felt like small boys from time to time, but she meant well so they forgave her.

All the women worked long hours. Anna was now feeling guilty that she'd ever doubted their ability and, bone-weary herself, would have given up and gone to bed but they wouldn't go home. 'It's because it's time out from our real lives,' explained Maddy. 'If we go home, we'll have to deal with nappy buckets and plates covered with baked-bean juice: all that domesticity.'

'But you'd be slumped on the sofa with a glass of wine by now,' protested Anna. 'It's ten o'clock!'

'Yes, but if we went home now we'd have to do all that stuff before we could slump. Men don't multi-task on the whole,' Betsy added.

'Talking of men, where's Rob when you need him?' asked Chloe, putting the kettle on, having decreed the area an alcohol-free zone until the house was done. 'Why isn't he here helping you?'

'I really don't think there's much he can do,' Anna said, 'and let's face it, the house isn't big enough for any more helpers.'

Chloe harrumphed.

Chapter Twenty

Anna had Saturday to herself, her helpers having returned to their families. It had been enormous fun getting everything finished together but there were several things that Anna needed to do without the accompaniment of chat and laughter. The bath had to be boxed in and the tongue-and-groove panelling fitted, and then painted. She loved carpentry and knew she was good at it, although she'd never describe herself as a professional cabinetmaker. There was a lot more sanding to be done before the first coat of paint went on the door frame. She spent most of the day up there, calling down to Caroline from time to time and taking her out often. Chloe and Mike were visiting grandparents with the boys, and after the bustle of the previous week, Anna experienced a sense of peace that sometimes felt like loneliness.

At about six o'clock, when Anna had realised she was hungry and needed to eat, there was a knock at the door. It was Rob.

'Hi,' he said.

She found herself very pleased to see him, possibly because she'd been alone all day and had become accustomed to company. 'Oh, hello! How nice to see you! Come in!'

'Thank you.' He smiled down at her but he seemed more serious than when they had gone to the novelty dog show together. 'I shouldn't have come really . . .' He paused. 'I just – I wanted to see how you've been getting on.'

Anna wondered why he appeared so reluctant, but didn't ask. 'It's nearly finished. Chloe organised a team of women who helped. It was like *Changing Rooms*.'

He laughed and relaxed a bit. 'Goodness, did they drive you mad?'

Anna laughed back at him. 'Well, sometimes. They were rather inclined to go for the quick effect, and some things you can't skimp on. But they were great fun.'

'I wish I could have come and helped you.' He sounded apologetic.

'But why should you? You've got your own house to renovate.'

'I would have come. Chloe told me you've got someone coming to see it tomorrow, but I was fantastically busy at work.'

'That's all right!' Anna suddenly realised that she would have enjoyed having him as part of the team. She could have left him to do things without feeling the need to supervise him constantly. 'Come and have a tour. Pretend you're Julian.'

'Julian?'

'He's the person coming to see the house. He's an old schoolfriend of my boyf—, Max's.' Then she wondered why she'd changed 'my boyfriend' to 'Max'. Did she feel ambivalent about giving him that title?

He paused. 'Ah. Well, let me say hello to Caroline properly and then lead on, sell me this desirable property.'

Anna hoped Julian wouldn't be quite so attentive to the fine details as he was. 'I really didn't have a lot of time,' said Anna defensively. 'And Maddy and Betsy aren't professional decorators.'

'It's fine. You've done a great job. Who did your plumbing?'

'I did my plumbing,' she said, failing to sound modest. 'Although it's not hard these days with plastic fittings,' she continued. 'It's not like I had to do brazing with lead and brass and what have you. The hard part was getting the bath up the stairs. It took Mike, Maddy's brother, and us four women. The newel post got a bit knocked about, but I sanded it down and decided it was character.'

Rob laughed. 'It is character. Your character. You've really put your stamp on this little house, Anna.'

Anna looked doubtful. 'I don't suppose that's a good thing with an investment property. Those television programmes always tell you to think of what most people want and to try not to be too individual.'

'Oh no, I didn't mean to imply that your taste is eccentric, just that you can tell this has been designed round the house, to suit it, not a standard Cotswold stone cottage. It isn't designed by numbers: magnolia paint, granite kitchen, top-of-the-range appliances.'

'I couldn't afford any of those things. I'm hoping Julian will appreciate the recycled iroko worktop and not yearn for granite.' She was flattered by Rob's appraisal, but still had her doubts. That might be what Julian preferred. After all, Max and Julian were friends. Could Julian possibly like anything so different to Max's icily glossy apartment?

Rob rested his shoulders against the wall and folded his arms. 'So, how do you feel about it, now it's finished and might be sold quite soon?'

Anna leant against the arm of what used to be Caroline's bed and now was an elegant piece of furniture – or at least, that was the idea. She took off the white cotton double bedspread that converted the elderly faded chintz-covered lump into a comfortable sofa. It wasn't supposed to be sat on, it was to be tucked neatly round to look like a proper cover and not a throw. She had been given strict instructions to put it on only moments before Julian arrived, to preserve its whiteness, but she had forgotten and Caroline had spent a comfortable night on it.

'Mm?' Rob prompted her gently, having watched her

shake and fold the bedspread, possibly guessing she was avoiding answering his question.

'I am very pleased to think that I might be able to pay back Will and Laura. They're not asking me for the money or anything, but I know they do need it. And I'm really pleased with how it's all gone. There've been no major problems, once I'd accepted I had to put it back to how it was before it was all stripped out.'

Rob ignored this reference to their early association. 'I'm sensing a "but",' he said.

'I know it's silly but I've grown attached to this house, it really feels like home,' Anna said wistfully. 'And I love Chloe, Mike and the boys, who've been so good to me. The thought of leaving it all is . . . well, it's making me quite melancholy.' She made a face to lighten her words but felt it hadn't really worked.

Sympathy and understanding crinkled the corners of his eyes. 'Well, we can't have you melancholy. When did you last eat? You're thin as a rail, I bet you don't eat when you're working.'

'I do get a bit absent-minded about it and I tend to live on chocolate.' But Max liked her thin, she remembered. He'd remarked on her slenderness in very flattering terms.

'Then you need to eat,' he repeated firmly but gently.

'I was thinking of getting myself something, but I couldn't bear to mess up the kitchen. The girls made it look so wonderful.'

'It is a very nice kitchen, but if you won't cook in it, you'll have to eat out. Let's go to the pub.'

'The appliances are all B grade, but I've managed to conceal the chips and things,' Anna said.

'I'm really impressed.' Rob looked around the tiny but immaculate space.

'I am quite proud of it,' Anna admitted. 'I bought every-thing over the Internet.'

269

'Great. But right now I insist on taking you to the pub. You need high-fat, high-carb food. Nothing like it for lifting your spirits when you feel a bit blue.'

'I shouldn't be blue, of course, I should be elated, and in a way—' Anna broke off.

'Stop trying to analyse your feelings,' said Rob, heading for the back door. 'I'll put Caroline in the garden for a couple of minutes and then we'll go.'

'OK,' said Anna, aware that she was being bossed about and not objecting enough. 'But it's on me. Otherwise I won't come, and will probably faint with hunger.'

Rob put his hand on her arm. 'Go and comb your hair or something. I'll see to Caroline.'

They walked through the footpaths to the pub. It was a lovely summer's evening and the pub garden was full of families and couples.

'Let's go inside, where it's quieter,' said Rob. 'You look too shattered for anywhere noisy.'

He guided her to a table in the corner where a large black settle formed a cosy seat. He fetched a couple of menus from the bar.

'Right, so you've had no breakfast—'

'I had a bar of chocolate!' she protested.

'No breakfast. Lunch?'

She shook her head. 'Last week Chloe kept making sandwiches and bringing them over. She was in her element. The other women – Maddy and Betsy – they loved it too, although it was such hard work. They were getting away from their families.' Anna was aware she was rambling a bit, but tiredness was scrambling her brain.

'I can imagine you had a ball. Now let me get you a drink and then you can tell me all the details.'

'This was supposed to be on me!' she called pathetically to his back.

'You're dreadfully bossy,' she complained, after he had persuaded her to order steak and chips when she said she just wanted a light meal.

'My sister is bossy. I'm just doing my duty as a friend. Have some more wine.'

The joy of spending an evening with someone who wasn't your boyfriend was that you didn't have to try and make yourself appealing, you could just say what you really thought, admit ignorance, fling your hands about to make a point. After the first few restorative mouthfuls, Anna began to tell him about the last frantic week of getting the house, if not finished, at least presentable.

He listened attentively and asked pertinent questions but the moment Anna put her knife and fork together he said, 'Pudding. I insist you have pudding.'

She looked across at him, about to refuse, and caught an expression in his eyes that confused her. Trying to interpret it, she held his gaze too long and looked away, suddenly embarrassed. He cleared his throat. 'Treacle tart. I prescribe treacle tart.'

'You're being very profligate with my money,' she said, trying to pretend there hadn't been a moment of unexpected intimacy.

'That's fine. I'm sure after tomorrow you'll be able to afford it. I'll get you another glass of wine, too.'

'It would have been more economical if we'd had a bottle,' she said.

'Yes, but unlike you, I have to drive.'

'I'm sure the treacle tart would blot up quite a lot of alcohol. My sister has a recipe that uses condensed milk or something. It's about a million calories a bite but so delicious.' She paused. 'I really don't know if I could manage any, really.'

'We could share one.'

'Oh yes! That is a good idea. Here, let me!' She made

to get up but he wouldn't let her move. She watched him go to the bar and thought that he was a fine figure of a man. A bit taller than Max and not nearly as well dressed, but he would definitely make someone a lovely husband. She closed her eyes to think about Max, but she found his image strangely hard to conjure.

She opened her eyes with a start when Rob spoke.

'I ordered it with cream and ice cream because I didn't know which you'd like best and was too idle to come over and ask you.'

He smiled and Anna suddenly realised that sharing a pudding was rather an intimate thing to do. But he was a friend; friends did share puddings.

'I think I'll just pop to the loo and wash my hands,' she said as she clambered out of her seat.

'Don't smudge your make-up,' he said.

'I'm not wearing any!'

'I know. Now go, and hurry back. If it arrives before you do I may eat it all.'

He was a bit of a conundrum, she decided, using a paper towel to blot her face, which, she realised rather too late, had been very dirty. Most of the time he was a really good friend, one she liked and respected very much, but every now and then he made her doubt her feelings – about him and about Max. She was overtired and not thinking straight, she concluded, and went back to the table.

'Oh my goodness. I've never seen anything so decadent in my entire life!' she exclaimed. 'Thank goodness we didn't order one each by mistake!'

'It does look fairly substantial, but as it represents about three meals for you, I think you should tuck in. We've got two spoons here.'

It crossed Anna's mind that however attentive and sophisticated Max was, with vintage champagne at the ready and rose petals on the bed, he would never have encouraged Anna to eat like Rob did. Of course, food wasn't love and one shouldn't confuse them, but somehow, at that moment, she found Rob's nanny-like caring appealing. However hungry she was, she would never have eaten with quite such abandon with Max watching her.

She picked up her spoon and, paying careful attention, cut off a piece of tart, making sure she took a bit of ice cream and cream at the same time. She smiled ecstatically at him and put it in her mouth. 'This is really fabulous,' she mumbled through a large mouthful. 'You'd better dig in before I eat it all.'

'Not a chance. Let me at it.'

An undignified race followed. Anna triumphantly speared the last piece of crust. 'I win!' she cried, rather louder than she had intended. 'That means I get to pay.'

She had reached the bar and was pulling her wallet out of the back pocket of her jeans before he had even started to move. As she handed her credit card over, laughing, the barman said, 'It's not often my customers are so keen to part with their money.'

'It was a really delicious meal. Thank you,' she said, having put in her pin number. She handed across a five-pound note. 'I'll definitely come again.'

They walked down past the village shop, through the summer night, in silence. The fragrance of a nearby philadelphus mingled with some tobacco plants. She was going to miss the village so much, she realised, and resolved to buy somewhere else as near as possible.

'You really don't need to walk me home,' she had protested to Rob.

'Yes I do,' he had said, brooking no argument.

'Nothing bad is going to happen to me, you know.' She realised that him walking her home would turn the evening into a date, and not just a meal between friends. A second later she knew it had been a lovely date, one she didn't really want to end.

'I know,' he said quietly.

As it wasn't exactly far out of his way – his car was only parked up the lane – Anna didn't argue further, but her mind was racing. Why had she enjoyed a meal in the pub with Rob so much more than the grand restaurant she had been to with Max? And how would it end? She suddenly felt funny about the simple kiss on the cheek that would finish any normal evening with a friend.

'That was a really nice evening,' she said quickly and slightly formally as they arrived at her front door. 'Thank you so much.'

'I should be thanking you,' said Rob. 'In fact I do thank you, very much.'

Anna looked up at him in a fog of confusion. All that she thought she'd been certain of had blurred, so she didn't know where she was any more. If Rob magically turned into Max she'd feel disappointed. She wanted friendly, easy Rob more than glamorous Max, whom she'd loved for years.

Rob put his hands on her shoulders. Then he brushed her hair back from her face and cradled it gently. Her heart began to beat faster as she anticipated his kiss. He bent his head and then they both heard voices along the lane and he straightened up, a flicker of frustration passing across his face.

'Hello!' whispered Chloe, carrying a sleeping child. 'What have you been up to?'

'We've had dinner at the pub,' said Rob shortly. 'What about you?'

'A day with my parents. They wanted to see for themselves that I was all right so they invited us to lunch. Very hard work, I can tell you.'

Mike appeared carrying a bigger child. 'Let's get these monsters into bed,' he said. 'Then I'll go back and get Harry.'

'Well, goodnight then,' said Rob when Chloe and Mike

had disappeared into the house with their bundles. 'And thank you very much for a wonderful evening. Good luck tomorrow.' He gave her a quick peck on the cheek and turned away.

As Anna watched him walk down the path in front of the cottages she wondered what would have happened if Chloe hadn't appeared just then. Once she was finally in bed, having let Caroline out and in again, she contemplated Max and Julian's visit tomorrow afternoon. It would be nice to see Max again, she decided. But when she closed her eyes it was Rob she thought of. How very odd, she murmured, when I'm not in love with him at all.

'All it needs now is a big vase of lilies on the coffee table,' said Chloe the next morning, wiping her hands on her jeans.

'Not with Caroline in the house, thank you,' Anna laughed. 'Although of course she won't be in the house because you lot are taking her for a walk.'

Chloe nodded. 'If there's one thing I've learnt about selling houses it's that you must remove all pets.' She frowned thoughtfully. 'Although I suppose if you had a very beautiful exotic breed of cat that was the same colour as the suede sofa, you might be all right.'

'I haven't got a suede sofa, although mine does look heaps better with that throw over it, thank you, Chloe.' She'd managed to brush most of the dog's hairs off it, after Caroline's nocturnal visit.

'As long as no one sits on it, it should stay tucked in like that,' Chloe said. 'That's the joy of throws. No one with children could have a white sofa, but you can have lots of throws and just chuck them in the washing machine when they get dirty. White does make everything look bigger. Very important.'

Chloe sounded so knowledgeable that Anna asked,

'Have you sold many houses, Chlo? I thought you bought next door when you were first married.'

'Oh, we did, but when I was breastfeeding Bruno, I watched an awful lot of daytime television telling you how to turn your slum high-rise into a penthouse flat.'

'I watched quite a lot of that sort of thing when I was a student.' Anna tweaked the throw once more for good measure.

'You can't do that when you've got more than one baby, of course, unless it's *The Tweenies*, or something.' She sighed, as if she missed those months spent on the sofa, switching her hungry baby from one breast to the other, with no apparent space in between feeds. 'All the houses had lilies when the people came round.'

'Well, even if you are removing Caroline' – Anna glanced at her dog who had been banished to her indoor kennel while the set-dressing had gone on – 'I'm not having lilies. They're terribly expensive and the pollen marks your clothes.'

Chloe laughed and perched herself on a stool. 'As if you care! But we haven't got time to go into town and buy some, and anyway those twigs look nice. Anyone would think you'd actually bought them. What time are they coming?'

'Half past two. They'll have had lunch with Max's mother. Lucky things.' Anna pulled a face and rearranged the twigs for the hundredth time.

'Aren't you invited for tea?' Chloe said mischievously.

'Yes, but I'm not going to go. I just couldn't face it. She's bound to recognise me and I'd have to raid your wardrobe, again.'

'She is the sort of person who'd judge you by your clothes.'

Anna bit her lip. 'Max dresses beautifully and I really like seeing the way his suits fit, but the trouble is, it makes me think I have to, too. That was what was so nice about going out with Rob last night.'

'What?' Chloe's matchmaking antennae leapt to attention.

Anna flapped a calming hand. 'Oh, you know, just being able to slob out together, sharing a pudding, letting him practically carry me home.'

'You weren't that drunk, were you?'

'Of course not. I was very tired and I sort of leant on him. Now, do you think the house looks all right?' Anna changed the subject before Chloe started asking more questions she didn't feel ready to answer.

'It looks fantastic!' Chloe reassured her. 'And it doesn't show that it's not actually finished. The staircase is to die for.'

'It's quite like your staircase, actually, and I haven't noticed you dying for that.'

'You know what I mean. It looks totally original. And the bathroom is posh enough to eat your dinner out of.'

'Now, Chloe, I'm aware that my appetite has increased somewhat over the last few days, but it's not fair to suggest . . .'

Chloe pushed her. 'You know what I mean. That bath is bloody gorgeous.'

Anna laughed. 'And so it should be, the torture I had to go through to get it! Naked in front of thousands of people, surrounded by bubbles! It would have been less trouble to install one carved from a single ruby.'

'Red wouldn't look right with all the stripped elm,' said Chloe seriously.

Anna made a face at her. 'And it would have been far too heavy. The structural engineer would have made me reinforce the floor even more than he did.'

'But all that went very well, I thought.'

'Oh yes, it did. I've been very lucky with my officials,' she said, thinking of Rob in particular. 'And with my friends,' she added, putting her hand on Chloe's arm. 'Thank you for helping me do all this. Not only did you get Betsy and Maddy along, but you've worked really hard today. And I know it wasn't easy for you getting the boys looked after, even with Mike around.'

'You know perfectly well I've loved it. So did Maddy and Betsy. And you didn't ask me to help you, I just summoned the team and we barged in and did it.'

'I know, but it looks super and I didn't have the right things to set it off.' She frowned. 'I just hope we haven't gone over the top and made it look like a show home.'

'Not at all! It looks like a really expensive magazine interior. It was good you managed to get a top coat on the woodwork. It does set it all off.'

Anna smiled and then looked at her watch. It was nearly two o'clock. 'They'll be here soon. I'm really nervous. Supposing they don't like it? Or rather, Julian doesn't like it?'

'That's fine! You've very nearly finished the house and it's all ready for the next viewer.'

'But don't forget the—'

'—market's very flat. You've said that a million times. Now can I be bossy and suggest you change your jumper? The welt from your sleeve is hanging off and it's got paint or something on it.'

'It was very expensive paint, rat-dropping brown, or some equally esoteric colour. But I will change.' She looked at her friend. 'I think I'm partly nervous about seeing Max again, too. This will be the first time he's seen me looking more or less au naturel.'

'You go and put on some slap. I'll take Caroline then you can put the cage outside.'

Anna didn't bother to remind her it was an indoor kennel, not a cage.

278

Chapter Twenty-One

❦

'Sorry we're late, darling,' said Max, kissing her cheek. He and Julian had finally arrived at three o'clock, smelling of brandy and cigars. 'We popped into the pub after lunch. Ma serves excellent wine but not a lot of it. You remember Julian?'

'Of course! Come in, both of you,' she said, gesturing for them to enter, a smile firmly fixed on her face.

'Oh dear, Julian, I do hope you haven't plans for cat swinging in the immediate future,' murmured Max, sending Anna a consolatory smile.

'It is small,' said Anna, refusing to be cast down by this criticism so early in the proceedings. 'But that's reflected in the price.' She wasn't sure that it was, actually. The enormous amount seemed to reflect a premium for really tiny cottages.

'Small, but very charming,' said Julian. His smile was genuine. 'Do give me the tour.'

'Well, the walls are painted in a colour called Sour Milk. It was the nearest thing I could get to a traditional lime plaster. I think it works rather well, don't you?'

'Certainly,' Julian agreed. Max was peering at the walls, a slight frown on his face.

Anna ignored him and kept her attention on Julian. 'This is obviously the reception room,' she said. 'The kitchen's at the back, as you can see. It's all fitted with brand-new appliances of very high quality.' If you didn't count the odd, well-hidden chip or scratch, she thought.

'You have done a good job in the kitchen,' said Max, 'I'll say that for you.'

Anna beamed at him, almost forgiving him for the remark about cats.

'It is a bit of a shame that the listings people didn't let you open up that end. It would have made it all seem much more spacious,' Max went on. 'Nothing to stop you doing that after you've bought it, of course,' he said over his shoulder to his friend.

'Except you'd have to put it all back when you came to sell,' said Anna, who was certain this wouldn't be Julian's final resting place. 'This is a very important row of cottages. The listings people are very keen to preserve it.' She would tell Rob personally if she got wind of anything being done that wasn't absolutely permitted. Chloe would spy for her.

'This is a very fine staircase,' said Max. 'Is it original?'

Anna's feelings were rent asunder. Should she express her huge indignation that Max had obviously forgotten her telling him, in painful detail, that she had built the staircase herself, or be absolutely thrilled that he'd made such a mistake?

'I think Anna made it herself,' said Julian approvingly. 'She told me all about it when we met before.'

The look on Max's face took all the sting out of him forgetting, or not listening to her. He was virtually speechless. 'Oh,' he said eventually. 'Well. Anna. What can I say? You are a clever girl.'

Anna winced at this slightly condescending remark and then put it down to the brandy.

'No one would ever have guessed it wasn't original,' said Julian admiring her work.

'I was lucky. I had some super wide elm boards I could use, to keep it entirely authentic.'

'You're extremely talented,' said Julian.

'Why don't we find out if they work and go upstairs?'

said Max with a laugh. 'You must have finished seeing the downstairs by now.'

One by one they went upstairs.

'As you can tell, there's one bedroom on this first floor and a small family bathroom,' Anna said.

'Excellent bath, sweetheart,' said Max. 'How did you track it down?'

Anna hesitated for a moment and decided she didn't want to regale Julian and Max with her Kylie Minogue impression at the Home Decorators' Fayre. 'On the Internet. We couldn't have got a bigger one up the stairs, even if there'd been room for it. As it is, it all fits in nicely.' This had been a huge relief, because although the bath had felt small, and she'd done her sums, she hadn't been quite sure it would actually fit until it had.

'I prefer a shower myself,' said Max.

'And for people who prefer a shower,' she said, regarding him sternly, 'there's one in the en suite upstairs.'

'An en suite? I hardly hoped for one of those,' murmured Julian, following Anna up the next flight of stairs.

Her bedroom (she had decided to move up here for the space, and the view, of course) had never looked so tidy. All extraneous bits and pieces had been put in a carrier bag and hidden under her dressing gown which was hanging on the back of the door. This was Chloe's tip, learnt from having exacting in-laws. With windows on both sides, a dormer in the front and a roof-light at the back, the space seemed much larger than it was.

'Very sweet,' said Max, who obviously didn't really appreciate sweet.

'Look at that view!' exclaimed Julian with a sigh. 'Fantastic! You can see for ever.'

'Oh yes,' agreed Max, barely glancing out of the window. 'Clothes storage?'

'Clothes storage is here.' Anna opened what seemed to be a wall, but inside was a hanging rail that swung forward to reveal drawers behind. Chloe had suggested she put some of her clothes inside to prove it worked, but Anna had felt it was perfectly obvious it did. The mechanism was so slick, she could have spent all day opening and shutting it.

'Hmm. Let's have a look at this en suite, then. Oh my goodness!'

Pleased to have his appreciation at last, Anna smiled as he and Julian inspected her bathroom.

'I did think about having it as a wet room,' she explained, 'but I felt a walk-in shower was better. I was only allowed to have it as there had been some sort of built-in cupboard before. I was able to extend it by putting piano hinges on the edge of the original door, making it big enough for an entrance.'

'It has the wow factor. I'll give you that,' Max admitted, 'but it is absolutely tiny!'

'It has everything you need,' declared Anna defiantly. Chloe had donated a cube of soap bought from a French market. Its chunky shape gave the little room masculine appeal. Chloe had, she assured Anna, more feminine shapes if Anna had to show any women round.

'It certainly has,' said Julian, inspecting the tiling and finding it perfect. 'You have done an amazing job. It's modern and yet totally in keeping. And have the listed people approved it all?'

'They haven't made an official inspection yet,' said Anna. 'But I'm not anticipating any problems.' Rob would have told her, she knew that.

'Let's go back downstairs,' said Max, somewhat impatiently, Anna felt. 'I'm beginning to feel a little claustrophobic.'

'I thought you said you had a dog,' said Julian when they were downstairs once more.

'I have. My neighbour's looking after her. She's rather large. And she doesn't like men very much,' she added, looking pointedly at Max.

'It's a shame there isn't room for a huge American fridge,' said Max, who had returned to the kitchen.

'It's a workman's cottage in the Cotswolds.'

'One does have to move with the times, darling. I would have thought you'd have known that, being an interior designer.' He gave her a teasing smile.

Anna felt the need to escape. Max, although being supportive in his own way, was irritating her. 'Perhaps you two would like a look round on your own?'

Julian gave her an apologetic look. 'I have brought a tape measure with me. If you wouldn't mind me measuring up a little? I've got one or two key pieces of furniture . . .'

'Of course I don't mind,' she said.

She went outside so she wouldn't hear them discussing her house. It was tiny, too tiny to sell except to midgets or possibly fairies. All her hard work and money had been a complete waste of time. She went back in and heard big, male feet tramping over her heart.

At last they came down. Julian smiled. 'I do really like it, but it is on the small side. Can I let you know when I've done some more measuring in my current flat?'

'Of course.'

'And if you get an offer in the meantime, let me know, but if someone wants to snap it up I perfectly understand.'

'Fine.' She didn't feel fine, she felt totally deflated. She also felt extremely foolish for assuming he was really interested in anywhere so bijou. He was a man. He had huge feet. He'd want more space.

'It's very good that Julian's so keen,' whispered Max, meaning to be positive but instead being patronising.

'Now make yourself tidy, Ma's expecting us for tea. We'll wait down here.'

She was too desolate to argue. The black trousers were shaken and put on, with a cardigan of Chloe's that had somehow not got back to her. A hasty swipe of lipstick and a scrub of mascara and that had to do. Fortunately it was a very nice cardigan in a pretty coral pink and the effect was fairly feminine. Laura's suede loafers sorted out her feet and she was ready.

They walked along the same lanes as Anna and Rob had walked the previous evening, but the atmosphere was utterly different. Then it had been a pleasant amble along scented lanes, now, wearing Laura's shoes, which were slightly too big, it seemed a stony, rutted path. Max's instructions didn't help. She was glad Julian was with them.

'If my mother realises you were one of the people who cleaned her greenhouse she'll be furious,' Max said. 'She has very old-fashioned views on servants being too familiar and it will embarrass her horribly.'

'But she won us in a raffle! That hardly makes us servants.' She was glad she hadn't ever told him about the jacuzzi incident, although she was fairly sure Mrs Gordon hadn't recognised her under the bubbles.

Max was walking rather fast and because of the narrowness of the lane, Anna had to trot behind him, her shoes flapping. Julian made up the rear.

'She just doesn't have a sense of humour about these things, so try and be tactful!' Max shouted back to her.

He didn't seem to have a sense of humour about those things either. 'It's hardly likely I'm going to say anything if she doesn't!' Anna said indignantly.

'I never know with you, Anna, you can be quite unpredictable.'

Another bad mark against her. Anna sighed.

*　*　*

Mrs Gordon looked at Anna a little curiously when Max made the introductions but she didn't say anything to make Anna anxious, so she tried to relax.

Max ushered them all into the drawing room where plates of sandwiches cut into tiny triangles were set out. An old-fashioned cake stand held a Victoria jam sponge and a coffee and walnut cake. The latter, of which Anna had eaten a few at Chloe's, was instantly recognisable as bought from the WI stall at the market. A spectre of fear that perhaps Mrs Gordon had witnessed that particular humiliation as well as everything else brushed Anna like a cold hand. She shook it off. The woman wasn't haunting her, after all.

A red and gold rose-covered tea set, which could well have been Mrs Gordon's best, sat next to a pile of silver cake forks. Tea was not a meal to be taken lightly, obviously, and Anna, imagining how Caroline would have reacted to such daintiness coupled with such accessibility, inwardly smiled.

As bidden, Anna sat on the sofa while Max and Mrs Gordon disappeared to the kitchen to bring in the actual tea.

'I expect Mrs Gordon warms the pot, don't you?' said Anna in a low voice to Julian, making conversation.

'Oh, definitely.'

He didn't say anything else, so Anna amused herself by admiring her surroundings. It was a pretty room with French windows looking on to the garden. It was filled with antique furniture and ornaments, and looked to Anna as if the contents of a much larger house had all been squeezed into this one as if keeping everything had been more important than making the room attractive.

There were a couple of large bureaux, a plethora of little tables and several small chairs, and every flat surface was covered with ornaments, silver photograph frames and crystal. If the contents had been reduced by two-thirds, it would have been a truly lovely, timeless room. The wallpaper was a faded Zoffany print that looked more like a painting than wallpaper, depicting parrots against a blue sky. Many of the ornaments were parrots and if Anna had been let loose on it, she'd have emphasised the parrot theme. Particularly when Mrs Gordon appeared holding a teapot stand and she realised that her hostess was a parrot, too.

Max poured the tea, leaving Mrs Gordon free to turn to Anna and begin her interrogation. She didn't need to interrogate Julian: his family tree and job history were well known to her.

'What is it you do again?' Mrs Gordon asked her. 'You seem faintly familiar. I wonder if I've seen you in a shop, or something.' It was quite clear that Mrs Gordon would have expected to find Anna behind the counter of any shop they might have shared space in.

'I'm an interior designer,' said Anna politely.

Mrs Gordon made an irritated flapping gesture, as if Anna had declared she did something arcane and possibly heathen, like training butterflies for a circus. 'Which is?'

Anna swallowed, wishing Max would hurry up with her tea, and tried to think of a way of describing what she did that wasn't just 'designing interiors'. 'Well, currently, I'm doing up a house for sale, but my work involves rearranging interiors for maximum use of space and light, things like that. It involves a bit of architecture. Max was one of my tutors at college.'

'A guest lecturer, darling,' he corrected her, handing her a cup of tea at the same time. 'One couldn't afford to have been one full time.'

'Oh,' said Mrs Gordon, light dawning. 'So if you'd been a man you'd have been an architect?'

Anna had never thought what career she might have chosen had she been a man. 'Um, maybe. Possibly. But

286

lots of men are interior designers and of course lots of women are architects.'

'Really?' Mrs Gordon seemed horrified at both these notions. She frowned at Anna again. 'If that's really what you do it can't possibly be how I know you, then.'

'Perhaps you've seen me at the market? I see you've bought a cake from the WI stall.'

Major faux pas! Mrs Gordon looked the personification of affront. 'All the cakes here are home-made!' she announced.

'Yes, but . . .' Anna stopped, flummoxed by someone prepared to lie about a thing like that. The cake was so recognisable, she couldn't have made a mistake. 'It couldn't have been there, then,' she mumbled.

'It's a small enough village,' said Max smoothly. 'You could have seen each other anywhere.' He handed Julian his tea. 'Did you go to a sort of cut-down Ideal Home exhibition at Horsecombe House, Ma? Perhaps you saw each other there? That's right up Anna's street.'

Anna went the colour of the roses on the cups. 'Oh no, I didn't go to that,' she said hurriedly. Lying must be contagious, she thought. The wretched woman's got me doing it now.

'Well, I'm sure it doesn't matter,' said Mrs Gordon, who obviously felt it did. She accepted a cup of tea from Max and sipped it contemplatively. 'Max usually goes out with models, you know.'

'Oh?' Anna fiddled with a cardigan button: this tea was proving more of an ordeal than even she had imagined.

'Mother, really, I don't think—'

She glanced at her son and forced a smile. 'It's nice that he's chosen an ordinary girl for once.' She made it clear that Max had only briefly dipped his toe into the soup of ordinariness, and that he'd be back to models any minute now.

Anna looked at Max, hoping for a sentence or two of

support, but got none, only a frown. Why has he introduced me to his mother if he knew she was going to hate me? she wondered. She caught Julian's eye and saw that he was smiling sympathetically. She smiled back with relief and decided she felt totally out of place, in this room and in Max's life. And what's more, she didn't want Max in her life any more, either.

This certain knowledge came like a bullet and she didn't immediately realise she'd been shot. It took her another cup of tea and a couple of cucumber sandwiches to reconcile this with her psyche: she'd loved Max from afar for so long. How could she stop loving him in a moment? And yet she had. But why? Was it because she'd discovered that an easy, laughing friendship was just as important as the hectic fever of passion?

She was suddenly aware of Mrs Gordon offering her a piece of cake. She took it, to cover up her mental absence, but she resolved that as soon as she'd eaten it, she would leave.

Putting her plate down on the occasional table at her side, she got to her feet. 'Well, Mrs Gordon, it's been lovely to meet you, but I really must go now.'

Mrs Gordon put down her cup and saucer in surprise. Anna should have waited until she'd been dismissed. 'Really?'

'Yes, I'm afraid I have another, rather urgent appointment.'

Max had risen when she had but she shook her head. 'I don't want to spoil the party, Max. I'll see myself out.' And she walked, with utmost dignity, to the door. It was a shame that she left one of Laura's shoes behind on the Persian rug and had to go back for it.

Max hurried after her. 'Anna! Where are you off to? This is so rude! My mother will never forgive you for this.'

Anna turned to face him in the hall. 'Quite frankly Max,' she hissed, 'I don't really care. We're over! I loved you

288

so much for so long but I realise now I was in love with a person I didn't really know.'

He looked at her in bewilderment.

She put her hand on his arm, to soften what she was quite sure was not actually much of a blow. 'It's been such fun and you've taught me a lot, but goodbye!'

Then she took off both shoes and, in spite of the stony ground, ran for home. Somehow she didn't expect she'd hear from him again.

She burst through Chloe's door with a groan and prostrated herself on the floor, mostly so Caroline could greet her without covering her with paw marks, but partly to add drama to the situation.

'Anna, love! What on earth happened?' demanded Chloe, satisfyingly impressed.

'It was awful,' said Anna, trying to avoid Caroline's enthusiastic licks. 'Like being in one of those ghastly plays where people just serve tea all the time. I kept thinking my hand was going to jerk, spilling the Earl Grey and breaking the Royal Worcester at the same time.' Anna closed her eyes.

'Oh, so she didn't fling boiling water from the silver urn all over you, then?' Chloe said in amusement.

'No.' Anna sat up. 'It was ghastly, but not dramatic.' She clambered to her feet. 'Do you mind if I wash my face? I'm covered with Caroline.'

'Help yourself. And don't worry about getting my best cardigan all covered in bits,' said Chloe as Anna headed for the stairs. 'I was going to wash it anyway.'

Anna grinned. 'Sorry!'

When she came back from the bathroom she said, 'You'll be glad to hear that you were right about Max! He's so wrong for me!'

'I never said a word!' Chloe pulled the cork out of a bottle of white wine and poured some into two glasses.

'No, but your thoughts were deafeningly loud.'

'I'm sorry, but he just is wrong for you!'

'Yes, but I'd loved him for so long! This was a little miracle for me, actually having him as a boyfriend, even if we didn't see much of each other.'

'You loved a mirage. Now, take this, purely medicinal, of course.' And she handed one of the glasses to Anna.

Anna sighed and took a deep slug of wine. 'I know. A pompous mirage.'

Chloe sipped her own wine and patted the sofa. 'The boys are upstairs in our bed, watching a video and eating crisps. I'll have to change the sheets to get the crumbs out, but it's worth it for a bit of peace. Sit down and tell me all about it.'

'There's not much to tell, really,' said Anna, settling herself next to Chloe and taking another very welcome slug of wine. 'You've met her,' she went on. 'Can you imagine, her drawing room is full of parrots! And other stuff. I'd take out the other ornaments and quite a lot of the furniture and keep it as a parrot theme. The wallpaper was to die for.'

Chloe sipped her wine, satisfied that her friend was not suffering from a broken heart.

'You should have seen the sandwiches! Tiny wasn't in it. I reckon she only used about four bits of bread. I wonder if she made them herself? Oh! And she definitely lied about the cake.'

'It seems a strange thing—'

'When she was trying to place me – thank God she didn't,' Anna gabbled on, 'the greenhouse thing was bad enough, but supposing she'd remembered the jacuzzi? Anyway, because it was at least respectable, I suggested she'd seen me at the market, and commented on her buying the cake from the WI stall. She was furious! Said it was home-made.'

'But the cakes on that stall are wonderful, and they are home-made!'

'I know, but she made out she'd made it. A woman who'd lie about something like that . . .'

'Well . . .' Chloe had turned a little pink.

'Don't tell me! You've told your mother-in-law you've made those cakes yourself?'

Chloe nodded. 'She is a special case. But tell me, what made you finally see the light about Max?'

'I realised he didn't have much of a sense of humour, really. He didn't think it was amusing at all that I'd cleaned his mother's greenhouse and couldn't mention it. I don't blame him for having an old bag for a mother, but he might have appreciated it was a funny situation.'

'I'm so relieved,' said Chloe, her eyes closed. 'I can't tell you.'

'Yes, so am I, but there is one thing that's worrying me.'

'What?' Chloe opened one eye.

'Julian. He was awfully nice, and I don't suppose he'd have bought the house anyway because it is titchy, but supposing he's put off buying it because I was so rude?'

'Oh, surely not.'

'Well, you can't tell, can you?'

'I don't think it would make any difference. You weren't really rude, you just cut it all a bit short.'

'I'm glad it's over, anyway.' Anna sighed and put her now empty wine glass down. 'Now, I must take Caroline home and phone Laura. It would be so wonderful if Julian buys the house. If he does, I'm definitely going to organise a party, a thank you to everyone who's helped me.'

'Oh fab, I love parties,' said Chloe, giving Anna a hug. 'And you will tell me if you've anyone else in mind as a love object, won't you?'

Anna chuckled at Chloe's blatant digging but refused to submit. She'd made such a terrible mistake over Max, she didn't want to get it wrong again. Her heart, she decided, was a very unreliable organ, and not to be trusted. But this sensible decision didn't stop her mind wandering in Rob's direction with tiresome regularity.

Chapter Twenty-Two

'It's not that I expected to sell it to the first person I showed it to,' Anna said to her sister the following day, having failed to reach her the previous evening, 'it's just having made the leap from homeowner to home-seller – which took some doing, I can assure you – I feel all confused. There's stuff I can get on with, but I've lost heart somehow.'

'Well, we'll definitely be down for the party if he does buy it, but if he doesn't, perhaps you should put it on the market at a slightly lower price?' Laura suggested.

This, Anna could tell, was a subtle way of Laura saying they needed their money back. Her sister would never use any pressure, but Anna could read the signs. 'Of course!' she said. 'That figure was a try-on, really. You couldn't expect anyone to pay that amount for such a tiny house.'

The conversation moved on and, soon afterwards, Anna took Caroline out for the last time and then went to bed. She wished she could have talked to Rob about it all but it was late, and although she did want to ask him about the buildings inspector coming round to check all her alterations were legal and hygienic, she didn't think she could do that at this time of night.

'It's just as well I didn't have much in the way of finger-nails anyway,' she said to Caroline, 'or I'd have eaten them all by now.' She inspected her nails, remembering how just a day earlier, she had scrubbed them so she could shake hands with Julian without shame. Already they were grubby again. Had it all been a horrible waste of time?

When Julian rang the following morning, she was so shocked, she could barely take in what he was saying. 'You want to buy it? Really?'

He laughed. 'Yes, really. I did some measuring and then decided that it wasn't worth letting such a gem slip through my fingers for the sake of a couple of bits of furniture.'

'Oh my goodness, I can't believe it. Thank you so much!' she stammered.

'There is just one thing, I need to be able to complete in a fortnight, or as near as possible. Do you think you can do that? I have a solicitor I could recommend, although I'm sure it's very unethical, but we need someone who can move really fast.'

'Brilliant! That means we can have the party!' said Chloe jubilantly when Anna hurried round with the news. 'I know the perfect place we can have it. We'll make it a bring-and-share picnic, then all you have to do is provide the wine. Oh, and I definitely think you should have a new dress. You are going to invite Rob, aren't you?' she looked at Anna, a mischievous glint in her eye.

Anna laughed fondly. 'Yes, I am going to invite Rob. He's been such a help.' Her heart gave a little skip of excitement at the thought but, luckily for her, Chloe didn't see it, and so didn't comment.

The morning of the picnic, the following Saturday, was wreathed in mist like a bride, as Anna observed to Chloe as they got ready, this time in her house, now it was fit to wash, change and live in.

'Mm. It's going to be really hot,' Chloe said, looking out of the window. She turned and smiled at Anna. 'I love your dress, by the way. You've got just the figure for bo-ho. All that lace and flounces make anyone remotely fat look like a lampshade, or one of those dolls used to cover up loo rolls.'

'Well, I am glad I don't look like that.' Anna laughed. 'Now, have we got everything?'

'Yes. Mike and the boys are coming on later with Betsy, who's got a people-carrier. We can get everything set up before they get there. Come on, we'd better get going.'

'Are you sure a dozen bottles of fake champers will be enough?' Anna asked anxiously as they loaded up Chloe's car. Caroline was coming later in the people-carrier.

'Loads! And we've got all that beer and cider as well, and people are bound to bring stuff.'

'As long as they bring food, or we'll all be paralytic.'

They drove along lanes flanked by wild flowers, barely a breeze coming through their open window.

'And Rob is definitely coming?' Chloe asked.

'Yes, for the hundredth time,' Anna replied, laughing at her friend's persistence. 'He's bringing ice cream. He's borrowing all the cool boxes and stuff from his sister. It's what we did when we went to that fête.'

'So you and he – you know – are getting on quite well?' Chloe pushed.

'Yes, he's a very good friend.'

'It's just that when I came down the lane with Tom the other evening, it looked to me as if . . .'

'As if what?' Anna wasn't going to make it easy for Chloe.

'He was about to kiss you.' Chloe's eyes remained firmly on the road ahead.

'To be honest, Chloe,' said Anna, 'I've had so much in my mind and going on, I really can't remember.' She was determined not to tell anyone about her feelings until everything was a bit more certain.

* * *

They parked the car neatly on the verge, and, carrying a box each, they headed over to the field.

Anna didn't usually wear white broderie anglaise with a daisy chain in her hair, but she was strangely pleased that she was when Rob appeared at the party, a huge cool box in his arms.

'Where do you want this?' he asked, putting it down on the grass beside him.

'Over there by the trees.' Anna pointed. 'Aren't we lucky Chloe knew this person with this bit of land? It's perfect for picnics.'

'What's it usually used for?' asked Rob, with something a lot like admiration in his eyes.

Anna was secretly pleased. 'Don't know,' she said. 'I think it's just attached to their house and they wanted to make it into a garden or something, but they're not allowed.'

'I see.'

'Which reminds me.' She smiled at him. 'I must ask you about getting the house signed off by the buildings inspector.'

'I'll look forward to it,' he said, laughing down at her and then heading off for the trees with his cool box.

Maybe it was her floaty dress, the beauty and sensuousness of the day, or the glass of champagne she'd already drunk, but suddenly Anna was aware of a wave of lust. 'Oh my goodness,' she told herself when she'd identified the unaccustomed feeling. 'No more to drink for you, my girl, or you could get into the most awful trouble.'

Seeing a large car pull up and what seemed to be an entire primary school's worth of children fall out, with one large greyhound, she ran across to greet her guests. She wasn't used to giving parties, and if it hadn't been for Chloe she might have backed out. But she definitely owed all these people a very big thank you, and this beautiful summer Saturday seemed almost an adequate reward.

'So, how many people are you expecting?' Rob came up behind her and she jumped. She was now standing beside a picnic table covered with plastic cups and bottles.

She was inordinately pleased to see him. 'I have no idea. I'm encouraging people to bring any friends they've got staying and all their children and dogs. Caroline is being led round by Tom, look!'

They both watched the little boy trotting along in front of the huge dog, a satisfying loop of lead between them, indicating that she was following, not showing the way.

'She's so good with children,' said Anna. 'I'm very lucky.'

'You are, but you handle her very well – now,' he added. 'When I first met you she was anything but in control.' He seemed tense for some reason and she wondered if he still worried about her having Caroline.

'I'd only just had her and she was scared by that car!' Anna fiddled with a plastic cup, feeling a little tense herself all of a sudden. It was obviously catching.

'I know, I'm being unfair, I just didn't want you to get complacent.' He gave her a half-smile. 'What will you do with her when you move?'

'Well, move her with me, of course.'

'Have you thought that you're going to have to find somewhere else to live very quickly?' he asked. 'The right sort of project takes some searching for.'

Anna sighed. 'To be honest I haven't thought that far ahead. I might have to rent for a bit, I suppose.'

Rob looked dubious. 'I should warn you, it might be difficult to find somewhere where they'll let you have Caroline.'

She put her hand on his sleeve, suddenly wanting

reassurance. 'Oh no! Now, instead of celebrating, I'm feeling all sort of – homeless.'

He put his hand on hers briefly and laughed gently. 'I didn't mean to make you feel homeless, I just wanted to tell you that if you need somewhere for Caroline she can come and stay with my pack for a bit.'

Anna turned to him and put her hands on his arms. 'Can she? That could be a lifesaver. Thank you so much!' Then, aware she was still holding on to him – his arms seemed to have a magnetic attraction for her today – she let him go.

'Is Max Gordon coming?' he said abruptly.

Anna frowned. 'No, why on earth should he be?'

'I assume that, as your boyfriend . . .'

She looked at him in bewilderment for a moment and then realised he didn't know. 'Not any more. We split up the same day Julian came to see the house.'

Rob suddenly seemed much more relaxed. 'Oh? Why?'

'Well, his mother was the catalyst.'

'What do you mean?' He looked puzzled.

Anna made a gesture with her hand as if explaining all. 'She's so stuck up, with no sense of humour and a crashing snob. And' – Anna's eyes grew wide with shock – 'she *lied* about the cake! Who would do a thing like that? Then I realised Max was fairly pompous without much of a sense of humour either.'

'Wow,' said Rob, obviously impressed. 'I promise you, my mother is absolutely charming. She would never lie about cake.' He frowned, indicating he didn't really understand that last bit.

'Chloe admitted that she did, sometimes.' Anna smiled, glancing up at him with her head on one side. 'And why do you feel the need to tell me that about your mother?'

'It wasn't a need, exactly, just information, in case you should ever meet her.'

'But that's hardly likely, is it?' Flirting with Rob was

much more fun than flirting with Max, she decided.

Rob sent an eyebrow skywards. 'Well, you can never tell.' He glanced at the table. 'Why don't you leave this and come for a walk. We can take Caroline. The others can help themselves to what they want.' He indicated the bottles and plastic cups.

Anna suddenly felt diffident; their relationship had changed from just friends to something potentially more. The thought of being alone with him, even with Caroline as a chaperone, was suddenly unnerving. 'Oh no, I must be a proper hostess. I don't think I've ever had a party before; at least, not on my own. I must stay.'

A group of little children came up at that moment, and Anna dispensed fizzy elderflower, proving to Rob, she hoped, that her presence really was necessary. In fact, although in many ways there was nothing she would have liked more than to go for a walk with him, she was worried her feelings for him might be false. She had spent so long pining for Max, loving him, and in the end her feelings there had been so misplaced. Supposing Rob only wanted a brief fling: how would she feel then? Having a broken heart was so wearing!

'You could get me some food,' she asked him when they were alone again. 'I've only had one glass of champagne but I—'

'Didn't have breakfast. You really need someone to look after you, you know,' he said, putting a couple of empty plastic bottles into a designated rubbish sack.

'That's fighting talk, mister! I'll have you know I'm an independent woman—'

'Who hasn't the sense to feed herself.' He laughed. 'What would you like?'

'Oh, anything that's handy.'

'I'll see what I can find.'

She watched him disappear across the field with a contented little sigh. He was gorgeous, and he did seem to like her. It was possible falling in love with him wouldn't make her a complete slut.

People drifted over to say hello and thank you to her. Anna dispensed drinks, insisted that no, it was she who should be thanking them. Everyone who had helped had come. Eric the plasterer; the tiler; Betsy and Maddy; Mike, of course; and, a little late, Laura and Will.

'You look positively bridal!' exclaimed Laura, hurrying with difficulty across the grass towards Anna, her kitten heels sticking into the soil with every step.

'Oh God, do I? That's awful!,' said Anna. 'Perhaps I shouldn't wear all these daisies, but these dear little girls – Betsy, who helped me, they were her daughters, I think – each made me a daisy chain because I was already wearing one. I felt I had to wear them all.'

'Of course you must wear them,' said Laura, enveloping her sister in a hug. 'They look lovely! I just want you to look bridal for real!'

'No chance of that, now. I've finished with Max. He was dreadfully pompous, really.' A stab of regret that she had actually slept with him before she discovered this made her frown.

'Just as well to find that out now,' said Will, who had followed his wife a bit more slowly. He kissed Anna's cheek.

'Will!' She hugged him violently. 'I'm so pleased I can give your money back! Did you bring the boys?'

'No, I'm afraid we left them with my parents. They were disappointed not to meet Caroline, though.'

'She's over there. Chloe's boys seem to have taken her in hand. I'll put her in the car if it all gets too much. Chloe's parked in the shade and we could leave the boot open for her.'

'That's all right then,' said Will gravely.

'It's all very well for you, you've only got children. Us dog owners have to look after them very carefully. Now, what would you like to drink?'

'Whatever you've got in that bottle. This is a great party!'

Laughter, childish giggles and squeals could be heard on the balmy summer air.

'It wouldn't have been great if it had rained, so it was a bit of a gamble,' Anna said. 'Although Chloe did have the village hall on standby in case, but it wouldn't have been the same.'

'Right,' said Laura when she and Will had both got drinks, 'I'm going to find Chloe and Mike. And later on I want to see what you've done to the house – I can hardly wait.'

Will was already making for the food table.

'I have to get it signed off by the buildings inspector, but he's coming on Monday,' Anna said.

'What does he do?'

'Checks all the head heights are adequate, bathrooms properly ventilated, stuff like that.' Anna searched for Rob in among the mass of people over by the food. She had sent him glibly away, and now she wanted him back. 'Rob will talk me through it.'

'I can't wait to meet him.' Laura regarded her sister closely. 'Are you and he – um . . . ?'

'Laura! I've only just dumped Max!'

'I'll take that to mean you'd like you and Rob to be an item, but you're not an item just yet.'

Anna tidied the bottles and cups, not looking at her sister. 'I've got so much to think about at the moment, my love life is really last on the list. Julian only wanted the house if we could complete in a fortnight. If I can't I'll have to put it back on the market.'

'And a fortnight's not long,' said Laura. 'On the other hand, I could stay with you next week, and help you look for a new place.'

'Could you?' Anna was touched by her sister's offer. 'That would be fantastic! It's quite hard house-hunting without being able to drive.'

'That's what I thought. Will and I have already discussed it and he said he'd have the boys if you did want me to stay. You can't see all that much in a week, but it would be better than nothing.'

'And I need to find somewhere to rent first.' Anna felt her spirits sink a little.

Laura picked up a bottle. 'Perhaps you'd better have another drink. Oh, there's Chloe. I must say hello.' Laura waved and tottered over to greet her properly.

As Anna was tearing cellophane off more plastic cups, Dorothy and Ted, whom Anna hadn't seen since Chloe's dinner party, came up. Anna felt as if she was in a receiving line. 'Anna, you probably don't remember us . . .' Dorothy began.

'Of course I do!' Anna embraced them one at a time. 'That amazing dinner party at Chloe's.'

'You look so – different,' said Dorothy, as forthright as ever.

'Well, I'm wearing a dress and I've got daisies in my hair.' Anna laughed. 'I'd got dressed in rather a hurry before the dinner party.'

'I gather your house is great. Would you mind if we came home and had a look at it finished?' asked Dorothy.

'Now, don't be nosy, Dor,' Ted chided. 'I expect Anna's got enough to do without showing you round. You've got to complete in a hurry, I hear?'

'Yes, but I expect I could show you round, too. I have to wait in for the buildings inspector on Monday. If you arrange to arrive at roughly the same time, you could lie in wait at Chloe's until the coast is clear and then come over.'

Dorothy laughed. 'So, will you be wanting somewhere to rent while you look for a new house?'

'You must be psychic!' said Anna, amazed.

'Not really,' said Ted. 'It's obvious you won't be able to find a house and move into it in a fortnight, but what

Dorothy is going to say is, we have a holiday cottage that's not rented at the moment.'

'Have you?' This seemed too good to be true.

'Yes,' agreed Dorothy, 'but I'm afraid we couldn't let you have your dog with you. It's just the whole wear-and-tear thing. They are a bit hard on the paintwork.'

Indignation rose and then fell again in Anna as she remembered what Rob had said about it being difficult to find somewhere to rent where she could keep Caroline with her.

'That shouldn't be a problem. Ro— A friend could look after Caroline for me. And it shouldn't take me too long to find somewhere to buy.'

Dorothy rubbed Anna's arm in a friendly way. 'It's a dear little house. I have no idea why no one wants to spend their holidays in it just now. If you took it on for at least a month, you could have a special rate.'

Ted laughed. 'Specially large!'

While his wife was giving him a playful push, Sue and Ivan, who had also been at the dinner party, appeared. Like Dorothy and Ted, they wanted to see her house.

Later, having told Chloe about the offer of a holiday cottage to rent, Anna complained to her that if she wasn't careful she'd have to spend the whole week showing people over her house. 'I'll have to keep it permenantly tidy.'

'Horrid,' Chloe agreed, 'but if people see what you do, it'll help you get commissions in the future.'

Anna acknowledged this truth with a sigh as Chloe rushed off to tend to Harry who'd fallen over and wanted 'Mummy'.

Anna was feeling tired and hungry and just a little disgruntled when Rob reappeared at her side. He had a paper carrier bag in his hand, something rolled up under his arm, and Caroline.

'Sorry it took so long. I got caught chatting. Anyway,

come on. Caroline's fed up and needs a proper walk, and you need food. We're taking a picnic into the woods.'

This time she didn't argue and took hold of the carrier bag. It was surprisingly heavy and it clinked.

'I brought a bottle of my own, to celebrate the house being finished, and stole some food. There's enough to feed a regiment.'

Anna peeked into the bag. 'Oh, champagne! As long as you haven't brought rose petals . . .'

'What?'

'Never mind. I was distracted for a moment.'

'I've got a rug to sit on as well.'

Anna took hold of Caroline's lead thinking that if they didn't have so much to carry, they could have walked arm in arm. But then the whole world would have suspected them of being an item, not just Chloe and Laura.

'It's a shame we couldn't find anywhere a bit more private,' said Rob a little while later.

'This is fine! There's a lovely patch of sunshine here.'

'But we're right by the path.'

'I know, but it's so tiresome when people keep trying to find better picnic spots and keep moving on. In the end you always find yourself somewhere not nice at all, because you're so hungry and desperate.' Anna paused. 'Laura's a bit obsessed with the right picnic spot.'

'Here it is then,' said Rob, smoothing down the rug.

Anna arranged all the food while Rob did the honours with the champagne. She got the giggles. It was partly because of the champagne, which she shouldn't really have had on an empty stomach, partly the food, which had got quite mushed up on the journey, and partly because Caroline insisted on sharing the rug with them. Nothing either she or Rob did could get her off it.

'It's not funny,' said Rob, laughing himself. 'I planned

a nice romantic picnic and I've got to share it with a bloody great dog and any number of passers-by!'

Several sets of party guests had decided to take a woodland stroll and had seen them fighting to keep a bit of rug dog-free, and trying to rescue bits of quiche from the bottom of the bag.

'It is funny, and it's very nice.' Suddenly the sun and the champagne got to her. 'I think I'll just sunbathe for a bit.'

'This is very peaceful,' said Rob, beside her.

'Mm.' Anna shut her eyes, feeling wonderfully relaxed.

'You must have been working so hard lately.'

'Yes. It was fun, but now I don't need to do it any more I feel really tired.'

'You could go to sleep. I'll guard you.'

She opened her eyes. Although the thought of Rob guarding her while she slept made her feel she was in a Gothic novel, it was rather a waste of his company. 'No need to do that. You'd get bored waiting for passing dragons out to snaffle sleeping maidens.'

He chuckled and she glanced at him. He was lying on his side with his head supported by his hand and his hair had flopped forward a bit. His mouth, Anna decided, looked particularly sexy from that angle.

To stop herself reaching up and touching it with her fingertip, she said, 'Oh, I nearly forgot to tell you – one of Chloe's friends has a house to rent. It's a holiday cottage but, as you said, I can't have Caroline. So can I take you up on your offer?'

'Mm,' he murmured. 'I can, of course, have Caroline but I'd very much rather have you.' He ended on a husky whisper and Anna closed her eyes again, waiting for the feel of his mouth on hers, when she heard her sister's voice.

'There you are!' said Laura, with Chloe close behind her. 'Dorothy who's renting you the house? She's been looking for you. She wants to make some arrangements. Oh, sorry,' she added belatedly. 'Have we interrupted something?'

Rob sighed. 'Oh no, that's fine. I've realised that attempting to run your love life on a public footpath is fraught with difficulties.'

'Tell you what,' said Laura, trying to make good her blunder, 'give me a key and then perhaps Rob could drive you home?'

'Of course I could,' said Rob. 'I'd be delighted.'

Anna produced the key from a cord around her neck and handed it to her sister. 'We won't be long,' she said. 'Put the kettle on and get out the Chinese menu. Are you up for that, Chloe?'

'Mm. Absolutely,' said Chloe, excitedly.

'And what about you, Rob?' Anna was suddenly shy. 'Will you join us?'

'Yes, do,' said Laura, 'I'd really appreciate a chance to get to know you better.' Chloe nodded in agreement but Rob shook his head ruefully.

'I'm afraid I can't. I promised I'd babysit for my sister. Her usual girls have all got something on and there's only me left.' He looked at Anna. 'I was going to ask if you'd like to help me, but if you've got your sister . . .'

'Sisters need to be attended to,' said Anna resignedly. 'Especially older ones.'

Rob chuckled. 'Come on then, on your feet.' He put out a hand and pulled Anna up.

'Don't forget to have a word with Dorothy,' Laura called back. 'You can move in really soon. I'll be able to help you!'

'And me,' Chloe added.

'Lovely!' said Anna, not sure that she meant it.

'And I'll make sure she and Caroline get home safely,' Rob said firmly.

The moment their voices were no longer audible, Rob

pulled Anna into his arms. 'I don't think I can wait any longer for this.'

Anna was still fuddled from champagne. It took her no time at all to fit her body to his, close her eyes and submit to the waves of pleasure his mouth created with hers. They paused momentarily for breath and then locked back together. Rob's hand moved to her waist and lingered there longingly. She put her hand behind his head and gently stroked the back of his neck: the space between his hair and his collar. Anna never wanted to be anywhere else, ever, except in Rob's arms. As Caroline's confused whimpering penetrated her consciousness she realised that Max, accomplished kisser that he was, could take lessons from Rob.

Reluctantly they separated, both breathing deeply. Anna swallowed and cleared her throat. She looked up at Rob. 'I think we'd better be getting back.'

He too sounded husky. 'Yes, stay here much longer and who knows what might happen?'

Anna knew very well what would have happened and was only sorry that neither the time nor the place was right.

They walked back to the car arm in arm. The field was nearly empty; only a couple of families playing French cricket were enjoying the late afternoon sunshine.

'Much as I love my sister, and Will, I kind of wish they weren't staying the night,' said Anna.

'Well, I don't mind them staying the night at all. I've got to be at my sister's, remember?'

Anna sighed deeply. 'I know.'

'There'll be other times, Anna,' he said gently.

'Oh I do hope so!' she replied.

It was a sociable evening. Anna and Laura went round to Chloe and Mike's to eat their takeaway, and the air was full of chat about Anna's new rented house to be visited the next day, and laughter and reminiscence about the party. Anna struggled to concentrate. Her mind was full of Rob. When she finally got to bed she tried to think about the following day. After they'd checked the rented house, and if it was OK, moved some stuff into it, Laura and Anna were going to pick up the keys of a couple of houses. She knew she'd have to say sensible things about them. They were both empty, and both in need of major renovation, but now all she could think about was Rob's mouth, his hands, his soft, crisp hair under her fingers. I don't know about being in love, she thought as she drifted off to sleep, but I'm certainly in lust!

Chapter Twenty-Three

It seemed a lifetime had passed since the picnic, but as Laura drove Anna and Caroline to Rob's house, it was, Anna realised, only just over a week.

With Laura staying and Rob's heavy workload and own family commitments it had been hard to get away, but Anna and Rob had managed to snatch a walk together early one morning. Anna had left a note for Laura, taken Caroline and stolen out of the house and along the lane to meet Rob.

Mist wreathed the fields and valleys, transforming the landscape with its gauzy whiteness. As she looked over to the distant hills she felt separate from her everyday life, as if she really had been transported somewhere more magical than a village in the Cotswolds. When she saw Rob waiting by the car her heart leapt and she smiled, half laughing at herself for her imaginings, realising that nothing more mysterious had happened to her than falling in love. But what was more mysterious than that?

He wrapped his arms around her while she was still holding on to Caroline's lead. 'I can't be long,' he murmured into her hair. 'I've got a site visit at nine.'

'I can't be long either. Laura and I have got a very lengthy to-do list.' She muttered this into his fleece, unable to get her arms round him because of holding Caroline.

'And am I on the list?' Rob muttered back.

'You were number one, only of course I didn't actually write you down. Can we put Caroline in the car?'

Reluctantly, Rob let her go and took hold of Caroline's

lead. Caroline, unaccustomed to being ignored, looked up at Rob reproachfully. He chuckled, stroking her head and ruffling her ears, then led her round to the boot of the car and put her inside.

Anna got into the front seat and waited for him. She wished they could just drive off and leave everyone and everything behind. She sighed. She was being silly. They were very lucky; they had found each other and nothing was likely to stop them being together – except their respective sisters. She sighed deeply again, but smiled.

'Do you want a wood or a view or both?' he said as he joined her in the car.

'The nearest, but a wood for preference.'

'Right. Only a little way then.'

Anna felt giggly and wistful at the same time. It felt strangely illicit, sneaking out of her house so early. 'This feels a bit odd,' she said.

'It's because we're both so frantic. There's a guilty pleasure in stealing time away from what we should both be doing.'

Anna laughed. 'Which is sleeping.'

He glanced across at her. 'I'm find it very difficult to sleep just now.'

She nodded. She was too.

'Come on, let's walk.'

He parked the car in a lay-by near a wood and let Caroline out.

'Do you think we can take Caroline off the lead here?' said Anna, thinking how frustrating it was having one arm trapped when she wanted both of them round Rob.

'Probably, but not just yet. I'll take her.'

He put his other arm firmly round Anna and they stumbled down a steep dip before they reached the path on the other side. It would have been easier to walk if they'd separated, but neither of them was willing to do that.

310

'This is like a three-legged race,' Anna said. 'Can we let Caroline off now?'

'In a minute. There's something I want to check.' He pulled Anna up the opposite side of the dip. There was a break in the trees and Anna was just about to exclaim at the beauty of the view when Rob put his finger to her lips. 'Look,' he breathed.

There in the clearing, just below where they were standing, was a herd of deer, about half a dozen of them. They were downwind of Anna and Rob and weren't aware of them. Anna gazed in rapture at this unexpected sight until a pheasant squawked its way in their direction and the lead hind raised her head and saw Rob and Anna, with Caroline, ears pricked. The deer set off into the woods at a gentle gallop.

'That was unbelievable,' she breathed, still finding it hard to take in that she had actually seen a herd of wild deer.

'I've seen them here before,' said Rob, 'although not often. Often enough for me to want to keep Caroline on the lead, though.'

'It was magical.' She looked up at him in wonder, only partly because of the deer.

He sighed, let go of Caroline's lead and took her in his arms.

After that they had had to make do with phone calls and now Rob was about to go away, but they'd promised each other they would meet up for a proper, grown-up date when he returned.

It was now early in the morning. Rob was waiting for them to arrive before he went to work and later that morning Laura was going to drive back to Yorkshire. Anna was feeling very anticlimactic. Laura, aware of this, was being bracing.

'I can't believe so much has happened so quickly,' she said, checking her rear-view mirror and getting a good view of Caroline's head. 'You've done really well!'

'Sit down, Caroline,' said Anna, half-heartedly and ineffectually. 'It's amazing what you can get done if you've got a really good incentive, and you've been wonderful. If I hadn't had you to drive me to look at houses, I'd have had to make do with Cirencester's answer to Kirsty and Phil.'

'They probably would have been excellent, but an estate agent is never going to give you totally unbiased advice.'

Anna didn't comment. She felt she could have managed without Laura's advice actually, but didn't say so. She would have preferred to search for a new project with Rob; she respected his opinion, it would be a huge advantage knowing in advance what the listed buildings people would accept or reject, and it was always useful to have someone to help with the measuring up. The fact that she was in love with him was, she tried to convince herself, completely beside the point.

'Mm,' she murmured.

'And your holiday cottage is sweet!' Laura went on brightly. 'With a garage for your extra stuff. Couldn't be better, really.'

'No,' Anna agreed flatly. 'Except if I could have had Caroline, of course.'

Laura sighed with a patience only a mother could muster. 'Well, that would have been the icing on the cake, naturally.' She frowned. 'I don't know why you're so depressed, Anna. You've sold your house; you've had an offer – a very low offer – accepted on a new one. You've got everything going for you!'

'I know. It's just . . .'

'What?'

'Rob's going away for work. It's not long, but . . .' she stopped again.

'What?' Laura's sympathy was waning but she was valiantly trying not to show it.

'While I think we've got something – something really lovely – going on, I was so horribly wrong about Max.'

'But Rob's wonderful! He's good-looking, he's kind to animals, he seems to have a steady job. How could you be wrong about him?' Laura was now losing her battle to remain patient.

'Max was very good-looking, much more affluent, and while I don't think you'd describe him as an animal lover, he didn't kick puppies, I'm sure.'

'Well, *I'm* sure Rob's much more suitable.'

'You never met Max!' Perversely, Anna felt the need to defend him. 'And whoever fell in love with someone because they're suitable?' She shot her sister a sideways glance. 'Except possibly you.'

Laura laughed. 'That proves my point! The fact that a man ticks all the boxes for a mother-in-law doesn't mean you can't fancy the pants off him.'

Anna smiled and patted her sister's hand on the gear lever. 'I've kept you away from Will for too long, but I do want to thank you. You've been a real star. I couldn't have done it all without you.'

'Yes you could,' said Laura briskly. 'But something I can't do without you is find the way to this bloody place. Do we turn left or go straight on?' They had come to a crossroads Anna vaguely recognised.

'Straight on,' said Anna after a moment's thought. 'I would have gone mad if I'd had to show all Chloe's curious friends round the house on my own. I was beginning to sound like a demonstrator who has to learn their lines by heart.'

'I enjoyed it. It reminded me of when we did up that flat together,' Laura said. 'Anyway, you might get quite a bit of work from them. It's important to have a showcase.'

'I hope so. And at least Dorothy came at the same time as the buildings inspector.'

'He was nice, wasn't he? Very helpful, I thought.'

'Yes, he could have been much worse. In fact, he was excellent. He didn't demand any more fire-resistant walls or air bricks or anything like that. He could have done, and I would have had to have done it before I let Julian buy it, I'm sure.'

'Right,' said Laura a few moments later as they set off through the wood towards Rob's house, 'I'm going to sit in the car while you hand over Caroline. I think you and Rob need a little time alone.'

Anna thought she and Rob needed a lot of time alone but as she knew that Rob had to go to work and Laura had to go to Yorkshire, she would have to be happy with what she could get.

She led Caroline up the path and Rob, who had been watching for her, came out of the house to meet them. Anna felt suddenly nervous. Supposing she'd imagined the electricity between them during that kiss and that lovely romantic walk together? Supposing it was just lust or something? She was still fretting about her mistaken feelings for Max. How could you be sure you'd found gold just because it glittered? A proverb wandered vaguely around in her mind. She might be as wrong about Rob as she was about Max. She was such a noodle!

Seeing Rob smile made her realise that her feelings were perfectly real, which was a relief, but she was left with a shyness that made her talk too much and too fast.

'Hi! Sorry I'm a bit later than I said. I hope I won't make you late for work! Oh, of course, you do flexitime, don't you?' she rambled.

He smiled. 'Yes, I do do flexitime, and no, you haven't made me late for work. But on the other hand, I'm afraid I haven't even got time to offer you a cup of coffee.'

'Well, Laura's in a hurry, too, so I couldn't have had one,' she said, disappointed all the same. 'I'll get Caroline's bed. Will she be all right with your lot, do you think?'

'She'll be fine,' he reassured her, bending slightly to

stroke Caroline's ears. She leant in to him adoringly.

Anna smiled. 'And remind me what's happening to them while you're away?'

'My neighbour is going to come in twice a day, but there'll be people here, too – I'm having some work done – so they won't be on their own much. She'll let them out, feed them, and take them for a long play in the field. She even watches television with them after she's fed them in the evenings. Just as well: we wouldn't want them watching anything unsuitable.'

Anna smiled politely. 'I'd better get Caroline's things. Then we must be going . . .' He hadn't even kissed her cheek.

'Why don't you stay and have a look at what I've done since you were last here? I'll get Caroline's stuff. I can say goodbye to Laura at the same time.'

Anna helped herself to a drink of water to ease her dry mouth and then wandered through the house. There were lots of signs of activity. One of the kitchen walls had been demolished and Anna could see where he intended to put in an extension. It would be very nice, she thought. A cement mixer, a couple of sawhorses and some electrical tools were pushed into one corner.

'It's going to be jolly nice, Caroline,' she said to the dog, who seemed to sense her imminent abandonment. 'You'll be fine. You must be used to living with other dogs, after all, and I'm sure Rob's dogs have very good manners.'

'They have,' said Rob, coming back with his arms full of bedding, 'and I suggest you say goodbye to Caroline now. I'll get them settled together before I go to work.'

'OK,' said Anna, suddenly near tears. She knew that Caroline would be fine, would probably forget her the moment she met her new friends, but the hectic time Anna had had and the fact she was saying goodbye to Rob, too, had stretched her nerves.

'All right, Caroline,' she said, trying not to let her voice betray her emotions, 'you're going to stay with Rob for a bit, but it's only for a short time, while my house sale goes through and we can move into our new home.'

She put her arms round Caroline's neck and laid her head on Caroline's for an instant. Then she straightened up. 'Right, now I must let you get on.'

'Oh, come here,' said Rob and pulled her into his arms.

He hugged her so tightly she couldn't breathe, but that was fine because this was where she wanted to die, held tightly in Rob's strong arms.

'I'm only going away for ten days,' he murmured into her hair moments before asphyxia set in. 'Then I'm going to take you somewhere really nice for dinner.'

Anna kept her eyes closed and didn't let go. 'That would be wonderful,' she muttered into his shirt. 'Or fish and chips would be OK.'

He laughed and released her, 'I think I can do a bit better than that.'

'Whatever.' Pulling herself away was like prising a limpet from a rock. 'Anyway, I must go. Bye bye, darling,' she said.

'Is the darling for Caroline or me?' asked Rob with a hint of sadness in his smile.

'You decide,' said Anna, trying for playfulness and not quite bringing it off. 'I'm going now. Goodbye!'

His bear-like hug had gone a long way to restoring Anna's spirits. It had made her feel more sure of her feelings and his. They had plenty of time to build on their friendship and, in Anna's case, the sudden spasms of lust could well become real and lasting love. Caroline would be all right; everything would be all right. The future was fun and exciting. But she'd still had a break in her voice when she'd said goodbye.

* * *

Laura left later that morning and Anna spent the next couple of days distracting herself with odd little jobs that weren't absolutely essential, but she wanted to leave the house as near perfect as possible for Julian. For her professional pride. Then, still feeling proud of her achievement, but with a huge wrench, she left the cottage for Dorothy and Ted's holiday home. Only frequent calls and visits to Chloe kept her spirits up.

'I know,' said Anna brightly, just after she had had lunch with Chloe and her younger boys the following week. 'Why don't we find that place you told me about? Where there are trees that are easy to climb? You'd like that, wouldn't you, guys?'

Amid the general agreement Chloe said, 'And would you like to call on a certain person on your way home?'

Anna gave a confessional sigh. 'He might not be back yet. He was away for about ten days, I think. He has rung me a couple of times but he found it really hard to get a signal so I'm not quite sure what he's up to.'

'What did he go away to do, exactly?'

'It was to help out in the office where he worked before. He took holiday to do it!' Anna was indignant to think of Rob using his much-needed time off to work, especially as it took him away from her. But that's why she adored him – he was so generous. 'Although they will pay him of course,' she went on, 'and his house is going to swallow money, so he does need it.'

'So why did they need him exactly?' Chloe was gathering sauce-garnished plates and stacking them in the dishwasher.

'Oh, a huge backlog. They'd lost a member of staff, apparently, and had to wait for the new person to join.'

'So you've been in touch enough to find out all that, at least.'

'Yes,' said Anna, sighing again. 'But not the exact date he's coming home. It depended on how much he could do, and how quickly.'

'OK, boys, give the table a wipe someone. I'll just switch on the dishwasher. We won't need boots, just hoodies. Let's go!'

Tom and Harry, and even Anna and Chloe to a lesser extent, had spent a happy afternoon climbing trees, eating digestive biscuits, and swigging orange squash out of a bottle. They were now on their way back, having picked up Bruno from school, taking the diversion necessary to visit Rob, if he should be home.

'How will he feel, us all turning up, if he's just got back from a trip?' asked Chloe.

'He'll be thrilled to see us! Well, he might not be, but considering he's probably not there, I'm sure it won't be a problem. I might get a glimpse of Caroline!' Anna added, to give the impression it was not just Rob she wanted to see.

'I thought you said the other night it was better for you not to see her, so you didn't get all emotional about it,' Chloe teased.

'I know, but I'll see her when I visit Rob anyway, and it shouldn't be too much longer before I complete on my new house.'

'I thought there were problems with the searches?'

'Chloe! You're not supposed to make a note of every-thing I say and hold it against me when I want to change my mind about something!'

Chloe laughed. 'OK, guys. We're going to see if we can find Rob.'

'Oh goody,' said Bruno. 'I like Rob.'

They got a little lost and had to negotiate the lanes until they thought they were going in the right direction. Chloe, who knew the area best, was fairly confident they were on course. Anna didn't think it looked right, but kept her thoughts to herself.

Suddenly, Chloe said, 'Hang on – is that smoke?'

It was definitely smoke, a very large cloud of it. 'Either someone's having a massive bonfire,' said Anna, 'or . . .' She felt all the moisture drain from her mouth, and the blood from her bones. She felt very sick. 'Oh my God!' she whispered. 'Are you sure we're where you think we are?'

''Fraid so,' said Chloe, biting her lip. 'I would so like to be wrong.'

They drove towards the smoke. Even the boys seemed aware that the atmosphere in the car had changed and sat quietly in the back. Harry had fallen asleep in his booster seat.

Anna felt as if her insides had turned into a pit of snakes. She was sweating and unconsciously she leant forward in her seat and brought her knees up, to try to quell the churning. He's an adult, she told herself. He's perfectly capable of walking out of a burning building.

Chloe glanced across at her. 'It's terribly unlikely it's Rob's house, Anna,' she murmured, hoping the boys wouldn't catch on to what she was saying. She didn't want them asking questions she couldn't answer.

'There are no other houses around. If it isn't a bonfire, it must be Rob's house. But he might not be back yet.' A thought suddenly hit her. 'The dogs! Caroline!'

Chloe brought the car to a halt. 'Listen, even if it is a fire, we can't go there.' She nodded towards the back seat, indicating the reason.

Anna wiped sweat from her forehead. 'No. We must call the fire brigade. See if they're on their way.'

'OK, do that.'

'Damn,' said Anna, a few minutes later. 'No reception. We'll have to find a telephone box.'

Chloe started the car again and pulled back out into the road. 'We can be home in just over five minutes. I know exactly where we are now.'

'OK, but if we see a phone box, I want to stop,' Anna insisted.

'All right. It probably is just a bonfire. The fire brigade will think we're a nuisance call.'

'No they won't. If it is a fire they want to know about it, and if it isn't, well, better a false alarm than not telling them.'

'I'll turn on Radio Gloucestershire and see if there's any news,' said Chloe.

Anna didn't answer; she just sat in silence, willing Chloe to go faster along the lanes, concentrating on not being sick. The five minutes or so that it took them to get home could have been five hours in a torture chamber.

The moment Chloe had lifted the still-sleeping Harry out of the car, Anna said, 'Look, you phone the fire brigade. I've got a driving licence, I want to borrow the car and go back.' She paused, seeing the shock on Chloe's face. 'I know the car isn't insured for me to drive, but if anything happens to it, I'll buy you another one. I have to go back and see what's happened.'

Chloe looked utterly bewildered.

'I want to borrow the car!' said Anna, desperate.

Chloe gulped. 'Fine. But I could get someone to come round and look after the boys and go with you.'

'No. No time. I can't wait.' But she did pause. 'I mean it about buying you another car.'

Chloe shook her head. 'It's OK. It's insured for any driver. It was in case I was ever stuck; but when did you last drive, Anna?'

Anna almost smiled. 'The day I passed my test.'

'OK,' Chloe said, seeing that she wasn't going to be able to dissuade her. 'Here, take my keys.'

As Anna went through all the procedures her driving instructor had drilled into her (seatbelt, mirror, ignition, mirror, gear, mirror, and a final look over her shoulder) she realised that all doubt about the genuineness of her

320

feelings for Rob had vanished the moment she saw smoke rising from his house. If Max had lived there, it would have been Caroline who would have been uppermost in her anxiety. While she was worried about her dog, she knew that she was even more worried about Rob.

She probably didn't need to check her mirror so many times, but she was in such a state she couldn't let herself take chances. She moved off, fractionally slower that a snail with a Zimmer frame. A little further on she realised that her tongue was welded to the roof of her mouth. There was a leftover bottle of water rolling round in the footwell. She pulled over and drank quite a lot of it and it calmed her. She set off again to Rob's house, hoping she could remember the way.

The smoke and a sense of direction she didn't know she had led her to the house. There were fire engines and firemen everywhere. Anna felt a moment of relief. At least it hadn't mattered that they couldn't get through. The moment she was spotted, one of them came over to her.

'Keep out of the way please, love. We've got enough on our hands.'

Anna could see that he was right. Half the house seemed to be up in flames and the heat would have kept her back if the fireman hadn't. It was horrible to see. She forced some moisture into her mouth so she could speak. 'I just have to know. My friend lives there. Is he all right?'

There was a pause. 'Someone went to hospital in an ambulance. Would that be your friend?'

'Oh God, I don't know.' Anxiety was making it diffi-cult for her to speak, and when she did, her voice was so croaky it was barely audible. 'I'm not sure he was even here. And the dogs? There were four dogs at least, and one of them was mine.'

'They're all right.' Anna sighed with partial relief. At least Caroline was safe. 'That's how the bloke got injured, rescuing the dogs,' the fireman continued. 'Apparently they were in the bit where the fire started. If only people would get their wiring fixed!' He smiled at her, obviously aware she was in shock. 'I'd be out of a job.'

'Do you know which hospital he might have been taken to?' Anna asked, her legs almost buckling beneath her.

"Fraid not, love. It could be the local one, or it could be Gloucester. I suggest you go home and ring round. Now, you're just in the way.'

Anna turned away from the flames, frantic. Knowing that the dogs were OK was one good thing, but until she knew about Rob, she would be beside herself. And the house! Even if Rob wasn't badly hurt, his house was destroyed and with it his dreams. As she walked towards the car she heard a great timber crash down and realised that her face was wet with tears.

She sat in the car and thought about getting it back to Chloe. On the way she'd had Rob to focus on: she had to get there to see if he and the dogs were all right. But now she had no incentive other than that she'd borrowed Chloe's car and needed to get it back to her in one piece. The elastic seemed to have snapped in her limbs. She remembered hearing that on safaris, if a rhino or something was chasing a group of people, it was no trouble getting them to climb up the trees out of the way, but it was hell's own job getting them down again. This was her version of climbing down the tree with no fear or adrenalin to help her.

Breathing deeply in an effort to calm herself down she sat in the driving seat with the door open. She finished the bottle of water and then had an overwhelming urge to pee.

'OK,' she said to herself. 'Find a tree and go behind it. No one will see. They're all preoccupied with the fire. You can't drive if you can't concentrate.'

Finding a place and getting herself organised seemed incredibly complicated. 'If only I was wearing a skirt!'

she berated herself, and then went on, 'Don't be stupid! You hardly ever wear skirts. Just try not to get it everywhere.'

The mechanics of it seemed extremely difficult and she realised that this was where penis envy, if such a thing existed, sprang from. God obviously was a man. At last she zipped up her trousers, feeling slightly damp. As she walked back to the car she said, 'If you can't even have a wee without making a mess of it, how on earth do you think you're going to drive a car?'

And it was so much more important that she got that right. Cars were dangerous beasts, intolerant of mistakes. And if cars would put up with the odd scrunch or scrape, Anna wasn't sure that Mike would. It was only now that the impact of driving someone else's car hit her. She really mustn't make a single mistake.

She got back into the driving seat. It was properly adjusted. There wasn't any traffic. Getting out of the wood would be easy. 'You drove here all right; you can drive back all right. And there are no towns or anything between you and Chloe. It'll be a piece of cake.'

Apart from having to do a hill start once, something she'd avoided on the way there, her journey back was surprisingly easy and it was with a certain amount of pride that she knocked on Chloe's door, dangling the keys.

'He's in hospital. They don't know which one. The dogs are OK.' Then she burst into tears.

Chapter Twenty-Four

❦

'Come in,' said Chloe. 'I'll get the Rescue Remedy. You're covered in soot. It's all right!' She put her arms round Anna and steered her to the nearest kitchen chair. 'I'm sure Rob's not badly hurt. We'll telephone all the hospitals and find out where he is. Sit down.'

Anna sat and, a moment later, obediently lifted her tongue while her friend squirted fluid into her mouth. 'It tastes like brandy,' she said.

'I know, but it can't be the brandy that makes it work because you'd have to drink a whole bottle.'

'I can't believe I drove your car. Oh, Chloe! Supposing he's badly hurt! I love him so much. And his house. It's all so dreadful.' She looked stricken.

'I've called Susannah,' said Chloe, taking charge. 'She's going to pop over and mind the boys. While we're waiting for her to do that, we'll ring round and find out where Rob is.'

'Can you do that if you're not a next of kin?'

'I have no idea! You'll – I'll have to pretend I'm his sister or something if they're difficult.'

'You're a star, Chloe.' Anna blinked at her friend, fighting back tears. 'There's no way I could be sensible at the moment. I expect the Rescue Remedy will kick in soon.'

'Perhaps it already has; you're sounding a bit more rational. It's such a pity Mike had to go away again. Still, that's the way it is. Now I'm going to go upstairs and check on the boys. They seem quite happy; they're all exhausted. Then I'm going to phone. If I have to tell lies I don't want an audience. Here, read a magazine. Chloe threw a copy of a gossip magazine at Anna and ran upstairs.

Anna looked at the magazine without seeing it. She couldn't concentrate on facelifts, wonder diets and who was sleeping with whom when her mind was full of Rob. He was such a good, kind man, and incredibly sexy. Max had been sexy in theory, but in practice – Anna shuddered and picked up a pillow to hug. 'Oh, Chloe, please hurry up,' she crooned into it. 'Let Rob be all right.'

Chloe came down the stairs really quite quickly. 'I said I was his sister, and they said: "Another sister?" Obviously his real sister is already there. I said a man could have more than one sister. Anyway, he's in the local hospital which is good because it means he can't be badly hurt. Good news, huh?'

Anna blinked so she wouldn't burst into tears again. 'Excellent.'

'And Susannah won't be long. Her mother only lives next door and can pop over to look after her tots. Shall we make Marmite sandwiches? You never know what the food's like in hospital. I never like to go anywhere without Marmite sandwiches.'

'What?' Anna stared at her friend as if she had gone mad.

'It'll give me something to do while we're waiting,' said Chloe, trying to instil calm in her friend. 'And they might come in useful.'

Seeing the sense in keeping occupied, Anna said, 'I'll help you.'

Chloe valiantly refrained from saying she could have got on much quicker without Anna's dubious assistance. Her concentration was all over the place and she kept putting the Marmite on before the butter. They'd managed about two between them when there was a knock on the door.

'Thank goodness!' said Chloe, flinging down her knife and rushing to the door. She flung it open. 'Hi! I'll babysit for you any time at all. I'll have all your children to stay so you can go off on a romantic weekend.'

Susannah, who looked like a typical earth mother in an ankle-length skirt and slightly grubby T-shirt, shooed them out of the door. 'You go and find out about this chap in hospital. I'll take care of the boys. Do they need a bath?'

Chloe's face took on an expression of extreme guilt. 'Yes they do, they're filthy!'

'Supposing they won't let us in,' Anna said to Chloe as they drew near the hospital. 'They might not, if he's really ill.'

'They would have told me if he was really ill and said he's only allowed to see one person at a time,' said Chloe matter-of-factly. 'I'm sure it can't be that bad. Do try not to worry. I know it's difficult, but we'll be there in a minute. Oh look, there's the car park. Let's see if there's a space.'

Anna was so anxious she could hardly get her legs to work, but somehow she went up the steps to the hospital entrance. At reception Chloe asked which ward Rob was in, and Anna followed her along the corridors.

'It's just as well it's a small hospital,' said Chloe, chattily. 'You can walk miles in big hospitals.'

Aware that her friend was making conversation for her sake, Anna attempted some sort of reply. Luckily they reached the ward and she could stop trying.

Her heart flipped when she saw Rob from the door to the ward. He was lying on top of the bedclothes and even from here she could see he was looking murderous. The kind, funny, teasing Rob she had come to know had been turned into the angry man she had seen a glimpse of when Caroline got away from her all those weeks ago.

Although she badly wanted to see him, at that moment Anna wanted to go home even more. Cassie was with him and she suddenly felt like an intruder. He wouldn't want to see her in this state. She grabbed Chloe's arm, about to tell her that they must leave, when Cassie spotted them.

'Oh look, here's that nice girl who helped at the fête. Anna, isn't it? Come on in. Rob's in a stinking mood, I'm afraid.'

'Um, I think I'll go and get a coffee,' said Chloe and disappeared.

Anna walked across the ward to the bed. 'Hi!' she whispered, wishing his sister wasn't there. She wanted to fling her arms round him, to check he was really all right, but she couldn't because Cassie would read too much into it. And she wasn't really for that just yet. Denying herself a proper embrace made her feel she couldn't even kiss his cheek.

'Hi Anna,' said Rob. He smiled ruefully at her. 'This isn't quite how I'd imagined seeing you again. I—'

'He's a bit upset,' Cassie interrupted him without even noticing she was doing it. 'They won't let him out until tomorrow. But he was very lucky I was in town and able to get here straight away. Fortunately he remembered my mobile number and could get the hospital to phone me. His phone stopped working when he dropped it in the flames.'

'Well, it would,' muttered Anna.

'Luckily I was able to phone the fire brigade and Geoff before the fire got too bad,' said Rob.

Then Cassie turned to her brother and raised her voice slightly, as if he were very elderly or of limited intelligence. 'Tell Anna how you rescued the dogs. She'd like to hear that.'

The fact that he hadn't yet brained Cassie spoke volumes for his patience; he was obviously longing to. She was worse than Laura. 'You tell her. I'm fed up with telling people.' He looked exhausted, thought Anna, and wasn't surprised that he closed his eyes. She perched on one of the plastic chairs at the side of the bed.

Cassie seemed quite pleased to take on the role of reporter. 'Well, he'd just got back from being away, hadn't you, Rob?'

'Yes,' he breathed.

'And you saw smoke coming out of the place where the dogs are kept. Well, of course he had to get into the main part of the house to get through to their bit, and the smoke was really thick. I told him he should have put a wet cloth over his mouth to protect him from the smoke.'

'And if you'd also told me where I was likely to find a cloth and some water from outside the house in a hurry, that would have been a handy tip.' This was said with his eyes still closed and Anna couldn't decide if it was because he was exhausted, or just irritated to the point of madness. She longed to touch him as Cassie revealed every grisly detail, with some relish, Anna noticed.

Cassie gave him an older sister look. 'Anyway, the flames had taken hold but fortunately the bolt on the door to the garden was really flimsy—'

'I seem to remember you telling me to get that bolt changed,' said Rob. 'But as I hadn't, I could just kick it open and we all got out.'

He said this last bit to Anna, whose mouth was dry and hung slightly open. 'Thank God,' she whispered.

He managed a weak smile. 'The dogs are with a farmer friend. They won't get the five-star treatment that they're used to, but they'll be warm and comfortable and get a run every day.' He explained where the farm was.

Anna moistened her lips. It was the thought of what might so easily have happened that was freezing her into immobility. She made an effort to appear normal. 'Um, is there anything I can get you?' She remembered the

Marmite sandwiches left on Chloe's worktop and really hoped he didn't want them.

'You can get me out of here. Sorry!' He sent Anna an apologetic smile. 'I'm just so angry with myself. It's all my fault. If I hadn't let people in while I was away, I would have realised they'd rigged up the temporary electrics in an unsafe way.'

'Don't be silly, Robbie.' His sister, who had obviously looked after him a lot when he was little, patted his leg. 'You've got to stay here until the doctor's had another look at you and then you're coming home with me to recover.'

'I'm not ill! I've only got a sprained ankle!' he said impatiently.

'Don't forget the smoke inhalation,' Cassie felt the need to remind him.

'Oh, for God's sake! I'm fine! I don't need to come—'

Cassie snapped out of big-sister mode and into the kind of older sister that tells her brother he has BO and really needs to do something about his spots. 'Sweetie, I don't want to rub this in, but you've nowhere else to go,' she said practically. 'You're homeless, you've sprained your ankle and you can't drive.'

Rob closed his eyes again and sighed very deeply, then he looked at Anna, a ghost of his usual humour in the mixture of anger and frustration. 'If it wasn't so bloody annoying, it would be almost funny.'

Anna didn't think it was at all funny. It was tragic. She tried to think of something positive and encouraging to say but couldn't think of anything. Much as she would have liked to, she didn't feel she could invite him to stay with her in her rented house. 'It's awful,' was all she could manage.

'It's not the end of the world,' said Cassie. 'Everyone's OK. Think how awful it would have been if one of the dogs had been hurt – all of them, possibly.'

'Well, there is that,' murmured Anna. She looked at Rob, who was scowling at Cassie. 'Could I bring you anything to read? Solitaire? Pack of cards?' She searched her empty brain for ways to lighten his life. 'Scrabble, possibly?'

'Sweet of you to offer,' said Cassie before Rob could speak, 'but I can bring him anything he needs: a portable DVD player for one, then I may be able to get one of his nephews to give up his Game Boy for twenty-four hours.' She made Anna's idea of entertainment sound very old-fashioned. She smiled again. 'I'm hoping to take him back with me tomorrow.' She patted Anna's leg now. 'You must visit. Play chess with him or something. I know he's going to be a nightmare to entertain.'

Rob closed his eyes once more.

'I'd love to visit,' said Anna, 'but you'll have to give me directions. I'm not sure where you live, exactly.'

But Cassie had lost interest in Anna and had turned her attention back to Rob. 'I will. Now it looks as if my little brother needs a bit of shut-eye.'

Anna got up. 'If there's anything I can do, Rob?'

'Really, everything's under control,' said Cassie, chivvying her away from the bed. 'But I really look forward to seeing you.' She gave Anna a conspiratorial smile that made Anna want to hit her. 'I remember from when he was a little boy, he's a terrible patient.'

Anna didn't even have time to say goodbye to Rob as she was propelled out of the ward by Cassie.

Chloe was still drinking her coffee when Anna rejoined her. 'You didn't stay long. Was he all right?'

Anna sat down opposite Chloe. 'I think so,' she said, although she was still feeling rather shell-shocked. 'His sister stayed the whole time. Please do remind me how bossy she is if ever I moan about Laura. Poor Rob! Anyway, I hope she's going to invite me over – she can't

330

really expect me to just pop in, can she? She lives miles away. It's so awful to think he's lost everything. And he's sprained his ankle so he can't drive. He must feel so helpless.'

'It is bloody awful, but at least he rescued the dogs. He'd never be able to live with himself if anything had happened to them.'

'True,' said Anna, then fell into a contemplative silence. Some minutes later she said, 'I must buy a car. I'll need it if I'm going to visit Rob.'

'How long is he going to be at his sister's then?'

'I'm not sure, but she says I must come and visit, and then there's the dogs. I can drive over and take them out. Anyway, I need a car.'

'Shall we go?' Chloe gathered up her bag and put her plastic cup in a nearby bin.

Anna trailed after her friend. She felt so frustrated. Her visit to Rob had been completely taken over by Cassie, who treated Rob like a child, and she wasn't sure when she would see him again.

'I mean it about buying a car,' she said as soon as they were back in Chloe's. 'It would definitely be useful.'

'Well, why don't you hire one first, until you've got used to driving again.

'Why? Why not buy one?'

'Because you don't know the first thing about cars! You could get sold a lemon.'

Anna gave her friend a withering glance. 'I may not know much about cars but I'm quite good on fruit.'

'Idiot! No, much better to hire a car.'

'Surely it would be more economical to buy one?' Anna watched a car whistle by and wondered if she would ever feel competent enough to drive so fast.

'No! If you hire one it'll be new and reliable and if anything goes wrong you just ring them.'

Anna considered this. 'But I could buy a new one,

although I hadn't planned to. Really, I just want a big old estate that I can put building materials and several greyhounds – or at least Caroline – in the back of. Something really practical for a girl like me.'

'I can see that would be useful, but until someone – Rob, Mike, Will perhaps – is around to help you buy one, just hire something that can take you to and from Rob's sister's house.'

'But I couldn't put the dogs in a hire car, unless I hired something huge.'

'Why not?'

'Dog hairs! And although I do see your point, I'd really rather have my own old jalopy so it won't matter if I scrape a few walls.' Chloe raised an eyebrow. Anna smiled. 'Not that I will do. Anyway I quite fancy being a car owner, although I never thought I'd get back from Rob's alive.' She shuddered. 'I've never seen a house fire before. I wasn't there more than a few minutes, but it was so frightening. And to think of all Rob's hard work, gone.'

'The dogs could have been gone, too, if it hadn't been for Rob.'

'He is a bit of a hero.'

'He's a lot of a hero.'

Anna nodded. 'It's just a pity he sprained his ankle kicking down the door. That never happens to Bruce Willis.'

'Bruce Willis doesn't have much hair and is way too old for you.'

'True,' said Anna ruefully.

Once back in her rented house after having a restorative drink with Chloe, Anna spent some time looking at the local paper she'd filched from Chloe, and the *Yellow Pages*. She turned on her computer and checked her bank balance online. Then she dug out her driving licence. The local paper told her that she could buy the sort of car she wanted for very little money. She wouldn't buy one from an individual seller, even if there were a couple that seemed very cheap; she would be sensible and go to a dealer, who'd give her some sort of guarantee – but buy a car she would.

Since seeing Rob lying in the hospital, furious and unable to do anything, helping Rob had become Anna's raison d'être. And as she couldn't help him personally, she had to help him make his house habitable. All the energy and enthusiasm she had put into her little cottage she now wanted to put into restoring his house to a live-able condition.

It wasn't as if she had another project of her own she could get into immediately, she argued to herself as she cycled along the lanes to town the following day. The house she had decided to buy wouldn't be hers for a few weeks. She had time on her hands. This is what she would tell Chloe and her sister when inevitably they discovered what she was up to. But in her heart she knew she would have felt like that even if she had got possession of her own house, and could start measuring and drawing and, later, swinging a sledgehammer about. Rob had lost what meant most in the world to him; she had to try and give what she could of it back. Getting her own transport was the first step towards making that possible.

When she chained her bike up on the railings of the car-showroom forecourt, she was obviously a woman not to be messed with.

'Hi,' she said to the rather startled young man at the desk. 'I want to buy a car.' She put her cycle helmet on the counter and fluffed at her hair. It had got stuck to her head and felt uncomfortable. 'And I want to drive it away today. Can you arrange that for me?'

The young man took a breath. Anna couldn't decide which of them was the more unnerved by her request, her or him. She decided it must be her. He had probably sold a car before.

'What sort of car were you looking for?' he asked.

'An estate,' she said. 'It doesn't have to be fast, but it needs to carry a lot of stuff. It must be totally reliable, never break down, and it must be environmentally friendly – if that's possible for a car.'

The young man made some marks on the paper in front of him. 'Right. And have you got your insurance papers for your current car?'

'I haven't got a current car, that's why I'm buying one. I came here on my bike. Didn't you see?'

'So you don't own a car currently?' He obviously thought she'd been beamed down from another planet.

'No. I've never owned one. This will be my first time. I suppose you could call me a car virgin.' She wrinkled her brow. 'But I really would prefer you not to.'

The young man's own brow developed a film of sweat. 'Have you got a driving licence?'

Anna pulled it out of her back pocket. 'Oh yes. And it's clean. Unused, and totally unblemished.'

The man cleared his throat. 'Right. Well, if you'd like to come this way. How much were you hoping to pay?'

'That's not as important as getting the right car. But otherwise, as little as possible.' She smiled at him. 'I do have the money to pay for it, I promise.'

Anna drove her car very slowly out of the forecourt. She was fully legal and couldn't quite believe what she'd done. The young man had loaded her bicycle in the boot and persuaded Anna it was not necessary for her to wear her cycle helmet. 'It's a car you're driving now, and you'd look silly.'

As they'd been through a lot together she trusted him and smiled. She realised she knew him better than she'd ever known Max.

334

Now she looked both ways, several times, and drove her very first car out on to the road. She was glad that the traffic was light. She drove the car round the block and then round the town, following the cars in front, indicating when they indicated, and generally got to feel familiar with it. Then she drove towards her rented house. There she would collect her sketchbook, tape and pens and go and see for herself exactly what the damage to Rob's house was. Then, when she went to see him at his sister's, she could perhaps give him some good news. His sister had promised to ring her and invite her over, surely quite soon. She had to have as much ready to show him as possible.

Tears came to her eyes as she parked the car and saw the blackened beams, the empty windows and one wall completely collapsed. The smell of the fire was still appallingly strong. She had been so full of determination on the journey over, and in her head she had made the job seem quite do-able by a woman more than competent at DIY. Now she saw it she knew she couldn't possibly do it herself, not until a lot of the initial building work was finished, anyway.

It took an effort to push her emotions aside and be the practical woman she claimed to be but as she walked about the ruins she realised that the main part of the house was still mostly intact. What had burnt to nothing was an extension, probably from the twenties or thirties, going by the tiles left on the floor. It was where the dogs lived and Anna could imagine the panic Rob must have felt when he discovered the fire, and where it had come from. The thought of him kicking down the door in a room full of smoke and flames made her heart turn over. It was what might have been that was so terrifying.

In a way, she realised, getting rid of the extension, which had blocked part of the light from the kitchen, had improved the property. Inspired, she got out her note-book and began making rough sketches. If she could tell Rob that all was not lost, it might cheer him up when she went to visit him. He'd be getting enough grapes and Marmite sandwiches from his sister. From her he would want news of his house.

It would cost a fortune to do, of course, but as she counted paces and jotted things down, ideas began to crowd into her head and excitement began to replace her shock at the devastation. This would be a much bigger project that her own little cottage, something she could really get her teeth into. Of course it wasn't her house, and she wouldn't dream of suggesting Rob used her plans unless he wanted to, but doing the drawings would be a really interesting exercise.

A two-storey extension, to replace the one that had burnt down, could be put on to the west side of the building, where the remains of a conservatory now smouldered, broken glass glinting in the rubble.

Another conservatory, or sunroom, could go on the other side of the house, the cool side, so it wouldn't get too hot in summer. You'd have to get rid of the shed, of course, so the view was better, but already in her imag-ination the room was full of climbing plants that liked it cooler: plumbago, passion flowers possibly – she'd have to ask Laura.

When she'd done all the measuring and drawings she could without a drawing board, or even a table, she got back into her car, which was now feeling familiar and friendly, and set off in what she hoped was the direction of the farm and the dogs.

Once there, via a few minor deviations, it took Anna a while to track down the farmer, who was doing some-thing in a barn far away from the house.

'Hello,' she said. He was a youngish man of medium height, dressed in muddy jeans, an old and cracked waxed jacket and a tweed cap pulled down low. 'I'm Anna. I've come to take Rob's dogs for a run, if that's all right.'

The man regarded Anna contemplatively for a few moments and then said, 'Eh, you're all right. You can take them up into that field if you like. There's no stock in there at present, and the hedges are good. You a friend of Rob's then?' His curiousity was evident. Perhaps Rob didn't have many friends.

'Sort of. He's been looking after my dog for me. She's one of the ones you've got. I've just been to see him in hospital. He told me where the dogs were.'

'Oh aye.' He didn't comment, but she could feel him speculating about whether there was more to their relationship than just dogs.

'So – the dogs?' Anna realised he probably thought she was too young for Rob, and she did look young in jeans, a hoody and trainers. I should have put on some make-up, she thought. Then I wouldn't look quite so much like someone's kid sister. There was also the faint but pressing concern that she might have soot on her face.

Anna knew it was going to be difficult seeing Caroline when she couldn't take her home, but she braced herself, and although Caroline was ecstatic to be reunited with her, it didn't seem as if she'd been too miserable. Anna clung to her for a few moments trying not to think of her dying in a fire. Then, because Rob's friend was looking, she said hello to the other dogs, who greeted her politely, but with none of Caroline's rapturous enthusiasm.

'They've been fine there together,' said Geoff, who had warmed up sufficiently to introduce himself. 'But they'll be glad to be back with their master.'

Anna didn't add 'or mistress'. Laura and Chloe would have been ashamed of her.

'Do you know the way to the field?' he asked. 'You'll need leads to take them up there.'

'I've been to it from the other end, with Rob, but I don't know it from this way.'

'I'll find the leads for you.'

Anna felt a bit as if she was behind a team of huskies, crossing the Arctic wastes as she took hold of four leads attached to four huge dogs. They behaved perfectly, however, being accustomed to walking on the lead from their days as racing greyhounds, and she had no trouble. She had taken the precaution of buying some dog treats on her way, and she had two packets of ham slices for when they'd had their run in the field and needed to go back on their leads. Caroline was very good about this, seeming to like being back in contact with her mistress, but she didn't know if Rob's dogs would feel the same about it, particularly when she wasn't truly their pack leader.

As Geoff was present when she returned the dogs to their stable, Anna managed to hold herself together when she closed the door on Caroline. She missed her but she was excited about the prospect of putting together her plans for Rob's house.

'Rob rang me as soon as he'd got the dogs out of the house and rung the fire brigade,' Geoff said. 'And asked me to take the dogs out of the way. I reckon he's a bit of a hero, kicking down the door to get them out. I heard he'd broken his ankle doing it.'

'I think it's only sprained,' Anna said. 'As I said, I went to see him in hospital just after it had happened. I saw the fire from a distance, you see.'

'Ah.'

'Also, he had my dog. Naturally I was worried.'

'Ah, right.' He paused. 'I reckon it was the wiring.'

'Apparently it usually is.'

'Cost a fortune to repair the house. He'll have to sell it as a building plot, I reckon.'

Anna smiled as if in agreement. Over her dead body.

Chapter Twenty-Five

❧

For the next few days Anna first took the dogs out and then went on to Rob's house every afternoon. She was waiting for a call from Rob's sister, inviting her to visit, but none came. She tried not to feel downhearted, telling herself it gave her more time to get on with the job. She almost wished she knew exactly which house in that pretty village his sister lived at, then she might have just gone over without being invited. But she didn't fancy knocking on doors looking for her, so not knowing the address made this seem impossible.

Perhaps if she'd done it immediately it would have been all right. Now too much time seemed to have elapsed for her to do this. It would look as if she was desperate to see Rob. She was desperate, but she didn't want either him or his sister to know.

She put her caring into his house. It became her passion, more important to her than anything. She hadn't ever felt this fired up before, even over her own little cottage. Her drawing board now had layer upon layer of ground plans, roughs, different elevations, sketches of details he may or may not want. She'd carefully copied all remaining sections of architrave so they could be used as a template if necessary. She'd even drawn the remaining floor tiles so they could be reproduced in exactly the same, compli-cated pattern. She would have preferred something a bit plainer herself, but it was his house, she wanted to offer him all the options. Reference books with period details piled up around her desk, which she hadn't stored away

– she must have instinctively known she'd need it. She couldn't guess which of the several periods the house sprang from he would want to take up, so she did designs for all three.

She worked until late at night, barely noticing the time and falling back into her old habit of eating chocolate and snatched meals. She'd hardly seen Chloe, who was luckily preoccupied with various school and playgroup summer events.

On the fourth day she forced herself to do a rough costing. Without a builder to look at the site and the plans it could only be very rough, but even at the most optimistic estimate it seemed likely it would cost about the same as a small housing estate.

It would be very much cheaper to knock down the ruins and build a house from scratch. It seemed deeply depressing but these days a house that looked as if it was period could be built from scratch. Rob would need a fully qualified architect, as her training had only covered the first part, but anything was possible. Especially as she was perfectly willing to stop the purchase of her new house and put all her money into Rob's. Then she realised he probably wouldn't let her do that, and he would probably be right.

There was nothing else for it, she had to consult a builder. Rob had given her the name of one, when he thought she'd need more help than she'd had from Eric. She would ring him up and arrange to meet him on site. She'd need a structural engineer, too. And maybe Eric, whom she now knew and trusted, for extra support. She hoped they'd do it out of the kindness of their hearts.

Although she was totally committed to Rob's house, she couldn't help feeling hurt that he hadn't invited her over to visit him. She couldn't really blame it on his sister because she'd definitely said she wanted her to come.

Maybe Rob didn't want her to see him when he wasn't at his best.

But perhaps he just didn't want to see her. Maybe she'd imagined all that electricity between them. Or maybe it had it all been on her side? Had he just kissed her because it was a lovely summer's day and she was a woman, wearing, she realised now, only a very skimpy dress? Maybe all those fireworks had only exploded for her?

Determinedly she pushed aside these negative feelings. She had been wrong about Max, but she wasn't wrong about Rob, she was sure of it. She buried herself in her plans and made telephone calls. It took a little fiddling and negotiation, but eventually she found a time when everyone could be on site.

It was a truly beautiful summer's morning when Anna set off for the site meeting. Eleven frantic days had passed since she had seen Rob in hospital. She had put aside the hurt that neither Rob nor his sister had got round to inviting her to visit, and used every second of the time.

She had deliberately taken a bit of trouble with her appearance, to give her confidence and to stop her looking like the college student she sometimes felt she still was. It was important to make a good, professional impression on these people. Even now many men were wary of taking orders from a woman. Not that she'd be giving orders today, of course. Today was all about consultation. She had several copies of her plans in her drawings tube, so they could take them away and think about them. She was full of optimism and hope.

It was a lovely site for a house, she thought, as she'd thought every time she'd seen it. She parked her Volvo sedately beside the two other cars that were there already, although, checking her watch, she saw that she was early herself.

She greeted Eric cheerfully. The two other men, who

had come together, were strangers, but seemed nice enough. She'd had quite a long chat with them both before setting up the appointment so she felt she knew them both a little.

'I'm Arthur Baynes,' said one. This was the builder. 'I know Rob Hunter a bit. Terrible what's happened to his house. You must be Anna, the interior designer?'

Anna nodded and allowed her hand to be crushed in his.

'This is Phil Meadows, the structural engineer. You spoke on the phone.' Although he wasn't the same man who had given her own cottage a clean bill of health, he looked friendly as well as suitably professional.

And to Anna's relief neither of them made remarks about interior designers and scatter cushions. They seemed prepared to treat her as a fellow professional. She was sufficiently accustomed to being treated like a glorified window dresser to be able to swiftly disabuse people of their misconceptions, but it was nice not to have to.

Introductions made, they trooped over the site together, discussing the damage and Anna's potential plans. She was on her knees, unrolling a set of them on to a flat stone when she heard a car. A Land-Rover towing a caravan rumbled slowly on to the parking area.

She felt she was watching everything happen in slow motion. The Land-Rover stopped and Rob got out, obviously annoyed to find his way obstructed by the three cars already there. She started to get to her feet, to explain, but the plans rolled up and threatened to blow away. Arthur, the builder, got to Rob before she did and as she panted up, the plans under her arm, she heard him say, 'She's got some great plans for your house, Rob. Phil's had a good look round too, and Eric.'

'What?' Rob looked confused and then spotted Anna. 'Hello, Anna!' Although he was pale and rather gaunt, he seemed pleased to see her.

She was ecstatic. She hadn't expected to see him but now he was here, they could all go over the site together. She could tell him about her plans as well as the others.

'It's so exciting!' she said. 'I've done lots of plans and Arthur and Phil Meadows – he's the structural engineer, but of course you know that . . .' She stopped, aware that Rob was no longer smiling.

'What's going on, Anna?' he said, ignoring the three men, who were all looking rather puzzled.

She suddenly felt unaccountably guilty. 'Nothing's going on, I just . . .'

'Just what?' he demanded softly.

'I just thought it would be a good idea to have a site meeting.' She licked her lips, trying not to show how upset she was.

'A site meeting? At my house? Why? Is that a developer? Are you involved with them?'

Anna was distraught that he could so misunderstand the situation. 'No, there's no one else involved except me. I got them over here because there's no point in making plans—'

A look of anger flashed across Rob's face and all the blood drained from her. 'So you're the developer, are you Anna?'

'Not like that!' she squeaked.

'Like what then?'

Anna couldn't speak. The others stood like shop dummies, no one daring to get involved.

'Like what?' Rob repeated, tension straining his voice. As Anna could only stare at him, he finally lost his temper. 'What the bloody hell do you think you're doing!' he raged at her. 'This is my house! It's not for you to make plans for it, to employ people, in fact you shouldn't even be here at all! You're trespassing!'

She uncleaved her tongue from the roof of her mouth. She had no answers. It suddenly all seemed so silly, so quixotic, so thoroughly impractical. She couldn't say that

344

she'd done it for him, because she loved him, that she wanted to make it so his house wasn't just a burnt-out shell, but a project, something that could be achieved. She would look like, and indeed was, an idiot.

'Well?' he roared again. 'What have you got to say for yourself?'

Arthur looked at Anna. 'Didn't he know you were doing all this?' he said, finally finding his voice.

'I thought he was your client,' Phil spoke up. 'What are we doing here if he hasn't commissioned you?'

Eric, who knew her better than the other two, remained silent. In fact, he knew her well enough to be sure she hadn't been doing anything underhand, but couldn't have guessed her motives.

'We'll be going then,' said Arthur, and the three men walked swiftly back to their cars, leaving Anna and Rob to it.

Knowing no cataclysmic event would save her, she gathered what resources she could. 'I was trying to help,' she managed at last. 'I wanted to have something for you to work with when you got back.'

'Oh, did you? And why was that? Because you saw it as a good investment?' he accused. 'An opportunity to be exploited?'

'No, I just felt so awful about your house being burnt—'

'That you couldn't wait to move in your team and take over? What on earth makes you think I want to sell my house to you? I know it's worth nothing as it stands but it's mine!'

'I know it's yours—' Anna tried again.

'And how did you think I was going to pay for all the work you're so gaily planning?' he stormed.

'I was going to ask you to . . .' She realised nothing she was saying was penetrating his pall of anger. 'Oh, never mind.'

She turned from him and stalked back to the piece of wall where she had left her plans, her drawings tube and her notebook. She tried to roll up the plans but couldn't, so abandoned them and just took the tube and went towards her car. There was obviously no point in trying to reason with him.

'So you're just walking out, are you?' He came thundering after her and part of her noticed he was limping.

'No!' She took huge pleasure in contradicting him. 'I'm not walking out! I'm driving!'

She walked over to the car, ignoring Arthur, Eric and Phil, who were about to drive away, but aware of their fascination. They had obviously worked out exactly what was going on. She produced her car keys from her pocket and stabbed them into the lock of the Volvo.

'Now what are you doing?' Rob demanded.

'What does it look like I'm doing?' she snapped. 'I'm getting in my car!'

'But you don't drive!'

'Yes I do!' She pulled open the door but he put a hand on her arm to stop her.

'From when?'

'From when I passed my driving test.'

'But you go everywhere by bicycle!'

'Not any more. Now, let me go!'

He still held on to her arm. 'So if you've got a car, why the hell didn't you come and see me?' he hissed.

'Because you never asked me!' Anna was beginning to feel increasingly angry. Not only had he misconstrued her intentions, now he was accusing her of not caring at all.

'Surely to goodness you didn't have to wait for an invitation!' he said, his voice shaking. 'Since when has anyone had to wait for an invitation to visit someone who's ill?'

'According to you, you weren't ill! You just had a sprained ankle!'

'Oh, for goodness' sake, there was the smoke inhalation you know,' he said, glaring at her.

'You were staying with your sister! It was her house, I couldn't just turn up uninvited. Besides, I didn't know the address!'

'But you'd been there before!'

'I've been to Buckingham Palace before but it doesn't mean I know the way and it doesn't mean I'd go without an invitation!' She thought for a moment. 'Anyway, I haven't been there before. Just near.'

'Oh.' He paused for a second. 'I lost my mobile in the fire. I didn't have your number.'

'Oh.' Of course, now she remembered, and grudgingly admitted this was quite a good reason for him not getting in touch, but then again, he could have got hold of her via Chloe.

He read her thought. 'I tried to get in touch with you via Chloe, but she's ex-directory,' he said defensively.

Anna wasn't going to let him off so easily. 'Oh. So that explains everything,' she said. 'Good-o. Now, if you don't mind, I'll be going.' She just wanted to get away.

Although he'd taken his hand off her arm by now, he still stood in her way. 'None of that is any excuse for all this!' He made a sweeping gesture.

'I didn't start the fire, Rob.' She forced herself to remain calm, but she was now equally furious. How could he have read her so wrongly? He had totally over-reacted and she didn't went to be around him any more. 'All I tried to do was to make some plans for rebuilding,' she went on. 'I thought it was what you wanted. You obviously thought I was doing it for me!' She wrenched open the back door and threw her belongings into it.

'Well, what was I supposed to think?' he muttered. 'You were tramping all over my property with a lot of tradesmen. What else would you be doing?' He was now standing with his arms folded, daring her to deny this.

'If you can think that I'd do that then I'm sorry. And

you've got me as wrong as I've got you. Well, thank God we found out before we could make a terrible mistake – sorry, before *I* could make a terrible mistake.' She regarded him, shaking with anger and upset. 'It's just as well I'm used to being wrong about men, isn't it? It makes it all less of a shock.'

Then she got in the car and started it. As she'd left it in gear it bounded forward and Rob leapt out of the way. Then she kangeroo-jumped the car all the way out of the clearing. She was out of sight before she got the gears right and moved smoothly.

She drove as carefully as she could until she saw somewhere she could pull in, then she spent several minutes breathing deeply. She wouldn't let herself cry. That would serve no purpose. Now she needed to get home. She needed to reassess everything in a practical way. There was nothing else for it.

She didn't dare visit Chloe. A milligram of sympathy would fracture the brittle veneer of her courage. Nor was she ready to admit what a fool she'd been. How could she have made all those plans without consulting him? Of course he was furious. He had every right to be. She allowed herself one shuddering sigh. The fact was that she wouldn't have done anything he didn't like if she'd been able to see him. If she'd seen him she could have tactfully asked him what, if anything, he'd like her to do.

Did she believe his story about not being able to get in touch? Actually she did, and now it could be an advantage. This way, she could get in touch with him when she wanted to collect Caroline, but he couldn't get in touch with her. And she was angry too. He had no right to shout at her like that, to immediately assume the worst about her – surely he knew her well enough to know she'd never do anything like that. He'd looked at her with such fury, she thought she could almost see actual hatred in his eyes.

348

She got home, hardly aware of doing it, and realised that with so much on her mind, her driving had become more automatic. She got out of the car and closed the gate although, with Caroline miles away, it wasn't really necessary. How could she have been so mistaken about Rob's feelings for her? She had fallen in love with him, wanted him and was prepared to do anything for him. But how did he see her? As an interfering idiot? Well, she wasn't going to spend another three years mooning over a man. She was going to get on with her life.

She unlocked her door and went into the small, tidily arranged hall.

But not here, not in the Cotswolds. She couldn't carry on with her plans to buy that house because, much as she had loved the area, now it was nothing but a reminder of how stupid she'd been. She'd buy a house near Laura, and forget all about Amberford.

She went into the kitchen and put the kettle on, more for something to do than because she wanted to make anything with boiling water. Rob was a bastard, there was no other word for it! How could he think she was planning to take over his house behind his back? He couldn't have said or done anything that could have hurt her more. She hated him! And he was welcome to his burnt-out shell.

Forgetting the kettle, which was electric, she went into the sitting room and sat down. She was still wearing her fleece and it was a warm day, but she felt terribly cold.

'You've softened up,' she chided herself. 'Think how cold it was in your house to begin with.'

Reminding herself of her lovely little house, now owned by the elegant Julian, did not make her feel any better. Now she was safely home she felt exhausted, all the anger drained out of her.

She was sitting huddled on the sofa, losing the will to live, when the telephone rang.

'Hello, Anna!' It was Chloe and she sounded strange.

'Hello.'

'I'm ringing to see how you are.'

'Not great, actually, but, Chloe' – she changed her tone, to discourage Chloe's questions about her well-being – 'are you all right? You sound a bit tense.'

'I am a bit tense!' Chloe lowered her voice to the point of inaudibility. 'I've got—'

'What? You'll have to speak up. I can't hear a word.'

'I'm in the kitchen! Rob's next door. He wants to know if it's OK for me to give him your telephone number and address. He lost his mobile, his address book, everything like that, in the fire.'

Anna's lips went numb. The thought of seeing Rob made her shiver convulsively. 'Oh, Chloe, thank goodness you rang! No, absolutely do not give him my details! I really don't want to speak to him, ever again!'

'But I thought you two—'

'Well, you're wrong. I want nothing more to do with him.'

'But what about Caroline?' Chloe asked.

'I'll sort that out somehow. She's not with Rob at the moment, so I can get her back.'

'But you can't have her in your rented house!'

'No, but I'm not staying here. Oh, Chloe, there's loads I need to tell you,' Anna said in a small voice.

Chloe swallowed. 'I'll try and come over tonight,' she said so indistinctly that Anna could only make out the words because she could guess what Chloe would say, like the true friend she was.

'Great, but please don't tell Rob where I am! I really, really don't want to see him.'

'Are you sure?'

'Yes! I'm begging you, don't betray me!'

'Of course I won't betray you! I'll try and come round later, then.' And she hung up.

Anna went hot and then back to freezing cold again.

She reboiled the kettle and filled herself a hot-water bottle. She felt as if she was coming down with flu.

Anna was wearing her fleece and still clutching her hot-water bottle when Chloe arrived. Chloe was wearing a sleeveless dress which told Anna it was actually quite warm, and her arms were full of fish and chips, a bottle of vodka and a carrier bag full of books. 'Comfort reading,' Chloe said, it being the only item that needed explanation.

'Come in,' said Anna. She ushered Chloe into the living room that had a kitchen down one end. The rest was arranged as a sitting room, with a sofa and chairs. She regarded the fish and chips dubiously. 'I'm not sure I'm hungry, though.'

'Nonsense! When did you last eat?'

Anna considered. 'Not sure.' It could have been break-fast, but she might not have bothered. She'd been so excited about the site meeting she had arranged at Rob's house. Light years had passed since then.

'You're so lucky! When I'm miserable I eat, and then I get fat and that makes me more miserable.'

Anna hadn't been thinking of herself as lucky until then. It was a novel angle. 'Oh, Chloe, it's good to see you!' She hugged her friend. 'Now you've got to tell me why Rob went to your house.'

'Food first,' Chloe said stubbornly. 'Get the oven on, and we'll heat this lot up while we have a drink. Or at least, while I watch you have a drink.'

It took Anna some minutes to get the oven to work properly. It had a fan and several knobs and it was a while before she had heat and air, rather than just air.

'What have you got to put in the vodka?' asked Chloe.

Anna inspected her cupboards and the fridge. 'Elderflower cordial,' she said eventually.

'I would have brought something but we were out of tonic. Never mind, elderflower will have to do.'

'I might prefer mine without vodka.'

'Nonsense! Haven't you read *Bridget Jones*? There's only one cure for heartbreak, and it's vodka.'

'I'll find some glasses,' said Anna meekly, wondering how Chloe knew what she was suffering from. She certainly hadn't mentioned her heart.

Chloe started opening and closing cupboard doors in Anna's kitchen. 'Where on earth do you keep your plates? Oh, here they are. We must heat them.'

'Must we?'

Chloe nodded. 'I know it's only fish and chips but they won't taste nice if they're not hot. Now, pass those glasses.' She poured a small amount of cordial into each one.

'Are you sure about this?' Anna asked. 'We could just have boiling water. That makes it quite comforting.'

'Wimp!' Chloe poured a large measure of vodka on top of the cordial.

'What about the water?'

'There is no water! This is proper alcohol, not a cocktail! It would be better with ice though . . .' She looked questioningly at Anna who shook her head. 'OK, where's a spoon?' Chloe stirred the vodka into the syrup and then handed Anna a glass.

Anna regarded it as if it might contain poison. 'But you're driving. You can't drink practically neat vodka.'

'I know. I just want to taste what I'm feeding you. Have a sip.'

Anna sipped. 'It's incredibly sweet. But quite nice,' she added a moment or two later.

Chloe followed suit. 'Mm,' she said, making a face. 'Not my favourite mixer but not bad.'

When Anna felt Chloe was ready to sit down and discuss matters, she perched on the arm of the sofa and said, 'Now tell me about this whole Rob thing. I can't tell you how grateful I am to you for not giving him my address. You didn't, did you?' she added anxiously.

'Of course not! But don't get too complacent. He knows roughly where you live, just not which house. He found out my telephone number through the Greyhound Trust. He was kicking himself for not thinking of it before.'

'I can't think why he wants to see me. I certainly don't want to see him.' Anna clutched a scatter cushion to her, seeing the point of them at last.

'I rather get the impression he wanted to apologise to you. He said he'd said some dreadful things.'

'It's not what he said that bothers me, it's what he thought.'

'Which was?' Chloe asked, heading for the kitchen area.

'That I was making plans for his house – his burnt-out house – so I could sweep in and make a profit. Quite honestly, Chlo, if he can even think that, he doesn't know me at all.'

Chloe was opening and shutting drawers, looking for cutlery. 'The trouble is, you haven't seen each other for a bit. That's how misunderstandings develop. He was extremely keen to make contact with you while he was at his sister's.' Frustration can make people react in funny ways. Ah, here we are.' She brandished a couple of knives and forks and set about putting portions of fish and chips on to two plates.

Anna accepted hers and put it on her lap, evicting the hot-water bottle. 'If he was that desperate, why didn't he try harder?' Anna was starting to wind herself up again.

'Because he hadn't thought how to. You know what men are like.' Chloe joined Anna on the sofa, her own meal in her hand. 'And he kept thinking you'd get in touch with him, and get me to drive you over, or something. He knew *your* mobile phone hadn't been destroyed in a fire,' she said reasonably.

'It would have been hard for me to get in touch with

him! I don't know his sister's surname, let alone her telephone number. She's quite likely to be ex-directory anyway, like you.' Anna drew breath so she could continue her tirade. 'And although I have been to her village, once, I don't know if I could go back there without instructions. It's totally unreasonable of him to have expected me to get in touch with him.' Anna ate a chip savagely. 'It's his dippy sister's fault. She was the one who told me his phone was dead! She should have made sure she had my number before she hurried me out of the hospital.'

Chloe bit into a batter-covered morsel. 'She was looking after her baby brother. She was bound to be distracted.'

'Oh, stop being so reasonable!' Anna smiled ruefully as she heard herself.

'Sorry,' said Chloe. 'It's my birth sign. It's very irritating.' She ate a chip, chewing thoughtfully. 'I'm sure this isn't an irreconcilable difference, Anna.'

Anna shook her head vehemently. 'Yes it is, Chloe. Absolutely. You weren't there. It wasn't a lovers' tiff, it was a basic misunderstanding of my whole character. How could he have got me so wrong?' She forced a half-smile. 'I'm excused from getting him wrong. I have no judgement when it comes to men. Think of Max.'

Chloe put down her plate and got up. She went to the kitchen, looking for something.

'I haven't got any ketchup, I'm afraid, if that's what you're looking for. I don't like it,' Anna said.

'That's OK, nor do I. The boys do. I like mayonnaise. Got any of that?'

Anna nodded. 'In the fridge.'

'Right,' Chloe said, bringing the jar back with her and sitting herself down again on the sofa. 'Tell me everything.'

'No, *you* tell *me* everything!' said Anna, out of self-defence.

354

'I think, for continuity, you have to go first,' Chloe insisted.

'What's with the long words?' said Anna flippantly, feeling anything but. She was not looking forward to telling Chloe she was moving back to Yorkshire. But it did seem the only viable solution.

'Just tell me! Why did Rob fetch up at my house, furiously angry and very upset? What did you do to him?'

Anna sighed. 'I don't know why you think I've done something to him, but anyway, I didn't mean to do it. He just got the wrong end of the stick and wouldn't let me explain.'

'What do you mean?'

'Well, once I'd got the car, I started going to take the dogs out while Rob wasn't there. It was for Caroline's sake, really,' she explained, crunching into a large chip.

'And for Rob's,' Chloe pointed out. 'You knew he'd be worrying.'

'Yes, but as he didn't know about the car, he would still have worried, but that's beside the point.'

'OK, go on.'

Anna felt a little calmer now Chloe was here, she'd had a soothing drink and refuelled a little. Perhaps it would make more sense as she explained it to Chloe. 'Well, I went to what's left of his house, and because it's what I do, I started making plans for its rebuilding. After all, I can't get on with the house I'm buying – was buying – as it's not mine yet.'

'It's bound to cost a fortune,' Chloe said matter-of-factly.

'Oh definitely,' Anna agreed. 'Much cheaper to pull it down and start again. But I don't think Rob would want to do that.'

Chloe nodded. 'Nor do I.'

'I haven't been able to cost it properly, but it is going to be very expensive,' Anna continued. 'Although lots of the old house is still standing. Anyway, I'd arranged a site meeting with a builder, a structural engineer, and Eric – you remember him?' The whole scene replayed back in her mind in horribly vivid detail. 'Well, Rob turned up, saw us all there and hit the roof.' She smiled ruefully. 'Or he would have hit it if there'd been one.' Anna took another sip of her drink, which was growing on her, in a strange way.

'Go on!' Chloe urged.

'He thought I saw it as an investment opportunity. I just don't know how he could have thought that about me. It's so hurtful! The last thing I would ever do is try to exploit anyone's misfortune, least of all Rob's.'

'So you do care about him then?'

'Oh yes,' Anna sighed. 'Or at least I did. At the moment I just want to spit roast him over the flames of what's left of his house, but I don't suppose that'll last. But anyway, I'm going back to Yorkshire, to live near Laura. I can't stay here, where so much of the area is either listed, or in a conservation area: we'd keep running into each other.'

Chloe made a harrumphing noise and dipped a large chip in mayonnaise. 'But if you care for him,' she said slowly, when her mouth was free to speak with. 'I think you should give him a chance to explain.'

'What's to explain? He hates me!' Anna said dramatically. 'He thinks I'm someone completely different from who I am!'

'I'm sure he doesn't hate you,' murmured Chloe.

'Yes he does! Get with the programme! He couldn't think those things of me if he cared about me at all.'

'I didn't get the impression he hated you when he came round to my house, desperate to get in touch.'

'Well, anyway, I've decided to back to Yorkshire.'

Chloe, who had left her drink on the side, took a sip of Anna's. 'But, Anna, you've just bought a new house.'

Anna shook her head. 'I haven't completed. I can easily pull out.'

Chloe placed a hand on Anna's arm. 'Well, don't do anything in too much of a hurry. You're extremely upset—'

'That does pretty much describe it.'

'Why don't you just go and stay with Laura for a bit?'

'I can't stay with her with Caroline for long. I'd have to find somewhere to live anyway and, as we know, it's hard to rent with a dog.' Anna got hold of her cushion again and gave it a hug.

Chloe stayed silent for a few moments. 'I can't believe this is really the end. You two had so much going for you.'

'I thought we had, but then I thought I was so in love with Max that I thought I would die, and that was just infatuation. This probably is, too.' She hugged the cushion tighter, feeling astonishingly sorry for herself.

'I'm sure it's not!' Chloe said reassuringly. 'I'm sure he cares about you. Why would he be so keen to get in touch with you if he didn't have feelings!'

'He hates me. That's feelings.'

'Come on, Anna,' Chloe chided. 'He doesn't hate you. Now, are you certain you won't let me tell him where you live, or at least give him your number? Honestly, he's in a complete state. Since he got my number he's left three messages on my answer phone, and then came round.'

Anna sat up straight. 'Chloe, you've got to promise me, whatever else you do, you won't tell Rob where I am, or give him any way of getting in touch with me.'

Chloe regarded her friend, trying, by sheer effort of will, to get her to unsay those words.

'I mean it, Chlo. You've been such a good friend to me—'

'And you to me! Think of you and Rob taking over while I was in hospital – then it all just went away—'

Her voice broke. 'I can't bear it! And I'll never see you again if you move to Yorkshire.'

'Come on! It's me with the broken heart, not you. And you can come and visit.'

Chloe sighed deeply. 'OK, I know. And I will promise if you're sure that's what you want me to do.'

'It is.'

Chloe put her arms round Anna and they hugged for a long time.

Chapter Twenty-Six

After Chloe had gone, Anna realised she had to act quickly. She knew Rob would want to have his dogs back with him as soon as possible and that he wanted to see her. It was quite possible that he would go to Geoff's and be lying in wait until she came for Caroline. She'd have to start planning and packing immediately.

Although it was late, she rang Laura. 'Sorry for ringing so late. You weren't in bed, were you?'

'That's fine. Are you all right?' Laura sounded tense, and definitely as if she was in bed.

'Fine, but it is a bit of an emergency. Can Caroline and I come up to stay for a little while? I – I might even buy a property up near you, like you said I should.' This sounded a bit more positive than just needing a place to run to.

There was a silence. Anna knew Laura was imagining all sorts of emergencies and trying not to panic. 'Fine. When would you want to come?'

'Tomorrow, really, but it may have to be the day after.' Anna picked up a pen and started doodling, until she saw she was drawing houses and had to score them out.

'But, Anna!' Laura exclaimed. 'You've got at least three more weeks on your rented house paid for.' She sounded incredulous and a little hoarse. 'What's the rush?'

'It's complicated, but I promise you, it's urgent that I come.'

'And you have to bring Caroline? Not that I don't adore her, of course,' she said hurriedly. 'But I'm not sure there's room for her. And Will has turned the spare room into an office.' Laura obviously hated not being immediately and totally welcoming. 'I'm not saying don't come, but a couple of days' notice would be brilliant.'

'I'm not sure I've got a couple of days, Lo. It's hard to explain.' Anna picked up the pen again and started drawing: bars this time, crossing and recrossing.

'Is it Rob?' Laura said gently.

'Mm.' Anna had been so brave in front of Chloe, but she'd drunk a fair amount of vodka since then and her resistance was crumbling.

'God! Men are bastards! What's he done? You're not pregnant, are you?'

Anna could almost see Laura's imaginings, a crying baby as well as a greyhound in her shrinking house. 'No! It never got that far.'

Relief made Laura expansive. 'But you were so in love with him!'

'I know, but it's not reciprocated and I have to get away. I can't stay here, knowing I might bump into him at any moment. I just can't.' She heard her voice crack and tried to get herself under control. She couldn't let herself go. She had things to do. 'If it's hard for you, I could always go and stay with Mum.'

'No! We'll manage somehow. Come whenever you like.'

'Well, I won't be with you until quite late, I shouldn't think,' Anna said. 'I want to avoid the motorways and I'll have to work out a route. I need to buy a map.'

'Honey, why don't you hang on for a day? I'll come down by train and we'll drive back together. It's a long way for an inexperienced driver.'

'I can't wait for you to do that, although it's a wonderfully kind offer,' she added, trying not to sound too desperate. 'I have to be away from here as soon as possible.'

'Shall I get in the car and come down now?' Laura asked. Anna could hear the concern in her voice.

'Oh, Laura! You're such a star, but it's not that bad. Tomorrow will do. And I'll manage the drive just fine. I've got a lot of practice in recently, even though I haven't done any long journeys yet. I'm not worried about the driving.' This wasn't entirely true, but the drive was quite a way down her mental worry-list. There were so many much more pressing matters.

When Laura was satisfied, Anna assembled the few bits and pieces she cared about in bin liners. The furniture she had stored in the second bedroom, she would leave and let Chloe sort out. It was a shame, really, as Laura had given it to her and she liked some of it. But needs must, and there wouldn't be room in her car, large though it was, for occasional tables, bookcases and a greyhound. Except for a little painted cupboard that had been in her kitchen in her old house. It didn't take up much room, after all.

She hadn't packed the car but she'd made decisions about what she was taking and what was staying. An hour or so later she was lying in bed, considering her choices, trying hard not to think about Rob. Trying not to think about someone only meant you thought about them more, she knew that. But she couldn't drag her brain away from him. She had nothing else to focus on. At last, the vodka and the World Service took effect and she slept.

She awoke early, having slept rather fitfully. But being up at six gave her a start on the world. She had a very long day ahead of her, after all.

The first thing was to collect Caroline. Geoff would be about. He was a farmer and would be up with the dawn, that's what they did. She had loaded the car the night before, leaving the boot for Caroline. It was lined with Anna's duvet, the one that had once been Laura's. She

361

was confident of being able to take Caroline, but getting her bedding might be more difficult.

It was seven o'clock when she arrived at the farm. Geoff was there, fiddling with a tractor.

'Good morning, Geoff!' she called breezily, although she'd always been rather shy of him before. 'I've just come to collect Caroline. I know it's early but I'm off today and need to get her.'

He looked at her quizzically.

'Well, I'm afraid you've missed her,' he said. 'Rob came and got the dogs last night. Said he had somewhere for them to stay. It'll be a bit of a squash in the caravan, though.'

Bastard! He must have known she'd try to get Caroline. But why would he want to keep her when he had three dogs of his own?

'OK then! I'll go to Rob's and get her. I'd better hurry or he'll leave for work.' She hesitated. 'He didn't mention if he was going to work today, did he?'

Geoff shook his head. 'There's no knowing with Rob. He could be doing that flexitime thing. And he's taken leave, I think, to give him time to sort out the fire. Bad business, that.'

'Terrible,' she agreed. 'Now, I really must go. See you soon!'

She got back into her car and drove off, waving gaily out of the window. Quite why she felt she had to give this light-hearted impression to Geoff, she wasn't sure. 'It's probably the social equivalent of whistling a happy tune,' she said to herself. 'Goodness, I do hope talking to oneself isn't really a sign of madness. I've done nothing but lately.'

She found a lay-by a little way away from the entrance to Rob's house and parked. She needed to psych herself up. Seeing Rob again was going to be agony, but she'd better get it over with. As she got out and set off along the path she cheered up slightly. He might have gone back to work. Then she could just steal Caroline. A spot of breaking and entering seemed easy compared to confronting Rob.

Quite how she would achieve this she didn't have to work out because as she reached the clearing she saw the Land-Rover and caravan. Rob was standing there, as if he'd been expecting her.

Even being in the physical location of that awful scene was agony. Seeing him there was like a kick in the stomach and made it difficult to breathe.

'Hello, I've come to get Caroline,' she said, as clearly as she could manage.

Rob started to move towards her and then stopped. 'Look, Anna, I'm terribly sorry about the other day.'

She became aware of him looking pale and anxious but she couldn't allow herself to feel compassion: that might weaken her. She wasn't going to give him the satisfaction of seeing her cry. 'Yes, well, we don't need to talk about that. Just give me my dog and I'll be off.'

'But, Anna' – he pushed his fingers into his hair in a gesture of frustration – 'you must give me a chance to explain. I know—'

Anna interrupted him. 'You were perfectly clear the other day. There's no confusion.' She was impressed with how controlled she sounded: almost cold. If only she felt controlled inside.

Rob sighed deeply. 'Where's your car?'

'I left it a little way away. I thought it might be muddy. I didn't want to get stuck.' Where this thought came from she didn't know, but it sounded good.

His eyebrow went up in disbelief. 'We haven't had rain for weeks. There's a hosepipe ban.'

'Really? How awful. Now, can I have Caroline, please.'

He folded his arms and regarded her in a way that told Anna he was not going to let her have Caroline without a fight. 'Why do you want her now? Have you bought your new house? That was quick.'

Anna folded her arms, too, and squared up to him. 'As you know, it's possible to buy a house very quickly if you know the right people,' she said. Her voice was still cold but panic was beginning to rise. How much longer could she keep up this brave front?

'Yes, I do know that, but where is your house?'

'It's not anywhere you can reach me! I'm going to Yorkshire, to live near my sister.'

He seemed horrified. 'Why?'

'Because I like her! Now could you stop making inane conversation and let me have my dog!'

'I should point out that technically she's not your dog. She belongs to the Greyhound Trust. You just have the care of her.'

'Rob, I'm telling you that if you don't let me have my dog very soon, I'm going to start to get angry.' She could have added 'tearful' and really hoped he wouldn't notice.

He shook his head. 'You can't just take her out of the county without permission—'

'Then let me have the permission and then give me my dog!' She could hear the hysteria in her voice and hoped passionately that he couldn't.

'No.'

He was using Caroline as a weapon – a hostage to keep her here. It was an outrage. 'What do you mean: "no"? This is ridiculous.'

An expression Anna couldn't interpret crossed his features and he seemed to be thinking. 'Well, yes, it may seem ridiculous,' he said after a moment, 'but the fact is, Caroline's not here.'

'What do you mean, she's not here?' Anna went cold. 'Where is she? Is she all right? She's not at the vet's, is she?'

'No, she's not at the vet's, she's just – out.'

364

'Rob! She's a dog, she doesn't go "out"!' Anna said, almost stamping her foot in frustration. What was he up to now? Devious tactics to weaken the enemy?

'Well, she did!' Something that in other circumstances she would have thought was a smile flickered at the corner of his mouth. 'She said she had to buy shoes. You're a girl – woman – you'd understand that.'

Anna's exasperation overtook her anger and despair and she lost a little of her tension. 'No, I hardly ever buy shoes if I can help it. I just borrow someone's! And I don't believe Caroline's buying them!' The horror of the fire had obviously driven him mad. There was no other explanation for it.

'Well, maybe it's not shoes. It could be something else.' His head slanted a little, as if in query. 'Maybe a handbag. But anyway, she told me she doesn't want to leave me now.'

'She never said that! She loves me!' Anna wasn't sure where this was going but it was very irritating. She just wanted to get Caroline and go. It was so much simpler when he was angry. He wasn't making it easy for her.

'Yes, but she's fallen "in love",' Rob went on, as if he was making complete sense. 'That's different, isn't it?'

Anna sighed very deeply. She hadn't slept well, she'd been up early and was suddenly extremely thirsty. How much longer did this pantomime have to go on? 'Yes it is.'

'I mean, I love my sister, when I don't want to murder her but . . .' He paused, looking at her in such an intense way she blushed.

'What?'

'Never mind.'

This wasn't good enough. 'Well, what? Either explain, or let me have Caroline.' Anna felt her resistance weaken.

'I'd rather explain over a cup of coffee.'

'And I'd rather leave here with my dog!' she persisted,

but the fight had gone out of her.

One side of his mouth lifted in a half-smile. 'As my preference is easier than yours, shall we try it?'

Another piece of the iceberg of her tension broke away as she noticed something behind Rob's shoulder. She bit her lip to hide her smile. 'Well, I would really like to say hello to Caroline, who appears to be about to break the door down.'

Abashed, he spun round to see that the caravan door had swung open and Caroline was emerging from it. He turned back to Anna. 'She must have changed her mind about the shoes.'

Anna didn't have to reply. Caroline, seeing her, came bounding over, behaving like a puppy, jumping up, licking her face, nearly pushing her off balance in her enthusiasm. To stop herself being knocked over, Anna got on to her knees and flung her arms round her. They hadn't been away from each other for very long, but she realised how much a part of her life Caroline had become. She sensed tears prickling in her eyes, but also what felt decidedly like a flicker of hope.

Rob put out a hand and pulled her to her feet. 'Please, come and have some coffee. Let me explain about Caroline's romance.'

An overpowering need for a cup of coffee weakened her resolve further. As she became more aware of her surroundings, she noticed a brand-new shed near what was left of the house. He must have taken delivery of it just after she'd left last time. She shuddered and then smiled to herself. It did seem as if he was wanting to make peace. And he had a right to a fair hearing, didn't he? 'All right,' she said, 'as the romance is slightly more likely than a passion for shoes, I will.'

He saw her looking at the shed. 'That's Caroline and Dexter's love nest, although they will have to share it with the other two. If they love each other they won't mind a bit of hardship or cramped conditions.' He opened the door to the caravan.

'I see what you mean about cramped conditions,' said Anna, finding herself overwhelmed by greyhounds.

'I'll put them in their shed. I'll just get the bedding out of the back of the Land-Rover.'

Anna went to help him. She'd have felt awkward sitting in the caravan, waiting for him to come back. 'Is this yours?' She indicated the rather battered vehicle that looked as if it was still doing service on cross-country safaris.

'It's on a long loan. It belongs to my brother-in-law, who loves off-roading – you know, driving all over the countryside up muddy hills. But my sister doesn't approve and so she lent it to me.'

'It is very environmentally unfriendly.'

'Yes, though he and his mates own the bit of land that they do it on. But now he can come over here and use it whenever he likes and she won't know.'

'Oh.'

He handed her a huge, corduroy-covered dog bed and took another himself. 'These are a present from them both. They've been incredibly kind, if a bit irritating at times.'

Anna smiled but didn't comment. She found her own sister irritating sometimes but would have hated anyone else to agree with her.

Two more fleeces the size of tarpaulins, an old duvet and a collection of sundry stuffed toys (from the nephews, Anna presumed) were all arranged in the shed, which was already warm from the sun, and the greyhounds' comfort was assured.

Once all four were ensconsced in their new surroundings Rob turned to Anna and said, 'I don't think we should talk about Caroline and Dexter where they can hear us. They'll be fine in here for a while.'

Anna followed him back to the caravan. It seemed too small and intimate a space to be in when there was still so much awkwardness between them. On the other hand, in different circumstances, Anna would have found it cosy.

'Do sit down,' he said formally, suddenly nervous.

She sat. The dogs couldn't have been there long, but the place was already covered in dog hairs. She brushed at her trousers, more for something to do than anything else.

'You see why they have to have separate accommodation, don't you? Would you like coffee or tea?' he offered.

'Coffee, please.'

He handed her the mug a few uncomfortable minutes later. 'So, are we going to talk about Caroline and Dexter?' he asked. 'Although I wouldn't like them to feel it was an arranged marriage.'

'Even if you did arrange it?' She sipped her coffee, staring at the floor.

Rob stood there, taking up most of the tiny space. He bit his lip. 'Anna, I really want to apologise. I've behaved like an absolute idiot.'

She blushed into her coffee, more so when he came and sat next to her. The chemistry was still there. For all that she'd tried to convince herself that she hated him, she still wanted him, quite a lot.

'I saw your plans,' he went on. 'All of them. They're fabulous. You've put a great deal of effort into them.'

She knew that. It must be terribly embarrassing for him having to say all this. He had been utterly vile and got her completely wrong, but now he was making her feel as if he had to tell her she'd failed an exam, although acknowledging she'd worked really hard for it.

She didn't answer and took another sip of coffee. It was bitter and didn't have enough milk in it.

'Why did you spend so much time and energy on my burnt-out shell?' He took the mug out of her hands and put it down.

She wasn't going to admit to all her motives but she did owe him some kind of explanation. He had apologised and if she hadn't got quite so carried away, they would still be friends . . . She could afford to be magnanimous now, she felt. 'It was something to do, a project.' She managed a quick look at him. 'I'd had an offer accepted on a house, but you know how long these things usually take. I had to do something with my time.'

'You could perfectly well have started the plans for your own project, or looked for work elsewhere. Why work on mine?'

This time she looked at him for a bit longer. 'I just thought – I just thought that it was such a dreadful thing to have happened, I had to do what I could – which isn't much – to put it right. I was trying to be practical.'

He took hold of both her hands, as if afraid she might run away. 'Do you know, I thought having my house burn down was the worst thing in the world.'

'Absolutely!' His fingers were warm on hers and she longed to hold his hands back, but was afraid doing so would reveal her true feelings. Her gaze returned to the floor.

'But it isn't,' he said quietly.

'Isn't it?' She glanced up in surprise, meeting his eyes almost by mistake.

He shook his head slightly. 'No. The worst thing in the world came when I drove the most important person in my life right out of it.' He frowned slightly. 'Although, to her credit, she drove herself.'

She moistened her lips, not daring to believe what she thought he might be saying. 'Did she?' It was barely a whisper.

'Yes. She's eminently practical, you see.'

Anna sighed. 'Rob, all this joking around is all very well, but I was terribly silly. I know I like to think of myself as practical but what I did was barking! Of course

369

you'd resent it. It was just not seeing you, worrying about you, I had no focus for . . .'

'For what?'

'My – creativity.'

'Ah. I was hoping you were going to say something else.'

'What?'

He looked diffident. 'The "L" word.'

'I do like my work, yes.' She gave him a lopsided grin.

He growled and wrapped his arms around her and hugged her, so tightly she thought she'd never breathe again. Then she realised she didn't much care about breathing as long as she could stay in Rob's arms.

'I wasn't talking about work,' he said eventually, looking down into her eyes.

'I know you weren't.'

'So, do you think Caroline and Dexter would like it if we stayed together, so they could be together?'

'I think they might like it very much.'

His mouth on hers was everything it had been before, only much more so. There was an intentness about his kiss, a yearning, caused, no doubt, by their separation and quarrel.

'And what about you?' he said at last.

'What? What about me?' Anna had been to a place very far away and had no recollection of any conversation they might have just had.

'Would you like to live with me? You wouldn't have to, of course,' he hurried on. 'You could live in your house, the one you haven't finished buying yet, but I do think it's important for a designer to live near or preferably on site.'

'What do you mean?' She was confused again. Love seemed to have destroyed an awful lot of her brain cells.

'I mean, how can you do a proper job if you're not able to visit every day, every hour that's necessary?' He seemed to be explaining something that was blindingly obvious to him, but still obscure to her.

'I still don't understand.'

He took her hand. 'I love you, Anna,' he said, looking deeply into her eyes. 'Not only do I want you, for ever, but I want to use your designs.'

Warmth spread over her body as she blushed in pleasure. 'Oh.'

He nodded as he saw comprehension dawn. 'I think I might just be giving you a very large commission.'

'The biggest!' She laughed a little. 'But how on earth are you going to pay me? It's going to cost a fortune.'

Now he laughed, too. 'I was rather hoping to pay you in kind.' He started to fiddle with the hem of her jumper.

'What kind of kind?'

'This kind.' He led her to the double bed and they toppled on to it. Anna's last conscious thought was that she had not been wrong about the electricity. It was high voltage and potentially explosive. If not properly channelled it could be very dangerous. She decided to pursue it as the ultimate form of environmentally friendly power.

They stayed in bed until Anna became aware of a strange little sound. Eventually she recognised it as her mobile phone, growling in the bottom of her bag. Crawling over Rob to retrieve it was a mistake, and it had stopped ringing by the time he had finally let her go.

'Oh God, that was Laura. I'd better ring her back; she's expecting me in Yorkshire later.'

'You're not going to go?' He sounded suddenly worried.

She smiled lovingly and stroked his hair back from his face. 'Not if you don't want me to.'

He pulled her towards him again and said earnestly, 'I have only a caravan to offer you – at least, for ages. It's not what I'd want for you. Or even for Caroline, really.'

371

'A caravan is fine. A little alteration of the design and we'd fit much more in.'

'Oh, Anna, I do love you!' he said, smiling at her, emotion shining in his eyes.

'And I love you. Very much. But I must ring my sister.'

'And I'd better let the dogs out for a run. They're going to be wondering what's been happening.'

Anna smiled and began to gather her scattered clothes towards her. 'I expect Caroline and Dexter will explain.'

He chuckled. 'I am sorry about all that. I just had to make you stay.' She watched him pull on a sweatshirt and saw the muscles in his arms move. She only had the strength of mind to stop watching when he had gone out.

She picked up her phone. 'Laura? Sorry, I just couldn't get to my phone in time. Listen, I'm not coming to Yorkshire.'

'Oh, Anna! Why not? I've cleared you a room and everything.'

'I'm staying down here. In a caravan.'

'Now you really have gone mad. Why on earth do you want to live in a caravan?'

'Rob's living in it, too.'

Understanding leapt from mobile phone to mobile phone. 'Ah, you've made it up, have you? I thought it was probably just a lovers' tiff,' Laura said knowingly. 'I'm so glad. He's such a nice man.' She paused. 'You're not going to share a caravan with four greyhounds, are you?'

'No. They've got a very nice shed to sleep in.'

'So what's the deal? Can you talk?' Laura asked, keen for more details.

'There is no deal, but I can talk for a moment.' Anna sat on the bed, a smile on her face as she saw Rob with the dogs from the caravan window.

'You're not going to give up your job, are you? You must keep your independence,' Laura insisted.

Anna lay back on the rumpled bed covers and laughed. 'I promise I'll do that. I may stop doing up my own houses for a bit and concentrate on working for Rob in between commissions, because I wouldn't want to be doing up two places at once. We haven't talked about all that yet, but I think he'll let me help.'

'Well, make sure you do talk about it. Before anything irrevocable happens.'

Anna was still lying on the bed with a sunny smile on her face when Rob came back a little later.

'What did your sister say?' he asked as he closed the door behind him.

Anna sat up. 'She said we must talk before anything irrevocable happens. I said it already had.'

He looked startled. 'Has it?'

'Oh yes. I've fallen totally and utterly in love with you.'

'Snap,' said Rob and joined her on the bed.

Anna moved over slightly and smiled at him.

'If we were in a house and not a caravan this would be perfect,' he said as he straightened out a leg that had developed cramp.

'Practically perfect is good enough for me,' said Anna, snuggling into him. 'Perfection can come later. Much later. Let's have a bit more of this first.'

'Mm, OK.'

They didn't speak again for some time.